Tina Reilly
Flipside

D0892281

POOLBEG

Published 1999 by
Poolbeg Press Ltd
123 Baldoyle Industrial Estate,
Dublin 13, Ireland
E-mail: poolbeg@iol.ie
www.poolbeg.com

Reprinted February 2000

A catalogue record for this book is available from the British Library.

ISBN 1 85371 945 5

Cover design by Vivid Design
Set by Poolbeg Group Services Ltd in AGaramond 11.5/13.5
Printed by in Great Britain by
Cox & Wyman Ltd, Reading, Berkshire.

For Claire – my sister and friend.

Thanks to:

Colm, my husband, for being so supportive whilst I was writing this. For taking the week off work so that I could write and finish the story, for sending my caffeine levels sky-rocketing and for his patience and good humour whilst I became a semi-hermit who only appeared down at mealtimes.

Conor for being the brilliant child that he is. If he wasn't so good I'd never get time to write anything.

My parents, who think this whole book thing is brill. (Keep up the great PR work Mam!)

All of my sisters and my sole brother. Aunts, uncles, everyone in my family. (I can't mention names or I'll leave someone out.)

Claire, my sister, for staying up until three in the morning reading the proofs and discovering all the horrific typos I managed to make. For not embarrassing me over my spelling, just correcting it.

My in-laws, for being thrilled for me and promising to tell everyone to buy the book!

Dr Maurice Cowhey, for giving his time and knowledge to read my "medical" chapters to ensure that they are factually correct. It was a great help. As John Grisham is fond of saying, any errors are mine.

Isabelle Thompson, Chairperson of HUG – for sharing her experience with me and for being so patient with all my questions and so wonderfully frank with all her answers.

For the literature I received from The Irish Cancer Society, BACUP, The Green Party and any other society I contacted.

Thanks to Gabrielle Doyle, librarian at St Lukes, for her kindness in looking up information for me.

For all those people who wrote all the books I used for my research. I can't remember the titles, or the authors, but thank you all.

Thanks too to everyone in Poolbeg – Gaye and Philip for shocking the life out of me by suggesting that I write a book – Elaine, Paula, Nicole, Conor, Kieran, Simon, Trish, Emer, Derek and Andrew for all your help in the past while. Yer a great bunch of people altogether.

And finally, to Max and Tuppence, two of the most vicious dogs I've ever had the pleasure of living with. The inspiration for Buddy. Buy the book and you'll see what I mean.

PROLOGUE

"Janet, can you come here a moment?"

"Yeah?" I poked my head up from the latest issue of *Hello!* to find the manageress of Shop and Save beckoning me towards her.

"Over here please, Janet – we don't want the whole world to know our business, do we?"

She was standing beside the cooked-meat counter looking all prim and proper. Uneasily I wondered what she was going to nark about now. I'd cleaned out the fridges, dusted off the shelves, shone up the tins, cleaned the windows. I'd even arranged all my money neatly in the till in case she decided to carry out a tidy-till inspection. There was nothing she could catch me out on.

"Janet, here please."

She sounded cross about something.

"Coming," I tried to make my voice chirpy. Putting down my mag, I stood up from the seat beside the cash desk. My mug of coffee almost fell off the counter, but I saved it on time. It took me a few seconds to shove my

1

feet into the new ultra-high, ultra-narrow stilettos I'd got in Dunnes for a tenner. Then, assuming a confident but tottering step, I walked towards Charlotte.

"Yes?" I gave her a cheery smile, the one she'd told me to use on the customers.

"I'm afraid," her voice dropped and she looked grim, "that I'm going to have to let you go."

"Oh?" I asked, delighted and surprised. "Go where?"

For a second she looked puzzled.

Then I copped on. "The wholesalers, is it?"

"What?"

"Are you letting me go to the wholesalers? Only I can't drive. But I'll learn. I'll – "

She held up her hand. "I'm letting you go," she said again. As I opened my mouth, she said quickly, "Janet, I'm firing you."

"Oh."

Apparently it was the fridges. I'd cleaned them out but hadn't turned them back on. She wasn't mad on my dress sense either. It lowered the tone of her shop.

"Jan, can you come here a second?" Dr Lynch poked his head around his door.

"*Nah*, what's up Doc?" I did my impression of Bugs Bunny that had made him laugh so much in my interview that he'd hired me.

He wasn't laughing this time. He sat at his desk and motioned me to a seat in front of it. When I'd sat myself down and pulled my skirt over my thighs, he said, "I'm going to have to let you go, Jan – sorry."

"Let me go?" I was shocked. I mean, *really* shocked. The Doc was a good laugh. Even though the job was boring I never thought I'd lose it. The man was my dad's friend's second cousin for God's sake.

"Yes," he nodded. "Jan, you tried to diagnose Betty Carey today, didn't you?"

"I just – "

"The poor woman thought she was for the high jump." He leaned towards me and his voice got really slow and deliberate. "Apparently, you told her she had some weird disease."

"Endocarditis," I said, "She had all the symptoms and – "

"You have no business doing that." His face was going purple.

"It's just I got a medical encyclopaedia from me dad for Christmas, he thinks I'm going to be a nurse and – "

"I've warned you about this before, Jan."

"I know and – "

"I'm sorry."

It was very final the way he said it.

"Janeta, can you come here a momenta?"

I deftly caught the two frozen burgers I'd been juggling. "Hey, Mario, yo?"

Mario didn't look happy. "In the backa pleasea."

Julio gave a big wolf whistle when he heard that. "It's not burgers you'll be juggling in a minute," he sniggered, "It'll be meat and two veg."

"If you don't a shuta ya face, I'll fire you nexta," Mario snapped.

Stunned, embarrassed silence.

I was let go. Apparently Mario wanted a worker in his chipper, not an entertainer. He wasn't impressed at the way I could juggle frozen food, or the deft way I could catch onion rings in my mouth or the fact that his battered sausages came in for a lot of lewd jokes. He was sensitive about his food, was Mario.

The straw that broke his back came when I rechristened his curry chips "slurry chips". That was when I overstayed my welcome.

"Jan, can you come here a second?"

"I can." Up from my chair, hobbling badly. I'd drunk too much at the Christmas party, which resulted in me slipping and falling over a kerb which in turn resulted in a sprained ankle. A nice injury. It had kept me out of work for over a week.

Libby, my boss, was sitting at her desk in her office. "Janet," she began, before I'd even sat down, "I've been told to give you some bad news."

She was smiling as she said it, so it couldn't be too bad. I gave a hesitant smile back. "Yes?"

"The company has decided that your services are no longer required."

"What services?"

"Exactly," Libby nodded. "Exactly." She planted her hands on the desk and nodded even more vigorously. "There isn't a lot you do, is there, Janet?"

"Pardon?"

"Your leave record is appalling, you've been out sick more times than you've been in."

"That's 'cause I've had more sick days than I've had healthy ones."

"No one is sick that much." Libby scanned my leave sheet. "You're getting great mileage out of a bad back. It's been responsible for almost a month's sick leave."

"I have a bad back." I tried to stare her down. "LBP," I said. "Lower back pain."

"Mmm," Libby made a face and stared pointedly at my shoes. "Mmmm," she said again.

I didn't reply. Something was going on that I didn't really understand.

"Plus," and here she looked positively alight, "you managed to screw up the whole filing system, didn't you?"

"No."

That stopped her gloating.

"All I did was try another way of doing it. It wasn't my fault that no one could find anything. I was bored and I needed a challenge."

"Well, I've a big challenge for you," Libby said.

"Yeah?"

"Yeah," Libby stood up. "See how fast you can find another job." She handed me a pay packet. "You're fired."

I wasn't lucky with employment. I suppose I just didn't know what I wanted to do, I knew that when I found my particular niche in life, everything would fall into place. All my insecurities would vanish overnight, I'd be Janet Boyle, successful in life, love and the pursuit of happiness. I knew in my bones that that would happen.

All I needed was the right job and things would turn around.

So I did a course in *Word for Windows*. A night-time thing, a crash course. Literally a crash course – the guy running it said he'd never seen a computer crash as many times as mine. But I got a cert at the end of it. A cert to say I was *Word literate* – whatever that meant.

And then came the interview. I'd hit the jackpot. I went for an interview with McCoy, McBeale & Co. It looked like a real classy joint . . .

THREE YEARS LATER

CHAPTER ONE

"Jan!"

Half-way down O'Connell Street, struggling against the crappy March weather, I managed to hear him. So, it seemed, did the rest of the street. We all turned and saw a dark-haired twenty-something legging it towards me.

"Jan – hang on, willya!"

So I hung on.

"Feck's sake," Al had caught up with me now, "I turned around to answer the phone, next thing I look and you're gone."

He fell into step beside me. Usually we walked together down O'Connell Street after work, but that day, he'd answered a late phone call and I hadn't waited for him.

"'Course I was gone," I made a face. "I don't get paid to work after five."

"Yeah, well . . ." Al shoved his hands into his jacket pockets and bent his head against the wind, "you could have waited."

9

"What? To be your chaperone down O'Connell Street?" Even though his head was bent, I could see his face going red. "Is poor Ally afraid he'll be mugged by some big bad man?"

"Feck off!" He was grinning but he didn't look at me.

"It's just I'm in a mad hurry this evening," I said after a bit. I didn't know whether to tell him about going to the doctor's. I knew he'd make a laugh of me, but in the end I said, "I'm going to the doctor's."

Just like I thought, he exploded in a laugh, "Again?" He was looking at me now. "Feckin' again?"

"Yeah." I tried to say it nonchalantly.

"What's the matter this time?" He'd stopped and stood grinning at me. "Comin' down with some really nasty fingernail trouble or wha'?"

"Ha. Ha."

"So how long do you reckon you'll get this time?"

"Dunno." I began to walk again. "If O'Callghan is on, he'll probably do a cert for a week or so, but if it's the other fella – O'Brien – it's anyone's guess. He's as scabby with his certs." As Al laughed, I went on, "And I was with him about two weeks ago, so he mightn't believe that I'm sick again."

"I bet those doctors could retire on the amount of cash you spend in there," Al slagged.

"It's worth it." Anything was better than going into work every day. I hated my job. I suppose, I just hated working – full stop. I'd had a string of jobs since I left school and I'd dumped about three of them and been fired from four. How I'd managed to hang onto this typing job with Mc Beale and Co was a miracle. Three horrible years I'd been there. Well, if you didn't count my many illnesses, I'd been working for three years.

"D'you want me to collect your cheque on Friday?" Al broke into my thoughts. "I'll drop it around at the weekend."

"Oh, yeah, right." Opening my bag I began to root around for some paper to write a note to the pay clerk, Derbhla, telling her it was OK to give my cheque to Al. "Good thinking, Al."

I couldn't find any paper and Al hadn't a pen. "Great."

"I'll drop around to your flat tomorrow if you're out sick," Al offered, grinning as he said "sick", "and you can write a note then." We'd stopped walking as we'd reached my bus-stop. "Will you be there?"

"'Course I will." I pretended to sound offended. "I'll be sick, won't I?"

"Oh yeah." He laughed then and people looked at him. Al has a big loud laugh which is strange, 'cause he's a really quiet guy. He's nice though, really helpful, but really, really shy.

He tipped me a half-salute, "Hope you're really sick."

"Hope so too!"

I watched him walk away, his sports bag slung over his shoulder. I spent a few seconds admiring his rear view before I turned my attention to the bus timetable. There should be one in about five minutes which would leave me right outside the surgery. If I got there early, there wouldn't be too many people around.

For once, my bus came on time. I paid my fare and sat down.

Gently, I felt the small swollen gland in my neck, which I'd just noticed that morning. Maybe if I kept rubbing it all the way to the doctor's, it'd get a bit bigger. It was going to be my ticket to a week's cert – at least.

CHAPTER TWO

The waiting-room was empty. It looked as if it hadn't been in use all afternoon. The chairs stood neatly along the sides of the wall and the magazines were stacked up as if no one had touched them. Though looking through them it wasn't surprising. There wasn't even an issue of *Hello!* there. Instead there were things with titles like *Business and Commerce* and *Greening up your Home.* Riveting stuff.

Being a veteran doctor goer, I'd come prepared. I was just taking my Walkman out of my bag when the receptionist walked in. I don't know if I should've been flattered that she recognised me.

"Janet," she said, as if I was an old friend. "Dr O'Brien is free. You can go in to him now."

My heart plummeted. "Well . . . " I stood up and tried to look reluctant. "I was hoping to see Dr O'Callaghan." Lowering my voice, I whispered, "I think he's the better one."

For some reason, she didn't look so friendly anymore. "Dr O'Callaghan isn't on today," she snapped.

"Oh." I felt a bit put out at her tone. And the way she was looking at me made me feel about two foot high. "Oh, well, I'll see O'Brien so." I'd gone red, I knew I had and for some reason I felt guilty. *She* was making me feel guilty. I couldn't look at her as I made my way to O'Brien's room.

"In there." she opened the door for me and nearly flung me through it.

The doctor was sitting behind his desk, writing something, and he barely glanced at me as I sat down. I saw my file on his desk, a pink folder with my name on the front. It was a really thick file.

He was youngish-looking, in his thirties, I guess, He wore thick glasses and had fuzzy black hair. I suppose he was handsome for a doctor. He was swotty-looking though and I could just bet that in school the other kids would have called him a lick-arse.

I was afraid of him. He always made me feel like a complete fraud.

He let me sit there for a few minutes as he wrote. Then, when he finished, he did a swivel in his swivel-chair and stared straight at me. "Janet," he smiled. "And how are you?" He picked my folder up off his desk and thumbed through it. "You were only here about two weeks ago," he went on, not waiting for me to tell him how I was. "You had a cold – is that right?"

I nodded.

"Did it clear up all right?"

"Fine."

"So," he leaned back. "What seems to be the problem?"

I swallowed. Only Oscar-winning performances got a cert from O'Brien. "Eh," I pointed to my neck. "I, eh, have a bit of a swelling in my neck. A gland I think."

"I see." He nodded. "Where?"

"Just here." Again I pointed at the well-rubbed spot. "I, eh, well, I have a bit of a sore throat."

I hadn't, but I knew that swollen glands meant sore throats, so it wasn't strictly a lie. "And my neck feels sore too." It didn't, but it would, in time.

O'Brien leaned forward. "Just scoop your hair up," he said, "while I feel your neck."

I did as I was told and allowed him to rub my neck with his fingertips. He bit his lip as he was doing it, a sign that he was concentrating. (I knew him that well).

"Yes." Much to my delight, he was nodding. "You've a few glands up all right."

A few? This was better than I could have hoped.

"Let's have a look at your throat."

He took the light from his drawer and I obligingly opened my mouth for him. My heart was hammering, I knew he wouldn't find it sore.

"Doesn't look too bad," he said. He felt my neck again. "Still, you've a few glands up. There must be something." He wrote in my file. Then he took out his thermometer and shook it. Placing it under my arm he took my temperature. "Slight fever," he said as he shook it back to normal.

I'd a slight fever. Suddenly I felt as if I was burning up. This was great.

"All right," O'Brien said. "My guess is that you've a

slight infection there. A course of antibiotics should do the trick."

To my joy, he began to write out a prescription.

"A seven-day course should clear it up – all right?"

"Fine." I was trying not to smile.

He tore the prescription out and handed it to me. "I suppose you want a cert for work?"

I tried to guage the question, but his tone was neutral.

I made a face. "Well," I did my best to sigh with great reluctance. "I suppose."

So he wrote that out too. A cert for the rest of the week!

"Thanks." I took both from him and eventually a smile forced its way onto my face. "Thanks."

"No problem."

I knew he watched me as I left so any spring in my step was severely curtailed.

Walking out into reception, I gladly paid my bill.

The receptionist, still a bit distant, scribbled out a receipt for me and for the first time I noticed a big sparkler on her left hand.

"You got engaged?" It was my pathetic attempt to press her defrost button.

"I did." She was busy scribbling and wouldn't look up.

"Congratulations." I gave a cheery smile. "Anyone I know?"

"Dr O'Brien." With that bombshell, she handed me my receipt and stared straight into my face.

"Shit." That was all I could say. Then I stumbled out a thanks as I grabbed my receipt from her and fled.

CHAPTER THREE

It took me ten minutes to walk home. By home, I mean the flat that I share with two other girls – Beth and Abby. Beth's been there the longest, Abby and I moved in about three years ago. You know the saying, two's company and three's a crowd – well, it's true. For me at least.

Abby and I get along fine. She's the same age as me, twenty-four, but totally different. She'd look good wearing a sack, so would I – if it was over my head. Abby wears minimal make-up and I plaster it on, Abby cooks and I get take-aways. Abby gets into steady relationships, I've trouble even finding a rocky one. But we like each other. We don't fight.

Beth, on the other hand, can't seem to stand the sight of me. I don't know what I've done to her, but ever since I moved in, she's become more unfriendly all the time. Sometimes we get along fine and then, for no reason that I can see, she starts acting cold towards me, rolling her eyes and making sarcastic comments. She's untidy too, her room is like a bomb site and she throws her clothes and stuff everywhere. *And* she's the biggest sneer, though she doesn't sneer at Abby half as much as she sneers at me. If I'm honest, she scares me a bit. Sometimes she can be nice and when she's nice, I forget about her being horrible. Until the next time.

The two of them were watching *Coronation Street* when I let myself in. Abby had obviously been cooking as the two of them had some sort of horrible green pasta stuff on their plates. The stuff that looks like snot.

"There's more in the pot," Abby said, mistaking my look of revulsion for one of interest. "You can have some if you like."

"Naw, I'll pass." I dumped my bag on the table and flicked on the kettle.

"Make us a cup there, Jan," Beth, who was sitting in the only decent chair in the flat, turned and put her cup on the table.

Both of them turned back to watch the telly.

I began to root about in the press to see what food we had. There was a bit of bread and some beans. It'd have to be beans on toast.

Again.

For the third night running.

Bad-temperedly, I began to bang pots and tins about the place. It wasn't fair. We had a kitty that we all paid into. It was meant to buy things like drink and chocolate and occasionally food. The only food it bought was pasta and noodles and other stuff I'd never eat in a millennium. I liked plain food and my flatmates liked foreign slop and because majority ruled, all our money went on it.

Bang! The saucepan was stuck onto the tiny gas ring.

"Sussh!"

Big bang! I pulled the grill out to stick the bread under it.

"Quiet!" Abby hissed.

Obviously *Coronation Street* was nail-biting stuff tonight.

The break came and conversation resumed.

"You're late in," Abby said, as she came to dump her plate in the sink. "Did you go for a drink or something?"

"Nope." I grinned and pulled out the cert from the back-pocket of my jeans. In a sing-song voice, I said, "*I* was at the *doc*-tor." I waved it in front of her face. "A three-day cert."

"You went to the doctor again?" Beth was staring at me. "Again?"

"I've an infection in my glands." I gave the saucepan a shake, to hurry the beans up.

"My arse you have." Beth rolled her eyes. "Your bloody doctor has an infection in his brain if he believes all that crap out of you."

"He's the one who gave me the prescription for antibiotics," I said.

"Pity it's not arsenic," Beth sneered.

Abby gave a small giggle. It was her attempt to stop Beth going on at me. "She must be sick if he gave her a prescription," she said to Beth as she walked back to her seat in front of the telly.

"I am sick." It was as close as I could get to standing up for myself.

Beth gave a snort which I ignored. The music for the soap came on again and any sarcastic remarks she'd planned were forgotten.

The toast was done and I concentrated on buttering it and spooning the beans on top of it, to make it go all soggy. I love it when it goes like that. I ate my tea sitting at the kitchen table, there was no way I'd lower myself to watch *Coronation Street*. Everyone in my house at home watched it, even my dad, and that was warning enough to stay well clear.

Once it ended, the station was flicked to Channel 4 where *Brookside* had just started.

Abby got up. "Video it for me, will you?" she asked. When Beth nodded, she said breathlessly, "I have to go out."

Both of us looked at her. She was beaming around, only dying for us to ask the obvious. My mouth was too full of beans to oblige, so Beth asked, "Who with?"

Abby shrugged and said with forced casualness, "Aw, just some guy I sold an ad to. He liked my voice so," big smile, tight clasp of the hands, "he asked me out."

"What?" This was big stuff, *Brookside* was ignored. "Over the phone?"

Abby nodded and blushed. "Yeah."

I was seriously impressed. "Womanticc, huf?"

"Sorry?" Abby looked at me.

Swallowing my food wholesale in an attempt to talk, I began to choke. Abby rushed over and thumped me on the back, Beth got some water and shoved it under my nose. "Drink that," she muttered.

I drank it down and eventually I was all right.

"What did you say?" Abby asked.

"I said, romantic huh?"

"Yeah. It's weird." She looked at both of us and her voice grew all excited. "Every month I ring his company to sell ads, and whenever he answers, we always have a bit of a laugh over the phone and now," she sighed and looked all dreamy and soppy, "he's asked me out."

Abby's a sales-person in a crummy magazine and she personally saves it from closure every month by selling advertising in it. She could get Ian Paisley to take a front page advocating the Peace Process if she wanted. It's her voice - husky and gravelly. Many's the fella I've had ring me only to hear Abby's voice and make a date with her instead.

"It really is romantic, isn't it Jan?" she asked.

She just wanted me to say it again. "Yep," I agreed.

"Hope he's not a let-down," Beth said, staring fixedly at the TV screen.

"He won't be." Abby made a face over at her.

"He'll be great." I beamed. My lack of romantic entanglements only made it more exciting when I knew someone who was experiencing it firsthand. "You'll have to spill all the dirt when you come back, right?"

"I only hope there's dirt to spill," she grinned as she disappeared into her room.

Abby left around nine. She looked great, even though she'd hardly any make-up on. She didn't need it. Abby has nice clear skin.

Beth and I were left on our own. I hate being on my own with her, especially when she's got a face on. Tonight, I'd offended her, I don't know how, but I had. It was one of her bad nights, when she basically commandeered the telly and ignored me.

"You not working tonight?" I asked, hoping she was.

She flicked a glance over at me. "I called in sick," she said.

"Fun-ny."

She didn't say anymore.

She began to watch a film, I forget what it was called. I stayed up to watch it with her. I hadn't a lot of choice, it was either watch the film or go to bed. By the middle of it, we were falling about the place laughing. Not because it was funny but because it was crap. It was meant to be a thriller, but it had more holes in the plot than Bill Clinton is alleged to have had in the White House.

"This is so crap!" Beth giggled as someone got shot.

She looked different when she laughed. Younger-looking. Abby and I didn't even know what age she was – imagine. When Beth laughed, she actually looked quite good-looking. It sort of hit me and gave me a shock. Because Beth never really smiled at me, I just assumed she was ugly. But she wasn't. Her hair was that reddy brown colour and her skin was quite dark. When she laughed, her eyes glittered and lit up her face. She looked nice.

"Want a coffee?" I asked as I got up to make one for myself.

"Naw, get us a can," Beth waved her hand in the direction of the fridge. "Carlsberg."

I handed her a can and took one for myself.

"You won't be able to drink once you're on antibiotics," Beth announced as she saw me pulling the ring-tab off.

"Let me worry about that," I grinned at her and we clinked our cans together.

"Cheers."

"Cheers."

The film got worse. The plot became non-existent as bodies piled up on the screen. We stopped laughing after a while and opened another can each. We drank in silence.

Most times I have no problem talking to people. Sometimes I click with them and can chat about everything. Other times, pure nerves drive my conversation on. With Beth, I'm useless. It's like me and my mother all over again. Two people in the whole universe I can't talk to, Beth and Mam.

The film ended and I decided to hit the sack. Abby hadn't arrived in and I felt too tired to wait up for her.

Getting up from the sofa, feeling a bit light-headed from the drink, I made my way to my room. "Night," I said to Beth.

She was getting another can for herself. "Enjoy your

sick leave," she said. This time there was no sneer behind it. She meant it as a joke.

I smiled. "Anything you want done in the next few days, I'm your woman."

"I'll remember that."

We smiled at each other and I knew that, for the time being at least, she'd give her mouth a rest.

That night it happened again. Weird really. I'd be in bed, asleep, when suddenly I'd wake up. The fact that I'd wake up wasn't weird, it was the fact that my whole body would be covered, head to toe, in sweat.

That night, the sheets were soaking too. My hair was plastered to my face and I was drenched in sweat.

"Christ! Christ! Christ!" I muttered as I flung the sheets off the bed. This was the last thing I needed, especially when I had to get up the next morning.

Then it hit me. I didn't have to get up.

That was all right so.

Not feeling so bad, I found a tee-shirt in my drawer and pulled it over my head.

Pulling up the duvet, I snuggled back down under it.

It was probably just the Carlsberg.

CHAPTER FOUR – THURSDAY

The flat was empty when I crawled out of bed the next morning. It was after ten and lashing outside. Rain pelted off the windows and, as I looked out, I could see the trees in the back garden bent over with the force of the wind. Grinning to myself, I flicked on the kettle for a coffee. The more miserable the weather was, the happier I felt. It made me grateful that at least I didn't have to stand in the pissings of rain and wait on some dodgy overcrowded bus to ferry me to the end of O'Connell Street. Also, it meant that I didn't have to trek up O'Connell Street and arrive in work all sweaty and smelly from the raincoat I wore.

Instead, a few quid wisely spent ensured that I could stay inside, have a shower, a read, watch telly, stuff my face, make phone calls . . .

I had to ring work. That would be my first call of the day.

As I waited on the kettle to boil, I dialled the office. "Please let Lenny or Al answer," I whispered over and over to myself as the phone rang at the other end. They'd be the sympathetic ones, Liz and Henry would only make some smart remark or other.

"McCoy, McBeale and Co," the girl on the switch answered.

"Accounts." I deepened my voice just in case she recognised it.

"Just a minute," she said, putting me on hold and torturing me with ten minutes of *Greensleeves*.

"Accounts."

I was in luck.

"Lenny," I made my voice sound weak. "It's Jan. I'm off until next week. I've . . ." I sought for some way of making what I had sound dramatic. "I've a glandular infection."

His intake of breath let me know that my illness did indeed sound horrific. "'Tisn't glandular fever?"

I waited a second before I answered. "It might be. I don't know." How brave I sounded.

"Well, now, you take care of yourself."

His concern made me feel guilty. I had to get off the line. "I will," I muttered. "I'll see you next week."

I was about to put down the phone when he said, "Oh, Jan, hang on there now. Alan wants a word."

There were mutterings as he relayed my illness to Al.

Al came on the line. "How's it goin'?" He had a big grin in his voice. "How's the glands?"

I bristled at his jokey tone. "Infected."

I heard him laugh and then he coughed in an attempt to cover it up. "Sorry to hear that."

26

I said nothing.

"Write that letter for me," he said then. "I'll drop in later and get it off you."

I was half-tempted to haul him up on his grammar just to get him back for laughing at me, but Al was a bit strange. He seemed to hurt easily and maybe he wouldn't think it was funny. So I just said, "Fine. See you then."

"Take care now, won't you?"

I put the phone down to the sound of him laughing.

The water in the tank was cold so I had to flick the switch to heat it. While I was waiting, I had some breakfast and drew out a plan of what to do with my day. Abby had left a note asking me to get a video from the local video shop and a cheap bottle of wine. At the end she'd written: *Good night last night.* She'd left six quid for me.

Videos and cheap wine were a sign that we were broke. Beth would probably arrive in later with another few bottles that she'd got wholesale from the pub she worked in.

The whole wine business put me in a dilemma. If I got the antibiotics, I wouldn't be able to partake in the getting smashed routine. If I didn't get the antibiotics, Beth would have proven her point that I wasn't sick at all.

And I was.

The doctor had said so.

Reluctantly, I decided to get the medicine. I'd make

a point of taking it while Beth was watching. That'd show her.

The kettle boiled and I switched it off. We have one of those ancient shiny unautomatic kettles. The ones that, if you forget to turn them off, they turn the kitchen into a sauna before exploding.

I made some coffee and toast and flicked on the telly. Whoever invented breakfast television must've had me in mind. My idea of heaven is coffee, food and TV.

The water for the shower had heated and so, by twelve thirty I was washed and dressed and rearing to go.

I got my antibiotics in the chemist at the top of the road and then it was on to the highlight of the day. Visiting the guy who worked in the video shop. He was gorgeous.

"Have you got," I walked up to him, trying to sound sexy, "*Sleepless in Seattle?*"

"Yeah." He chewed his gum and didn't look at me. Instead, he concentrated on the *Friends* video that he'd put in to watch.

"Oh, well, can I have it please?" I'm not a video-shop browser. Beth and Abby spend hours in a shop choosing what video to watch – they pick them up, read the backs, discuss the reviews they've had before making their decision. I just go straight for the one I want by asking for it. They're always the one-pound rentals as well. Paying over two quid for a video that'll cost a quid to rent in five years time was not me.

Abby's into the new releases big time. She knows who's in what film, who directs what, who had an affair with who on what set. She's basically a walking issue of *Hello!* Beth'll watch anything bar weepies. She loves thrillers.

That's why I got a love story.

The video hunk got me my video and took my money and never even glanced at me.

"Thanks."

He kept chewing.

Next stop was the wine. That was easy. The cheapest bottle in the shop.

I was back in the flat after three.

I'd the whole afternoon to myself.

I watched *Oprah, Rikki Lake, Geraldo*. I wrote the note for Al and I got out my Flab-buster contraption. It had taken me three weeks to construct and even then it only vaguely resembled the picture on the box. I got it out and did the flab-buster stomach exercises. Feeling fit and healthy, I flicked the telly to the five-thirty edition of *Neighbours*.

Abby arrived in ten minutes later. "How's the patient?" she grinned. She put her coat in her room and came out to join me. "What's happening?"

Ignoring her, I asked, "Never mind *Neighbours*, how did last night go?"

Before she'd a chance to answer the buzzer went.

Abby went to the intercom and pressed. "Who is it?"

"Al."

Abby looked at me. "What's he doing here?"

Her and Beth didn't like Al much. Like I said before, Al's shy and sometimes it looks as if he's being unfriendly. That's what it looked to them the night I invited Al for a drink with us. I hadn't told Al that Beth and Abby'd be there because I knew he'd find some excuse to back out. When he arrived in the pub and saw them, he got tongue-tied. Simple questions made him get all jumpy and nervy and I was mortified for him. Beth had a field day. She'd been horrible, muttering questions in a low voice so that he couldn't hear. Then he'd keep going, "Sorry? Sorry?" And she'd shrug and say it didn't matter.

That night I'd really hated her.

But I hadn't said anything. There was no point in rocking the boat.

In the end, Al had begun to get really mutinous-looking and after a while he'd left.

Beth had laughed and Abby had stared at me and asked what on earth I was doing with such a weirdo.

Al hadn't come into work the next day and when I did see him he never mentioned it again.

"What is that weirdo coming here for?" Abby grumbled as she buzzed to let him up.

"He's not a weirdo."

"Come in," I yelled as I heard his footsteps along the corridor, "It's open."

Al came in and stopped dead at the sight of Abby. I could see him gulp and then he stammered out, "Hi, Abby."

"Al." She nodded at him and asked if he wanted a cuppa.

"Naw," Al came towards me. "I've just to get a note off Jan."

"Here you are." I lifted my letter off the table and handed it to him.

Al, pocketing it, said, "I'll drop your cheque around on Saturday sometime."

"Thanks."

"Take care now."

"You too." I walked to the door with him. "You sure you don't want a cuppa?"

He shook his head. "Have to head. I have training tonight."

Al's a runner. He goes out running every lunch-time in work.

"See you so."

I watched him walk right down the corridor before I closed the door.

"He fancies you rotten," Abby said from her position at the cooker. "It's so pukingly obvious."

She was stirring a huge saucepan of beans. "Want some?"

"He doesn't and no I don't want some." I leaned against the bench and grinned at her. "So, how'd it go?"

She took her time pouring her beans onto a plate and began to look for a fork. Abby liked to make a drama out of things. "I had a good time," she said eventually, "He was nice."

"And?"

She sat down. "And what?" She wouldn't look at me.

"Come on, Ab," I coaxed. She couldn't let me down, it was the only bit of romance in my life.

"He said he'll ring," she muttered.

"Oh."

She didn't need to say anymore. Abby knew, from my and Beth's experiences, that when guys said they'd ring, they never did. I'd even bought an answering machine to facilitate the men in my life who promised to ring and – surprise, surprise – it had never been needed. I was firmly convinced that I had a big sign saying *one-nighter* stapled to my forehead.

But it was a first for Abby.

"He might ring," I offered.

"And you might get a life."

She was in bad form, I said nothing.

She began to mash her beans up, squashing them onto her plate. "What video did you get anyhow? I feel like getting drunk."

"*Sleepless in Seattle.*"

Her moan made me jump. She put her head almost into her beans and wailed. "Why did you get a love story? *Whyyyyy?*"

So I watched it while she got drunk.

CHAPTER FIVE – FRIDAY

Friday night, Abby and I sat in front of the telly watching *The Late Late Show*. Yeah, we were desperate, we'd nothing else to do and there wasn't a thing on the other stations. Gay was interviewing some novelist or other and we were almost comatose on the floor with boredom.

There was just the two of us. Beth had taken off to Wicklow for the weekend, to visit her dad. Her parents were separated and she visited each of them once a month.

The novelist was American and she was just about to let us in on the secret of how to have a happy, fulfilling spiritual life when the phone rang.

Abby and I looked at each other.

"It's for you," I said, "I bet it is."

She was pale. "Say it's *him*," she whispered. "Wouldn't it be great?"

She was in a bad way. "Play hard to get," I said, knowing it was good advice but being unable to recognise the fact when it was my relationships. It was OK for other people, though. "Don't answer, let the machine click on and he'll think you're out."

I know she didn't want to do it, but Abby's sensible. She doesn't make mistakes the way I do. "OK so," she said.

We waited, barely breathing, for the caller to reveal themselves as the phone clicked onto the answering machine. Our message was great with Abby speaking, of course. At the time, Beth and I thought it was hilarious, until, as I mentioned before, fellas that were ringing me had defected to Abby instead. Nevertheless, as Beth said, if they were going to do that with someone as mediocre-looking as Abby, how would they resist real temptation?

They weren't worth it, she said.

And I agreed.

So the message had stayed. It was the tester of relationships.

The machine whirred and Abby's voice, deep and husky, said, "Hi. You've reached the flat of Beth, Jan and me, Abby. We're kind of," suggestive pause, slight chuckle, "tied up at the moment. However, if you'll leave your name, number and a message, we'll get right back," another pause, "when we're untied."

All we could hear was a gulp. That was normal, it was the way Abby's voice affected most males. Then a cultured voice spoke. "Eh, Abby, it's eh – "

So much for playing hard to get, Abby virtually

leap-frogged over me to grab the phone. "Mickey," she breathed, "Hi!"

Mickey! *What sort of a name was that?*

I looked on in amazement as my flatmate whispered and simpered into a phone with a guy called Mickey. In ten seconds flat, she'd been transformed from a mature twenty-something into a brainless giggling bimbo.

It had to be love.

CHAPTER SIX – SATURDAY

"Please, Jan?"

"No way."

"Aw, go on."

"Ab, I can't."

"Why?"

"Because," I searched desperately for an excuse, "I'm washing my hair this morning."

Abby glared at me. "What'll you do all day after that?"

I didn't answer. There was no way I was going into town with her.

"Well?"

"What!"

"What'll you do when you've finished washing your hair?"

I didn't need this first thing on a Saturday morning. "Go back to bed." I answered. And I meant it. I felt rotten. I'd a pain in my neck and it wasn't just from Abby's wheedling voice.

The gland in my neck hadn't got smaller either. I'd been four days on the tablets and it seemed to be feeding off them. It had been joined by two other glands. It was the only thing keeping me in good form. I was going to the doctor the next Wednesday if they didn't clear up. It'd be a week since I'd been before. Next Monday was my birthday – it'd be a present to myself if I got another cert.

"Please, Jan?"

"No." I got up from the table to escape her. She wanted me to tag along while she marched the length and breadth of the city looking for clothes to wear for her dinner date with Mickey. Shopping with Ab was about as satisfying as pig-farming in Israel. She went into every shop, tried everything on and pissed the sales assistants off big time. And I was normally the eejit that stood by while she did it. Well, not anymore.

"I really like this guy, Jan," Abby said sulkily. "And if it was you, I'd go into town with you."

"Only because you love shopping," I tried to make a joke of it.

She didn't laugh. Instead there was a silence.

"Oh, don't bother yourself then!" she snapped after a few seconds.

It worked, I felt guilty. "You've *piles* of stuff to wear."

"But I *don't*." She put her head down and stared at the table. "I need something new."

"Your wardrobe is stuffed with gear," I went on, knowing I was walking myself in deeper but unable to stop because she sounded so miserable.

She didn't answer. She gave a wretched sniff.

I really wished I could go into my room and close the door on her without feeling awful. But if I did that I'd feel awful. "Well," I muttered, and, as her head shot up, I said, "you go in and get something and I'll meet you at twelve thirty and see if I like it."

She looked horrified.

"See if I don't like it," I amended.

She gave a satisfied smile. What I hated, she loved. She joking called us The Smart and The Tart. Smart meaning herself and Tart which meant me. I didn't care 'cause I didn't believe her. I looked good in tight jeans and short skirts.

"Thanks, Jan!" Her face was brighter than Einstein.

"It's OK."

"Thanks!" She came over and gave my arm a squeeze. "Thanks!"

"Don't mention it."

"You're so good."

"I know."

"But you are!"

She'd be all over me now. I could call in this favour big time at a later date.

"No probs." I bestowed a smile on her and exited to the bathroom to wash my hair.

Hair washed and shining, make-up applied, it was time to head into town. Because the flab-buster had failed thus far to make any impression on the droopiness of my arse, I decided to walk to town. It was only three miles, it should be no problem. *Pm Live* on Friday had extolled the virtues of walking whilst squeezing the cheeks of the buttocks together, swinging the arms loosely and inhaling deeply. Pounds of flesh were guaranteed to tone up and disappear into the body as muscle, or something along those lines. Anyway, as Monday was my birthday, and I was going to be twenty-five, I decided that the last Saturday of my twenty-fourth year would mark a new beginning. It would be the day when I would walk somewhere for the first time. I left the house at eleven-thirty determined to make it all the way into the city under my own steam. By the time I got to the end of the road, I was knackered. My buttocks were aching and I'd also managed to belt a young fella who had been walking behind me. So I decided to just take my time and stroll.

I'd never known that walking could be so boring. Lifting my feet up and down, up and down was mind-bendingly uninteresting.

The swollen glands I'd discovered underneath my arm-pits that morning popped into my head as I walked and I had to concentrate hard on nailing the thought into a big box in my mind. There was no point in thinking about it, no point in worrying. I was a master of that. I never worried about things until the last minute. That's why I'd failed three subjects in my Leaving. Worry set in the last week in the run-up to the exams. Until then I'd gone out most nights and come home langered. Then worry had hit and knocked me for six. I'd puked up in the middle of History and failed. I'd frozen in Geography and failed. I'd written my name at the top of the Biology paper and failed.

I tried hard to think about other things, like the black pvc skirt I'd seen for twenty quid in A-Wear. If I got into town on time, I was going to buy it. Slowly, the impending excitement of my purchase pushed the other thoughts away.

Walking gave too much time for thinking. Next time I'd get the bus.

At the top of Grafton Street it started to rain. Huge drops began to plop on top of my shiny hair.

The rain got heavier and I pulled my rain-jacket out of my haversack. "It's a clever man that brings his coat when he travels!" My dad's saying. His pearl of wisdom, he liked to say. Well, I guess there had to be at least one pearl in all that sand he had for his brain.

I pulled my jacket over me and pulled up the hood as I stomped my way to the bus-stop.

I couldn't *possibly* be expected to walk in the rain.

I got into town early enough to grab myself the skirt. I even managed to get a size ten in it. It made my day – normally I'm a twelve.

At twelve thirty, I made my way to meet the shopper from hell.

She was standing where we'd arranged, at the bottom of Grafton Street and I knew by the look on her face that she hadn't found anything.

"I can't find anything," were her first words.

"Jesus Jan, will you take that yoke off you!" were the words that came next.

"It keeps me dry." The rain-coat is the only coat I possess. I hate buying coats, so the only thing I have is my blue rain-jacket. Every year, I get a new one. Every year, I always go for the blue colour. Blue is always in fashion.

"You look ridiculous," Abby made a face. "You're like . . ." she screwed up her face. "Like a walking triangle!"

"Yeah," I said, "The Bermuda triangle and I'll make you disappear if you don't shut up."

"Oh, touchy."

I wasn't actually, I'd meant it as a joke. "More witty than touchy actually," I said.

Abby didn't answer. For the first time it dawned on me that she might be embarrassed to be seen with me. The hurt of that flashed through my brain and I pushed it away. That sort of stuff was for kids, we were mature adults.

"So where to?" I nudged her. "Did you even see anything nice?"

That did it. Conversation was back on track.

CHAPTER SEVEN

We'd walked for two hours. In the pissing rain. And that was only up Grafton Street.

Nothing she tried on was suitable. The sleeves were too big, the waist was too small, it would crease, or it was too revealing. Or it didn't reveal enough.

It was getting harder and harder to be civil to her.

Bad-temperedly, I stomped along beside her as once again we found ourselves in O'Connell Street.

"We'll just head down Henry Street and across to Mary Street," Abby said brightly. "Just for a quick look."

I didn't answer.

We were just coming up to the GPO when a loud voice caught our attention.

"Stop the development of the mountainside! Sign 'ere!"
"Stop development of mountainside! Sign 'ere!"

It was pure cockney. And there is something really sexy about that accent. I'm the only person I know who can virtually have an orgasm at *Eastenders*.

I moved in a little closer, just to see did the guy look as good as his voice.

There was a crowd around a table and they all seemed to be signing something. At first I couldn't make out who'd been doing the shouting as there were about three people handing out pens and paper behind the table and they all had their backs to me. I stood waiting for them to turn around.

Abby grabbed my arm to haul me away. "What're you doing?" she demanded. "Will you come on, we'll never get anything at this rate."

"No, Ab," I corrected, "*you'll* never get anything." I shook her off, determined to get a glimpse of Mr Sexy Voice.

Slowly, one of the trio turned in our direction and raised his voice. *"Sign 'ere to save yahr mountains and woods!"*

I almost went weak. This guy was not drop-dead gorgeous. This guy was stay-alive-and-get-your-hole gorgeous.

I even heard Abby suck in her breath. "Fine thing or what?" she whispered.

The *Fine Thing* was tall, about six foot two. He was dressed in a green combat jacket and trousers. His shiny black hair was long and untidy and covered with a weird-looking multicoloured hat. From where we stood, you could see that he had big shiny dark eyes. He had *free spirit* stamped all over him.

"'Ow are ya, ladies?" he'd spotted us and grinned over. His teeth were like an advert for toothpaste.

He motioned us to come forward.

I nearly tripped over myself to get to him.

He had a stud in his nose and about twenty ear-rings marched up his ear-lobes. A small gold hoop dangled from an eyebrow.

He still looked lovely.

"Do ya want to sign 'ere?" He held out the pen to me.

Normally I don't go in for signing things. I'm convinced that these street petitions are an evil conspiracy by the government to see what my affiliations are. Or else they're a way to rope people into anti-government organisations. The minute I sign, I'm sure I'll start receiving all sorts of post looking for my support to uproot civilisation.

No such doubts besieged me when dark Adonis-like men with sexy cockney accents hold out pens and ask me to sign.

Abby made a grab for the pen too.

He laughed.

Oh, what a sexy laugh!

"Keep yer 'air on, I fink I 'ave two," he dug his hand into one of his numerous combat-jacket pockets and pulled out another one. "'Ere luv," he handed it to me.

I couldn't sign my name fast enough. Using my best writing so he'd be able to read it, I also added my address and phone number. Might as well be arrested for a sheep as a lamb and maybe I'd get a phone call out of it to join whatever group this guy was in.

When I finished, I handed the pen back to him. He

was looking at me with something that I thought was admiration. He was no doubt impressed by me being so radical as to give my name and address.

"I like the coat," he nodded at my rain-jacket. "Keep you nice and dry – does it?"

Had I got a board on my back that said *Target Practice*? "It does actually," I replied coldly, "It's a great jacket. Actually."

"Yeah," he gave an easy grin. "Where'd you get it?"

I was virtually monosyllabic. Well, triosyllabic. "In a shop."

"'Ow much?"

That threw me. Why wasn't he backing off?

"I don't think that's any of your business."

"Oh, right," he shrugged. "Sorry – I was only asking."

Abby nudged me. "I think he really wants to know," she whispered. Turning to him, she said, "Jan's a bit hypersensitive about her jacket."

Thanks a bunch, Ab!

"Most people laugh at it."

If she didn't shut up, I was going to kill her.

"In fact, everyone laughs at it."

She's dead.

The guy looked amazed. "But it's a great jacket."

I think he meant it.

"It's a great jacket," he said again.

I knew he meant it.

Shit! Shit! Shit!

"I need somefink like that for the site."

"Site?" Abby asked.

"Yeah," he pointed to the petition. "We're camping in the woods at the foot of the mountainside. They're gonna to build 'ouses on it, so we're protesting." He looked at me. "We've built tree 'ouses and stuff and we're staying as long as it takes."

I felt like beating myself with a machete.

"And it gets pretty wet and cold at night and a jacket like yours would be great." He looked at me when he said that.

"Oh, right." What was I like?

"So?" He gave me a smile. "Where'd you get it?"

"Frawleys," I said.

"Great," he grinned at me. "Thanks a lot."

"It's all right." But it wasn't all right. This guy probably thought I was a hysterical, hypersensitive woman.

Abby was yanking my arm to get going, but I didn't want to leave. I wanted to show him how nice I was when I wasn't being neurotic.

"So you live in a tree-house?" Abby gave an exasperated sigh behind me but I didn't care. "Where?"

"Jan, come on, we've shopping to get."

He sat down on the edge of the table and looked at me with gorgeous brown eyes. He had eye-lashes that I would have killed for.

"You interested in supporting us?"

"Madly interested." I couldn't take my eyes off his face.

"I'm going," Abby announced.

I ignored her.

"You should come on the protest march so." He reached behind him and pulled a bundle of leaflets from under the petition. "Tomorrow at eleven." He handed a leaflet to me and Abby.

SAVE OUR MOUNTAINSIDE was written in huge black letters.

I suppressed a grin – this guy was English.

"Beauty don't belong to anyone," he said as if reading my thoughts. "No country can claim the right to destroy the landscape." He leaned further towards us and the intensity on his face enthralled and excited me. "It's up to everyone to protest. It's our world, ya know?"

"Yeah," I breathed.

"So, we'll see you tomorrow then?"

"Sure," Abby shoved her leaflet into her pocket and began to drag me away. "Nice to have met you," she called back, trying to be polite.

I shook her off. "Just a sec." I never felt like this about anyone before. It was weird. I had fancied a lot of strange men in my time, but never strange men, if you know what I mean. I knew I had to see him again. "Eleven o'clock here?" I asked. Out of the corner of my eye, I could see Abby looking at me in disbelief.

"Yeah," the guy nodded. "Then we march to the developer's office, which is just across the city, 'ave a few speeches, get a few photos taken and then off to the local boozer."

The last bit sounded great. "I'll see if I can make it," I promised.

The smile he gave me made me feel that I'd just saved the world single-handedly.

"Great." He stood up and looked down on me. He was tall. "Look forward to seeing you." He touched my coat. "Maybe I'll have managed to buy one of those by tomorrow. Great coat." He winked and turned away.

Abby rolled her eyes as I rejoined her. "You're not going on the march?" she laughed. "Are you mad? They're all headcases."

"Handsome bloody headcases though," I grinned.

"Well, you needn't expect me to go with you."

"Aw Ab– "

"No way," she shook her head. "If you want to go and make a fool out of yourself, go ahead."

"I'd feel better making a fool out of myself if you were there too."

"No way."

She was adamant. I didn't know if I'd have the nerve to go on my own.

"Please?"

"No."

"Aw, Abby, it's for the good of my love life."

She rolled her eyes. "Jan, if I thought for one moment you'd have a chance with him, I still wouldn't go."

"Ha. Ha."

I didn't say anything more about it as we tramped through town. I pretended to listen to her as she talked on and on about what she was going to buy. All the time I was wondering if I should head off to the march on my own. Imagine if I went and I didn't see him there? Still, I could always come home then. I gazed at the leaflet he'd given me. Eleven o'clock.

" – woman?"

Abby butted in on my thoughts.

"Pardon?"

She was holding a long black dress up to her. "I said," she repeated, doing a twirl, "Does this make me look like a nineties woman?"

A nineties woman! That's what I was. Feck's sake, if I couldn't go to a march on my own, what did that say about all the years of women's liberation. If I couldn't chase a man in this day and age, when could I?

So I decided to bite the bullet and go.

I only hoped it didn't explode in my face.

CHAPTER EIGHT – SUNDAY

Nothing was going to deter me from getting up early on Sunday. The march was at eleven so I set my alarm for eight thirty. That's roughly how long it takes me to look my best.

At eight thirty, the alarm went off. I rolled over and fell asleep.

At nine thirty, I really woke up.

What woke me was the fact that, yet again, I was soaked to the skin. My hair was plastered to my skull and my sheets were sopping. It was definitely too hot in the room.

I didn't dwell on it. What worried me more was the fact that I was an hour behind in my preparations to look stunning for the march. Jumping out of bed, I made straight for the shower. The water was freezing. Shite, I thought, this is not going to be my morning.

The chip on my shoulder became a large single.

Showering in artic conditions caused my body to become numb after about five minutes. Blue and shivering, I exited the bathroom. I gave my hair a hasty rinse, wrapped it in a towel and put on my bathrobe.

The only good thing was that I was alone in the flat. Beth was still in Wicklow and Abby's date must have been explosive because she hadn't arrived home. It meant that I could have a nice leisurely breakfast, watch TV and ponder on what I was going to wear. Mentally, I went through my wardrobe.

I was just munching my last bit of toast and sneering at some MTV presenter, who could barely speak English, when the phone rang.

It could only be my mam.

Her usual 'don't for God's sake have a lie in on a Sunday when you've mass to go to' phone call.

If I didn't answer, she'd think something was wrong and she'd come haring around to the flat to investigate.

She'd done that once before and she hadn't liked what she'd seen. The rift had grown bigger.

I padded over to the phone. "Hello?"

"Janet?"

"Hi, Mam."

"Hello, Janet." I knew by her voice, she had something to nark about. "You never told me you were sick."

"So?"

She paused and I heard her taking a deep breath. "Well, you could have rung to tell me. I phoned your work on Friday and was so embarrassed when some guy said you were sick. Imagine not telling your own mother you were sick." When I made no reply, she continued, "You are genuinely sick, aren't you?"

I didn't need this first thing in the morning, so I tried to make a joke out of it. "Mam, if I told you I was terminally ill, would that ease your mind?"

As usual, she didn't laugh. "That's in bad taste," she snapped. "I just hope you're not on course to lose another job."

I hoped I was.

Her voice rose. "When are you coming to see us?"

"I dunno."

There was a silence. I couldn't think of a single thing to say to her.

"Well, it's your father's birthday next weekend, so I hope you'll oblige us with a visit."

"Eh – "

"He's fifty."

"I'll be there."

"He's building an extension to the house," she went on, her voice softer, now that I'd agreed to leave my den of vice to pay a call to the homestead. "All his builder mates are giving him a hand every Sunday. "

I didn't want to know. Dad and his mad schemes. The last time he'd attempted to build something, he'd knocked down the supporting wall of the house.

"Your dad and his mad schemes, huh?" There was a tolerant smile in her voice.

"Yeah."

"And Lisa's driving us all mad studying for the Leaving."

"Well, let's hope she doesn't bring in any calculators this time." I couldn't help it. My mam brings out the worst in me.

She missed the sarcasm. "Yes, we've warned her about cheating. She got that video out last week – what was it now?" she paused as she tried to remember. *"How to cheat in the Leaving* or something," she continued. "It's set her mad all together."

She fits right in so, I thought.

"She's a gas kid."

She'd never have said I was gas if I'd got expelled for cheating. In fact, the time I did get suspended from school, World War Three broke out.

"Well, it's good to know we'll be seeing you soon," Mam said. Then she took a breath and asked the question she'd really rung to ask in the first place, "Have you been to Mass yet?"

And I answered what she knew I'd answer. "No."

I rattled on before she could get a word in. "I'm going on an environmental march this morning. To stop developers from building on the mountains."

"Sounds like a good cause." I think she was impressed. "You can't be too sick so."

"I'm all right."

"So you'll get Mass tonight?"

"No, I won't." I was sick of this. Every week she rang, she seemed to convince herself that I'd had a sudden leap of faith since she last talked to me.

"I see." Deep disapproval. "I'll see you next week, say Saturday?"

"OK."

"And you'll stay for Sunday?"

"I dunno. I might . . . "

"Course you will. Your sisters'll be dying to see you."

"Ma, I . . . "

She cut me off. No one ever lets me finish what I want to say on the phone.

And now I'd have to spend two days at home.

After breakfast, I did my make-up. I can't go outside without wearing at least a tonne of foundation on my face. First, I dabbed concealer on all my spots. Twenty-five and still spotty. That was one of the great myths of our time. If I'd known when I was a spotty fifteen-year-old that my spots would still be there ten years later, I'd have slit my wrists.

Next it was time to get the trowel out and shovel on the foundation. I know when to stop when my face takes on a tangerine glow.

Then it was the turn of the eye-shadow, brown, to match my eyes, lipstick, bright red, and powder which went everywhere. I still couldn't put on powder without drenching my eyelashes and having to dust down my clothes at the end.

I stared at my reflection. I looked all right.

Unwrapping the towel from over my hair, I shook it loose. My hair's the only thing I have that sets me apart. It's long, glossy and black. Because it has a curl, I don't need to spend ages drying it. It's the only thing that always looks good no matter what.

It was almost dry and I turned my head upside down and ran my fingers through it to get rid of any tangles. Switching on the hairdryer, I finished drying it off.

After trying on all my jeans, I decided on my blue Levis. They looked better on me than I remembered. They even creased up at the thighs and the pockets fitted exactly on my arse. So it didn't look droopy.

I took out a denim shirt and put it on and then I pulled a pair of socks from my sock-drawer. Beth always slags me when I say things like "sock-drawer". She thinks it's mad to have a place to put your socks and another place for your clothes. Beth just dumps all her gear into her wardrobe and pulls it out when she needs it. She can never find anything. I like things tidy. The flat itself I don't mind being messy, but when I go into my room I like to know where everything is.

I put on my boots, the ones with the heels. They made me look slimmer than I did in my runners.

I took a last look at myself in the mirror and satisfied that it was the best I could do, I grabbed my rain-jacket and set off.

It was pissing rain and a gale-force wind had just started up as I made my way towards the marchers. They were standing in the shelter of the GPO. There weren't that many and feeling really self-conscious I walked towards them. There was a funny feeling in the pit of my stomach and my heart was beating like mad. As I drew nearer, I could see them in little clusters, talking away as if they all knew each other.

I began to walk more slowly, reluctant to intrude. To be honest, they looked a scary enough bunch – unwashed and unshaven, and that was only the women. Everyone seemed to be carrying banners and some of them were handing out leaflets to people as they walked by.

I suddenly wished I hadn't come. It had been a mad idea. My nineties image of the forceful woman began to evaporate.

I was just about to turn back when I heard his voice. "Oy, you! You in the raincoat!"

I saw him pushing his way through the crowd and his eyes crinkled up as he recognised me. "Raincoat girl – ya came." He stood in front of me with a huge grin on his face. "Ya came," he said again.

He'd remembered me! "Yeah," I nodded, suddenly feeling shy as his eyes looked me up and down.

"Great." He shrugged. "Loadsa people promise to turn up and don't." He stuck out his hand. "Dave."

"Jan," I clasped his hand in mine and savoured the first touch of him.

"Great to meet ya, Jan."

His handshake was firm and he looked me in the eyes when he talked. The wind blew his long hair over his face and he had to put his free hand up to keep it back. He was wearing the coloured hat again. It suited him.

"I never got to the shops yesterday but I told all the others about your coat." He kept hold of my hand and pulled me over to one of the groups of people. "Oy you lot, this is Jan."

They turned and stared and smiled at me. They didn't look half as threatening close up.

Dave began the introductions. Pointing to each person he gave me their names. "Sam, Orla, Chaz, Megan and Pete."

They were all young – in their twenties at the most. "This is the girl I told ya 'bout. The one with the – "

"Coat," Megan finished for him. She gave me a stunning smile and nodded. "Dave was singing your praises yesterday. Said he'd met this girl with a great coat." She eyed me speculatively, "I think he was a bit smitten actually."

I blushed, thrilled skinny. Well, not skinny, but thrilled medium-size.

Dave spoilt my euphoria by telling Megan in an affectionate voice to "Do one".

They all began talking again.

"We ready to start?" a fella asked, coming toward the group.

Dave quirked his eyebrows at Sam, who nodded.

"Right," Dave yelled above the chatter. "Let's get going."

I watched, suddenly feeling left out again, as everyone began getting their banners and holding them in the air. Dave left my side and picked up an enormous one with a slogan that read: SAVE THE TREES. Coming towards me, he asked, "Want to 'elp me carry it? We'll be right at the front?"

Help him carry it! I was honoured. This was even better than I'd fantasised. I'd lain awake last night imagining what would happen today. Carrying his banner and being able to look at him close up hadn't even featured.

Reverently I held my pole and followed him as we made our way through the crowd. We took our places at the top of the line. Dave shouted over at me, "We'll just wait for everyone else to get 'emselves sorted and we'll 'ead off – right?"

"Fine," I agreed. This was great.

He came to stand beside me, the banner drooping on the ground. "You'll come for a pint after – won't ya?"

"Sure."

"Great."

He'd asked me to go for a drink. Could life get any better than that?

The march started off brilliantly. With Dave and me heading the line, we'd slowly made our way down O'Connell Street. The wind whipped our flags and banners as they proclaimed our entry onto D'Olier Street. "SAVE THE MOUNTAINSIDE!" everyone chanted.

At first I was mortified, convinced that everyone along the road was gawking at me. I was glad it was raining because it meant that there weren't many people around. During my fantasies last night, I had a nightmare scenario where I met all the crew from my office. Of course, that couldn't happen, but if it did I would've died.

So, at first, as we marched down O'Connell Street, I couldn't shout out, all I could do was stare fixedly in front and imagine like hell that I was somewhere else.

Dave's voice broke in on my thoughts. "Goin' great, ain't it?" He had a big smile on his face, like a kid in a sweet shop, and it made me feel all funny inside.

It just seemed so brilliant and outlandish that he cared about what happened to a bunch of trees on some mountainside. A fella that cared so much about a flipping tree. It touched me something weird.

It was like the story of God taking care of the birds that fell out of nests. It had been my favourite bible tale when I was a kid. Animal-lover that I was, it had made me feel so safe and secure to know that God cared about birds and flowers.

Until I'd found out the truth.

When I was twelve, I found the body of a baby bird beside our house. He was so tiny that when I picked him up his body didn't even cover the width of my palm. He was warm and floppy and his feathers blew in the breeze. Despite the fact that he was dead, he looked perfect.

Puzzled and shocked, I brought him into my mother. She was peeling spuds beside the kitchen sink.

"Look what I found," I held out my hand and showed her the bird.

"Oh, Jesus," she screeched, dropping her knife into the sink and flapping her arms at me. "Get it out of here! Get it out of here!"

"It's OK," I said, "he's dead. He won't fly around."

"Janet," she screeched even more, "Throw it away, you'll get all sorts of germs."

I stared at her. "Why didn't God save him, I want to know?"

"What?" She was pushing me towards the door.

"Well, you told us that God looks after all the birds of the air. Why didn't he look after this one?"

It was a reasonable question.

She took the bird between her thumb and forefinger and dropped its little body on top of all the rubbish in the bin outside the door.

It didn't look right.

"Why didn't he save — ?"

"You're over-reacting, Janet. It's just a bird." She was on her way in again.

"You said that God would — "

"God was too busy, all right," she snapped. *"Just like me trying to make the dinner."*

It was like the Easter bunny and the Tooth Fairy and Santa all over again. Only this time, I knew I'd never believe any more crap from anyone.

I grew up that summer.

A group of students were gathered outside Trinity College. They stared at us as we marched by. One woman walking along with a massive blue umbrella yelled, "Shower a wasters! Get yerselves a job. Feckin' bloody trees, me arse."

The students joined in. "Hey man, any hash for sale?"

"Eco fuckin' wasters, man!"

"Oy you, you with the orange face in the front – it's not the twelfth of July, ya know."

I think the last comment was intended for me. My face turned red.

Dave grinned over at me. "Don't mind 'em Jan. They're the ones with the problem."

None of the marchers reacted to the abuse. They kept shouting and I joined in. No way was I going to be insulted by a bunch of Trinity heads. We all smiled at their ignorance.

The rain began to get heavier. It lashed on us as we made our way down D'Olier Street. The wind blew papers and bottles about our feet. It was a feat of strength to be able to struggle against what had to be a force nine gale and keep an enormous banner upright.

And my feet were killing me. I should've worn runners like everyone else.

At first, the pain was tolerable, a dull ache on the balls of my feet. Dullness began to mount in intensity. They began to seize up. Slower and slower until I was limping along.

I could hear rumblings of dissatisfaction in the background.

"Why're we moving so slow?"

"Hey, hurry up in the front!"

"It's not an all-night-march Davy!"

I was mortified but I couldn't go any quicker.

Dave looked over at me. "You all right?"

"My feet are hurting."

He glanced down at my feet. "You've big 'igh boots on!" He sounded amused.

I couldn't look at him, I knew he'd think I was a twit.

"You 'aven't been on many marches, 'ave ya, Jan?"

"I have," I fibbed. I raised my eyes from the ground. "I didn't wear my runners today because," I searched for a good excuse.

"'Cause you knew it'd rain?"

"Exactly!"

We grinned at each other.

Davy rolled his beautiful eyes in his beautiful face and turned around to the crowd. He handed his stick to a girl behind him. "Take that, luv," he said. He came over to me and holding my hand, he gently removed the pole from it. "Oy, Sam, hold that would ya."

Sam came towards the front and relieved me of the pole. He looked questioningly at Dave.

"Jan's done 'er ankle in – I'll go with her and we'll grab a drink. Meet ya later?"

"Sure," Sam nodded. He smiled at me. "Thanks for your support, Jan."

"No probs."

"Maybe we'll see you again?"

"Count on it!"

"Great."

The march set off again without Dave and me.

We were left alone in the middle of the street. I didn't want to say it but I felt I had to. "If you want to go on," I gestured towards the retreating crowd, "don't worry about me."

"Naw," he shook his head. "It's not as if I'm makin' a speech or anyfink. Anyhow," he gave me a crooked smile, "I want to find out more about ya. Come on." He grabbed my arm and pulled me along the street until he found a pub. "This all right?" he asked.

I couldn't believe my luck. Anywhere'd be fine, I wanted to say. But I didn't. "Suppose," I nodded with as much nonchalance as I could.

This hadn't been in my fantasy either. Sometimes reality is better.

CHAPTER NINE

"What you 'aving?" Dave shoved his hand in his jacket pocket, searching for cash.

I didn't think he'd have much money. "I'll buy."

"Nah." He looked a bit insulted. "What you 'aving?"

"All right – thanks. I'll have," I considered carefully, "a mineral water."

"You're joking?" He looked even more insulted.

This was not how I'd planned it. "I'm on antibiotics so I can't drink," I said. "Honest – water's fine."

He grinned. "You're sick and still you came on the march." He looked really touched. "That's great."

I shrugged modestly. "That's me."

I was glad Abby wasn't there – she'd have puked.

He told me to find a seat while he got the drinks.

There was no problem as the pub was deserted. I found a nice comfortable sofa-seat beside the stained-glass window. Sunlight was streaming through it and it lit up coloured dust motes in the air. I don't know what that said for the pub hygiene, but it looked great.

I watched Dave making his way across the lounge, he had a drink in each hand and two packets of crisps dangling from his mouth. He'd taken off his hat and stuffed it into one of his numerous pockets. His hair was a mad mop of black curls. There were little ringlets over his forehead and he reminded me of the guy in the Suzanne Vega song, "Gypsy".

Under his combat jacket he was wearing a CND tee-shirt.

He handed me my drink and taking a packet of crisps from his mouth offered them to me too.

"Thanks."

The two of us sat in silence in the half-empty pub just sipping our drinks and eating the crisps.

He broke it. "So, Jan?"

I looked at him. "What?"

"Tell us about yerself." He regarded me over his pint glass. Then, he put it down on the table and leaned back in the seat. I got the feeling he thought he was about to be entertained.

Bored rigid more likely.

I tried to change the subject, "Well, I guess my feet will take about ten years to recover."

He sat up again, all sparkly eyes and shiny white teeth. My heart did a slow flip-flop in my chest.

"Take 'em off," he grinned.

"Pardon?" This was definitely not how I'd planned it. These eco-warriors were something else. I wasn't too sure if I could handle it . . .

"Yer boots. Take 'em off."

"Oh," I tried to look like I knew what he'd meant.

"Take 'em off."

"I can't take my boots off in a pub."

"Sure ya can." He grinned. "Wot's a matter?" When I didn't reply, he nudged me gently with his elbow. His eyes were laughing at me. "Go on – I dare ya."

"You'll pass out with the smell," I joked feebly. Then, I realised, that if I wanted to get to know this guy, it was exactly the kind of off-putting thing not to say. "It's a joke," I clarified hastily.

"Prove it." He was studying me intently. He was probably wondering why on earth I wouldn't take my shoes off in public. I know he was about to call me a prude or something equally offensive and I didn't want him to say that.

Even if it was true.

Taking shoes off in public was something my dad always did, anywhere he went. "Bleeding shoes have me murdered," he'd mutter.

He insisted on buying bargain shoes. It didn't matter if they fitted him or not, once they were cheap. They were usually of the squeaky, plastic, sweat-like-a-pig variety. "A bargain is a bargain," was his motto. My mother's was "His bargain is our chagrin". But she never said that to him. The stench from his socks would knock an elephant out cold for a month. Many's the trip I'd taken with my father when he went shoeless. Many's the time I'd see people sniff the air wondering what herd of animals had died nearby. I blushed even now, thinking about it.

"Go on," Dave said again. "You a prude or somefink?"

"No."

"Well then?"

At least I'd put clean socks on. They were white and holeless. Reluctantly, holding my breath, I took off my boots.

"Up here," Dave pointed to the seat.

"What?"

"Put yer feet up here."

"I'm not planning on sleeping," I was trying my best to make light of the situation. I was afraid to breathe in case there was a smell.

Dave took no notice, he grabbed my feet and pulled them up onto the seat. I nearly fell off.

"Sorry," he smiled.

I couldn't reply. It would mean taking a breath. Were smelly feet hereditary?

"Now," Dave aligned my feet across his knees.

My lungs were about to burst. I slowly exhaled and inhaled. The air seemed fine. I felt my body beginning to relax. I was forced to catch my breath again though because he'd slowly begun to peel off my sock.

"What are you doing?" I gasped. *What was he doing?*

Very gently, he cupped my foot in his hand. His thumb on top, his other fingers supporting my foot. With soft circular movements, he started to rub his thumb across the toes. His head was bent, intent on what he was doing and my hormones went into overdrive. His thumb moved up the bridge of my foot, his other fingers caressing the sole. He moved his fingers in small erotic circles, gentle yet pressured. I wanted to faint with pleasure. Slowly and sensuously, his fingers made their way up my foot. I thought I'd died and gone to heaven when, with his two thumbs, he caressed either side of my ankle bone. Both his hands were holding my foot, smoothing it, stroking it and not once did he look at me. That turned me on more than anything.

"The pain gone now?" he asked, lifting his head up and looking at me with sleepy brown eyes.

"Yeah," I breathed, wondering when he'd suggest going somewhere and caressing the rest of me. I couldn't believe this was happening. It was like being in a book.

He beamed. "Wow, that was quick." He let go of my right foot and started on my left.

I got ready to enjoy it all over again. That was if my heart could stand it.

"I learned foot massage from a girl in the Amazon," he said as he pulled off my other sock. "Never tried it on anyone afore though." He gave my foot a gentle tweak. "You're my guinea-pig."

"I am?"

"Yep." He began his ministrations. Head bent, circular thumb movements.

A guinea-pig.

I hardly felt what he did with my other foot. All I know is that while he fiddled around with it, I was trying to get some sort of a smile back on my face.

"All right now?" he asked about ten minutes later.

I put my socks back on with a furious intensity. I figured I owed him a word of thanks. "Thanks."

"No probs." he relaxed his long body back into the seat again. "She told me I had healink hands."

"Who?" All I could think of was that I'd been his guinea-pig.

"The girl in the Amazon," he looked upwards as if trying to think. "Can't remember 'er name."

Well, I thought, she can't have meant that much to him.

"She was a lesbian, I remember that."

She can't have meant anything to him.

His attention flicked back to me. "So Jan, wot's your story?"

I'd been dreading this. "Aw, nothing major," I said airily.

"You gonna tell me?"

Didn't look like I had much choice. "I work in an insurance company."

"Yeah? Long?"

"Three years." I shrugged. "I'm supposed to be a typist."

He grinned at that and I smiled back. "I've had loads of jobs before that – shop-assistant, chief chip-maker in the local chipper, doctor's receptionist. I hated them all."

"And what would ya like to do?"

"Dunno." I studied my hands. "I haven't found out yet."

"'Aven't ya?"

"No." I looked up to see him smiling at me. "I'm nearly twenty-five and clueless."

Then I remembered something. "I exercise." I didn't elaborate. "And I live in a flat with two other girls."

He looked at me.

"That's it." It sounded like an apology.

"Oh, right."

He didn't look disappointed. It was a relief.

"You seeing anyone?"

The question caught me on the hop. Why did he want to know? Was he interested? It could be just a casual inquiry, in which case, I suppose I should have said that I was. That way I could save face.

On the other hand, why the hell had I come on this march? "No, no one," I said, and added hastily, in case he'd think I was desperate, "at the moment."

"'Ave you not?" He sounded interested, yet not interested, if you know what I mean.

"No." I gave a little laugh as if having a fella wasn't a big issue for me.

"I'm surprised," he looked straight at me, "A good-lookin' girl like you." He drank down the remains of his pint and stood up. " . . . one?"

"What?" All I could hear were the words, "good-looking girl like you".

"D'ya want another one?"

"Oh, I'll get these," I could barely manage to get the words out.

"Right so."

I left the table and seemed to float all the way to the bar.

"Yeah?" the barman asked.

"He said I was good-looking." I had to tell someone.

"Yer all right – not exactly Miss World, are ya?" He sniggered. "Now, what are ya drinkin'?"

Voice barely civil, I gave the order. "A pint and . . ." I wondered would I need any Dutch courage. "A double vodka." Then I remembered the antibiotics. "No, no, a water," I said.

"Comin' up," He pulled the pint and left it to settle, then went to get the water.

I had time to compose myself as I waited. I knew that if I didn't do something, I'd probably never see Dave again. I had to let him know, without throwing myself at him, that I was ready for a steamy sexual relationship without further notice. Well, any kind of a relationship actually. Adrenaline flowed, thoughts raced. He was an eco-warrior. What kind of a woman would he go for? He wandered all over the place. First, I had to show an avid interest in his ideas, agree with everything he said. That should be no problem. Easily led was my middle name.

The pint was banged down and it slopped out of the glass onto the counter. "Pint and water." The barman took my tenner, cashed it up, then virtually threw the change at me. "Naomi Campbell you are not," he said.

That was it. "In training for arse-hole barman of the year, are you?" I asked. Without waiting for an answer,

I picked up the drinks and ran back to our table. I was afraid he'd come after me.

He didn't.

I handed Dave his pint and he nodded his thanks.

Sitting in beside him, I lifted my glass. "Cheers."

"Cheers."

"So, what about you?" I asked. Grinning ruefully, I added, "I betcha your life's more exciting than mine."

"Depends," he shrugged. "Depends what you like."

"Where have you been?"

"Loadsa places."

He wasn't being too forthcoming. Valiantly I persisted. "Amazon? You said you'd been there?"

"Yep," he nodded. "We were there, and a few places in Europe."

"Protesting?"

"Yep." He grinned. "The best I've been was this town in California. Davis, it's called." His voice became animated. "Aw, Jan, it's somefink else. It was the first town in the US to become an eco-village." He took a gulp of his pint and continued, "Everyfink they plant is edible, they mainly use bikes instead of cars, they recycle most of their gear . . ."

He's beautiful, I thought.

" . . . half their ground is cultivated . . ."

I wish he'd kiss me.

" . . . double deckers . . ."

Maybe if I concentrate hard enough.

" . . . communal compost heap . . ."

Kiss me. Kiss me. Kiss me.

" . . . supportive of human . . ."

Kiss me. Kiss me. Kiss . . . it wasn't working.

He stopped. "Interesting, ain't it?"

"Yeah. Brill," I agreed.

"So then, we decided to come over 'ere," he grinned. "I'll probably stay on until the end of the protest, but some of the lads move from place to place."

I hoped the protest would never come to an end. "How long before a decision is reached?" That sounded a knowledgeable question.

"Dunno," he shrugged. "Could be a few months. Could be a year."

Despite the lack of Dutch courage, I knew I had to move in. Face burning, I asked, "So, do you have time for . . . " I gulped, "relationships?" I took a swig out of my glass. "You know, moving from place to place?"

He shook his head. "Nah. Impossible to commit. I 'ave gone out with a few people but, ya know, it never lasts." He grinned. "I like my freedom too much."

"Oh, me too," I agreed delightedly. He'd given me the lever I needed. "Commitment is not big on my agenda either – I like casual flings."

"Yeah?" Interest sparked in his eyes. At least, I think it did. "Two of a kind." Dave clicked his glass with mine and winked. "Down with commitment, hey, Jan?"

"Absolutely."

But when he really got to know me, he wouldn't say that. I knew he wouldn't.

"Do you miss home much?"

He shrugged. "Nah." Then he grinned. "*'Ome is in me where ever I roam.*"

"Really." What was he on about?

"*Waterboys.* 'Further Up, Further In'. Me favourite song."

"Oh."

"Tell ya wot I do miss though, Jan." He leaned nearer to me, "I miss a proper dinner and a bed."

Was it my imagination or did he look meaningfully at me when he said the 'B' word.

"Yeah, potatoes and veg, that's wot I miss."

He was looking meaningfully at me now.

"Sure, come to my place and I'll rustle you up some grub." Eagerly I looked at him. "I'll cock, eh, cook you something."

I don't know why I said that. Somewhere at the back of my mind a voice was reminding me of the only obstacle to my invitation. I couldn't even boil an egg.

"Great," he beamed. "Thanks." He looked thrilled. "And you wouldn't mind?"

"No."

I'd ask Abby to cook.

"Thanks."

I gestured to the bar. "Ask the barman for a pen and paper. I'll write down the address for you and we'll arrange a day." I hadn't the courage to confront the barman again.

"Right." He kept smiling at me. "The others'll be mad not to be invited." He paused and raised his eyebrows.

I had no intention of having hoards to dinner. I pretended not to hear.

"Right," he said again and left.

I couldn't believe I'd actually done it. I asked him to dinner and I was going to see him again.

We arranged to meet the following Friday, five whole days away, and I drew a map for him to the flat. I gave him my phone number too, just in case he wanted to ring.

When we parted, at about four, he reached out and ran his index finger lightly down my face. "I like you," he said. "I like the way you turned up at the march today and I like your interest in our work. You're committed."

"I am," I said, feeling only a little guilty that he seemed so taken in by my eco air.

And I vowed, as a nineties woman, that when I was finished with him, he'd be committed too – to me.

CHAPTER TEN

Abby was sitting at the table eating some horribly healthy green food when I got back. She was dressed in the clothes she'd worn out the night before.

"Hi, Jan," she greeted me. I could tell by the cheery way she said it, that she was in good form. When Abby was pissed, she'd usually wail something like, "Where were you? And why didn't you invite me? Don't you know I'm on my own?" etc, etc. Obviously she'd had a good night with Mickey.

And with a name like that, it wasn't surprising.

"Abby – hi," I smiled back. I decided to go for it. Strike whilst the iron was smiling.

"Eh, Ab . . . "

"I had a great night last night." She put some of the revolting green food in her mouth. She looked meaningfully at me. "Great night," she repeated pointedly.

"I'm glad. Eh, Ab . . . "

"And I'm seeing him again," she stopped dramatically, "tonight!"

"That's great." I smiled. The fact that she was happy would make my request easier for her to accept, "Abby, I need . . . "

"You don't sound too interested." Abby looked offended. Her voice rose on a wail, "This is a big deal for me, Jan."

"Yes, I know." I jumped into the seat opposite her. "It's just that I have to ask you something."

She looked through me. She flicked her attention back to the magazine she'd been reading when I came in. Idly she began to turn over the pages.

"It's just that I have to ask you something," I said again.

She started to hum to herself.

Third time lucky? "I have something to ask you."

She got up to make herself a coffee.

There was no way of avoiding it. It was to be a tit-for-tat situation. Obviously Abby was making sure that it was in my interest to be interested. I half-grinned as I asked, "So how was it with Mickey then?"

Abby turned back to face me. She smiled beatifically. "What was that, Jan?"

"How was it with Mickey?" I asked. "Tell me what happened." Mentally I prepared myself for the onslaught of information. Abby is the most boring story-teller on the planet.

She beamed. The fact that she'd blackmailed me into listening to her didn't spoil the moment one bit. "We had a great time," she gave a little shiver and a small private smile. "We went to an Italian place and had the most gorgeous meal." She proceeded to tell me what she'd eaten and it all sounded revolting. I'm a chips-and-battered-sausage person.

"Sounds gorgeous."

Then she'd told me what they'd talked about – at length. It was of the "and I said and he said" variety.

Half an hour later, green slime congealing on Abby's plate, I tuned back in. She was telling a joke that Mickey had told. It was a very subtle joke all about the stock market. Too subtle for me. But I laughed.

I thought she'd think it was decent of me to laugh at her fella's jokes.

"Do you get it?" She sounded surprised.

"Uh-huh, it's a good one all right." This 'licking Abby's arse' routine was going well. So I tried again. "Abby?"

"Oh." She sounded put-out. "I hadn't a clue what the joke was about – I just pretended to laugh." She half-glared at me and asked resentfully, "Will you explain it, Jan?"

"Well . . ." I stalled for time. "It's, eh, not the sort of joke you can explain." Not the sort I could anyway. At her crestfallen expression, I said, "Well, you either understand the stock-market or you don't."

She looked even more miserable.

"I'm thick, aren't I, Jan?" She poked her food around.

"No. Don't be mad." I couldn't let her get upset. So, I came clean, "I didn't understand the joke either, I just

pretended to laugh." Maybe now I could slip it in? "I
wanted to get on your good side because – "

"You're only saying that! You did so understand it."

"I didn't."

"Huh!"

I don't think she believed me. "Everyone is good at
something," I said, not trying to sound the least bit
patronising, but doing it anyhow, "You're good at
selling ads." Encouraged by her smile, I continued
cautiously, seizing my chance, "And . . . well . . . you're
good at cooking."

"Yes, I am." She sat up straighter. "And he's into
good food."

"Everyone likes your food, Ab." Biting the bullet for
the second time in twenty-four hours, I said, "You
should cook more often, Ab."

It worked. "You're right, Jan," she said smiling.
"You're right." She paused and said, "I think I'll cook a
meal for him and invite him to the flat."

"Yeah." I nodded. "Maybe you could do it on – "

"Mickey is clever," she whispered, cutting me off yet
again. "Really clever. I don't want him to think I'm
stupid."

"He won't."

"But he might."

"No. He won't." I was getting the tiniest bit pissed
off at this stage.

"How won't he?"

That stuck me. "Just agree with everything he says,"
I replied hastily. "Men like that."

"Yeah, it might work," she said slowly. "If he says something stupid and I agree, he can't call me stupid, can he?"

"Nope." Yet again, I tried to get back to a part of the conversation earlier. "I definitely think you should cook him a meal, though."

"Oh, I will," she nodded. "I will."

I gulped. How did I get this one out? "Next Friday night, maybe," I finished weakly.

Her eyes narrowed. I think she saw right through me. "Friday?" Her voice was quiet.

"Uh-huh."

"I might." She paused, considering. "If you'll promise to be out."

Trying to appear unruffled, I said, "No can do, Ab."

Arched eyebrows. "Why?"

Her voice was serene. The calm before the storm.

"I, uh, I invited someone over that night."

"So?"

"For a meal." I attempted a casual laugh.

"And you thought I'd cook?" Still the calm voice.

"I'll pay," I began to grovel. "All the food – I'll pay. All you'll have to do is . . ."

"All I'll have to do! All I'll have to do!" She stood up and glowered at me. "I don't believe you!"

"I'm telling the truth." A feeble attempt at a joke.

"Here I am, thinking what a great friend you are and all the time, all the time," her voice rose, "all the time you're scheming to get me to slave over a meal for you and whatever dead-beat you've managed to acquire."

"I did say that I had – "

"This is too much." She was on her feet now, pacing agitatedly about the room.

"So you're not interested?" I strove for calm.

"HA!"

"Please Ab . . ."

"HA!"

"Spuds and vegetables – nothing fancy."

"Well, it won't be when you've finished cooking it, that's for sure." She tossed this slur over her shoulder as she made for her room.

"It's the eco-warrior," I shouted finally through her closed door.

Silence.

"You know the guy we met in town yesterday and you thought he was a ride?"

"No way!" The disbelief in her voice was insulting.

"It's true."

"I'm still not cooking."

"*Aw* please, Ab," I begged desperately. "I promise I'll help. I'll peel all the vegetables."

"*That's* helping?" Scorn poured all over me.

"I'll pay for everything. You name it, I'll pay." This was desperate. She couldn't let me down.

"Wow."

"I'll even wash up."

"Pardon?"

"I'll even wash up." Resentment came through.

"Sorry, don't believe you."

"I promise I'll wash up." When she didn't reply, I said, "I promise on my mother's life."

"HA!"

"On your life then."

"No way."

"OK. OK. I promise on my life that I'll wash up on Friday."

Slowly the door opened. "You'll pay for everything, peel everything and wash up everything?"

"Yeah." I wasn't sure that Friday was such a good idea now.

"We'll have to get Beth out of the way."

"She's working."

Abby smirked. "Oh, you had it all planned, didn't you?"

I hadn't planned on you and Mickey being there, I wanted to say, but didn't. "Most of it."

"What time is he coming around?"

"Eight."

"Fine. I'll leave all the stuff out and when you get home, start peeling."

I didn't know whether to feel grateful or conned. "Thanks."

Abby shrugged. "Anytime." Knowing that she had got the better of me, she emerged from her doorway. She wandered back out into the room and, looking over her shoulder at me, she asked casually, "Is it *really* the eco-warrior?"

Now it was my turn to smile. "Yeah. Oh, Abby, he's gorgeous."

Her face softened. "I can't believe it. Fair play to you. I'm glad. I really am."

"Do you want to hear about the march?" Now I knew how she felt when she wanted to talk about Mickey.

"'Course I do! Did you get off with him?" She gave my arm a squeeze. "No, no, don't answer, I'll stick on the kettle and you can give us the low-down."

I was happier than I'd been in ages.

CHAPTER ELEVEN – MONDAY

I was five minutes early for work. Al was the only one there when I got in. I was glad because it meant I could get used to being depressed again. Depressed because I was back in work and that today was my birthday and everyone would probably forget it.

The Insurance Company has its offices in an old building in the city centre. From as far back as I can remember, I wanted to work in a high-tech chrome and glass office block. With plush carpets, obscure pictures and marble floors in the foyers.

Reality bit me really hard when I started work for McCoy, Beale & Co. I was lulled into a false sense of security when I went for my interview. It was held on the ground floor, which is gorgeous. The public see this facade and so did thick gob-shited gullible me.

Full of hope and joy, I started work. On my first day I was led past the deep-blue-carpeted offices and cash desks. Led past the fuzzy-felt wallpapered walls. I was brought high up into the attic part of the building. The further I went from ground level, the worse things got, until at last, I was deposited outside a brown wooden door, situated on a mustard-tiled corridor. Fungus growing on the damp, yellow-painted walls lent the whole hallway a certain Stephen-King-like ambience. And it was freezing. Siberia had nothing on this.

At twenty-two, I learned the truth. That plush offices and central heating were for Beauty Queens. Downstairs was where all the good-looking typists worked. What did it say about me that I was stuck right at the very top? And three years later – still there. The only good thing about working in a cold, damp office at the top of a building is the privacy. Phone calls are not listened to like on open-plan floors. Details of your private life are not transmitted via e-mail to the whole building.

We share a quiet understanding in our place: no one tells how little we do, no one rats on anyone else's life. It works great.

Al was sitting at his desk reading a sports magazine. He looked up and grinned at me. "How's the patient?"

"Crap," I sat on the edge of his desk. "All I want to do is get plastered."

"That's what people do on birthdays."

I gave him a delighted punch. "You *remembered* it's my birthday?"

He smiled and pulled an envelope from his drawer. "After last year, I'd be afraid to forget."

"Bastard!" I'd spent all day last year humming *For She's a Jolly Good Fellow* and saying how much I was dreading the coming of the big Three Zero in a few years and no one in the office had reacted. Instead, they'd all said how lucky I was that at least I didn't look my age.

"Well," Al shoved the card at me, "you gonna take it or not?"

I was touched. "Bloody sure I am."

He sat grinning at me as I opened it. It was a picture of a big fat person on an exercise bike. Inside it read, *Fancy a ride?* He'd just signed it Al.

"I wouldn't ride you if you stole Brad Pitt's face and wore it."

"Thanks, Jan. My ego needed that." He shook his head and grinned. Then, shoving his magazine into his drawer he asked casually, "Do you want to go for a jar tonight? My shout."

"That'd be great." Then I remembered about the antibiotics. They were really getting in the way of my social life. So I decided not to take them that day. "Thanks, Al."

"No probs."

We grinned at each other.

"Can we go somewhere local to me?" I asked then. "The thoughts of getting a taxi back home after a session might be expensive."

"I said a drink."

"Feck off."

Al laughed and nodded. "Anywhere you want to go is fine by me."

It was funny how normal Al was when it was just me

and him. He changed when other people were around. He was weird. In fact everyone in my office was weird, so he fitted in grand. Al had joined us about eighteen months ago and for the first week he hadn't said a word, just sat at his desk and did his work. The fact that he did any work marked him out as unusual anyway.

There'd been high hopes for him. He was good-looking. Dark eyes, floppy dark hair and cheek-bones that'd cut you. And what a body! It was from training every lunch-time. Ten miles he'd run and not a bother on him.

Good looks in a previously trollesque empire.

A stampede had ensued.

Women, previously unknown and never seen since, had found reasons to come for a gawk and a flirt. The long trek up the stairs to the polar regions of the company was undertaken with gritted determination. It was better than the Diet Coke ad.

Al had remained unimpressed by all the attention. In fact, I think he'd been terrified by it.

He was a hopeless conversationalist. On a one to one, he was great. In a group, he fell to pieces. He refused invites to go out drinking, he committed the mortal sin of not going to the Christmas party and as a result most females in the place lost interest. Even me (and I was desperate).

But then, after a while, I noticed something about him that made me think I'd like just to get to know him. You'll probably think this is crap, and stupid, and it probably is, but it fascinated me.

So here it is.

Whenever someone in our office cracks a joke, we all laugh. I mean, the joke could be rubbish and more often than not, it's in really bad taste, but we laugh anyway. Just to be polite. Everyone laughs. Everyone *except* Al. He only laughs if he thinks it's funny. Otherwise, he just sits there, with this bewildered look on his face. And, you know, I liked this.

I thought it was cool.

So I decided to get to know him.

I made Trojan efforts to drag conversation out of him. I'd talk about my weekend and stuff and I'd ask him about his. He'd shrug and mutter, so I'd just keep blabbing away. It was great – he never interrupted me once. I like that in a fella. Plus, and this is a big plus, I found that I could boss him about. No one takes me as seriously as he does. It's great.

Then, bit by bit, he began to crawl out from under his shell.

He told me bits and pieces about himself. He's the eldest. He has a little brother. And he (Al) still lives at home. With Mammy and Daddy. *That* was a black mark against him. But other than that he was OK.

We're good friends now. He doesn't talk a lot – he's just like that, shy.

Sullen, Beth said, the day after the disastrous pub date. He's a sullen pig.

Unfriendly, Abby said, wrinkling up her nose. Good-looking but no personality at all.

But I like that in a fella. Not in a boy-friend of

course. No, a boy-friend has to have a personality so that his wit and looks can make your friends puke with envy. But a friend who says very little and lets me do all the talking is my kinda friend.

We stopped talking as we heard Lenny coming along the corridor.

"Do-be-do-be-dooo."

I got off Al's desk and sat at my own.

"Folks," Lenny greeted us as he arrived in. He's in charge of us. In other words, he does nothing. Except shamble up and down the office humming the same five notes of a song endlessly. *Do-be-do-be-dooo*. All day. Every day. At first, I thought I was going mad, then the notes blended into the back ground, like the way the ticking of a clock does. *Do-be-do-be-do.*

"How ye?" Lenny nodded and sat at his desk.

We nodded back.

Silence.

Lenny began to shuffle about with a few papers.

This was our cue to shuffle ours.

Liz arrived, hair flying, face red. A keg on legs. Panting, she flung herself onto her desk and apologised for being late. Liz the lick, that's what we call her.

Lenny waved her away. "Away with ye." Shuffle, shuffle, shuffle. *"Do-be-do-be-doooo."*

When we were all sitting shuffling our papers, Henry arrived.

Late as always.

No apology from him. He marched in wearing a lurid red v-neck jumper.

I thought of suing him for eyesight damage. This jumper was seriously red.

He marched proudly past our desks, beaming from ear to ear. At the top of the office he did a twirl and marched back down its length. "How much did I pay for this fuckin' jumper?" he boomed, arms outstretched to give us all the benefit of his attire. He strode over to Lenny's desk, put his hands flat on it and asked cockily, "Go on, guess. Go on. You'll never guess." Grabbing Lenny's hand, he made him feel the jumper. "Feel tha'! Lambswool! Fuckin' *lambswool*."

I braced myself. Lenny and Henry were always trying to out-do each other.

Al rolled his eyes at me across the office.

Liz buried herself in her work and tried to ignore what we all knew was a potentially explosive exchange.

Lenny made a big deal of rubbing his thumb and fore finger along the jumper.

"Guess!" Henry ordered, shifting from foot to foot and grinning around manically.

Lenny frowned, perplexed. "I'd say, eh . . ." He put his finger to his lip and began to tap it.

"Yeah?"

"I'd say . . . about . . . in the region of . . . " He wrinkled up his face, "One ninety-nine."

I tried to turn my laugh into a cough.

Al winked over at me.

"Fuck off." Henry was offended. He glared at all of us and thumbed to Lenny. "One shaggin' ninety-nine, he says. Fuck off." This last sentiment to Lenny. He glanced down at his skeletal frame and pulled at the jumper. "Lambswool. This is fuckin' wool, ya bloody culchie moron."

Lenny grinned. "Well, ye must've got it cheap or ye wouldn't be blowing about it. So that's what I think." He smirked. "That's all I'd pay fer it anyhow."

"Bastard." Henry stomped over to his seat. He glared around at the rest of us and alighted on me. "How much would you fuckin' pay for this, Jan?"

Why did he have to pick on me? I tried to be tactful. "Eh, did they have it in any other colour?"

"No." He sounded really annoyed now.

"Oh, right. Eh – a tenner?"

His face lit up. "A fucking foiver! That's all. A foiver! Good value, wha'?"

"Great." I smiled back at him. "Great value."

He marched back over to Lenny. "A foiver. I paid a foiver fer it – ya scabby bastard!"

Lenny looked puzzled. "What'd ye say?"

"I said, ya deaf shite, I paid a foiver fer it."

"Pardon?" Lenny raised his eyebrows quizzically.

Henry faltered. "A foiver. A bleedin' foiver. And Jan," he pointed at me, "thought I paid a tenner."

"What?"

"You bleedin' deaf or wha'?"

Lenny shook his head. "Sorry. Can't hear ye above that ould jumper."

Me, Liz and even Al, cracked up.

Lenny beamed around at the success of his joke. Then he wiped his nose.

90

"Shower of bastards!" Henry spat. "Jaysus, I'm fed up with the lot of yez." He marched out.

"Hurry back," Lenny called winking at us, "I've piles of stuff here just waiting to be delegated."

"Fuck off!"

At lunch, I was glad I'd come to work. I wasn't hungry as Lenny too had remembered my birthday and he'd bought a little cake for the office. "To celebrate you making it to the quarter century," he'd said. I hadn't been too pleased with that. But the cake was gorgeous. We'd all eaten it between us.

As a result, all I'd bought for lunch was a yogurt and a juice. I joined Liz and Angela (a girl who works on the cash desk) at their table in the canteen.

Angela glanced triumphantly at Liz. "I told you," she said.

Both of them turned to me.

I looked at them, smiled and began to open my yogurt.

There was a silence. They were obviously waiting for me to say something. It was like being in a play with no script. "Yeah?"

Liz smirked. "Yeah, she says." She sounded a bit pissed off.

I raised my eyebrows. "Have I missed something?"

Angela hauled herself across the table. "How long have you been on that diet?" she asked accusingly.

"And what diet is it?" Liz looked at me with

narrowed eyes, "I mean, you could have told us and we could have done it together."

"Come again?"

"Yogurts and juices," Angela spat.

Light dawned. I began to grin. "I'm only eating these," I indicated my lunch, "because I ate a pile of cake about an hour ago." I stuck a straw into my orange and looked at Liz. "Remember?"

"Yeah." Liz sounded annoyed. "So, how come you look like you've lost weight?"

It took a second for it to sink in. Liz thought I'd lost weight! Me? Thunder thighs?

"Have I?" I asked, trying not to smile in case they were having me on. "Really?"

Angela pursed her lips. "You have." It sounded like I'd just murdered someone.

"Do I look like I've lost much?" I tried to inject a vein of worry into my voice, but the huge, radiant smile cracking my face apart belied any attempt at this.

"Those jeans used to be tight on you," Angela said sulkily. "In fact, they were a bit of a show actually."

"Tarty," Liz agreed.

"Painful to wear, I always thought." Angela added, getting into her stride. Thinness was not something she admired in a person and now her disappointment was directed toward me – it was great.

"How much have you lost?" Liz asked eagerly. "And how did you do it?"

"Far better to be happy with your own body shape, Liz," Angela pronounced. She lifted herself from the table. "Far better," she repeated, wobbling away. Her backside was like a two-tonne jelly on springs.

Liz rolled her eyes. "She's furious, you know," she whispered delightedly. "She was watching you from the minute you came in. She thinks you've bought a bigger size jeans and won't let on."

Silence.

"Have you?" she asked hopefully.

Liz always got under pressure when people lost weight. Any time I go on a diet, she does. If I lose more weight than her, she flips.

And what really annoys me is that she keeps making out we're the same – but I'm *thinner* than her. I have legs. I'm not round. I'm not a Mister Man. In fact, if they were giving us Mister Men names, she'd be Mr Rotund and I'd be Mr Flat-Chested, Big-Arsed.

"Have you?" she asked again.

I nearly thought of saying yes, just to get her off my back, but pride wouldn't let me.

"No."

Her face dropped. "What foods do you eat, so?" she demanded. "How did you do it?"

"It's no big secret," I leaned in toward her, "Chips, sausages, plenty of fluids, especially of the alcoholic kind, Mars bars, Bountys, cakes of . . ."

"Feck off," she was annoyed now. "You don't!"

"I do. I'm not on a diet, Liz." I looked down at myself, "Maybe my jeans stretched in the wash."

"Jeans don't stretch," she said sulkily, "they shrink."

And they do. She was right!

Maybe it was true, I thought joyously, maybe I had lost a few pounds. I decided that I'd have to weigh myself, to see if it was true. Ignoring Liz, I racked my brains. Where would one find some scales?

"I'm going back to work," Liz eventually broke in on my thoughts. "Coming?"

"Gimme five minutes." I watched her leave and just sat for a few minutes in contented happiness. I'd lost weight! Maybe it was belated puppy-fat falling off a decade late.

Getting up from the table I dumped my rubbish in the bin and braced myself for the long trek upstairs.

Roches Stores! They sold scales. I could always test them out by standing on them. Next time I went down town, I'd weigh myself.

CHAPTER TWELVE

After lunch, I floated into the office on a tidal wave of good will. Headache receding and weight receding too. It was the best birthday present I could get.

I was last back, but Lenny didn't seem to notice. He and Henry were having a heated argument over something or other.

"You fuckin' did!"

"I didn't!" Lenny began to chuckle. "I wish I had but I didn't!"

"You fuckin' did!"

Lenny shrugged. "He must've just said it out of the blue."

"Out of the red," Liz piped up and Al gave a shout of laughter.

I tried to sneak into my desk without them seeing me.

"Shut up you," Henry shouted over to Liz.

"What's the story?" I asked. "What's happening?"

"I'll bleeding' tell you," Henry began to advance on the three of us.

I could hear Liz suck in her breath and Al, by the look of him, was doing his best not to laugh.

"This culchie bastard," Henry thumbed toward Lenny, "only got Jimmy Madden to slag off my jumper in the canteen at lunch-time."

"I didn't!"

Henry was red in the face. It clashed with his jumper. "Do you know what the fecker said to me, Jan? Do you know what that Jimmy fecker said to me?"

"No." I cloaked my face in sympathy. It was always best to agree with Henry.

Henry lowered his voice in outraged uprightness. "He said," his voice quivered, "he came over and he said to me, where did I get this – this – whore of a jumper?"

I tried to look shocked, I really did. I gulped so hard that I began to choke. I didn't want to offend him, but I couldn't help it. Henry was looking at me for a reaction and, at the strangled sounds coming from my mouth, a look of bewilderment crossed his face. That did it! I ate myself laughing. I couldn't help it. Al and Liz began to laugh too. I don't know if they were laughing at me or Henry.

"Jimmy Madden said that?" I spluttered.

"Yeah," Henry was looking slightly unsure of himself. "He called my jumper a – a – whore of a jumper."

"Oh, God," I begged, "Don't, Henry. Don't tell me any more."

"It's not funny." He began to scowl. He pointed to my jeans. "How would you like it if someone called your jeans 'whore jeans'?"

"I wouldn't believe them," I gasped out.

"She could have you up for sexual harassment with that comment," Lenny called over from his corner.

"I wasn't saying they were whorey," Henry spat back, "I was only fuckin' makin' a point – "

"Yeah, yeah."

"Culchie bastard." Henry glowered at him and then at me. I felt a bit guilty for laughing.

"Unsympathetic wagon," he snapped. He appealed to Al for support then. "How would you feel if someone said that about your clothes?"

Al shrugged and grinned. "I'd be as mad as hell," he said slowly. Encouraged by Henry's beam of delight, he continued, "I'd march right over to them and demand an apology."

Henry looked impressed. "Now, yer onta somethin'." He wagged his finger and began to pace up and down. "Good thinkin'. Good idea." His pacing got faster and we all moved our heads, left, right, left, right, to follow him.

He stopped. Almost tripping over himself in the process.

"You can't go asking the likes of Madden for apologies," Lenny said. "He's our boss."

That decided him. "I can't let him slag off me shaggin' gear, can I?" Henry spat. He started to psych himself up. "I'm going down. He is gonna apologise and that's it!" Without looking at any of us, he flung open the fragile wooden door, and banged straight into Derbhla with some letter for us.

"Hey, watch it!"

He pushed her out of his way.

"What is up with him?" Derbhla stared after him. "Moron."

"He's a man on a mission," Lenny pronounced gleefully, rubbing his hands. *"Do-be-do-be-dooo."*

Derbhla made a face at him behind his back and rolled her eyes. As far as she was concerned, the five of us were all mad.

"Here's the gorgeous Derbhla with a letter for us," Lenny beamed at her as she flung his letter straight at his face. He had to duck, but gave a good-natured chortle at her lack of accuracy.

"It's not a letter, Lenny," she snapped. "It's a memo – right?"

My memo was fired at me in the same courteous manner.

She shoved Henry's behind a folder on his desk to get him back for knocking her down and she barely looked at Liz as she gave her hers. Then over she went to Al's desk, with the usual vampish smile she reserved for him.

He ignored it by bending his head and trying to appear as if he was working.

"A memo for you," Derbhla sat on the edge of his desk.

"Thanks." Al was monosyllabic, as usual.

Liz began to hum, "You'll never get the ma-an," to the tune of 'You'll never beat the Irish.' She always did that whenever Derbhla came in and made tracks for Al's desk.

Lenny, oblivious to all the undertones, began to read the memo.

I watched fascinated as Derbhla made her regular fool out of herself.

"Doing anything exciting tonight?" She touched Al's sleeve to show that she was beginning a conversation.

His face flushed. "No, not really."

She gave a tinkley laugh. Her voice took a nose-dive into sexier, huskier waters. "Come for a drink after work so. There's a gang of us going."

Al jumped. The word "suffocating" was almost lit in neon on his face.

Liz stifled a giggle and I watched with interest, wondering what he'd say.

"Are you heading for a drink after?" Derbhla repeated.

There was a silence. Al's flush got deeper. "Eh, well," he stammered, "I eh . . ."

"Actually," I said, feeling I had to rescue Al before he combusted, "Al's bringing me for a birthday drink."

The look on her face would have stopped an Orange parade.

"Yeah, " Al agreed. "It's Jan's birthday today."

"I see," she said slowly, getting up from his desk with as much dignity as she could muster. A snake wouldn't have been able to compete with the venomous look she shot me.

"Hey, Derbhla," Lenny said as she swept by. "This letter's about promotions coming up and I don't think – "

"Memo, Lenny," she snarled. "And talk to me tomorrow, right!"

Slamming the door she was gone.

"What's eating her?" Lenny gazed after her bemused. "Women. Jesus."

I looked at Al and winked. He gave a shy smile back.

Liz asked, looking at both of us, "Was it true? Are you two really going for a drink?"

"A platonic drink, nothing else," I clarified.

"Oh, you're in luck boyo," Lenny said, leering at Al, "Three drinks and she's anybody's, right, Jan?"

"And four and I'm yours," I slagged back.

It's not the sort of thing to say to your boss. He wasn't happy.

Just as well I'd never be looking for promotion.

CHAPTER THIRTEEN

After work, Al made me walk to the pub.

"It'll do you good," he said as he pushed me along.

"I don't care. A nice bus trip is all I want."

"Three miles, Jan," he caught me by the hair and began to pull me. "It's nothing."

"If you don't let go of me I'm going to scream."

"Sure you will."

So I did. I opened my mouth and yelled. "HELPPPP!"

It worked quicker than I thought. He let go of my hair and, turning around, I saw that his face was white. He kept looking at his hand and he mumbled, "Sorry. I'm sorry."

"Al?"

"I didn't mean to hurt you." His hand was trembling. "I'm sorry."

"It was a joke." I gave him a shove. "You were supposed to laugh."

I could see him trying to compose himself. Why, I

wondered, did I attract weird people into my life? It was probably the way I was reared.

"So," he looked at me and his smile was back in place, but his eyes slid away from my face, "you want to get a bus or what?"

How could I get a bus now? "No." I rolled my eyes and pulling him towards me said, "You win – let's walk."

"Good girl yerself!"

In the end I was glad I'd done it because it was a nice evening. A real spring evening, when the sky stays blue for ages and people busk along Grafton Street 'till dark. We didn't say much as we walked. We just listened to the music and gawked in shop windows and wandered into the record shops for a browse. Al bought a Steve Earl album and promised to tape it for me.

Wandering back out of HMV, we began to make serious tracks back to Rathmines.

At the rate I walked, I think it took about ninety minutes.

"So," I asked Al as we stood in the main street, "where to now? Any pub is fine by me."

"Once I can get drunk, I don't care," he grinned.

We did get drunk. But more of that later.

That night, it started off with me clinking his glass and saying "Cheers."

"Cheers," he lifted his pint and took long thirsty gulps. "Happy Birthday."

"Thanks."

"Do anything interesting at the weekend?" Al asked,

as he opened a packet of dry roast and began to shove them into his mouth.

"I went on an environmental march yesterday," I said. "That was pretty interesting."

He began to choke on a peanut. "You?" he said, between coughs, "March?"

"Yeah." I was a bit insulted at his tone. "I marched most of the way anyhow."

He grinned. "Most of the way – like how much?"

I decided to ignore him. He'd only laugh if he heard I'd marched straight into the nearest pub. "There were some great people there."

"What were *you* doing there so?"

"Feck off." I tried to look offended. "I'm interested in the environment."

"Right," he took a gulp of his pint and I could see his eyes laughing at me over the rim of it.

"I *am*."

"I believe you." I knew from the way he said it that he didn't.

"And I've a date on Friday with one of the guys." I couldn't resist it, I had to tell someone.

"Yeah?" He looked surprised.

"Don't look so surprised," I said feeling huffy. I had been about to tell him all the details and that it wasn't strictly a date, but his surprised tone annoyed me a bit, so I just tapped my nose, with what I hoped was a mysterious air and said, "Scorching hot."

"Oh, right." He gazed into his pint glass and swirled the last bit of Bud around. "Have a good time so."

"I intend to." Huh – that'd show him. "You?" I asked then.

He looked up. "What?"

"Did you do anything exciting this weekend?"

"I ran a ten-miler on Sunday." He drained his glass and wiped his lips.

"A what?"

"I was on me running club team. We did a ten-mile road race yesterday."

"Oh, great. Sounds great." *How boring.*

Al laughed. "Convincin', Jan."

He knew I hated exercise. The walk up to the office every morning killed me.

"Another?" Al nodded towards my empty glass and stood up.

"I'll get it." I stood up too.

"My shout – remember?"

"I'll get the next lot, I can't have you paying for everything."

"Willya feck off."

I watched him leave and head up to the bar. He has a nice backside, I thought objectively. He had the bum for jeans, especially those faded Levis he wore. And he walked like a man too, in a casual "hey ma man" kind of way.

Pity he wasn't a bit more dynamic.

He arrived back and put the drinks down. Raising his glass he winked at me. "To your red-hot date."

"I'll drink to that."

It was after about four drinks, when I thought he'd

relaxed a bit, I asked, "Why don't you ever come out for a few drinks after work with the rest of us?"

"Aw, I'm not much of a mixer." He grinned as he said it, obviously not giving a toss that he was considered an anti-social oddity in work.

"But you know everyone now," I pressed. "And they all like you. I mean, it'd be different if you were like Henry or anything."

He laughed. "Thanks. That boosts me confidence."

"So you'll come out with us?"

"Aw, maybe, I dunno." He turned away from me, so I knew there was no way he would.

"Does Mammy give out if her little boy is late?" I don't know what made me say it, only the fact that I knew everyone wanted to know why he never went out much.

His head shot up and he looked at me. He looked weird, as if I'd hurt him or something. I saw him swallow hard before nodding to my empty glass. "Another?"

The abrupt change of subject startled me. "Eh, yeah, all right." As he stood up to go, I touched his sleeve. He flinched, but he didn't shake me off. "It was a joke," I clarified.

"I know," he brushed past me.

I didn't spend time admiring his rear view when he left. No. I just sat, feeling miserable and guilty and angst-ridden until he arrived back.

"Here y'are," Al dumped what must have been a treble vodka in front of me. "A teenager drink like you ordered."

"It's not a teenager drink," I sneered. "It's a beautiful drink." To prove it I took a huge gulp.

"All the feckin' kids drink that when they want to get smashed." He was smiling at me and I knew I wouldn't have to make another apology and that things were OK again.

He sat down beside me and grinned. "Let's get locked."

So we did.

Short after short after short.

Pint after pint after pint.

I could see him loosening up. His shoulders lost their hunched up defensive look and his eyes seemed to light up in his face. I'm sure I began to relax as well, I mean it's not every customer who sprawls all over the sofa when they come in, is it? And, at another stage I actually lay my head on Al's shoulder. That was when I felt I was going to puke.

"So tell me," I asked, unable to mind my own business, "why are you still living at home?" I wouldn't have dared ask this unless I was well tanked up.

There was a pause and I could feel his shoulder stiffen (this was when I'd been lying my head on it). "I live in Dublin – what's the point of havin' a flat here too?"

"I'm," I gave a big exaggerated point to myself, "from Dublin too. But I," again the point, "moved out." I waited for him to say something and when he didn't, I went on, in a weary, life-is-a-bitch kind of voice, "I had to."

"Yeah?"

"Oh yeah." Big exaggerated nod this time. "My family," I dropped my voice, "my family are mad."

Al's pint sprayed from his mouth onto the table. Some of it came down his nose and I was jerked from the comfortable position of snuggling up to him, to being shot across the sofa.

Ignoring me and the fact that I'd nearly broken my elbow, he began to mop his nose and wipe his mouth with his sleeve.

"I've nothing else," he apologised as he caught me gawking at him.

When his wiping-up operation had ceased, he turned to me and said, "Come again?"

"Are you being disgusting?"

For a second he looked baffled. "No," he said, as if I was thick, "what was that you said about your family?"

"Oh that," I nodded. "What did I say?" My train of thought was getting a bit muddled.

"That they were all mad?" Al prompted.

I wished I'd said nothing. "Oh yeah," I tried to wave it away, "yeah, they are, all right."

Silence.

I looked at him and he gave an encouraging nod. He looked sceptical.

Huh, I thought, I'd show him. He thought I was exaggerating, making a big deal about things. He probably thought I was over-reacting! A famous one-liner of my mother's: "You're over-reacting, Jan", she always said in a big bored voice. As if I was the one that was mad!

"Oh, they're mad, all right," I confirmed. "All of them." Usually my family are a sensitive, if not a taboo subject but because I was drunk, that didn't matter. Being drunk always made it easier to talk.

"None of our neighbours will talk to us," I began in a low voice so that no one else would hear. "None of them."

"Serious?"

"Yeah." I took a gulp of vodka. "It's because of our garden."

He looked puzzled and then I realised that he'd never seen our garden. "My dad decided, years ago, that he was going to fix cars in the garden – right?"

Al nodded.

"And then, after wrecking every car he tried to fix, he gave up. There's car parts all over our front garden. All over. And he won't get rid of them. And some of the neighbours say there's rats hiding in them."

"Yeah?" Al didn't look disgusted or horrified. In fact, I think he was smiling.

So I went on.

"And my mother, right, she's a member of the God Squad. Up at Mass every Sunday singing louder than anyone else. And she keeps going off key and everyone laughs at her." I gave a small laugh myself, just to show how mad I thought she was. "All the kids on our road used to slag her – all the time." I stopped. "All the time," I repeated. I couldn't look at him. Instead I gazed into my glass. It was nearly empty. The vodka was almost gone.

Al said nothing.

"And, Sammy, my sister, right, she's unbelievable. She studied psychology and now – right – now she won't use it because she thinks that it puts fellas off her." I was getting into my stride. "All she'll do is work in a restaurant in town. And you should see the clothes she wears – combats and tie-dyed tee-shirts. And she never wears make-up. My mother's afraid she's a secret lesbian – it's awful. And my other sister, Lisa, she was expelled from her first school for cheating in the Junior Cert – imagine. And it was all over the papers and everyone knew." I leaned nearer toward Al. "It was her history exam and guess what she did?"

Al was staring into his pint. "Dunno."

"Guess," I ordered. I wanted him to understand about them. "Guess," I said again.

Al shrugged. "It was written on her sleeve."

"No," I shook my head. "No." I took up the beer mat and began tearing it apart as I spoke. "She brought her calculator in and had all the dates of stuff pre-programmed in."

Al didn't look as shocked as I'd expected. In fact he looked a bit pissed off. "And?" he asked.

"And she got expelled." I gave a deep sigh. "It was terrible, everyone knew about it, all the neighbours and all our family. I'm telling you," I tried to focus my gaze, "sometimes I hate them." There. The words were out and I didn't feel guilty like I normally did when I breached all the family-loyalty regulations. "I do," I nodded, "and I hate that I hate them."

He half-grinned. "You're joking – right?"

"Pardon?"

"About your folks, it's a joke – right?"

He couldn't be serious. He thought my family were a joke? "Al," I spoke with deliberate slowness. "A joke is funny."

There was something weird in his face. He looked as if he wanted to laugh and at the same time he looked a bit angry. "Get a grip, Jan," he said. "So what? What's the big deal?"

I gulped. It was like he'd slapped me sober. *Get a grip?* I wanted to tell him more but the look on his face told me to shut up. He seemed to have changed into someone I didn't know. Suddenly, I wanted to go home.

"Let's go."

Ignoring me, he stood up and announced that he was going to the jax and did I want a drink on the way back from the bar.

See? That's what I mean when I say he's weird. He doesn't react in a normal way.

So, I told him to get me another vodka. At that stage I just wanted to forget that I'd almost told him about the green and white paint and all the trouble that had led to. But he wouldn't have understood about that either probably.

CHAPTER FOURTEEN

When I was thirteen, Dad got a job lot of paint. There were two colours, green and white. And because our house had never been painted he decided that it was high time he tackled the job.

Mam was worried. "Are you sure you'll be able to manage the ladder, Des?" she asked. Dad was climbing up the ladder at that stage. It was enormous, stretching all the way to the roof.

"No problem," Dad announced from mid-way. "Heights don't bother me."

He had wedged the ladder up against a black mini that he'd decided to rejuvenate. The mini had been hauled across the grass and stood in the middle of the lawn. Tyre tracks had hacked up the lawn.

I stood looking up at him, feeling thrilled that at last our house would be like everyone else's. In fact, it'd be better because it'd only have been freshly painted.

Sammy and Lisa joined Mam and me on the lawn and we all gazed up in admiration as Dad began to paint.

"Do you not have to wash the walls down first?" I asked. Jesse, my best friend's dad had done that.

Dad stopped. He gazed down at me. "Wash the walls?"

Now they all looked at me. "Yeah, clean them off before you paint?"

Dad shook his head. "No, I don't think so." He looked puzzled. "Sure I'll just paint over all the dirt."

And he did. He ran out of white half-way through the job. So he started on the green. At the end of the day, we had a two-tone house.

The other three were delighted with it. Sammy thought it was really radical. Lisa was four, so she basically didn't have a clue and Mam was proud as punch of all the hard work my dad had done.

The ladder was removed and they all stood admiring his handiwork. Dad tweaked my ear. "Wash the walls!" he scoffed.

I tried to smile. The house looked better than it had done but at the same time it was striped.

Dad was on a roll. Pushing the mini off the grass, he decided that he'd cut the bit of grass we had. The bit of grass was about four feet high.

I was given the job of asking the Johnsons for their lawnmower. They were still talking to us at that stage.

And so Dad cut our grass. And all the grass blew on top of the green paint. And stuck there.

And the lawn-mower gave a terrible shriek as a huge stone embedded itself in its motor.

And Mrs Johnson flipped.

And there was war. Even though we bought her a new lawnmower and everything. She called our family some awful names.

I remember hiding in my room as my mother got stuck into her.

Other people on the road kept passing by and looking.

It was one of the worst days of my life.

CHAPTER FIFTEEN

Drunk and laughing, Al and I exited the pub. I wasn't too bad, but Al was twisted. He looked lovely when he was drunk, all smiley and laughy. Not a bit like his usual uneasy and dour self.

"You look lovely when you're drunk," I said as he tripped over a bad bit of path and ended up on his hands and knees in a puddle. It had rained while we were imbibing.

He laughed and hauled himself upright and swayed about a bit. "And you," he caught me by the shoulders, "just look lovely anyway." His earlier humour was forgotten.

"Get off, you're plastered," I pushed him away and laughed at the offended look on his face.

"Come on," I grabbed his arm and began to pull him along. "You're walking me home whether you like it or not."

"I like it a lot."

I ignored him, the guy would be mortified

tomorrow if he knew what he was saying. Instead, in a gloriously unsubtle attempt to change the subject, I gave a shiver and said, "It's gotten cold."

This made matters worse. Al attempted to take off his jacket.

"Can't have you cold," he said, as he wrestled with it in a futile attempt to take his arms out. In the end I had to help him. He insisted on wrapping it about my shoulders.

"There," he said as he draped it over me. "There." He pulled my hair out from under the collar. "Great hair. Great hair." He stopped.

I love my hair. I was pleased he'd noticed.

"Like a horse," Al said. "Hair like a horse."

"Sorry?" The temperature was dropping rapidly and if he didn't notice it soon, he'd be deep frozen.

"Shiny. Like a horse." He gave a vacant grin. Blinds up, no one home.

"Fine, thanks Al."

"No probs." He slung his arm over my shoulder and pulled me near him. His face up to mine, he asked groggily, "We're friends, aren't we, Jan?"

"Yeah, sure we are."

"Good." He nodded. "Good." He kept his arm around me but he gazed away. "I had a good night tonight."

"So did I."

"Did you?" His eyes widened, astonished. His face came nearer mine. "Really?"

"The best," I grinned. "It was great."

"Good. I like you, Jan. I really do."

"I like you too." We were outside the gate of my flat.

He turned to face me. "Yeah?" He caught me by the arms. "That's great. Good."

"Come on in for a cuppa?" I didn't want the night to end, tomorrow I'd have work and no birthday to cheer me up.

Al shook his head and swayed slightly. "Naw." He lowered his voice, "They don't like me."

"Who?"

"Them." He pointed to the flat. "Those girls you hang about with."

It was the first time he'd ever mentioned them since he'd met them.

"I'm not good with people, Jan," he said mournfully. "People don't like me. That night I fucked up big-time. I let you down."

"You didn't." I tried not to laugh. Al was really going to die tomorrow morning.

"I did." His hands tightened on my arms. "That girl, the dark one, she made me fuck up. She kept laughing at me."

I couldn't deny that, so I kept my mouth shut.

"I don't," he stopped and faltered, "I don't like to get too near people."

"Well, you're near enough to me now," I joked, shoving him off.

He didn't smile. "They let you down, always they let you down."

I don't know if he was talking to me or to himself, but all of a sudden, I wanted him to go.

So, I removed his jacket from around my shoulders and held it out. "Thanks, Al."

He took it and nodded, "Anytime."

"See you tomorrow?"

"Yeah." He was staring at me.

"Good luck getting home."

"Thanks." He grinned but he was still staring at me. "See ya." He was looking directly into my eyes and for one panicky second I thought he was going to kiss me. Instead, he gently brushed a strand of my hair away from my face and turned away. "I'd better be goin'," he muttered.

I watched him make his way down the road, simultaneously attempting to negotiate puddles and pull on his jacket. He was weaving badly.

Before I had a chance to close the gate, I saw him stop and turn back around to me. He cocked his head to one side as if a thought had just struck him. "Oy," he bellowed, waking the entire street, "Brad Pitt said he'd lend me his face if ya want a ride." He tipped a drunken salute and grinned.

"Piss off home," I yelled back, equally loudly. To the sound of his laughter, I ran up the path, opened the door and legged it inside before anyone had a chance to complain.

Beth had arrived back. She was sitting in the good chair, legs curled up under her, reading the evening paper.

"Good weekend?" I asked as I came in.

"All right." Beth never said much about her visits home. She never talked about her parents and I never asked. It suited me, because when I went home, I hated being quizzed about it too.

"You?" she asked then.

This was what I'd been waiting for. A chance to talk about Dave to someone other than Abby. So I launched into a blow-by-blow account. Beth, for once, didn't scoff or sneer. Instead, she asked, "So, he's coming here on Friday is he?"

"Yeah, for dinner."

"I'll have to be here so." She ignored my look of horror and went back to reading.

"You can't," I said faintly.

"Why?" She looked up at me from her chair.

I'd done loads of self-assertiveness courses and confidence-building courses and in every one of them they'd said that if you wanted to be in a position of power – stand up. Be higher than your aggressor.

How come I was standing up now and Beth was curled up in a foetal position on the chair and still I was intimidated?

"Why?" she asked again, mildly.

"Because," my mouth was dry. "it's a couples night."

"So you and he are a couple then?"

"Well – "

"Have you got off with him?"

"No, but – "

"Well, there you are then," she stood up to face me

117

and despite myself, I backed away. "All I want to do is meet Abby's fella and your Dave, that's all."

She walked off into her bedroom without looking back. I waited until her door was closed before muttering, "Well, you'll have to help with the vegetables, you needn't think I'm peeling yours and paying for you and . . ."

"Sorry, Jan?" She poked her head around, "What was that?"

"Nothing," I answered, biting my lip. I'd get Abby to tell her. Abby was well able for her.

I was hopeless at confrontation. I'd trained myself to be.

I made sure she was safely in her room before giving her the two fingers, then, spotting the evening paper, I curled up in the good seat to read it. There was a scurrilous article about Brad Pitt having a girlfriend and I was just reeling from the devastation of it all when Beth came out of her room. "Oh, by the way," she said, making me jump as she'd come up behind me. "There's a letter for you on the mantlepiece. It looks like a card. I took it up in the post this evening."

A card. Brilliant.

Beth watched as I opened it.

It was from my mother. A pink birthday card with a lurid bunch of roses on the front. Inside, a horrible verse proclaimed her love for me. She'd signed it *With love from Mammy, Daddy, Sammy, Lisa and Buddy.*

I shoved it back into the envelope.

"Put it up." Beth grabbed it off me and put it on the

mantle-piece. Looking at me, she said, "You should have told us, Jan, we could've gone for a drink."

"I went for a drink with Al." Remembering, I found my bag and took his card out. I put it beside my mother's.

Beth picked it up and read it. "Who'd ride him?" she sniggered.

"He's all right," I surprised myself by grabbing the card from her and putting it back in place. "He's dead nice actually."

"Sure." She made a face and then said, "Happy Birthday anyhow."

"Thanks."

We'd run out of stuff to say, so in order not to prolong the agony Beth went back to bed.

It was after one when I went to bed. I conked out as soon as I hit the pillow.

I dreamt of Louise Johnson, Mrs Johnson's daughter and my nightmare schoolmate. I dreamt of the way she'd made me so angry . . . I dreamt of the way I'd dealt with her . . . the only way I could've stood up to her . . .

I woke up sweating. Drenched to the skin again. But this time I knew what had caused it. Talking of my family had made me remember Louise. I shouldn't have said anything to Al about them.

It only made me get angry later.

CHAPTER SIXTEEN – TUESDAY

Al was late in the next day. When he did arrive, he looked like he'd had a major blood loss on the way to work. He was pale – big time.

"Hard night last night?" Lenny gave a big leery wink over at me.

Al staggered to his desk and put his head in his hands. "Don't remember."

"Oh, ya boya!"

"Jaysus, she's a goer is our Jan!"

"Hang on here a sec," I shouted over the other lewd and unprintable comments, "Al drank too much, it was nothing to do with me."

Al closed his eyes and laid his head on his arms.

"He's even tired," Liz squealed. "You must've worn him out!"

"Pathetic." I refused to be baited.

"You look a bit tired yerself," Lenny said. "Tired and pale."

"Oh, will you give it a rest!" I was tired that morning. Tired and irritable. It had taken all my strength to drag myself out of the bed. And what had I done it for? To listen to this crap.

Al groaned, it sounded as if he was dying.

"Shut up Al!" I didn't need him doing the martyr all morning.

"Someone's filled me stomach with hydrochloric acid," he groaned. "I'm dyin'."

Henry began to rummage around in his desk. He pulled out pens, papers and millions of jars of vitamin tablets. Eventually he produced a king-sized bottle of Milk of Magnesia. "Here," he strode over to Al and banged the bottle down on his desk. "Take that. It'll run the guts outa ya."

"Jaysus," was the only response Al could make.

"No. Magnesia." Henry gave a loud guffaw at his wit and the rest of us grinned. "You can keep the bottle," he bent down on his hunkers and began to yell in Al's ear. "I fuckin' showed Jimmy Madden who was boss yesterday – "

"He has a hangover, Henry," Liz said, trying to be tactful. "He's not deaf."

"I fuckin' marched inta his office. Here, says I, I want a bleedin' apology off a you. Feck off, says he. I will not, says I. Feck off, says he. I fuckin' won't, says I."

"And?" Lenny prompted.

"Oh, Christ." Al jumped from his desk and shot out the door.

Henry stood up. "In the end, he sorta grinned and said fine. If I wanted to get his back up that was fine, he said. Then he apologised."

"Madden apologised!" Lenny looked shocked. "Me arse he did."

"You callin' me a liar?"

Lenny waved his hands about a bit. "I didn't say that," he placated. "I just said . . ."

At that point I left the office. The debate could last all morning. Deciding to make myself useful, I walked down to Sales to ask for their first aid kit.

"Any solpadine in the first-aid kit?" I asked. There was a silence as I entered. "Any solpadine?"

"How did your drink go with Al last night?" Derbhla was perched on Angela's desk and the two of them were staring at me.

"Fine." I felt like Daniel in the lions' den. Doing my best to ignore their whispers, which I knew were about me, I walked over to the press where the kit was kept and began to rummage about. Files fell out all over the place. It was rumoured that Sales was the worst section in the company.

"She probably only drank low-fat water or something," Angela hissed.

The two of them started to snigger.

"Have you lost weight, Jan?" one of the typists asked. "You look like you have."

"I dunno." I was glad that my back was to the office. They were probably all staring at me.

"She's on a secret diet," Angela said. "Aren't you, Jan?"

Ignoring her, I continued my search for the kit. Eventually, I found it and sitting cross-legged on the ground, I tried to prise the lid off.

"It suits you, Jan," one of the lads said. I don't know what his name was. He looked pubescent.

"Thanks." Compliments from any source were very welcome.

"More mature men," Derbhla said, making a big deal of the word mature, "prefer curvier women."

The young fella was mortified.

Maybe it was that that gave me the guts to say, "Well, Al doesn't – after all it was me he went out with last night."

Derbhla went a furious explosive red. Some of the other girls began to laugh, I got the lid off the kit and grabbed the solpadine, then I legged it out the door and up the stairs in case she came after me.

I met Al sitting on the top stair nursing a glass of water. "Here," I sat beside him and put the tablets under his nose. "These might work."

His hand shaking slightly, he took it from me. "Thanks." He swallowed the tablets down and after a few seconds, he turned and gave me a lop-sided grin. "I'm dying, Jan."

"I believe you."

"I must've drank loads."

"You did."

He smiled and looked away. In a low voice he asked, "Did I say anything I shouldn't have said?"

"You said loads you shouldn't have."

"Yeah?" He still wouldn't turn to me, but I saw his shoulders hunch up. "Like what?" He began to rub his hands along his face. "Like what?" he asked again.

"Ohh," I leaned back and put my hands on the floor to balance, "Like how I was the most sexy, most desirable woman you've ever seen."

"I said – " He was staring at me now.

He'd swallow a brick.

"And how you couldn't get me out of your head. And how I had the most amazing body for someone who never exercised."

Doubt was beginning to cloud his face. "Naw," he grinned. "I didn't say that."

"You did."

"Look, Jan," he grinned. "I was drunk, not blind."

"You were blind drunk though."

We both laughed at that.

I stood up and held out my hand. "Ready to go back in yet?"

"Yeah." He allowed me to haul him up.

We were standing close to each other, and he kept hold of my hand. He held onto it a bit too long and I could feel myself going all hot and flustered. Trying to gauge what he was up to, I glanced up at him.

He was just staring down at me and there was a funny look in his face. I'd loved to have said it was unbridled passion or lust or whatever, but it wasn't. He looked sad.

I turned away because I don't think I was meant to see his eyes. It was like they were unguarded or something.

"You are sexy though," he said then. "Very sexy."

"Shag off."

"If only I could, it'd be great."

"Al!" I tried to sound shocked, but all I could do was grin. It was nice to be told I was sexy, even if he'd meant it as a joke. I grabbed him by the arm. "Come on back to work."

Lenny was reading the memo we'd been given yesterday when we got in. He stopped mid-sentence and observed Al shuffling back to his desk.

"You feeling better?"

"Sort of."

"You should've gone sick," he announced.

That was the great thing about Lenny. Sick days to him were days to be used for hangovers. Other bosses got really annoyed when half their staff rang in sick after the weekend. Not Lenny. *You're only young once* was his motto.

"Next time," Al said as he sat down. "Next time."

"And don't let that young wan corrupt you," he pointed at me. "She's an alco."

"I'm not!" He'd a poor opinion of me for some reason.

Lenny didn't reply. Instead he thumbed his memo. "Have ye all read yer memos?" he asked.

"I can't fuckin' find mine," Henry was throwing everything on his desk onto the floor. "That bitch Derbhla mustn't have given me one."

"Oh she did, begod," Lenny nodded vigorously. "Ah, now, Derbhla's a grand lass. She's a great ould worker. She wouldn't forget about you."

I hated reading memos. "What's it about?" I asked.

Lenny strode over to me. He put his letter on my desk and tapped it. "Promotions," he said importantly. "Inside promotions."

"Oh." That didn't impress me.

Looking around, I saw Liz devouring her letter. "I'm definitely going for that," she said. "Definitely."

"That's the spirit."

Lenny looked at me. "Jan?"

What did he think I was? "No way."

Everyone gaped at me, even Al. "What would I want to get promotion for?" I said in surprise. "If I got promotion I'd get more money."

"Exactly!" Lenny beamed.

"And if I got more money, I'd be tied to the job. It'd make it hard to leave if I wanted to."

A gob-smacked silence ensued.

"So – no thanks," I handed Lenny back his letter.

He was offended. Lenny was the kind of person that felt it was a reflection on him if one of his staff wouldn't go for promotion.

"Load of codswallop," he muttered, turning from me. "What about you, Al, hey?"

"Uh-huh, I'll go."

That shook me. "I'd never have taken you for a suit-and-tie merchant," I scoffed. All Al ever wore to work was jeans or wrecked cords.

"Naw, but I'm inta earning a few extra quid."

"Selling yourself out."

"I wouldn't put it that way."

"Yeah, well I would." It was like he let me down. I always thought Al was the same as me, that he hated work and couldn't wait to get out of it.

He shrugged and went back to resting his head on his desk.

Henry was still turning the place upside down for his application form.

"Have mine." I made an aeroplane of it and flew it across the room at him.

"Thanks," he grinned at me and, turning to Lenny, said, "I'm going for promotion an' all, the sooner I can get outa this poxy office the better."

The sooner I could get out of the whole poxy job the better.

I decided to try for another few days off. I rang at lunch-time and made an appointment to see the doctor the next evening.

It wasn't as if I was worried or anything.

I just needed a break.

CHAPTER SEVENTEEN – WEDNESDAY

I stood outside the surgery and felt my neck.

The gland was still there.

In a way, it was a relief, because normally, whenever I go to the doctor, any pain I have inevitably disappears just before I see him.

Feeling along the length of my neck I could make out another few glands beginning to swell up. The antibiotics hadn't worked at all.

There was a lump under my armpit too. Quite a big one. I decided not to tell the doctor about it. If it was important, he'd find it.

Pushing open the door, I went into the waiting-room. It was jammed with people and my heart sank. I'd be here for hours! Maybe it wasn't such a good idea. I had just begun to back out when the doctor's receptionist came up behind me. Thank God it wasn't Mrs O'Brien to be. "You are?" she asked.

"Eh, " I looked around in a panic.

"There are two doctors on," she said, as if reading my mind. "It shouldn't take too long."

I had no excuse now, I thought glumly. "Janet Boyle," I muttered.

"Have you been here before?"

"A couple of times."

"Whom did you see the last time?"

"Dr O'Brien."

She told me to go on in.

I found the very last seat and squashed in beside a woman with a child. The kid had the worst cough I'd ever heard. Still, he couldn't have been too bad because he was tearing the wallpaper off the walls and making flags out of it.

There were old people in abundance and just across from me was a girl with the biggest blister on her face that I'd ever seen. It was massive. The more I tried not to look, the more I looked.

"Burnt it," she announced about ten minutes later, glancing up from her issue of *Hello!*. She gave a sweeping "are-you-nosey-feckers-satisfied-now" look at everyone and returned to reading.

I went red.

The woman beside me whispered, "Burnt it, my arse!"

I smiled politely at her and at the same time scanned the room to see if I could find something to read. I'd no Walkman as, in my haste to escape the office, I'd left it behind.

The only half-decent thing was the Hello! magazine which was currently being perused by – for lack of a better name – Burnt Face. I resolved to grab it when she got called to go in.

She left about ten minutes later, but someone else had the same idea as me and she got there first. I ended up with a two-year-old issue of *The Car Owner's Manuel*.

Cursing silently, I slithered back to my seat, trying to make it look as if that was what I wanted to read.

"Janet Boyle."

The receptionist startled me. *"Anseo."*

A few of the school-going kids began to snigger. I blushed and stammered, "I mean – that's me."

"This way," she said leading the way.

She must be new, I thought, I could find my way blindfolded to any part of the surgery at this stage. All the receptionists knew that.

Opening the door, I could see O'Brien perusing my file. He didn't notice me, so I could see a bit of a pissed-off look on his face. A smile replaced it once I closed the door behind me.

"Janet," he said jovially. "What can we do for you now?"

He sound like a shop-keeper.

"Hi." I smiled and then decided not to. "Hi," I said again.

"So what brings you back again." He looked at my file. "You were here just a week ago, yeah?"

"Uh-huh." I began to feel edgy. This guy could see right through me. But I wasn't spoofing, the glands had got bigger. "The antibiotics didn't work."

He did a double take. "What?"

"The antibiotics didn't work. My gland," I made it singular, "is still swollen."

O'Brien put his pen down on the desk and leaned towards me. "Janet," he said, in smooth practised voice, "you probably haven't even finished the course yet, have you?"

"No," I replied in a small voice.

"They're not wonder drugs," he said. "They take time to work. I did say seven to ten days."

I didn't know what to say to that.

"Just give it another week or so, all right?" He began to write. Glancing at me, because I hadn't moved, he said, "There'll be no charge."

My heart was hammering. I wanted to go and believe I was fine, but instead I blurted, "The gland is bigger now."

He stopped writing and was about to say something when I cut him off.

"And more have come up since."

Now he looked curious. "More?" He sounded sceptical.

That was all I needed. I had to prove I was right, that I wasn't over-reacting. "Yeah, feel them if you like."

I scooped my hair up and coming over, he began to feel one side of my neck and then the other. *"Mmm,"* he said. Then he pressed and said, *"Mmmm"* again. "There's a few all right," he conceded.

He motioned for me to get up onto his couch. You know, the thing you lie on, I think it's called a couch. "Let's see if there's any more," he said.

I had to open my shirt while he felt underneath my arms. My heart began to hammer as he felt my right armpit. I studied his expression as he came to *the lump*. His forehead creased up a bit but he didn't say anything. I let out a slow sigh. It was probably nothing.

"You've glands up there too," he said eventually. He felt my right armpit again. "Really up," he muttered.

Then he began pressing my stomach and ribcage, though what swollen glands have to do with some doctor feeling my stomach and ribcage and yes, breasts, I don't know.

I do know, for all doctors out there, that the guy was only doing his job. I'm not suggesting for one second he was a pervert or anything. My breasts wouldn't excite too much male attention. In fact, one guy at school once told me that if breasts were cabbages then mine were Brussels sprouts.

Next, and this was embarrassing, he felt my groin. It didn't take long and he didn't look half as perplexed when he'd finished. "There doesn't seem to be any glands up there," he gave me a smile and I smiled back. "You can get down now," O'Brien said, not looking half as sceptical as when I'd come in.

There was a silence while he wrote, and then he thought a bit to himself. I think that's what he was doing. Then, and my heart took a nose-dive, he opened his drawer, pulled out a syringe and announced, "A blood test wouldn't go amiss."

Putting on a pair of gloves, he tore open the packet containing the needle, saying, "It's no big deal, just a precaution."

I couldn't answer. It wouldn't be an exaggeration to

say I was transfixed with horror. He pulled a tight thing around my arm and I began to feel all faint as a huge vein popped up.

"Lovely," he said, grinning at me.

If I'd known this was going to happen, I'd never have come. Maybe it was his way of ensuring I never came again. I closed my eyes as the needle point came closer to my defenceless vein.

"And another," O'Brien's voice broke in on my frantic thoughts.

Slowly I opened my eyes. I hadn't felt a thing. And this was the second sample he was taking!

"All right?" O'Brien removed the needle, unaware of the elation taking place in me. He dabbed something on my arm and handed me a plaster. "Good girl."

He put my blood away and labelled it. Then he turned back to me. "I think we'll do a chest x-ray too," he said. "Just to see if there's any glands up there."

"Now?"

I stared at him as he spluttered with laughter. "No. I eh, don't have an x-ray machine handy at the moment."

"Oh, right." These intelligent people had weird senses of humour.

"You'll get an x-ray as an out-patient in a hospital," he explained, still grinning. "So, will I book it for you? The sooner the better I think."

I wanted to ask him what he thought was wrong with me, but what was the point? If he knew, he wouldn't be sending me for x-rays would he? "Fire away."

"I'll ring first thing in the morning, book one for you and let you know when it'll be – all right."

"OK." I'd gone off the idea of a cert. All I wanted to be was at home drinking coffee and whinging to Abby about my horrible life.

O'Brien wrote a note to remind him to ring the hospital, then he asked, "So, anything else unusual happening with you?"

Why was he so determined to talk now? A small ball of fear began to tense me up. Pushing it away, I shrugged. "No."

"You're not tired or feeling bad or anything?"

"I'm tired sometimes." He was looking at me expectantly, I didn't want to disappoint. "Most mornings I'm wrecked."

He raised his eyebrows. "How wrecked?"

"Tired and stuff."

"Tired and stuff." He bit his lip. I think he was getting a bit annoyed again. "Do you sleep all right?"

"Yeah, but I wake up most nights all sweaty. I think that could be . . ."

"All sweaty?"

I had his attention now. "Yeah. Covered in sweat. I think that could be . . ."

"Drenched or just warm?"

"Eh, I have to change my pyjamas." I didn't tell him that I rarely wear pyjamas. But if I did wear them, I'd have to change them.

"And the sheets?"

"Yeah, the sheets are pretty soaking too. I think that could be . . ."

"How long have you had these night-sweats?"

I stopped. Night-sweats? There was a name for them? "Eh, I dunno."

"One week? Two?" He was staring at me now, pen in his mouth.

I had to concentrate. They started soon after I'd been home to visit my family the last time. "Six, maybe seven," I said eventually.

"Days." He started to write.

"Weeks."

He stopped writing. He looked at me. It was a very disbelieving look. "You've had night-sweats for six or seven weeks and you're only telling me now?"

I was about to answer when he started to write again. "Anything else besides sweats?" he muttered, scribbling furiously.

"No."

"Have you lost weight?"

"Huh?"

"Have you lost any weight?"

"Dunno." Then I thought about it. "I could have," I nodded. I pointed to my jeans. "See these jeans?"

"Uh-huh."

"Well normally I have to lie on the bed to pull them on but today, right, today they went on no bother."

"Really?"

"Yeah – really." I wanted him to know I was being

serious. "And," I'd just thought of it, "people at work think I'm on a diet."

"Stand up on the scales there." He pointed to some weighing-scales in the corner of the room. "Let's see how much you weigh."

I felt sick. The marvellous thought that I might have lost weight would soon be shattered by reality. Taking a deep breath, I approached the scales cautiously. I wondered should I take off my shoes, that might help shed a few pounds, but I didn't. Gingerly I stepped up onto them. O'Brien was standing beside me, ready to watch my shame.

The dial went up. And up. And stopped.

"Eight and a half stone," O'Brien muttered. He looked at me. There was a big smile cracking my face apart. "Is that your normal weight?"

"I have no idea," I grinned. "But the last time I weighed myself I was over nine."

"And when was that?"

His voice only just managed to intrude on the euphoria now making its way through my body. Eight and a half stone. It was great.

"Oh," I waved him away, "ages ago, when I lived at home."

"Years ago?"

"Years ago."

O'Brien didn't look as happy as I felt. "I'll just write this down and then I'll just give you a quick examination, all right?"

"Sure." Eight and a half stone was all I could think of.

The room was nice and peaceful. The only sound was the clock ticking away on the wall.

Finished writing, he pulled his chair over to mine and began to do all the usual doctor things.

He stuck a thermometer under my arm and left it there, while he proceeded to gawk in at my ears, shine lights into my eyes, stick that horrible stick thing halfway down my gullet. He even peered up my nose.

Then he took the thermometer out and looked at it. "You have a slight fever," he remarked, shaking it.

"Yeah, I feel hot every so often."

He wrote a bit more.

"Anything else?"

"Nah."

"All right so, Janet." He looked at me. "I'll get your blood test off tomorrow and we'll have the results by next week sometime. Meanwhile, I'll try and get you an x-ray and when I get it back, we should have some idea what we're dealing with."

"Right." I tried to keep my voice steady. Was there something wrong with me? Really? I didn't know whether I should ask or not. So I didn't.

"It's probably nothing," O'Brien went on, "but you might as well get checked out anyhow." He stopped for a second as if he was expecting me to ask something.

I stared at him.

"It's just a precaution." Bending over his desk he scribbled off a letter. His handwriting was terrible so I know that if I did steam the letter open, I'd never be able to read it. Not that I would anyhow. He shoved the letter into an envelope, gave it a big wet sloppy lick and banged it closed.

I didn't even ask about a cert. I just wanted to get out of there.

"Take it easy, all right?" he said as I left.

It was a rotten way to end the day.

Still, it wasn't all bad. I was eight stone seven. I bought myself a massive bar of *Fruit and Nut* to celebrate.

CHAPTER EIGHTEEN – THURSDAY

"Here," Abby shoved a piece of paper across the table at me. "It's the menu for Friday night."

"Oh, right." Absently I took it from her. I was more concerned with dabbling some spot-concealer on a massive spot that had appeared overnight. It was typical – the day before *the* dinner, a huge pustule stood like some kind of homing beacon at the tip of my nose. If I closed one of my eyes I could see it.

"Do I look spotty?" I asked Abby.

"Yeah."

"Oh no." Furiously, I rubbed in more cream. "Is it gone now?"

"No."

"Don't say that. Don't say that!"

"OK, it's gone," Abby smirked and I stuck my tongue out at her.

"Do I look awful?"

"You don't want me to answer that."

She always thought I looked awful, she kept telling

me I wore too much make-up and not enough clothes. "I think I look fine."

"Good," she replied mildly. Indicating the list, she said, "Will you read the menu and see what you think?"

"Does it matter what I think?" I was contemplating squeezing it.

"You're the one paying for it."

Shit! I'd forgotten that part of the deal.

"Well," I picked up the paper and stared at it. "I'm not paying for Beth – she's gate-crashing."

"Who's gate-crashing?" Beth was up.

I clamped my mouth shut and went the colour of liver.

"Jan offered to pay for the food for tomorrow," Abby explained, "And now, it seems as if you're the extra expense that broke the camel's back."

"Don't call me a camel."

Beth shrugged. "No probs. I'll just sit around and eat nothing while you lot stuff yourselves. The poor at the table of the rich."

She would too. Beth didn't give a shit.

"I wonder what sort of a person will Dave think you are then, Jan?" She frowned, pondering. "Horrible, most likely." With that she disappeared into the bathroom.

"Just 'cause she's no one, she's trying to ruin things for me," I whispered furiously.

"I made it out last night," Abby indicated the list again, obviously not caring that Beth was going to ruin me financially. "It's a list of all the stuff you'll need and the approximate price."

"He only wants spuds and veg," I muttered as I scanned it.

I thought the list was written in some foreign language. There was stuff on it I'd never heard of. The price was something I'd never heard of either. "I'm not spending that much on food," I gasped.

I'm not tight, really I'm not.

Abby folded her arms. "You want a nice dinner, it's up to you."

"I want a dinner that I won't have to take out a twenty-five year loan on." I shoved the list back at her. "Spuds and veg, that's what we'll have."

"Suit yourself."

I wanted to do just that.

But I couldn't.

"What vegetables go with spuds?" I asked a few minutes later.

"Most everything." Abby kept her head buried in her Bran Flakes bowl.

I couldn't go far wrong then, could I?

Yes. Yes, I could.

The cooker and I were old enemies. Five years spent in Home Economics taught me to leave it well alone. Once incinerated, twice shy. Only I was a million times incinerated.

"I suppose I'll get the stuff on this," I sighed picking up the list again. "I suppose it'll be fine."

"It's up to you."

I hated when she did that. Wouldn't pretend to be glad when I'd given in. I hated that.

Abby didn't look at me as she went to get her coat.

"See you later," she called as she was on her way out the door.

"See you," I muttered.

"Bye," Beth yelled as she emerged all washed and cleaned from the shower. She smirked at me. "Make us a coffee, Jan?"

"I'm not paying for you tomorrow night," I said, at the same time going to get her her coffee.

"Fine."

There was silence.

"I'm not." My heart was hammering, she'd probably go mad.

"I know." Calmly said. "Fine."

"I'm really not, Beth." I put her coffee in front of her. She said nothing, but I thought she grinned a bit.

"I only said I'd pay for Ab because she's cooking it." Silence.

I braced myself. "I don't think it's fair."

"Will you stop," Beth put her hands over her ears. "I can't take it any more," she moaned. "Jan won't pay for me."

"No, I only said I'd pay for Ab." I was trying to sound nice about it. "You were meant to be working. If I'd known . . ."

"Sure. Right."

"I might have paid a bit . . ." I couldn't lie. I stopped mid-sentence.

"I'll just sit and watch the four of you eat then – will I?"

"You can't!" To my horror I felt my voice go wobbly. Beth began to laugh. "Joke, Jan?"

"Yeah, right." I felt miserable all of a sudden, it was probably the lack of sleep. Turning away from Beth, I picked up my cup, I didn't feel like talking to her. She was being a horrible tight-fisted bitch.

"I'm not that hard-necked to expect a free meal off you."

"What?" I couldn't look at her.

"Here."

She put twenty quid on the table. She was looking at me all concerned. I think she knew I was going to cry.

"Oh, well," I was all flustered now. "Eh, I would've paid . . . it was just unfair but I . . ."

"Shut up Jan," Beth waved me away. "Just take the money before I snatch it back – right!"

I went shopping that evening. Once again I studied the list Abby had given me. She was going the whole hog – starters, main course and desert. Starters was stuffed mushrooms. Then there was going to be a cassoulet, whatever that was. It contained things like cervelat sausage and haricot beans. The beans I think I'd heard of, but the sausage sounded very obscure. She'd said that dessert was up to me but that she'd recommend ice cream, the biscuit Vienetta was nice. She said it'd be a nice contrast.

I got everything, except the sausage yoke, in the small local shop, aptly called Rob's Foodstore. Abby had seriously underestimated the price.

Resentfully, I handed over the amount the shop-girl asked for. And because I never normally shopped in there and, due to the scary pricing system, was unlikely to ever again, I said to the shop assistant, "Rob must have a great imagination."

"What?" The shop-girl smiled.

"To invent all the prices," I said pleasantly.

The smile faltered and she pumped it up again. "There's your change. Thank you."

Feeling pleased at my wit and slightly happier now that I'd managed to pass my bad form onto someone else, I studied the list. The only thing I hadn't got was the sausage.

Then I noticed that Abby had written at the end of the page, *Get sausage in Joan's Delicatessen.*

That was cool.

I'd never been in Joan's Deli before and I'd always wondered what it was like. If I ever passed it, all I'd see would be weird-looking food hanging from the ceiling or stored in fancy jars. In my opinion, people either had to be rich, arty or gay to buy stuff in it. They were the ones, in my totally, I'll admit, narrow-minded view, that ate weird foods.

In I went, feeling very right-on about the whole experience. The place smelt like it was infested with garlic termites. Up to the counter.

"Yes?"

"Five ounces cervelat sausage, please."

"Fine." The lady behind the counter went and got

me some quite disappointing-looking stuff, rolled it up and charged me the earth.

I took my change and exited.

Mission accomplished.

I was broke.

Dr O'Brien had left a message for me about the x-ray on the answering machine. I erased it before the others came in. For some reason that I didn't understand, I wanted to keep things to myself for the moment. I mean, I was probably all right. There was no point in telling anyone.

After O'Brien had proven himself a gullible male by inhaling sharply at Abby's message he informed me that my x-ray was scheduled for Monday morning at ten. "Bring your letter with you," he said as he rang off.

I wrote the date and time on the envelope and pushed further thoughts of it from my mind. I'd more important things to think of, like what the hell I was going to wear tomorrow night.

CHAPTER NINETEEN – FRIDAY

I hadn't eaten a thing since breakfast. It wasn't nerves, just the fact that I had to make my stomach flat so that when I ate my dinner, the new black dress I'd bought would be able to take the expansion. The black dress was a one-meal deal.

I studied myself in my bedroom mirror and tried to pick out faults. The biggest one was my lack of breasts. I had my wonder bra on to enhance what wasn't there, when what I really needed was a miracle bra, but no-one had invented those yet. Big flaw number two was the spot. The biggest one I'd had in ages. But a lot of foundation had camouflaged it – now my nose just looked as if I'd broken it. Other than that, I thought I looked fine.

From the mirror, a glamorous me looked back. I looked like a real grown-up. I pulled myself up straight. I was someone who knew what I wanted and wasn't afraid to get it.

The buzzer sounded and I went weak.

"Answer that, will you Jan," Abby called from her room.

"Oh, I can't, I can't," I was hopping from one foot to the other. "I won't know what to say. Oh, please don't make me answer it."

"Jan!"

My heart was lurching. I thought I'd be sick. Nerves, which I'd kept at bay all week were hitting me all at once. My face, despite having half a tube of foundation on it, went white. "JAN!" It was Abby again.

"Let Beth answer it," I pleaded. "She's not having anyone here."

"Oh, for Christ's sake . . ." Abby began to say.

"I'll get it!" Beth, laughing, strode out of her room. She pressed the intercom. "Yeah?"

My ears strained to hear who it was.

"It's Mickey."

Beth buzzed him to come up.

My heart began to resume its normal beat.

Opening the door of my room I walked into the kitchen. It didn't look like our unwashed, dishes-piled-in-the-sink kitchen. It had been cleaned. Abby had done a great job of ordering me about and the place shone. The table was set with steel knives and forks that sparkled and glittered in the candlelight.

Yeah, we even had candles.

They looked cool. Really high class. As if we were used to having fancy dinners.

The smell in the flat was all garlicky and spicy and made my stomach rumble.

147

And, the coup de grace, a real table-cloth on the table!

"Looks brill," Beth remarked as she surveyed everything. "You and Ab did a great job."

There was a timid tap on the door.

"It's open," Beth yelled.

Mickey's face entered followed by the rest of him.

Beth and I stared at him and then stared at each other. Her face reflected my own aching disappointment. There was no easy way to say it, but Mickey looked like a prick. He suffered from the unforgivable side-parting and creased trousers syndrome.

"Hi, girls," he nodded to us and deposited a bottle of wine beside the television. "How's things?"

"Hi." I attempted to smile. "Jan." I held out my hand and he shook it.

His palm was all sweaty and I had to stop myself from wiping my hand down my dress.

"Hi." Beth too shook his hand.

There was an awkward silence.

Beth took up his wine and began to study the bottle.

Mickey began to shuffle from foot to foot, overlong hands dangling by his sides. "All well?"

"Eh, yeah," I answered.

"Good, good." He stood, shuffling about and rubbing his hands together. Every so often he did a flick with his head to stop his side-parting from encroaching on his forehead.

"Looks nice," he nodded towards the table.

"Yeah," Beth was examining the label on the wine. "Good year," she pronounced.

Mickey laughed. Then he stopped. Then he grinned. Then he stopped. "Heh, heh," he nodded.

We looked at him until he went red.

Beth laughed. Quite unkindly, I thought.

Then I joined in.

At least Dave would be a bigger hit with her than Creased Trousers was proving to be.

Silence.

"Sit down, won't you?" I indicated a chair. "Abby'll be ready in a sec."

"Oh, oh, right, thanks, so." He walked and sat down. Well, perched down. Sitting on it as if he was afraid of it.

Beth was rolling her eyes and making puking faces behind him. I tried to ignore her. She could be a right bitch and, at the back of it all, I think she was a little bit jealous.

Abby came out then and I felt like joining Beth in her puking, because what I saw made me mad jealous.

His face lit up. I didn't know guys could look like that. A big smile. All for her.

"Hiya." He spoke softly. Not a big raucous "How's she cuttin'?" that John, my last boyfriend, used to throw at me every so often.

I liked the way he said it. So I rolled my eyes at Beth.

"Hello," Abby said back. She went over and they kissed each other. Just a quickie, or as Beth said later, a sickie.

"I was telling the girls how good the place looks," he said as he gave her hand a squeeze.

"Oh, yeah, we were having a right ould chin-wag, weren't we?" Beth smiled like a shark.

They ignored her. Abby started to tell him what was on the menu. "All your favourite things," she said. "Stuffed mushrooms, cassoulet, ice cream . . ."

I gaped at her. All *his* favourite things. Pardon, but I thought this meal was for my benefit? Hello? Hello? Ethics, where are you? I really wanted to say that, but I couldn't. I turned away instead and made a face at her.

"Anyone else coming?" Now that he had Abby by his side, Mickey had developed a voice.

"Some weirdo that Jan knows," Abby said dismissively.

Now that was a bit below the belt.

"Some weirdo that you think is gorgeous," I said.

She didn't even blush. "Yeah, sure Jan," she scrunched up her nose and giggled down into Creased Trousers' face. He reached up his hand and pinched her cheek. And they looked at each other. For ages.

Beth and I were beginning to freeze, being left out in the cold. Beth began banging open the oven door as she checked on the food. I started rattling serving spoons in an effort to get attention. I was terrified she'd keep gawking at him and let the food burn. So was Beth. Neither of us'd have a clue what to do.

Eventually, after they'd gooed at each other, Abby looked at her watch. "It's eight-fifteen, Jan," she frowned at me as if it was my fault. "Dave is late."

"It's rude to be early."

"I vote we serve up," Beth said. "Anyone else?"

"He'll be here," I said frantically. "Give him a chance." Uneasily, I wondered if he'd forgotten. He'd hadn't been in touch all week.

"I'm hungry."

The nerve, she wasn't even meant to be there! "Give him a chance."

"We'll hang on for another ten," Abby said hastily. I think she was afraid we'd show her up in front of Mickey.

It only took five.

At twenty past on the dot, the buzzer rang.

"It's me," his beautiful voice floated down the intercom.

"Come up," I said, relief making my voice joyful.

I tried to imagine what he'd look like. I knew for a fact, Beth would be even more jealous of me than she was of Abby when she met him. But, he was mine. I'd bagged him first.

Just like Mickey, he knocked on the door.

"Come in," I called, not going forward to meet him. I wanted him to walk straight into the kitchen without me blocking Beth's first glimpse of him.

In he came. Covered head to toe in the most horrible rainwear I'd ever seen.

"All right?" He grinned around.

"Christ!" Beth said from behind me. I couldn't look at her. I just couldn't.

"Like it, Jan?" Dave indicated himself. To make

matters worse he twirled around. "Frawley's, like ya said."

Realisation dawned. It was the same jacket as mine!

Oh God, did mine look as awful on me?

"It's great." A feeble attempt at a smile.

Dave grinned around at everyone. "Ow's tricks?"

Everyone smiled back. I wished he'd dump the jacket.

"Why don't you take the jacket off and we'll eat?" Abby said to my intense relief. At least underneath he couldn't look awful. "You're late, you know." Abby was all business. This was an Abby I'd never seen before.

"Yeah, sorry 'bout that," Dave began to heave himself out of the jacket. "I 'ad to help rebuild a tunnel that collapsed."

He wasn't lying.

His T-shirt was black. His jeans were slightly blacker.

There was silence as we all digested his appearance.

"Where will I put . . .?"

"Give it to me." I took the jacket from him and he grinned a thanks.

My heart went frantic at the smile. Despite the lack of suitable dress sense, he was still a babe.

"You might want ta look in the pocket of that," he nodded to his jacket. "Somefink for ya."

They were all looking. Feeling thrilled, I pulled out a plastic bag from his pocket.

"So it wouldn't get wet," Dave explained as I unwrapped it.

It was a drawing. A drawing of a tree. "It's lovely," I said, touched.

"An oak," Dave said. "I drew it for ya yesterday." He looked around the flat. "Be nice for ya walls ta 'ave a picture 'anging up."

"Look," I held up the picture so that they could all see what I'd got.

"Why in the name of shite would anyone draw a tree?" Beth asked caustically.

How I wanted to brain her.

"It's the tree I live in," Dave said mildly, obviously not offended. "One that'll be knocked down soon if the developers 'ave their way."

"That's sad," I said, smiling with pleasure. I was going to treasure this picture.

"It's just a thank-you for dinner," Dave nodded at all of us.

When I came back after depositing his picture reverently in my room and trying to find somewhere to dump his jacket, he was sitting down at the table. He seemed totally oblivious to the fact that we were all in our dinner best and he was in his trench-warfare worst.

In the candlelight at least, he didn't look as dirty.

"Jan," Abby ordered, "you sit here, beside Dave."

He grinned at me as I moved in beside him. "Nice place you have 'ere," he said.

I noted that his hands and nails were clean.

First course, stuffed mushrooms.

Abby dished them up, artistically arranged on the plate. Wine was poured and conversation was stilted.

I introduced Dave to Beth and Mickey.

Beth wasn't as impressed as I'd anticipated. "So what is it you do?" she asked.

Dave explained and I found myself getting all fluttery inside as I listened to him. The Mountain Mission was top of his agenda. "An' it is a mission," he stabbed his fork in my direction, nearly knocking my eye out. I didn't care. The passionate look on his face was enough for me.

When he'd explained all about his mission – it was like listening to the new Christ – he went on about the type of money-grabbing industrial tycoons that would allow houses on a mountainside. County councils got it between our second and third mushroom. Then, just as we all thought he was finished he launched the heavy artillery. He gave out about animal testing, nuclear testing, whale hunting, air pollution. Then he assassinated the workplace. Tippex, glues, coloured paper-clips, window envelopes were all major threats. Into the home now. Economic use of resources, oil, gas, petrol . . . on and on.

Beth was pretending to yawn.

I glared at her. I thought he was great. Really impassioned. In the middle of the paperclip diatribe, I wondered what all that passion could do between the sheets.

Then, he stopped. It was like the calm after the storm.

We were all finished our mushrooms and he hadn't started.

"Are you eating those?" Abby asked abruptly.

"Wha'?" He shook his head as if coming out of a daze. "The mushrooms?"

"Oh, right," Dave grinned. He lifted one up on his fork. "I get carried away sometimes."

"I wish he would get carried away," Beth muttered, beside me. This caused her and Mickey to splutter with laughter.

I wanted to give her a really hard dig.

The noise of Dave munching the mushrooms was quite off-putting. But he was only trying to hurry up because Abby had made him feel under pressure.

So, I glared at Abby.

"Great cookin'." Dave had finished. He smiled at Abby. "You do all this?"

"Yeah."

Not a word about how I helped!

"Great food."

"Thanks." She smiled back at him.

I sat, waiting for his attention.

"So," Dave leaned back in his chair and I got ready to talk, "how 'bout you, Beth, what do you do?"

Great.

"Oh," Beth threw her eyes up to heaven. "A spot of turkey-killing around Christmas. Other than that I'm a dole-drawer."

Another laugh from Mick the very annoying prick.

Dave sat, looking stunned.

"Don't mind her." I said 'her' as if Beth was a freak. "She's a barmaid."

"A barmaid," Dave managed a smile. "My favourite kinda ladies."

"Really?" Beth was doing her shark smile.

"Any woman with a drink in 'er hand is my kinda woman."

"Jan, stand up there and dig a few cans out of the press."

I blushed.

"I try never ta drink cans," Dave said. "D'ya know the plastic ring-pulls they come with take four hundred years to biodegrade."

"Someone's measured it, have they?" Beth asked dryly.

Dave laughed. I tried to laugh too.

"Naw. But, also, when they get thrown away, animals can get trapped in them. Fish an' stuff get caught. Birds that dive get caught. They strangle."

"That's awful." I really did think it was awful. I wasn't saying it to get his approval. Truly.

"Sure is." Dave shrugged. He looked again at Beth. "So how's life as a barmaid?" And he gave her a smile. I think that's why she decided to change from being her normal insulting self to an entertaining dinner companion. Once started, she kept going on and on about the pub. And then, just as Abby was putting our dinner in front of us, Beth launched into the hundred funniest barmaid stories. At least it seemed like a hundred.

Soon everyone was laughing and Dave was grinning over at her.

I hadn't made him laugh like that.

Mickey offered to pour us all some more wine.

I badly needed to get drunk. If I didn't do something, I'd lose him.

To my immense satisfaction, Beth ran out of steam and Mickey began to talk. He seemed to have gained confidence due to the fact that Beth's chopping, cutting artillery had been redirected towards Dave. As he talked, he turned occasionally to Abby who smiled encouragingly at him, the way you would at a kid learning to walk.

"I'm a stockbroker," Mickey began. "I'm in the stock market."

We all gazed blankly at him.

"Tell them about it," Abby said. She turned to us. "It's fascinating."

Mickey glowed with pleasure. "It's pressured, though – " He stopped abruptly as Dave, hand to his mouth, made a dive for the sink.

"What's wrong?"

"Are you sick?"

"Jan, he's disgusting." That was Beth.

Dave began to spit out the cassoulet.

"He's spitting out my dinner!" That was Abby.

Spitting out Abby's food is not recommended. Especially if Abby has slaved over it. Especially if Abby is there when you're nearly vomiting it up.

"Oh, shit!" Dave continued to make a big deal of hacking up his dinner. After that he ducked his head under the tap and filled his mouth with water. Sloshing the water around in his mouth, he spit it out again. "Christ!"

They all turned and looked at me. As if I should know.

"What's the matter?" I felt I had to ask.

Dave stood, leaning against the sink. He looked really shaken. Wiping his mouth, he pointed at the dinner. "Is there meat in that?"

Abby nodded. "Sausage." She tapped her fingers gently on the table. "Expensive sausage."

"It's lovely," Mickey said.

"I haven't touched meat in the last fifteen years. And now – Jesus." He sounded devastated. He looked at all of us. "Meat is murder, ya know."

Abby shrugged. "We didn't know."

"And didn't care." Another poisonous whisper from Beth.

She was going to be sorry.

"Yeah, well . . ." Dave shrugged. He looked at me. "Did I not tell ya I don't eat meat, Jan?"

"No," I said. I tried to think of something to keep his attention on me. "I can make you some toast, if you like."

"How about," Beth screwed up her face, "a toasted tuna sandwich."

"Yeah, how about that?" I looked at him hopefully.

Beth exploded in giggles beside me. Mickey tried not to and Abby rolled her eyes.

"No." Dave said, sounding a bit pissed off. "I don't think so."

I felt like someone who'd caught the wrong train. Everyone else knew where they were going except me. "So just toast then?" I managed to say.

"No butter."

"All right." I left the table and went to stand beside him. Deliberately, I let myself brush off him as I reached up to get some bread from the press.

He moved out of my way and went to sit back at the table. This was not going like I'd planned it.

Mickey poured more wine and was soon boring everyone with stock-market stories. I think he was getting drunk.

I was left, on my own, making toast. The scrape of dinner plates began to grate on my nerves as I waited for the gas to reach a sufficient temperature to actually toast the bread.

My dinner solidified as the bread browned. I wasn't even sure I could eat it now, anyhow.

"What do you eat?" Beth had interrupted Mickey in the middle of some new cryptic stock-broker joke. She was looking innocently at Dave. Too innocently. "Roots and leaves and stuff?"

"Mickey wasn't finished," Abby said.

"Vegetables," Dave replied.

"So you murder vegetables!"

"Mickey wasn't finished."

The first side went brown and I turned the bread over.

Dave's laugh twisted me inside. He'd laughed at Beth insulting him, only of course he didn't realise Beth was aiming to crucify him.

His laugh bought him some time. She didn't object as Abby ordered Mickey to finish his joke.

At last, side two was done.

I brought the bread over to him. "Thanks, Jan, you're great," he grinned up at me.

"All the ears of wheat that went into making that," Beth sighed dramatically. "Made to go all brown and burnt under the grill."

"This bread," Dave tapped it. "A lot of the nutrition is gone out of it." He stared around at us. "D'ya know the reason brown bread is made white?"

"No, but I'm sure you'll tell us!" Beth again.

I wanted to kick her. Really hard.

"'Cause it cuts the cost of baking and makes higher profits for the manufacturers due to the fact they use a lot of air and water in it."

"Really?" Abby said.

So, as we ate the dinner, Dave ate his air and water.

The dinner, despite the dead-flesh references, was gorgeous. We all signed up for a refill.

"Factory pigs have an awful life," Dave said, eyeballing me as I received my second helping.

"Do they?" A particularly delicious bit of sausage entered my mouth. I couldn't look him in the eye.

"Yep."

"Do tell," Beth shoved her food into her mouth before saying that. She chewed virtually into his face.

Dave was undaunted. "All white meat suffers," he said, bits of dry toast spraying everywhere. "The broiler chicken, roight, is a bloody meat-machine. Stuck for six months in a cage, not able to move, fed crap and then slaughtered in an assembly line."

"No." Now Beth was being sarcastic.

"Yeah, and bloody pigs aren't any better off." He nodded at Abby's dinner. "Think about that next time you eat a sausage."

"Now come on . . ." Mickey tried to intervene, but Dave was on a roll.

Knocking back his glass of wine, he said calmly, "No, you come on. Wake up to the world."

"I don't think – " Abby tried to intervene. He was annoying her big-time.

"No, that's right," Dave nodded vigorously. "Ya don't think. No one does. Wake up to the reality. The cruelty, the global warming, the greed of nations. Don't close yer eyes to it."

"I feel like closing my eyes right now." Beth did a big bored yawn.

I felt I had to salvage things for him, to win his approval. "Dave's right," I piped up.

His smile and the hug he gave me nearly made me collapse.

"See," he said, holding hard to my arm, "she understands what we're about."

I was just beginning to feel thrilled when he let me go. "Honest. She does." He gazed hard at my face. Then, he caught my chin in his hand and twisted my face around so they could all see it. He ran his hand down over my cheek. "The only sad part is all the make-up she's wearing." He gazed at me. "All that make-up is animal-tested."

I heard Beth laugh.

Abby gave a squeal, that I guess was a suppressed laugh.

I wanted to die with shame.

"Some companies test their make-up on animals that can't blink or cry," he went on. "They've no tear ducts and it . . ."

"Dessert?" Abby's voice cut through him.

It turned out that Dave didn't eat ice cream either. But it didn't bother him. "Next time you'll know," he grinned at me. And my heart soared. So there would be a next time!

"Oh, no, there'll be a next time," Beth pretended to whimper. "I can't take any more of this scintillating dinner conversation." Then, aloud she said to him, "How about fresh fruit salad, Dave?"

I was taken aback. Fresh fruit salad? I didn't know we had that.

Dave nodded. "Great, yeah."

"Fine. Hang on so."

I didn't know whether to be pleased or annoyed that she was taking care of him.

Beth grabbed an apple and an orange from the press, stuck them on a plate a handed to him to him. "There you go."

Dave laughed, totally missing her sarcasm. "Nice one." He began to peel the orange.

Beth was forced to smile at his complete lack of guile. "Anytime," she said, rolling her eyes.

After dessert, we all had more wine.

Abby bought out some after-dinner mints.

Guess what? Dave didn't eat them.

So he had more wine.

It was after twelve when Mickey left. "Have to go," he said, as he crashed into the door. Abby hauled him up. He couldn't stop laughing and neither could she. Solemnly he shook our hands. "Jan," he said, bending over my palm.

"Mickey," I said, extracting my hand from his *asap*.

Next he went to Beth. "Beth, pet," he belched.

"Mick, prick, dick . . . head, thick . . . as a brickhead, gick . . ." she stuttered to a halt.

"Shit-head?" I offered. I was drunk.

"Doesn't rhyme." So, instead, she did a huge belch. One that I reckon must have hurt her.

Abby trod really hard on her foot. Beth was too drunk to feel it.

"And Dave, save . . . the world, see ya man," Mickey, with Abby supporting him stumbled out the door.

"Just getting him into the taxi," Abby called back.

"What a dupid stork," Dave muttered.

"You mean a stupid dork."

"Uh-huh." Dave closed his eyes.

Terrified he'd go to sleep on me, I tried to give Beth hints to go to bed.

I said, "Going to bed, Beth?"

"No." She belched again and reached for more wine.

Dave, eyes still closed, handed her the bottle. He was sprawled out in the good chair. Very drunk.

The minutes ticked by. Abby hadn't come back,

Beth was drinking, Dave was almost comatose and I was drunk enough to make a fool of myself but sober enough to cringe the next morning. So I took another glass of wine and lashed it back.

At last, Beth stood up. She was swaying like mad. "I'm heading to bed."

We didn't answer her. I was afraid to in case she'd prolong the conversation. I held my breath as she walked to her room. I exhaled as she closed the door. *"DON'T DO ANYTHING I WOULDN'T!"* she yelled.

My chance had come.

As long as that wasn't the only thing to come.

I stood up, swaying slightly and moved towards him.

He began to snore.

No! No! No! Tell me this isn't happening. How could he do this to me?

I gave him a gentle kick. It didn't work. I kicked him harder, but he still didn't move.

I wanted to crucify myself.

And him.

CHAPTER TWENTY – SATURDAY

The dress was dumped in a corner. I pulled my nightdress from under my pillow and kicked it around the room before I put it on. It was the best one I had. All satin and polka-dots. I'd been saving it for tonight. And now, now I wouldn't need the feckin' thing.

How I hated my life.

I'd put a cover over Dave in the chair and even touched his face with my hand. But that was as much as I'd dared. It was awful tempting to kiss him but I resisted. I mean, if Beth had come out and seen me kissing a drunken sleeping man she would never let me forget it.

Climbing into bed, I pulled my one blanket over me. It was a cold night and to be honest I was freezing, but last night I'd been cold and I'd had three blankets on the bed and still . . . still I'd woken up all sweaty. Too many blankets. Made me soft. So I'd reduced my stockpile to one. A thin one.

Snuggling down, as best I could in a freezing, semi-blanketed bed, I wondered what it would be like seeing Dave first thing. If I had the courage I'd wander out in my nightie and pretend that I'd forgotten he was there. That would be great.

I was drowning and I couldn't free myself. Water was filling me up, in my mouth, in my nose. Drenching my hair, my skin, my clothes and dragging me down. I tried to get away. My head jerked, my body bucked, my eyes shot wide open.

I gasped and heaved and closed my eyes tight. The sexy nightie was clinging to me, the sheet under me was saturated. I kept my eyes tight shut so that I wouldn't cry. What was wrong with me?

I'd drunk too much, maybe it was a reaction.

Then why did it happen other nights too?

I couldn't answer that. I just sat in the bed, numb. Afraid to think. If I thought too much I'd worry. No point in that.

Might as well dump the sheet onto the floor and put something else on the bed so the mattress wouldn't get wrecked. I got out and in the semi-darkness I began to strip the bed.

Taking my nightdress off and putting on a tee-shirt, I fell back asleep.

The sound of Beth stomping about and cursing woke me the next morning. I lay in bed, determined to ignore her but after a while, I got the feeling that much of the cursing was aimed at me. Every time she passed my door, she'd shout, "Wanker."

I decided that if she did it ten times, I'd ask what the problem was. I really wasn't in the mood for confrontation. Washed-out was the word that described me that morning.

She got away with it fifteen times, before I called out, "What seems to be the problem?"

And in she came. All guns blazing. "Your eco-warrior wanker has gone," she snarled. "And . . ."

"He's gone?" I couldn't get my head around it.

"And he's eaten all our bread."

"Gone?"

"It couldn't have been too awful, if he ate it all! And the apples are missing!"

"When did he go?"

"I don't know," Beth roared. "I don't fucking care. All I know is that he's taken all the fucking fruit."

I said nothing.

"I bought those apples." Beth jabbed herself. "I bought them to eat healthily." She took a whoosh of air. "And what happens? What fuckin' happens? Your – your jerky friend takes . . ." She stopped.

I think it was because I was crying.

Hastily I wiped my eyes and looked at her.

"Are you all right?" She stared at me but she didn't come over.

"I'm – I'm fine." But I wasn't.

Her eyes narrowed. "Are you trying to make me feel guilty?" She didn't wait for me to answer. "Because you won't."

I said nothing. I couldn't, otherwise I didn't think I'd ever stop crying.

Beth stared at me for a second, before muttering, "He didn't just leave – he left you a note." She gulped. "I'm – I'm sorry if I made you think he'd done a bunk. I'm sorry." She left the room and came back a few seconds later with the note in her hand and offered it to me.

I took it from her. I didn't even read it. "It's not that." My eyes filled up. "It's not because he's gone."

"Is it 'cause you wanted some apples too?" She was joking now, I saw her smile.

"No." More tears ran down my face.

She said nothing for a second. Then, jerkily, she walked over to me. Even more awkwardly she put her arms about my shoulders. "So what's wrong?" Her voice was gruff.

Snot was coming out my nose. I wiped it on Dave's note. Her sympathy made it worse. Eventually, I blurted, "I think I'm sick."

Silence.

I'd begun to heave. "I think I'm sick, Beth."

"Sick in the head if you liked that eejit last night."

I gave a bit of a laugh that turned to a sob that turned to a wail. "I'm serious. I'm serious." More snot.

"You look fine to me," Beth said. "Healthy as anything."

"Every night I have these – these sweats and all the time I feel tired, especially in the morning."

"Sweats?"

The tone of her voice made me look up. There was something in her face but as soon as she realised I'd seen it, she closed down. "Sweats?" she said again, totally differently.

"At night," I said. "It's horrible."

She didn't say anything for a second or two, then taking her arms from around me, she stood up. She gazed all around the room. Finally, staring out the window, she said, "Sure, this is the warmest room in the flat, the sun shines in here. You're probably just too warm."

"I thought that," I said slowly. "I even took some blankets off the bed."

"There you are then."

Hope rushed through me. It seemed to fill every part of my body, from my toes up to the big smile on my face. "Do you think so? Do you really think so?"

She moved away from me towards the door as she said, "Yeah."

I hugged my blanket to me. How could I have been so stupid? "You're right, Beth. It's probably nothing."

Her smile was funny-looking. Though I didn't notice that 'till much later.

"Thanks, Beth." I couldn't stop smiling. "I'll be up in a sec."

She said nothing as she closed the door.

Once she was gone, I lay back in the bed feeling happy again and then I remembered about the note. Now that there was nothing wrong, I had my previous priorities to consider. I flung my blanket off the bed and began to conduct a search to find the scrunched up, snot-laden note.

Mucusy and wet, it lay in a ball beside the door. I tried to open it without it tearing. Some of the ink had smeared, but I could still make it out. *Jan, Sorry to go like this but I have to go into Dublin to hand out leaflets. Will ring. Thanks for dinner. Made some brekky. You should think of investing in a new kettle, an automatic one, as it saves energy. Cheers. Dave.*

I read it about ten times before I put on my slippers. He was going to ring again, that was the major thing. Another ten reads before I left the room.

The kitchen was a state and, with a crushing sense of depression, I knew why. I had to clean it. I stuck on the kettle, determined to have a coffee before I began. "Do you want one, Beth?" I called out, resolving myself to be nice to her because she'd been so nice to me.

Beth had gone.

I thought that was weird – she wasn't due in work until after lunch.

I half-wished I hadn't told her about the sweats. I didn't want her talking about it if I wasn't in the mood. Discussing them was out of my control now and I didn't like that feeling.

I needn't have worried.

CHAPTER TWENTY-ONE

April the first.

April Fool's Day.

My dad's birthday.

The irony was, it wasn't ironic. My whole family should have been born on April the first.

I hated going to see them. And I hated that I hated it. Usually, I could get away without much contact for a couple of months and then, the reproachful phone call would come. "When are you coming to see us?"

And I'd have to pack my overnight bag, get on a bus and call over.

And it was always the same. I don't know why Mam kept inviting me, because we usually ended up bitching at each other. Then the dog would come in and growl. Sometimes he even bit me. Lisa and Sammy would attempt to lighten the atmosphere by jeering either me or Ma. And Da would retire to his mate, Alfie's, house. And the two of them would go for a jar and come back singing and Ma would go ballistic at both of them, and somehow, it would all be my fault. And she'd say, "Oh, the sooner you go back to your flat the better."

And a month later she'd be on the phone again. "When are you coming to see us? You never come over."

Still, I thought, as I got off the bus, the worst of today was over. Cleaning the flat had been a nightmare. Food gone hard is disgusting, but other people's food gone hard is gross. I'd managed to wash most of the plates without touching them. Bits of half-eaten sausage kept bobbing up at me in the water. Even thinking of it now made me shudder.

My mother's house was coming into view. Our road was an advert for *House and Home* with Beirut on a bad day stuck in the middle. Everyone else had a nice house, we had Beirut. Hitler's blitz of London couldn't have competed. Every time I came home, I got angry at the sight of it.

Instead of green grass like everyone else, we'd muck. Instead of flower-beds, we'd rusting car engines and oil. The walls of our house were striped. Flaking now, bits of paint dropped all over the car parts.

Mam never cleaned windows, she said why should she be cleaning them for everyone to look in. So, our windows were black.

I approached the house with caution. There was no way I wanted to be seen going into it. I did a swift assessment of the road. All clear. Big deep breath as I clenched my bag in my hand and began the home run.

Trot. Trot. Trot. Nearer, nearer, nearer. Prepare to sprint.

Past O'Grady's, O'Briens, Doyle's, Murphy's, Reilly's, McPhearsons, Johnsons, and . . . in. Pounding up the path, tripping on a wheel or something, stepping over an exhaust pipe, jumping across bricks and bags of cement and banging on the door.

"Hang on! Hang on! Keep your knickers on."

The door opened and I jumped into the hall. Dad closed it after me and beamed. "Jan, it's yourself."

I nodded. Breathless after my run, I couldn't speak.

"Have you no key?"

"Lost . . . it. Last time."

He nodded. Up on his toes, he rocked back and forward. Huge grin. "I hit the big five-oh today."

"Oh, yeah. Happy Birthday, Dad."

"Thanks." He led the way into the kitchen. "Your mother's getting her hair done, she's going somewhere tonight. Sammy and Lisa are out."

"And Buddy?" I asked, looking around in case he was going to attack me.

"Outside. He's in disgrace. He ate a huge chunk of the garden shed last night."

Dad put on the kettle and, knocking a pile of old newspapers from a chair, he motioned for me to sit. "Your mother thought it'd be nice for Buddy to be in out of the cold at night, you know?"

I nodded.

"So she put him in the shed. She thought 'twould keep him warm like."

"Oh."

"And up she gets this morning and who does she see running about the garden?"

He was waiting for an answer. "Buddy."

"The very man. And she thinks he's after opening the door somehow. But not at all. Eating the door. That's what he did." Dad began to laugh. "Ate the feckin' door out of it. So she's ragin' with him, so she is."

The kettle boiled and he switched it off. Then he had to look for cups, so while he was doing that I opened my bag and pulled out his birthday present. It wasn't wrapped, they don't go for that sort of thing in our house. I left it on the table.

Dad was having problems finding a cup. He had to go upstairs. I heard him banging about in all the rooms before he came down with about ten in his hands. "Lisa and Sammy are divils altogether for using cups and not bringing them down."

He rinsed one, not very well, and filled it up for me. It was a blue cup, with big brown dried-on tea-stains running down the sides. I never enjoyed tea in my ma's.

"Thanks, Dad."

He's spotted his present. "For me?" Not waiting for an answer, he opened the bag and hauled his present out. I'd got him a green Aran jumper. "Well, well." He put it up to himself. "Well, well."

"Do you like it?"

"Oh, I do. I do." He stripped off the jumper he had on and put mine on instead. "It's grand. Lovely job. Thanks."

"It's nice on you." And it was.

The sound of the key in the door sent him out. "Jan's here," he said.

"Is she now?" That was my mother. Unimpressed. Then, *cackle, cackle.* "What is that you've on? It's like an American's wet-dream of an Irish jumper."

"'Tis not." Lowered voice. "Jan bought it for my birthday."

"Did she now?" I heard her coming nearer. She poked her head around the door. "The stranger returns." Sarcastic as usual.

"Hi, Mam." I was going to be nice.

"Did you get the card we sent for your birthday?"

"Yeah."

"You could have phoned and thanked us."

"Now, now . . ."

"She could have, Des," Mam cut him off, "How were we supposed to know she got it?"

"I suppose . . ."

"If I phoned everyone that sent me a card, I wouldn't be able to pay my phone bill," I tried to make a joke of it.

Dad at least laughed, Mam just pursed her lips and told me to take my coat off and not be acting as if I was a special guest in the house.

I did as I was told and, throwing it over the back of the chair, I turned to find her gaping at me.

Her eyes widened. She came in further. "What's happened to you?"

"Pardon?"

"You're like a skeleton!"

It was the nicest thing she'd ever said to me.

"Stand up. Stand up and let me have a look at you."

So I stood.

"Turn around."

So I turned.

"Like a skeleton." She came nearer. "Have you been eating?"

"Yeah." There it was. Auto-pilot. The special antagonistic voice I reserved for her.

"Have you lost weight?" She had her arms folded. "Have you?"

"Maybe, I dunno."

She clutched my dad. Ashen-faced. "Anorexic," she whispered dramatically.

"Now, now," Dad began to pat her arm.

"I'm not anorexic." She was always like this. Going off the deep end over something or other. "I just lost a bit of weight. No big deal."

The dog had begun yelping in the garden.

"Shut up, fecker!" That was directed at the dog. Turning her attention back to me, she went on, "You look sick-looking."

The words made my heart go cold.

"Doesn't she, Des?" Mam appealed to my dad. "Doesn't she look wretched?"

Dad frowned and studied me. "*Mnnnn*. She's a bit peaky-lookin' all right, now you say it. A bit pale too." He hadn't a clue. He always agreed with *her*. "And a bit thinner."

"A bit thinner!" Mam's voice had developed her habitual Janet-screech, *"She's fading away!"*

"I'm fine." My voice wobbled. I tried for more conviction. "I'm fine."

"I'll be watching what you eat. Losing weight at your age. You're too old for all that carry-on."

"Right." Despite my best efforts, my eyes rolled heavenwards of their own accord. Then, just in case she was going to say any more, I picked up my bag and walked by them out of the kitchen.

"You're with Sammy," she yelled after me as I ascended the stairs.

Sammy's room, which had once been mine too, was in bits. She had clothes dumped all over the place and I had to virtually wade through them before I found my old bed. It was hiding under piles of socks and discarded CD's. Dumping my bag on the floor, I groaned.

I promised myself that I'd do my best to stay calm until I left.

Just like I did every time I came.

I stayed in the room until tea, lying on the bed and staring at the ceiling. To be honest, I felt tired and the rest was great. No one came near me. Mam was on the phone most of the time, rustling up friends to go out with her that night, and dad had gone for a pint.

Lisa poked her head around the door when she came in, just to say hi. She'd been ready for a long conversation, but the way I kept yawning soon gave her the hint. She drifted off to her room to do some study. Her Leaving Cert was in two months.

Sammy arrived home about ten minutes before tea. I heard Mam telling her I was upstairs and to go and get me for tea.

"TEA!" Sammy stood at the bottom of the stairs and yelled.

"Don't shout," Mam shouted. "Just go up and tell her."

"I heard," I shouted down.

"Don't shout!" Mam yelled even louder.

"Is there some for me?" Lisa stood at the top of the stairs and shouted down.

"Only if you stop shouting!"

"I'M HOME!" Dad yelled, banging open the front door.

"Des!"

"Sorry," Dad said to Mam and he gave a sheepish smile at the three of us.

Tea consisted of a mountain of sandwiches on a plate in the middle of the table. The idea was that we all took as many as we could get our hands on and then went back for more. Sandwiches were my mother's speciality. No one can make a sandwich like her. She puts weird things between slices of bread and the taste is unbelievable. The whole three of us were brought up on them. In fact, if it wasn't for Abby, that's all I'd ever eat.

"Eat up now," Mam said, looking pointedly in my direction.

So, to spite her, I took just one. I pretended not to see her watching me as I delicately took a bite.

She nudged my dad.

Another ladylike nibble.

Whispering in his ear.

I shoved the whole lot wholesale into my mouth.

Open-jawed they gawked at me.

"Oh, you're very funny all right," Mam said. "Very funny. Shoving good food in your mouth won't get you very far."

A laugh came but I couldn't get it out – the food was blocking it. I could see Sammy winking at me behind Mam's back and that made me want to laugh more. Food started to go down the wrong way and I started to cough. Coughing and laughing with a full sandwich in your mouth is a scary experience. Tears ran down my face as I gagged on the bread. I couldn't spit it out, I just couldn't.

"Spit it out," Dad ordered, banging me on the back.

I shook my head and continued to choke.

"Spit it out!" He walloped me.

Out it came. All over my plate.

Sammy and Lisa were grinning and Mam sat at the top of the table, arms folded, with an I-told-you-so face on.

I don't know why I do these things. Whenever I come home I always seem to revert to being fifteen again.

Dad took my masticated sandwich and dumped it in the bin – the big huge green sack that stood like a tower in the middle of the floor.

He got me another plate from somewhere. "There."
I laughed into his face.

"It's the shock," he said to my mother. "It does funny things to people."

She didn't answer. She didn't look at me for the rest of the tea.

"So," Sammy asked, when I'd calmed down. "How's life in flatland?"

"Great." I couldn't say too much because good old Catholic-guilt mother would start on about the time she'd come to my flat.

Or maybe she wouldn't because Lisa was there. Lisa the pure.

"Brilliant actually," I went on, knowing she'd never corrupt Lisa, "We had a dinner party the other night."

"Wow."

And I launched into a description of everyone who'd been there. When I came to Dave, I omitted the dirty-clothes part and the staying-overnight part, even if it was in a chair. And the getting-drunk part.

"He sounds great," Sammy was impressed. She was the libber in our house.

"He's lovely," I agreed, dreamily.

"Beauty's only skin deep." The voice of doom from the top of the table.

"Yeah, but when you're horizontal-bopping, it's time to go beauty-shopping – huh, Jan?" Angelic Lisa had spoken. Smiling serenely, she gazed at the lot of us.

"True for you," Mam said.

Sammy and I and Lisa exploded in giggles.

Mam and Dad smiled indulgently. From the mouth of babes and all that.

The tower of sandwiches was depleting. I had discarded my anorexic tag as I'd eaten a load of them. She wasn't secretly watching me anymore.

After the sandwiches had gone, Mam, with a big theatrical flourish, took out a cake and they all began singing *Happy Birthday* to my dad. I couldn't. I just couldn't. It was so corny.

He was thrilled. "What a surprise, " he said as he blew out his candles.

This was the same as every year.

The only thing that was different was that the cake was red and square. Normally he just had a round cake.

"Why the red cake?" I asked.

Four faces turned towards me. "I told you last week," my mother's voice held an accusing note. "Your father is building an extension. This cake is a brick."

Something clicked. "Oh, yeah."

Dad's chest swelled. "Starting tomorrow. The mates got all the building materials at cost. A few of them are coming out to help." A knowing wink. "Who needs all that measuring and stuff when you've friends who'll help you out."

"And you should see his friends," Lisa licked her lips. "Huge lads."

"Physical work, plenty of it," Dad said, "That's what makes them huge."

"Very physical," Lisa agreed, nodding vigorously.

"Oh, yes. Yes. Indeed." Dad was thrilled with all the

attention. He swung back in his chair. "Whacker, now there's a man. He'd dig a foundation all the way to Siberia if he had to. Then, there's Claude, he's a young fella I met in the pub one night. Sure, he's always up here, offering to help me."

"Yeah, can't get more obliging than Claude." Lisa winked at me and Sammy.

"You're right there," Dad beamed at her.

Lisa smiled sweetly.

"You'll have to meet them tomorrow," Dad said to me. "A nicer bunch of people you could not hope to meet."

Mam muttered something about working on a Sunday but Dad ignored her. "Well, Jan?"

"Aw, I don't know." I'd planned on leaving first light.

"They'll arrive around dinnertime," Dad said. "Sure, stay around and say hello."

I knew he wouldn't leave it. "All right so," I agreed glumly.

I didn't go out that night. I rarely went out when I was at home. The embarrassment of emerging from a white and green house is as bad as going back into it.

Instead, I went to bed early.

Over the past few weeks, I developed a dread of going to sleep. Every night I'd go to bed hopeful, only to wake most nights drenched in sweat. It was like being on a roller-coaster ride, only more exhausting.

Tonight, I was in a different place to normal. If it

happened here, it was me. If it didn't, there was something wrong with the room in the flat.

Turning off the light, I managed, half-hopping in pain, to make my way into bed. I'd stubbed my toe on something that was left on the floor.

Cursing Sammy for maiming me, I closed my eyes and tried to forget about the pain.

I was asleep in seconds.

It was me.

Drenched to the skin I woke. The sheets were sopping and so was I.

The sickening feeling of something awful happening returned. I thought of what Beth had said earlier on and I knew, gazing at the saturated bed-clothes, that I wasn't over-reacting.

I hadn't drunk, it wasn't that.

It wasn't my room's fault.

All the stories I'd told myself over the past weeks didn't cut it anymore. Fear crept up my spine and seemed to clench my heart really tight.

Of course it could be nothing.

And if it was – why be so afraid to find out?

CHAPTER TWENTY-TWO – SUNDAY

"AAAAGGGGHHHHH!"

The screech woke me. I sat up in bed, heart thumping. Then it came again. *"AAAGGGGHHHH!"*

Sammy was snoring peacefully in the bed across the room. There was a banging, thumping, pounding sound coming from the kitchen. Then, *"BASTARD DOGGGGG!"*

It was only my mother.

Getting silently out of bed, I pulled the sheets off the radiator where I'd put them to dry out. Then I remade the bed. Snuggling back down in the warm sheets was lovely.

"Where is he – *BAAAA–SSSTARD!*" Mam seemed to be conducting a noisy search of downstairs all the while giving a commentary on what the dog had done. "He's wrecked the kitchen . . ."

Something was nudging open the bedroom door. A hairy face peered in, followed by a black body. Buddy, the most vicious dog in the universe, had paid me a visit.

"And he's overturned the bins, the fecker!" My mother again.

Silently, Buddy entered the bedroom, crawling along the carpet. I held my breath.

Please get out, Buddy. Please get out, Buddy.

"Cocoa all over the floor . . . "

Buddy climbed onto my bed began to nudge the end of the duvet up over his head.

"The chicken eaten. *AAAGGGHHH!*"

Buddy began to burrow underneath the covers. I stayed still. He was not a dog I, or anyone else, messed with. He wouldn't think twice of eating my leg off if I told him to get out.

He was Sammy's dog, though it wasn't a reality she liked to face. An ex-boyfriend of hers had bought him for her when he was still a cute puppy – the dog, that is. From cuteness, Buddy had developed into an enormous vulpine-like creature. Sammy swore that her fella had known all along the dog would turn out like that and it was his sick joke to the family.

At first Buddy had gambolled happily in the garden. We'd all loved him and Sammy had brought him on long walks. She'd bought him a lead and a brush and a bowl. She'd invested in Pedigree dog food and crunchy munchies. And all the while, a monster lurked. "A wolf in dog's clothing," Dad said as he nursed his lacerated arm. *A wanker*, Sammy had spat as she received a tetanus injection. She didn't buy any more dog food after that. Mam bought it instead. I remember going shopping with her one Friday and she'd startled everyone in the aisle by firing the dog food into her trolley with wails of *"And Muggins has to pay for the fecker's food now. Oh, yes, I knew the novelty'd wear off!"* I'd cringed as everyone looked at us.

Moving my foot slightly, to get comfortable, I froze as Buddy began to issue warning growls. He was totally covered now, the only indication that he was in the bed at all was a huge hump.

Mam commenced pounding up the stairs. I heard her entering her own room and yelling at Dad. *"Do you know what that dog has done now?"*

He muttered something.

"Only wrecked the kitchen! And overturned the bins!"

Mutter, mutter, mutter, went Dad. Or it could have been, nutter, nutter, nutter.

"And eaten the chicken. And the Cocoa."

More muttering from dad.

"AAAGGHHH!" She stomped out, slammed the door on him and went into Lisa's room.

The only one Buddy is afraid of is Mam. I was praying she'd arrive in soon, as he'd started issuing low don't-give-me-away-or-I'll-attack-your-feet type threats.

Sammy was still snoring away, oblivious to all the commotion.

At last, Mam exited Lisa's room and appeared at mine.

"Where is heeee!"

She came into the room like a storm trooper. Holding the sweeping brush, she began poking about the place as if she were on a witch hunt.

I couldn't move, Buddy was shaking underneath the covers.

Whirling towards me, her eyes narrowed as she took in the huge, trembling blanketed hump in the middle of the bed. *"Fecker!"*

Buddy seemed to take this as his cue to re-emerge. He stumbled out, falling onto the ground. Picking himself up, he stared up mournfully through brown eyes. His ears lay flat against his head, his tail tucked between enormous legs.

Huge sigh of relief from me.

"Out!" Mam pointed the brush towards the door.

The dog crawled from the room.

I prepared to get some more shut-eye.

"Do you know what he did?"

Oh no. She was going to lay it all out for me. I made my voice deliberately sleepy. "Yeah, Mam."

"He overturned the bin, raided the presses, ate the cocoa, ate the chicken."

Pause.

Waiting.

"That's awful, Mam." Little yawn this time.

"Rubbish all over the place. The kitchen's in a state."

So, what was new? "That's awful, Ma."

"I hate that dog. I really hate him. And who's the one who has to look after him?"

Oh, God, will she ever just go and let me get back to sleep. "You, Mam."

"Yes, Muggins, that's who."

Pause.

"And who buys all the fecker's food?"

"You." No point in giving subtle hints any more. I hauled myself up in the bed and prepared for the onslaught.

"And whose dog is it?" She raised her voice for the benefit of Sammy in the other bed.

Sammy slept on.

"Sammy's."

"And do you know that *WAGON* never buys anything for that dog?"

"Uh -huh."

"God help her if she ever has a child, that's all I can say."

I wished it was all she could say.

"I'm going to get her to come and clean the kitchen. Huh, she needn't think I'm doing it just because I buy the fecker all his food. It's her dog after all . . ." And over she went and began to poke Sammy with the brush.

"Up! Up! Up!"

Sammy moaned and snuggled further down.

Mam prodded harder. *"Get up! Get up! Get up!"*

Slowly Sammy woke. "What?" She rubbed her eyes. "What?"

I tried to switch off, to close my eyes and ignore them, but it was impossible.

The sound of Mam and Sammy arguing was enough to wake Dad never mind the dead.

I crawled out of bed to escape the confrontation. As I made my way to the bathroom I heard Sammy say,

"It's not my fault if someone bought him for me. I didn't ask for him."

"He's your dog." My mother.

"He's the family dog."

"There won't be any family left if he keeps attacking us the way he does." Mam was screeching.

I closed the bathroom door and the yelling turned into high-pitched muffles.

The five of us sat eating breakfast to a backdrop of howling from the back garden. Buddy had perched himself on the backdoor-step and, face skywards, he was bellowing mournfully.

Mrs Johnson, the neighbour from hell, who lived in the manicured-to-within-an-inch-of-it's-life house next door had already been in to complain.

Our kitchen was even worse than normal. Buddy had certainly done a commendable job. The huge green bin-sack was shredded and it's contents littered the floor. The chicken for the Sunday dinner was sitting in all its skeletal glory in the midst of the cocoa. Mam had ordered Sammy to clean up everything, so the two of them were glaring at each other across the table.

Dad was attempting to lighten the atmosphere. "Maybe I could accidentally run him over or something." He was referring to Buddy.

"In what?" Mam was in foul humour. "Going to build a car out of all the bits of junk in the front garden, are you?"

"Now, now . . ."

"Or maybe ten cars," she sniped. "God knows there's enough pieces out there."

Dad attempted a laugh. "Good one."

"I wasn't joking."

"Oh."

The rest of us stared hard at our toast.

Normally we never ate together. Sunday was a make-your-own-breakfast day. Get up at noon or later, grab a cuppa, watch telly and eat. Today, due to the assault on the kitchen and the impending arrival of the huge physical friends of my father's, we were all up early. All up early and knackered.

Mam was dressed in her Sunday best. She was going to Mass at eleven.

"She's only going so she'll get out of doing the dishes," Lisa whispered.

"I think I'll go so I won't have to clean the kitchen," Sammy muttered.

"Who's going to Mass?" Mam glared at the four of us.

Sammy's hand shot up.

Mam smiled knowingly. "It won't stop you doing the kitchen – it'll still be there when you get back."

"So will the dishes," Sammy shot back.

Mam's smile faltered. She looked at me. "Jan will do them." She observed me coolly. "She's a real radical since she moved out."

Mam had never forgiven me for leaving home. As far as she was concerned, you stayed at home until you married. I'd been gone nearly six years and still she bore the shame of having a daughter live in a flat when she'd a perfectly good home a few miles away. She took it as a slur on her maternal abilities.

I stared at her. Funnily enough, I'd been toying with the idea if ingratiating myself once again with Our Lord. At least until I went to see the doctor. But her barb got my back up. I knew it hurt her that I never went to Mass, not even on Christmas, so I nodded. "Yeah, I'll do them."

Her face dropped. I think she'd been under the impression that I would have done anything to get out of housework. Serve her right.

Lisa said she'd go to Mass later. With the ability of the expert liar, she looked Mam straight in the eyes as she said it. "I study better in the morning – I'll go to Mass tonight."

Dad hummed and hawed. Eventually he agreed to go, as she knew he would. Anything to get her to smile at him again. He was pathetic.

Why couldn't I ever meet pathetic men like that?

Off they went. Mam and Dad with a mournful Sammy in tow.

Lisa perched on the edge of her chair as I began to clear off the table.

"What diet are you on?" she asked as I deposited the dishes in the sink.

I could feel my hands stiffen. Jerkily, I tried to turn on the tap but my fingers kept sliding and I couldn't get the water to run.

"Well?" Lisa asked.

"I'm not on a diet." A week ago I would've been delighted, now I wasn't so sure. "I just lost weight."

At last the tap turned and hot water splashed into the sink.

"Mmmm." I could tell she didn't believe me. "You look slimmer than you were. I remember those jeans on you the last time you came home and they looked – "

"Don't say it," I snapped. "Tarty."

"I was going to say tight, but yeah, I guess they were tarty too."

I didn't answer and there was silence except for the scrubbing of breakfast dishes.

"That must've been around six weeks ago," Lisa mused. "And now, they fit you."

I scrubbed the dishes harder.

"Mam thinks you're anorexic," Lisa giggled. "She thinks everyone who loses weight is anorexic."

"I know," I smiled back.

"She worries about you all the time," Lisa grinned. "She thinks you're leading a life of debauchery in that flat."

"She's right to worry so."

Both of us laughed.

"I think it must be great to have your own place," Lisa said. "I can't wait to move out."

I said nothing. If Lisa moved out there'd be ructions. Nuclear warfare sprang to mind.

"Mam said, once I have my own job, I can do as I please."

"What?" That didn't sound like my mother.

"Yeah."

I smiled indulgently at her, pretending I believed. She was in for a right old shock. There'd been big hassle when I moved out.

Lisa lifted herself off the chair. "Must study," she chortled. She left the kitchen and I heard her go in to the telly and switch it on. Music blared.

The lads arrived at lunch-time. Dad went to the pub where they'd agreed to meet and rounded them up.

Full of bravado he marched them in through the front door of the house. "Marg," he called out to my mother. "Stick on a bit of lunch for us, will you, we're all starving!"

We were watching something on the telly and at Dad's voice, I could see Mam's eyes narrow. "Starving from being in the pub," she muttered. "Suit them better to do a bit of work."

"Hello," Dad boomed, opening the telly-room door, "come on lads and meet the family." He was stopped in his tracks by Mam's face. "Hello dear," he gulped. "I, eh, was just wondering if . . ." his voice trailed off. "Well, later maybe."

"After some work gets done, Desmond," she said sweetly.

"Of course, of course." Dad was nearly backing out the door.

The lads however crowded in behind my dad. There were six of them. Dad gave a hopeless glance at my mother and said weakly, "I'll just introduce them to Jan."

Great, I thought.

Five hulk-like men plus Dad and Alfie crowded into the room.

Dad lined them up and began to introduce them one by one. Because Mam, Sammy and Lisa had met them already, I was the one getting the real introductions.

Dad put his arm around me. "This lads," he said, "is my twenty-five-year-old daughter, Janet. My eldest."

Why, I began to wonder, was my age so important all of a sudden?

The lads nodded and smiled.

"Now," Dad was all business. Pointing to a slimy, greasy, lanky individual, he said, "This is Alfie." He laughed. "But sure, you know him already, Jan. He's an ould fella, like meself."

Alfie snorted away at the non-existent joke.

Mam rolled her eyes.

Alfie shut up.

Dad dragged another guy forward. Admittedly, this fella wasn't too bad. "Claude," Dad said. He looked up at the seven-foot Claude. "How old would you be now?"

"He's twenty-three," Lisa spoke up. "He's *much* younger than Jan." She shot me a malicious look.

Claude winked at Lisa who reddened. Coyness and sweetness replaced the malice.

Dad dragged someone else over. "And this is Lowe," he said. Lowe was actually rather badly named. He towered over Claude.

"Hi, Lowe," I smiled.

Lowe thought this was hilarious. He laughed for about twenty minutes.

Dad informed me, amid Lowe's irritating laughter, that Lowe was thirty – at least.

"At least," he said meaningfully, winking at me.

And then, light dawned. My welcoming smile vanished at the thought that Dad honestly considered this motley crew as potential suitors.

Whacker, the foundation digger-supreme, was like an ape. He was twenty-five.

"Same age as you, Jan," Dad beamed.

"Yeah, like about two-hundred million other people on the planet."

Sammy chortled and began to cough but Dad missed the sarcasm. He wasn't deterred. Adam was nineteen. "A bit young," Dad said. *Adam* pronounced *'At them'*. They all thought this was hilarious.

Bellowing big male laugher and slapping each other on the back so hard I hurt, they left to start building.

"You can get to know them later, Jan," Dad called back.

"*Where* did he get *them*?" I asked.

"From the Catalogue of Disaster," Mam pursed her lips.

I believed her.

An hour later and I knew I had to go. The sound of banging and hammering, cursing and shouting was doing my head in. Claude kept looking for jugs of water to keep the lads going. Every time he came in, Lisa rushed to oblige.

"She's such a helpful kid," Mam observed fondly. "Really into helping people out."

I shrugged and grinned. Whatever about into helping people out, she was certainly into Claude.

"Listen," I said, after I'd heard a particularly nasty crash, "I, eh, have to go. I'm heading out tonight."

"Stay for your tea," Mam coaxed.

"No, it's all right," I indicated the lads in the front garden, "you'll have enough to feed with all them."

She shot me a strange look. "Fine so," she said. "Off you go."

I left as fast as I could.

CHAPTER TWENTY-THREE

The sense of relief I had, knowing that I wouldn't have to visit home for another six weeks would ensure that I'd be in good form for five weeks at least.

It was great walking up the road to the flat, the sense of freedom of just being ordinary. Of not being one of the Boyle's that lived in the weird house.

If Abby was in I'd ask her to come for a drink with me. I felt like I needed one. Or maybe, if Dave had rung, I could go with him. Delicious sensations floated up and down my spine at the thoughts of sitting in a cosy pub with Dave.

And, the sensible-mammy part of me decided, it was probably for the best that I hadn't been in when he rang. It would look like I had a life.

I couldn't wait to get to the answering machine.

It seemed to take ages to open the front door of our building, and then I legged it up the stairs to the flat. It was knackering. Outside, I had the prolonged agony of fumbling about with the lock on that door.

And then I was in.

And so was Abby.

And Mickey.

The two were lying side by side on the sofa. Mickey had his pristine white shirt open to the waist, displaying his white, hairless chest. A two-pack would have been a gross exaggeration of his muscle tone. His ribs stuck out like dangerous weapons.

"Hi fuc – folks," I said, tactfully averting my eyes from Mickey's sticky-out bits. I stared hard at their faces.

Mickey blushed, and his white hairless chest was suddenly a crimson hairless chest. Almost ripping his shirt apart he tried to pull it on. Trying not to be noticed he surreptitiously began pulling up his fly. "Jan," he said. He might as well have said, "Bitch."

"What the hell are you doing back?" Abby had no such modestly, more's the pity. She glared at me as she pulled down her skirt. "I thought you were staying over Sunday."

"Ha!" I dumped my bag on the ground. "Stay Sunday? When have I ever done that?" I walked to the window and pretended to look out.

Mickey was still fumbling with his shirt.

"Will you relax," Abby snapped at him. "It's only Jan. She's seen more chests than I've had . . . " she tried to think of something.

"Periods?" I suggested, turning around and grinning. Normally I'm not so crude, but hell, I wanted to go for a drink with Abby and now, he was here, ruining it all. Most guys I had gone with never saw me on Sunday. Not in the afternoon anyway.

I suppose I was a tiny bit jealous.

Not that I'd have touched Mickey with a barge pole, but still, he was male and obviously interested, a rarity as far as my experience went.

Anyway, my comment succeeded in making Mickey look revolted.

"Don't be crude," Abby tried to look offended. "Hot dinners, that's what I was going to say."

"Oh, right."

There was a silence.

Maybe I was being awful? "Sorry."

Mickey sniffed and continued to dress himself. Abby started to pull her jumper over her head. "Are you going anywhere tonight so?" she asked.

Subtle as the two fingers.

"Might be." The look of delight on both their faces was pathetic. "First," I made a big deal of walking to the answering machine, "I have to check for messages."

Abby's face dropped. "He didn't ring," she said.

My face dropped. "Who didn't?" It was a cheap cover-up.

"Mr Save the Earth." Then, Abby grinned at Mickey. "What was it you called him, Mick?"

Mickey made a shut-up face.

"Something funny," Abby screwed up her face as she tried to remember.

"I think we – " Mickey was looking anxiously at me.

"No. No." Abby flapped her hands about. "It was a good one. Jan'll laugh."

I really didn't think I would.

Neither did Mickey. "I don't think – "

"Oh, yeah," Abby chortled. "The guy in the Infamous Blue Raincoat."

I stared blankly at her. Mickey smiled uneasily.

"You know," Abby giggled. "The Leonard Cohen song "Famous Blue Raincoat?"

"Yeah, I know it." You cow, I wanted to add, but didn't.

"Well, Mickey thought that Dave should be called Infamous Blue Raincoat – see?"

"Oh."

Pause.

Bigger pause.

Guilty looks from both of them. Just as I saw Mickey about to apologise, I smiled. "I think I will stay in tonight so."

Bang!!!

Down to earth they came.

Mickey gave Abby an exasperated 'what the hell did you say that for?' look.

And that kind of cheered me up. But just a little.

He hadn't rung!

He hadn't rung!

He hadn't rung!

Flicking on the television and trying to ignore the horrible looks I was getting from both of them, I stuck a determined smile on my face and pretended to watch some comedy show on RTE.

That in itself was enough to make me cry.

Maybe Abby had made a mistake? Maybe she'd accidentally wiped his message! Maybe now I'd never hear from him again.

I chortled at some joke or other.

Maybe I'd ruined everything by going away for the weekend. I should've stayed in and waited. Why did I have to go home that very weekend? It was all my mother's fault!

Another woeful joke. I groaned. Just to show I was watching it.

Maybe if I'd come home yesterday, this would never have happened. Maybe if I had been awake when he left on Friday. Maybe if . . .

"We're going out," Abby broke in on my thoughts. "And we'll be back later."

"Fine."

I knew what she meant. She wanted me to be in bed when she got back. Well, I'd see how I felt. But just to annoy her for sneering away at Dave behind my back I said, "See you later so."

I knew she wanted to kill me.

It was great.

I felt good about that.

The slam of the door as they exited the flat did make me feel guilty though.

It also made me dive for the answering machine.

Just in case.

Nothing.

Shit!

Now another sign to add to my collection: *Free*

Meals, No strings. The only string I wanted was one to hang myself from.

And I'd want to slim a bit before it'd hold my weight.

After effing the answering machine until I felt better I slouched over to the chair and flicked through the stations until I found a film just starting. *Untamed Heart.* A real *two-boxer.*

Ab and I measure weepies by the amount of tissues they use up. *Untamed Heart* was fairly high. *Beaches* was the top of the list – *a three-boxer.*

Not having anything better to do than cry my eyes out at something I'd seen twice before, I settled down to watch it.

The bedroom scene was just coming on when Beth arrived in. She plonked herself on the sofa, offered me some of her chocolate and started to watch it with me. I didn't tell her it was sad, I didn't think I had to. I didn't think it was a big issue.

Just before he got sick, she zapped the station over.

"Hey – " I attempted to grab the remote from her.

"I'm not watching it," she said. "It's crap."

"You've never seen it before," I said. I had my hand on the remote and was admiring myself for my bravery. "It's good."

"It's shite, the fella is thick. Imagine thinking he has a baboon's heart inside him. It's shite, Jan." She wouldn't let go of the remote.

"I was watching it first," I said. Then thinking that that sounded childish, I said, in a mature tone,

"There's only a few minutes to go, just let me see the ending."

"No." She wouldn't look at me.

"Beth!" I couldn't believe it. I was contemplating giving in when she startled me.

"Oh, fuckin' watch it then," she spat, almost firing the remote at me. She flounced off the chair and grabbed her coat. "Forget the fact that you've probably watched it a million times before and that you know the ending and that you'll have a headache from crying." She rolled her eyes. "You are pathetic, Jan."

Stunned, I looked at her.

She made her way to the door. "Sad," she flung back into the room at me.

Then she was gone.

I didn't cry at the end for the first time ever. She'd spoiled it on me.

CHAPTER TWENTY-FOUR – MONDAY

I was half an hour early for the x-ray appointment. By nine thirty, I sat in the waiting-area clutching the doctor's letter in my hand as if it was some sort of talisman. Already there were people ahead of me and I dreaded to think what ungodly hour they must have got up at to be in the hospital at this time.

I hadn't got out of bed so early in decades. Normally for work, it was a rush job, throw on a few clothes, grab a cup of tea and plaster on the camouflage, then out the door and on the bus. This morning, I was up at seven thirty and eating my breakfast by eight.

Beth, who also had decided to get up early, had done a double-take as she saw me at the table idly flicking through the Sunday paper.

"What's the story?" She turned on the radio and began to make herself some toast.

"Huh?" I pretended I didn't know what she meant.

"You. Up so early. What's the story?"

"Early bird catches the worm." It wasn't exactly a lie, just a saying.

"You don't need to get up early," she remarked, as she opened the press to look for a clean plate for her toast. "You catch them anyhow."

"What?"

"That eco-waster fella you had here the other night," she rolled her eyes and banged her plate on the table. "What a loser."

"I don't think so."

"Yeah, well you wouldn't." She took her toast out and began to scrape it with some revolting pretend butter. Taking a bite, she said through a stuffed mouth, "I mean, remember John, or whatever his name was."

"It was John." I didn't like to be reminded of him. John had been the greatest con-artist on the planet.

"You thought he was a computer whizz-kid."

"Whizz-man," I interrupted.

"I work in computers, Jan," Beth was into her stride now, doing a perfect take-off of John's Dublin 4 accent.

Despite myself I began to smile, though it hurt to remember. I'd liked John.

"And where did he work?" Beth made a stabbing motion with her fingers. *Where . . . did . . . he . . . work?*

I didn't answer. This story was one of Beth's all-time favourites. Whenever she'd a few jars on her and it got around to telling tales, this was the one she told about her gullible swallow-a-brick flatmate.

"Where did he work?" she said again.

I didn't answer.

"He worked in computers all right. As a fuckin'

porter in the computer section of a computer company." As always, she dissolved in giggles.

Then it went on to the time she'd asked him to have a dekko at the computer in the pub's stock section. He'd gone white and pretended to fiddle about with it and somehow succeeded in crashing the whole system. That's when he'd confessed.

"And he wasn't a worm?" Beth jibed, amid giggles.

"Dave isn't a worm." I gave a glare into my empty mug.

"Naw, he just likes to save them." And she was off again.

Just because she couldn't get a man . . .

Well, that wasn't strictly true, she'd been engaged once. I remember her telling us, when she was locked, he'd done something really selfish and it had –

". . . you?"

My thoughts were interrupted by a woman digging me in the ribs. "Is that you?" she asked.

A nurse was calling out "Janet Boyle?" and looking around at everyone.

"Me!" My hand shot up, as if I was answering a question in school. I smiled at the woman sitting beside me, gathered my things together and followed the nurse.

They brought me into a room where this enormous camera thing stood.

The woman took the letter from me and had a read of it.

"You're not pregnant, are you?" she asked as she began to fiddle about with the machine.

I have to say, I found that question a bit insulting. After all, I'd just lost weight.

"It's just if you are, x-ray's are not good for the foetus." She finished aligning the machine and looked at me.

Relieved at the explanation, I answered, "No. No. I'm not."

"Fine so." She made me cover myself with a heavy jacket thing, except that my back wasn't covered. Then she went out of the room and told me to stay still. She took an x-ray of my back.

After that it was all over.

"We'll hopefully have the results to your GP this week," she said as I left.

I couldn't get out of the place fast enough.

It was after eleven as I walked up the street to work.

"How's it goin'?"

Al's voice in my ear made me jump. "Don't sneak up on me like that."

"In good form, huh?"

"I was." I stressed the "was".

"Oh. Oh." He was smiling.

"So what's the story?" he asked. "Why were you off this morning?"

Ignoring him, I pointed to my watch, "What are you doing out here? You should be in work."

"I am workin'," he shoved a file under my nose, "Lenny made me get this from the other office."

"You lick-arse."

"Yeah, I know." We both laughed a bit and then there was silence.

"How come you were off this mornin'?" he asked again, after a few seconds. Another laugh. "Sick, were ya?"

"Don't be so smart," I didn't think it was funny. "I was on leave."

"Sick leave?"

"No – holiday leave actually."

"Must be a first," he jeered gently.

I decided not to dignify his comment with a response.

"So what were you doin'?" He was still laughing at me. "No. Hang on," he said, "don't tell, let me guess." He made a sort of humming noise, to make it sound like he was thinking deeply, I suppose. Then he said, "You were . . . eh, you were inhaling poisonous fumes in an attempt to get sick?" He stopped and before I could say anything, he was off again, "Or . . . you were standing beside someone with pneumonia and trying to waft their germs in your direction?"

"Shut up! You're pathetic."

He kept laughing.

"It's not funny."

"Maybe it's true though?"

"Piss off."

Al had a nice laugh, the kind that made you want to laugh with him. Luckily, he stopped just as I was beginning to smile. "So," he said, "How was your weekend? Crap, I suppose?"

"And why do you suppose that?"

"'Cause you're in shite humour."

"I'm in shite humour 'cause I met you, Al," I answered, feeling pleased with my wit. "No other reason."

"Funny, Jan," he punched me on the arm. "You're cracking me up here!"

I ignored his good-natured acidity. "I went home for the weekend," I answered. I didn't want to say anymore because he hadn't exactly been all tea and sympathy the last time I'd mentioned my family.

"Oh, right." He stopped for a second and asked, "You, eh, didn't meet your marcher friend then?"

For a second I didn't know who he was on about. Then it clicked. "Oh, Dave," I said, as if I met Dave every day of the week. "No, I, eh, I'd promised to go home last week so I, eh, couldn't meet him."

"So," Al went red, "it's not a mega-serious relationship then?"

I looked at him in amazement. "What is this?" I began to giggle, "Do you get a sick pleasure out of my private life? Is that it?"

"Don't be stupid," Al said a bit narkily, "I just wanted to know, that's all."

"It's not serious yet," I answered, humouring him, "But I hope it will be."

"Oh, righ'." He continued to walk beside me. For a few seconds neither of us said anything. Then, clearing his throat, he asked hesitantly, "So, eh, he wouldn't mind if, eh, I asked you to a concert on Saturday, would he?"

"What?" I couldn't believe this. "Are you asking me out?"

Al stopped walking, we'd just reached the steps at the front door of work. "Well," he gulped, not looking me in the face, "I got two tickets about a year ago for this gig and well," he stopped, "the girl I asked to go can't go now, so I was wondering . . ." He stopped and looked at me.

"You have a girlfriend?" I couldn't believe it.

"Had," he clarified.

"And what happened?" It was out before I could help myself.

"Shite," he cracked a smile. Then gazing down at me, he said, "So will ya come?"

"Who's playing?"

"Dylan."

"Bob Dylan?"

"The very man."

"Wild horses won't stop me going."

Al gave a delighted grin. "And your fella won't mind?"

It was nice to hear him say "your fella". Even if it wasn't strictly true. I smiled and said, "I'll sort it."

If only.

When we arrived in, everyone was there. Lenny was humming, Henry was rummaging about under his desk and Liz was trying to look busy.

"Ah, Jan," Lenny smiled at me as I came in. "You're here."

"Yes," I was cautious. He never usually greeted me so warmly.

"I've just stuck your name down as going for promotion." The last part of the sentence was said in a suspicious mumble.

"But I'm not going for promotion, Lenny," I said, walking over to his desk. "I said so before."

"Aw, sure that was before," he gave a flustered look at me. "You were probably just being . . . just being . . ." he stopped and cocked his head. "Just being a woman," he finished.

"Pardon?"

"What?"

That was myself and Liz.

"What are you saying?" Liz leaned over her desk towards him. Despite the fact that she was about ten feet away, she did succeed in looking threatening. "What are you implying?"

Lenny looked like an actor with stage fright. "Oh, oh nothing," he attempted to laugh.

"Are you saying that women don't know their own minds?" Liz was pinning him with her stare. "Are you?"

He was petrified of Liz. She was the most productive one in the office and if he fell out with her, he could say good-bye to any work being done. So he muttered "Mnnnn," which could have meant anything. He lifted himself out of his desk and walked from the room. *"Do-be-do-be-do."*

"Thick culchie," Liz glared at all of us.

"Where's this list?" In a panic I began to rummage through all the rubbish on his desk. "The nerve of him putting my name down."

"He took it down this morning," Henry announced. He grinned, "Face it, you're fucked, Jan."

I bit my lip. I suppose I wouldn't get promoted anyhow, not with my leave record, but I didn't want to go for interview and make a complete fool of myself.

"You probably won't get it anyhow," Henry said, very tactlessly I thought. "I mean," he went on, "you're not exactly a fuckin' Trojan workhorse, are you?"

Henry the Blunt – it was the most polite thing I could think of. I tried to stare coldly at him as I made my way to the desk. He was still wearing his red jumper – he'd worn it continuously since last week. I wanted to tell him that he reminded me of a woolly version of scarlet fever, but I didn't. Instead, I ignored him.

"Do you think I'll get promotion?" Liz asked, preening herself in advance of his answer.

"You might." Henry, unaware of the devastated look on her face, stood up. "I'm goin' on me tea-break."

"Dublin shite," Liz spat after the door had closed.

Al grinned at me and I managed to smile back.

This was not turning into the most promising of days.

Henry came stomping back from his tea-break. He came in and slammed the door, making Al and me jump. We were the only ones in the office.

"Fuckin' shit!" Henry began to advance on Al's desk. "Do you know what you've done? Do you?"

Al went white and looked bewildered. "What?" He cast a panicky glance at me.

"Don't fuckin' look at her," Henry snarled. "She's got nothing to do with it."

"Henry," I said, "Calm down, willya."

"Calm down, me arse!" Henry pointed over at Al. "That fecker with his marvellous ideas has just ruined any chance I ever had of being promoted."

"Come on . . ." Al said.

"DON'T!" Henry roared, making Al physically jump. "DON'T SAY THAT!"

"What's he done?" I tried to calm the situation down. Henry was hyper at the best of times.

"I go down to my fuckin' tea-break," Henry was pacing agitatedly about the room, "and everyone's talkin' about interview boards."

"So?" Al genuinely looked confused.

"SO!" Henry roared, "SO FUCKIN' JIMMY MADDEN'S ONLY FUCKIN' ON IT!"

If he hadn't been so mad, I would have laughed.

I saw Al trying not to grin, but so did Henry. He began once again to advance on him. "You and your fuckin' stupid ideas!" His fist was pounding into his palm. "It was your fuckin' idea that I tackle Madden over what he said about me jumper." He inhaled furiously. "And now look . . . and now fuckin' look at what's happened."

Al said nothing. Slowly he stood up to meet Henry. He had gone pale and with a jolt, I saw that his fists were clenched.

"You're going to wreck my career, you little fecker!"

Still, Al said nothing. His eyes were fixed on Henry, yet not fixed on him. He looked strange.

Henry was oblivious. "Fuckin' Madden's havin' the last laugh now, the wanker. And it's all your bloody fault you little . . ." a few inches nearer, still slamming his fist into his palm. "toerag. And . . . "

Al's body sagged. His eyes blinked and he stared hard at Henry.

" . . . I'll get you for this. I'll say that you don't . . ."

"Piss off," Al said contemptuously. He took a huge gulp of air, sat down and waved Henry away. "Just piss off, right."

I've never seen Henry speechless. His mouth opened and closed like a goldfish. He sucked in a whoosh of air in an attempt to recover his composure. "Don't talk to me like that," he said. "Don't dare."

Al looked at him. "I just did," he said.

Henry was gob-smacked. He did a double take. He blinked and then hauled himself up to his lanky six foot one. "Don't ever do it again," he said. "That's what I mean." He glared at Al's bent head. "I'm your superior. Don't forget it."

Al gave an indifferent shrug and I closed my eyes. What was he playing at? Was he looking to be fired?

"Are you looking to be fired?" Henry asked as he swaggered back to his desk. "Any more of that and you will be."

"Wow," Al spat. He stood up and without looking at anyone he left.

"I'm going on me tea-break," he yelled.

He didn't arrive back until after half-twelve. There was

just me minding the office, everyone else had gone off somewhere. Liz was photocopying, Lenny was gone for a quick smoke and Henry, I suppose, was busy slitting his wrists.

I was attempting to decipher Lenny's writing when I heard the door open. Looking up I saw Al.

"Where have you been?"

He walked over and sat down at his desk.

"Al?"

"Nowhere," he said quietly. "Just out." He picked up his pen and began to sieve through his files.

"Henry is on the warpath."

"So?" He didn't look up.

"You were fine this morning," I went on.

"And I'm fine now," he snapped back. "Drop it, Jan. Forget it."

I'd never seen him like that before. He was angry about something. "What's the matter?" I watched how he flinched and I continued, "I'm not being nosy, just, you know, it's not like you."

"What's not?"

"You're usually quiet." I attempted a grin. "Boring even."

It was exactly the worst thing I think I could've said.

He rolled his eyes and again I caught a glimpse of someone I didn't know at all. "Am I?" he sneered. "Well, Jan, hate to say this, but you don't know me – all right?"

Now, that hurt. It's awful to have your concern walloped back in your face. Especially from someone I thought was a mate. "Aw, get lost so," I spat. "I was joking. It was a joke, Al," I said the last bit as if he was thick. "I only asked because I care." I could see his face changing when I said that, so I decided to rub salt and acid and whatever else I could find into the wounds. "But, just fuck off, 'cause I don't care anymore."

"Jan . . ."

I stood up. "I'm going on tea-break." I didn't look back at him as I slammed the door.

It was the first argument I'd ever had with someone I worked with. I felt sick. I wanted to get away from the office as quickly as I could.

Serious cheering up was needed.

Going on tea-break with Liz was not the answer. She wasn't as friendly as normal. I think she was jealous because I'd lost weight. Every time I got up from my desk I'd feel her eyes following me around.

At first it was flattering. Now it was annoying.

I decided to go for a walk. If asked, I'd pretend I was getting a file from someone.

Opening the door, I saw that it had stopped raining, which was just as well as I hadn't brought my coat with me. There was no way I'd have gone back to get it either. I couldn't face Al just yet.

The row with him kept nagging me as I walked down Parnell Street and turned towards The Ilac Centre. I tried to push it out of my head – if he wanted to act like an ass-hole, that wasn't my business. But the image of him drunk and laughing kept popping into my head and I felt really bad about the things I'd said.

Maybe I'd been a bit over the top? No, it was his fault.

Are you sure? Bloody right I'm sure!

Before I realised where I was, I'd arrived at Roches.

The place where they sold weighing-scales.

My internal voices quietened as other, more beguiling thoughts took their place.

Maybe I could sneak a *weigh* on one of them? Just test it out as it were.

That might cheer me up.

Of course, if it said that I weighted thirteen stone or something, it might just send me over the edge that at the minute I was precariously close to. Still, nothing ventured nothing gained.

"Or lost," pessimism chortled.

But that was defeatist talk.

My heart began to thump as I walked into the shop and I knew that everyone knew what I was up to. It was like being a shop-lifter. The scales were downstairs, so I had to make my way to the escalators first. I felt I couldn't just saunter straight over to the weighing-scales, I had to browse, making it seem as if I was looking for something and I wasn't sure what. I meandered through the baby clothes section, I examined prams and handbags, I sniffed the flowers and tried on a few scarves. When I was sure that I'd convinced sales assistants, store detectives and anyone else who was watching, that I was a serious shopper, I made my way to the escalator.

Heart beating with alternate fear and anticipation I descended to the basement. On shaky legs I casually sauntered over to the bathroom section. And there they were. A veritable mountain of weighing-scales. So I browsed through them, moving my mouth in pretend concentration. Picking them up, putting them down. There was an unboxed one right on the left hand side of the shelf. Like a shark moving in for the kill, I gradually eased myself over towards it. Then, just in case anyone was looking, I did an "ooh" of surprise with my mouth, as if I'd just found my dream scales.

I turned it over, turned it sideways, examined the little dial. Then, as nonchalantly as I could, I put in on the ground. Heart hammering, I wondered if I'd have the nerve to stand on it. I put an expression on that said, I wonder will this fit in with the colour scheme of my bathroom?

I stared at it for ages.

Just as I was about to stand on it, my heart began hammering away like mad. Next thing I knew, I was gently touching the gland in my neck. I hadn't felt it since Wednesday at the doctor's, but for some reason, I was fingering it now. Painless but bigger than I remembered.

I yanked my hand down from my neck so fast it hurt.

I wanted to stand on the scales but I couldn't.

I wanted to be eight seven but at the same time, if I was, what did it mean?

Without looking back, I turned, ran up the stairs and out of the shop.

The rest of the day crawled. The atmosphere in the office was delicate. Liz wasn't talking to me, I wasn't talking to either her or Al. Al wasn't talking to Henry or me. And Henry wasn't talking to Al.

The only one unaffected by the tension was Lenny who hummed mindlessly through the day. His words, when he talked, fell into wells of silence as each one of us waited for someone else to reply to him. Normally, I hate a bad atmosphere but today, I just tried to block it out.

At about three, a call came for Henry saying that there was a package down in the hall for him. This got a bit of interest going. What could it be? Liz wondered. I mean, who'd send Lanky Legs anything.

Lenny chortled a bit at the nickname. "That's not nice," he chastised Liz, his face wreathed in smiles.

"Better than being called shit-head," Al spoke up. He hadn't said a word all day. As we looked at him, he explained, "The lads on my tea-break call him that."

"They call him Boney on ours," Lenny said.

We looked blankly at him. It wasn't funny.

"Because he's Boney," Lenny went on to explain.

Liz and I did a passable attempt at a giggle. Al shrugged and went back to work.

The door was banged open and the boney, shit-head, lanky-legged Henry entered. He was carrying a huge brown sealed cardboard box. Staggering under its weight, he deposited it on the floor beside his desk.

"Fuckin' heavy," he began a massage of his back.

None of us wanted to give him the satisfaction of asking what was in it. We ignored him.

He began to tear the seal off and one by one our heads looked up.

He began to pull apart the flaps.

Glaring red items.

Henry pulled one out. "Bought a job-load to flog," he announced as he held it up. "Two hundred red v-necks. Seven quid each."

It was surprising how we all found something very urgent to do.

I had just managed to get out of my seat with the intention of going downstairs to the photocopier, and staying beside it for the afternoon, when he latched onto me.

"Jan," he stopped me as I got half-way between my desk and the door. "Would you like one?"

I considered ignoring him. I considered telling him I'd spent the weekend in an army barracks and was suffering from temporary deafness, but I hadn't the nerve.

He was advancing towards me, holding the jumper up to his chest. I don't know which looked more off-putting, him or the jumper.

Everyone else was busying themselves with work, glad that they hadn't been picked on.

"Well?" Henry demanded. "What d'you think?"

He wouldn't want to know.

"You thought it was worth a tenner," Henry chortled. "I'm fuckin' giving it away. Seven quid."

"I don't wear v-necks," I said weakly.

"'Cause you don't have any!" Henry was swaying left to right trying to make the jumper look more appealing.

It looked like sun-stroke.

"You could buy it as a present," he continued.

Out of the corner of my eye, I could see Liz scurrying out the door.

"Anyone would fuckin' love a jumper like dis."

Lenny slowly and noiselessly got up from his desk.

"A fuckin' bargain!"

Lenny's hand was on the door.

"A fuckin' bargain, I'm tellin' you!"

A bargain.

A BARGAIN!

I could buy it for my Da. For Christmas or something. It'd get Henry off my back too.

"I'll take one," I said grinning. Then, thinking that spending seven quid on my father was a bit scabby, I stunned everyone, including Henry, by saying, "Gimme two."

He couldn't off-load them fast enough. "Clever girl," he kept saying. "Knows when to buy."

Lenny exited.

Al was the only other potential customer-cum-sucker left in the office, but due to the fact that they were incommunicado, I don't think Henry had the nerve to ask him. Instead, he took an armful of jumpers from the box and announced, "I'm going to see if anyone else is interested in a good buy."

He was gone.

Al and I were left alone.

I wanted to talk to him, but couldn't. I didn't know what to say or how I could start a conversation off.

He kept staring over at me and in the end he asked, "Are you mad? What did you buy two jumpers for?"

"I wanted to." Now that he was talking to me, I saw no reason why I should make the effort.

"Right," he said and turned back to his work.

The minutes ticked by.

He wasn't going to say another thing.

"For my Dad," I said, "He'd like a jumper like that."

Al looked up. He put down his pen. "Jan, about earlier . . . "

I waved him away. "Forget it." The hurt was still a bit raw.

"I think you over-reacted . . . "

"I don't fuckin' over-react. I don't." I glared at him.

He quirked his eyebrows. There was a smile on his face. "No," he said in a mocking voice. "You don't."

I threw my Tippex at him and he laughed. Especially when it opened in mid-air and dumped its contents all over Liz's desk.

We cleaned it up together and the row was pushed into the background.

Al and me were mates again.

We didn't talk anymore about earlier.

CHAPTER TWENTY-FIVE

Lying on my bed, I tried wriggling into my PVC skirt. It was hard work but I knew the effort would be worth it.

I was showing Abby what I was planning to wear when Dave eventually got in touch. Out of pity she'd agreed to look. I knew she didn't think he'd ring.

As I took a trembling heaving intake of breath, before attempting to button the top button of the skirt, I glanced up at my huge Brad Pitt poster on the ceiling. His was the last face I saw at night and the first face in the morning. It was meant to cheer me up on my way to work but it didn't work. I doubt even him being there in person could have done that.

"Help me, Brad," I mouthed and like the good thing that he was, he galvanised the button into buttoning.

I was ready to face Abby's critical eye.

"Da-na-na-naaah!" I did a twirl to add to the effect.

Abby frowned.

"Don't you like it?" Well, that was a stupid question, she hated everything I wore. But the least she could do was lie. Abby was good at lying – she normally tried to spare my feelings.

"It doesn't match," she said tentatively. "The blacks are different."

I didn't need this. I wanted to be told I looked wonderful. I'd spent the best part of thirty quid on the black cardigan to go with my black PVC skirt, because black was always in. Or so it said in Bella. With a black skirt and black top, how could I go wrong? "Not majorly different," I made a face. "You're too particular, Ab."

"It looks funny though."

"I don't give a shit." My mood was not the best. My faith in the simple cardigan was taking a nose-dive. "Look, Ab, it was dear, almost thirty quid." She didn't look impressed. "Anyway," I continued hastily, "I can take off the cardigan," off it came, "And . . . *voilá*." Underneath I'd a lovely orange sequinned belly-top.

"Have you lost weight, Jan?"

"Sorry?" The question surprised me. I thought I was in for a justify-your-taste routine.

"You look really thin," Abby sounded a bit shocked. In fact, she even looked a bit shocked. "You shoulders are really boney-looking in that." She came over and pressed her hands against my shoulders.

"Ouch!" I shoved her off and began to rub where she'd pressed. "That hurt, Ab."

"You *have* got thin."

"Have I?" I didn't know whether to sound pleased or not. I don't think she'd meant it as a compliment.

Abby didn't answer. She was gazing at me and making me feel uncomfortable.

"Are you all right?" she asked. "I mean, you're not sick or anything?"

"I'm fine." I know she was startled by how abrupt I sounded but I was past caring. I had to be like that, I had to shut it away. I pulled my cardigan around me. "Well, I don't care what you think," I said. "I like it."

Before she had a chance to reply, I went into my room to take it off.

It was being kept for good wear.

CHAPTER TWENTY-SIX – THURSDAY

Work on Thursday was even worse than usual. The only good part about it was that Henry seemed to have disappeared off the face of the planet. No one knew where he was, he hadn't phoned in sick, he hadn't applied for leave.

We all secretly hoped he'd been run over by a truck though none of us had the guts to say it.

I was in bad form and talked to no one all day. Al had tried but I'd chewed him up and spit him out. That had put everyone off talking to me. Lenny did big exaggerated tip-toes around the office and Liz kept sniffing and making comments about taking your troubles out on everyone else.

I'd just sat there and pondered on how I could avoid seeing my two flat-mates for the rest of my life.

There'd been a bit of a row. It had blown up out of nowhere and it was all my fault.

Abby had made me model the PVC skirt and short cardigan for Beth.

I wasn't in the humour for being teased. Dave still

hadn't rung and I had to put up with Beth's told-you-so face every time the phone rang and I leaped to answer it and it wasn't him. Plus, I was tired. Very tired. Washed-out tired. I just wasn't up to their messing.

So I'd put on the clothes just to shut Abby up. I'd thought that there was a chance Beth might like my outfit. That way, Abby would be put back in her box.

"It's horrendous," Beth said as soon as I emerged from my room. "Sure, the blacks don't even match."

"See?" Abby said smugly.

"I can't believe you like that," Beth walked around me. "You don't actually want to wear it?" She didn't wait for me to answer. She threw back her head and did a pretend guffaw. "It's a joke – right!"

Abby giggled.

I felt like I was back to being thirteen again. Standing in the freezing cold kitchen of the flat, wearing my new clothes and being laughed at by two people that I loosely considered my mates, I felt all those weird adolescent feelings rush in on me. An incident I'd forgotten about worked its way to the top of my brain and I stunned Beth, Abby and myself by losing the cool.

First, I started trembling, then I could feel tears at the back of my eyes. "Fuck off, both of you!" I yelled. "Just – just – fuck off!" I stormed into my room and slammed the door.

There was a silence from outside in the kitchen. I heard muttering, then I think Abby said, "Do you think we should go in to her?"

Beth had mumbled something and obviously they'd decided to leave well enough alone.

Both of them had gone out.

Then I let the tears come.

I don't know why I was crying.

Maybe because I was tired.

When I was thirteen I got all Sammy's hand-me-downs. She was taller than me, even though she was younger.

I didn't care, I wasn't fashion-conscious. I just wore what was given to me.

Then Fame came on the television. The programme about the American school for the Performing Arts. The place where people danced and sang about learning to fly and living forever. Danny and Bruno and gorgeous Leroy. Suddenly, everyone was wearing leg-warmers and rah-rah skirts and fame sweatshirts.

All I wanted was the leg-warmers. Big sloppy open-ended socks that were meant to keep your ankles warm. Everyone in my year had them. Being 'in' meant wearing leg-warmers.

I begged my mother to buy me some.

"We'll see," she kept saying. "We'll see."

So I knew she wouldn't.

But, one day, coming home from town, out of her bag came a green and white pair of leg-warmers. Hugging her really hard and saying thank-you to her over and over, I put them on over my jeans. Out I went. I saw Jesse and Louise and a whole bunch of others coming down the road.

FLIPSIDE

I was sitting on the wall of our house, swinging my legs and admiring the leg-warmers.

As they drew nearer, I waved. They stopped in front of me and Louise said, "Oh, you've new leg-warmers Jan."

"Yeah."

"They're a nice match for your house all right," Louise said giggling, "but not for Sammy's old green trousers you've got on."

They all broke their hearts laughing.

They walked on and left me there.

CHAPTER TWENTY-SEVEN

For the first time ever, I dreaded going back to the flat after work.

Al, obviously deciding that being called a stupid fecker by me was not something he wished to have repeated, left work before me that day. I had to walk alone down O'Connell Street. I caught the bus and despite the fact that it was rush hour, no one came and sat beside me. That pleased me in a sick way.

I managed to contain all dread until the bus actually stopped at the end of the road and then with every step I took closer to the flat, I remembered some part of the incident of the night before that I'd forgotten.

I was ready to vomit by the time I walked in.

"Jan." It was Beth.

This was worse than I had expected. "Yeah?" I tried to keep my voice neutral.

She gave a small smile and indicated the answering machine. "There's a message on it for you."

"Yeah?" I tried to keep the hope from my voice.

Beth pressed the button and *his* voice filled the room. Well, it seemed to fill the room as far as I was concerned. "Hiya Jan, it's me – Dave. I guess you're workink but I wonder if I could see ya after work tomorrow. About half-five." He stopped and began to talk to someone. "Yeah, Jan, if ya can't make it, call this number." He gave a mobile number. "I'll meet ya in O'Connell Street under Clerys."

For a second I was stunned.

He'd actually rung.

He wanted to meet me in O'Connell Street.

Under Clery's clock.

The next second I was elated.

He'd actually rung!

He wanted to meet me in O'Connell Street!

Under Clery's clock!

I'd always wanted to meet someone under that clock. I know it sounds corny but to me that was the pinnacle of romance. The fact that it'd be Dave made it even better.

"He rang," I said and the state I was in I thought I was going to burst into tears. "He rang."

"Not such a worm after all – huh?" Beth was smiling at me.

"No." My voice was very small.

"He must like you."

"Yes." I began to sniff.

"Sorry about last night."

"Huh?"

"Abby and me, we're sorry about last night."

231

Beth wasn't used to apologising. She was biting her lip and shuffling from one foot to the other. "We didn't mean to hurt your feelings," she said softly, "it was just a joke."

"I know that." I gulped and said one of the hardest things I ever had to say. "I think I over-reacted a bit."

"A bit?" There was a smile on Beth's face now. She pointed to my bedroom. "Your door will never be the same again."

I gulped out a laugh.

We smiled at each other and then, when we'd smiled all we could without actually saying how relieved we both were, Beth turned to the fridge and pulled out two cans.

"Cheers," she said, handing one to me.

"Yeah. Cheers."

Beth sat down in the good chair, obviously she wasn't *that* sorry.

Still, I just wanted to be by the answering machine. I kept looking at it.

I wandered over towards it. "Tomorrow," I said.

"Yeah."

I knew by her voice she was rolling her eyes.

"Under Clery's clock."

"Yeah."

Even bigger roll.

Slowly I ran my hand over the machine. After all, it was mine and I should be able to play . . .

"Will you ever just play the feckin' thing again," Beth jibed, "and don't be making a meal of it."

It was all I needed. I flicked the switch and re-ran the message five or six times. Mentally, I analysed each word he'd said. It was nice the way he'd not taken it for granted that I could make it. It showed that he thought I had other things to do. That he thought that I was someone in demand. I liked that.

John, the great pretender, used to phone me when his mates weren't available. "Shove on something tarty and let's hit the town."

"I wonder where he'll bring you?" Beth broke in on my John-thoughts.

"I don't know." I really didn't care. Just being with him would be enough, but I couldn't say that to Beth – she wasn't so sorry that she wouldn't make vomiting gestures.

"Just one piece of advice, Jan."

"Yeah?"

Beth grinned. "Don't wear the skirt."

This time I could laugh.

CHAPTER TWENTY-EIGHT – FRIDAY

Half-five saw me waiting for Dave outside Clery's. Because of Dave's objections to make-up, I'd tried to ease up on my use of it.

I felt as if I'd stepped out with no clothes on.

It had been even worse trying to figure out what to wear. I mean, where was Dave going to take me? Hoping that where we were going was to be nice, I'd worn a red tight sexy skirt. Over it, I had a white satin shirt and Abby had lent me a jacket. I still hadn't got around to buying a new coat for myself though the rain-coat had been binned.

To make myself look tall and slim, I'd worn my high boots. All in all, I thought that Dave would be quite pleased to be seen with me.

I'd deliberately chosen to stand beside a girl that looked all set for a hiking trip. She wore black faded jeans and a huge pair of brain-damaging boots. Keeping her warm was a duffle coat that Paddington Bear would have coveted. Her hair was a mangled unwashed mass.

Her fella arrived as the clock showed five thirty. He gave her a great big bear hug, which was appropriate considering her coat, then arms about each other they walked off.

I wished it had been me.

By a quarter to, Dave still hadn't arrived. But it was only fifteen minutes, I told myself. That girl had probably been waiting for ages for her fella. Six o'clock, no sign of him. My smile grew brighter and my interest in the shop windows reached an all-time high.

Quarter past six came and no Dave. Self-conscious phobia set in. People were staring at me, I knew they were. They were feeling sorry for me and talking about me.

I decided I'd give him five more minutes.

The five stretched to ten.

That was it, I was going!

Maybe something had happened? Imagine if something awful had happened and I hadn't been here to wait. So I gave him five more.

I really was about to go when I spotted him. He was coming from O'Connell Bridge, walking slowly his hands in his pockets. The raincoat had been discarded in favour of the combat jacket, which was a relief.

Just looking at him sent my heart thumping and I went all weak at the knees.

I didn't know whether to disappear into the shop and come out just as he reached the door so that he'd think I'd just arrived or stay and ask him why he'd been so late.

I stayed.

He spotted me and raised his hand to wave.

I smiled and waved back.

He still didn't hurry himself.

"Been 'ere long?" he asked when he did eventually reach me.

"No, just got here," my voice was too cheerful. I lowered it. "Just got here," I repeated.

"It's great ya could come."

I loved that. As if he thought I was doing him a favour by turning up. "I wanted to," I said simply. The smile on his face told me that that was the right answer.

He looked me up and down. I preened myself for his compliment.

"No raincoat?" he asked.

"Wha–? Eh, no."

He looked up at the sky. "'ope it doesn't piss rain on ya," he remarked.

So we must be going somewhere outdoors. Maybe it was some rooftop restaurant or a romantic walk or –

I hadn't time to think much further because he grabbed me by the hand and began to pull me along. "Come on," he said, "We'll be late."

So it was something he'd booked!

We were half-running along and I was desperately trying to keep up without letting him see that my boots were killing me. "So how's the protest going?" I asked.

It was as if I'd turned on a light. "It's goin' great!" He gave my hand a squeeze and his voice grew animated. "There's about fifteen of us on site now and we've got loadsa tents built. People from around 'ave donated stuff." Turning to me, he grinned, "We're gonna be there for the long haul."

"That's great." I meant about him being around for the long haul. The other stuff was good too.

"You should come out and see us."

"Yeah." I gulped hard. "Yeah I will."

"Bring a tent and join us. Get your mates to come too. That Beth one could do with it."

"I don't have a tent." And even if I did, there was no way Abby and Beth were coming.

"Aw, well," Dave screwed up his face, "Ya could always spend a night in my tree-house."

I thought I would be sick. That's the way I get whenever I get some incredible unexpected good news. My heart lurched. I didn't know what to say. "Your tree-house?"

"Yeah." Dave gave me a prod. "Not scared, are ya?"

"No," my voice was high, bordering on hysterical.

He was bringing me through a maze of streets. I hadn't a clue where I was until I saw a whole bunch of people that seemed vaguely familiar. This whole bunch of people that seemed vaguely familiar were marching around holding placards and chanting about the destruction of the rainforests.

This couldn't be happening to me.

"'Ere we are," Dave let my hand go and began striding towards the crowd.

This couldn't be happening.

"Come on, Jan," Dave had reached his friends and

was beckoning to me. "Told yez she'd come," he said as he pulled me into the group.

"Hi," I smiled around at them all, wondering if they could see the devastation etched on my face.

They were all dressed as if they were going on a hike.

I could see Megan looking me up and down. I kept my smile glued in place.

"So what's going on?" I asked, my voice sounding desolate.

Sam indicated a furniture shop behind him. *Loyd's Furniture* it was called. "We're holding two weeks of protest outside this guy's shop. He sells furniture made from rainforest wood."

"And it's our turn to protest today," Megan went on, "So that's why we rang you."

"Right." I was numb.

"We figured you could hand out leaflets," some other guy said whose name I'd forgotten. Suffice it to say, he was the hairiest of the bunch. He split his leaflets in half and handed me a bundle. "There you go."

"Thanks."

"We're here until nine," Sam said, shattering me totally. "You'll stay around – huh?"

"Sure."

This really was happening.

I wanted to go home.

"So let's get cracking," Sam was the guy in charge. He lifted his banner and him and about five others began walking around in circles chanting.

Hairy was busy walking up to people and handing out leaflets.

I just stood where I was, too mortified to do anything. I felt really stupid.

Hairy saw me and yelled, "You do your side, Jan. Let's nab them all."

I looked around for Dave. He was chatting to Megan. It looked like she was telling him what to do and then they both began to set up a table and get out a load of pens. They both stood behind it and started to shout about the mountains. It looked as if this was a killing-two-birds-with-one stone protest.

I read the leaflet before I began to hand it out. It basically said that people were destroying the rainforests for their own gain. It wasn't really radical or anything. My heart began to thump as I realised that I'd actually have to approach members of the public and give it to them. The combined noise of the rainforest group and the mountain group was overpowering.

But I couldn't leave. I'd never see him again.

I selected a very harmless old lady to be my first victim. She was hobbling towards me. "Please take one," I shoved it under her nose. "This shop uses wood from the rainforests. Read all about the destruction of the rainforests." My voice was quivering. What would I do if she started to hurl abuse at me?

She lifted her face and smiled. "I will certainly," she said. "It's great to see a young person so concerned about the world."

"Oh, eh, yeah," I felt like a charlatan and a saviour all at the one time.

"Good on you!" The old woman raised her fist and the others laughed and cheered. She hobbled away after first stuffing her leaflet into her handbag.

"Good one, Jan," Dave shouted over winking at me.

It gave me the confidence to continue.

At about seven it began to splatter rain. I had just managed to corner another old person into taking a leaflet. I was making an effort to pick on old people, I figured they'd be too afraid of the group to protest. "It's about the rainforests," I said to him as a huge drop landed on my head.

"The what?" he shouted back, shoving the leaflet so far into his face I thought he was going to eat it.

"Rainforests."

He peered up at me. "And what are they when they're at home?"

"They're big forests in the Amazon and in other places too."

"A forest." He didn't sound impressed. He pulled a soft hat out of his pocket and stuck it on his head. "You don't say."

If I didn't get out of the rain soon my mascara was going to run. "Read the leaflet and you'll understand."

Again he peered at it. "The printing's very small."

I said nothing, I was looking for somewhere to shelter.

"Can you read it out to me, do you think?"

"Eh – "

"There's a great girl. You read that out now." He pushed the leaflet back into my hands and looked at me expectantly.

"Rainforests are the lungs of the earth," I began.

"The lungs. You don't say."

A deluge didn't describe the amount of water now pissing down on top of me.

". . . and man is destroying them by cutting down the very trees that make up most of the world's oxygen."

"Say that again now, I didn't get that bit."

". . . and man is destroying them by cutting down the very trees that make up most of the world's oxygen."

"Ohh," he rocked back and forth on his heels. "It's fierce complicated now. I don't think I'd be up to all that stuff."

"Oh, right." I wanted him to go. I didn't force the issue. All I wanted was to get out of the rain.

"But it's interesting, mind you. Good luck with it."

"Thanks."

"I'll take that leaflet now and maybe give it to my son, he knows all about stuff like that."

"OK, fine." I had to wait as he folded it up, patted it down and eventually stored it in his pocket.

"Nice to meet you," he tipped his hat at me.

"You too."

I turned back to the others and I nearly died. In my absence they'd all donned big plastic raincoats. Dave must have bought a pile of them.

Him and Megan were standing at their table and the

two of them were dressed in them. I was the only thick in a nice double-breasted jacket.

There was no way I was carrying on. Abby's coat was getting drenched and she'd kill me when I got in. There were goosebumps the size of golf-balls on my bare legs.

I dumped my leaflets down on Dave's table. "I'm going somewhere to get shelter."

He pointed to a coffee shop up the street. "Go in there and get yerself a coffee. I'll join ya in a minute."

It was great to get inside where it was nice and dry. Taking off Abby's jacket I dumped it on a chair. Walking up to the counter I ordered a coffee and a cake.

Dave joined me a few minutes later. He ordered water and plonked himself down beside me. At least I had him to myself now, I thought a bit despondently.

"So 'ow you enjoying it then, Jan?"

"Having a ball," I said flatly.

"Good," Dave leaned back in his seat and smiled. "I knew you'd be up for it."

Was he thick or just naive?

"What 'appened the rain-jacket today then?"

"Aw, I just wanted to wear this instead." I pointed to the now sodden double-breasted coat.

"Not very 'andy for 'anding out leaflets in the rain, is it?"

"No."

Dave was a master of understatement.

We drank in silence. There was still over three hours

to go on the date from hell. What would I tell Beth and Abby when I got back? They'd laugh their heads off.

Dave had finished his water and he began to play with his cup, tearing bits off it and rolling them up. "These feckin' paper cups are full of crap, do you know that?"

"No."

"Oh yeah, all it is is paper bleached with chlorine, roight? This leads to dioxin contamination which in turn pollutes waterways."

"Really?"

"Yeah, and the plastic cups are no betta."

"So the ould trusty pottery mug is me best bet?"

"Absolutely."

Dave smiled at me, once again turning my insides to butter. "How do you know so much?" I asked in a gauche attempt to flatter him.

He shrugged. Flattered, I think. "I read a lot. I like readin'."

He didn't look the reading type. "You do?"

"Uh-huh," he nodded. "Most a the stuff I read now is environmental stuff, but before that, I useta read everything I could get my hands on."

"And what were you before?"

"Wot? Before I went on the road?"

I nodded, dying to find out about him.

He flicked a half-ashamed glance at me. "A fuckin' builder."

"And what happened?" I asked. "Was there no work going or something?"

As usual, without fail, Janet Boyle said exactly the wrong thing. Luckily enough, Dave thought I was joking. He started to laugh. "Too much bloody work," he grinned. His voice changed. "I 'ated it, ripping trees down to make roads. Bulldozing over fields to build bridges. It was 'orrible, Jan, all that destruction." Smiling again, he said, "It was kinda serendipitous – one day I was out and I saw a bulldozer rippink the crap out of a green field, and I just said, no way, not anymore. So I left me job, started a protest of me own and been doin' it ever since." His smile grew wider. "It was the best decision I ever made."

I didn't know what serendipitous meant, but I wasn't stupid enough to ask. I'd look it up later. Instead, I asked, "And what do your folks think?"

"It's my life, ain't it?"

"Do they mind?"

He didn't answer, just peered over into my cup. "Ya nearly finished yet?"

I drained it in one gulp. Dave stood up and let me by him out of the table. "I'm glad ya came, Jan," he said as he opened the door to let me out.

That made my day. "I'm glad too." And I almost meant it.

CHAPTER TWENTY-NINE

We ended up in a pub in Westmoreland Street. Not all of us, just me, Dave, Megan, Sam and Chaz. This was the part of the evening I'd been looking forward to since five thirty. Of course I hadn't bargained on squelching into the pub in crippling wet boots or rubbing my mascara out of my eyes to stop them stinging or being joined by three extra bodies, but at that stage I wasn't choosy.

Just as well.

I ended up bored out of my skull.

Chaz was going to BNF on a protest.

Dave, who'd done a stint over there already was chief advisor. Megan was second in command and Sam interjected every so often with some unintelligible comment. I'm sure what he said made a load of sense to the others but I hadn't a clue.

Who were BNF?

What were they doing?

And – why did they have to ruin my feckin' date by existing?

"I have to go," I stood up after a particularly boring

speech against English nuclear policy, courtesy of Megan. She'd just started to rant on about English politicians when I decided that enough was enough. Not that I minded political debates, I couldn't care less, but everything Megan said was treated with so much respect by Dave that it made me panicky. I wanted to drag him away from her.

They looked at me. "I have to go," I said again. I picked up Abby's coat from the chair and, with as much dignity as I could, I put it on. It dripped everywhere. It was like wearing a swimming-pool on my back.

"See ya," Dave gave me a salute and turned back to Chaz.

"Yeah, thanks for showing," Sam grinned. "We'll be in touch."

Megan smiled. "Are you all right for getting home?" she asked. "Do you want one of us to go with you?"

I hesitated only slightly. "Eh, no." I went red, "I'll be fine." I wasn't that hard up to ask Dave to tag along. I do have a little pride. "I think," I added.

"Dave, bring the girl home," Megan gave Dave an elbow. "You can't let her go on her own." She turned to me and winked. "He's a gentleman really."

"Wot?" Dave looked at the two of us.

"Jan wants someone to walk her home," Megan said, "Don't you, Jan?" It was said in an innocent tone but I think she knew I fancied the shit out of him.

"Do ya?" Dave asked. "Really?"

"Oh, eh, no," I said, making an effort to sound as unconvincing as I could. "It's only about three miles in the dark, I'll be fine."

"All right so." Dave took a gulp of his pint and smiled. "If you're sure."

I was devastated. The rain forests had nothing on me. So near and yet so far.

"Walk the girl home," Megan ordered, giving him another rib-shattering dig. "Jan's only trying to be polite about it." She threw her eyes heavenward and said to me, "Dave has no concept of subtlety Jan. He's basically thick."

"Ta." Dave dipped his fingers into his pint and flicked it at her. She squealed and took a fistful of alcohol and threw it back at him.

"Mind me pint," Dave grumbled as he got to his feet and shook the drink out of his hair. He ignored her laughter. Turning to Chaz, he gave him the thumbs up. "Good luck, mate."

Chaz grinned and nodded back.

"See yez later," Dave got out from the table and saying goodbye to everyone we left the pub.

I could have got the bus back, but I wanted to be with him as long as I could. I told Dave I only got buses in emergencies. "Don't like polluting the ozone layer with all the fumes," was my brilliant excuse.

"Great stuff," Dave beamed at me and I inwardly applauded myself for my resourcefulness.

I'd never tried walking from the city centre to Rathmines in six-inch heels in the pouring rain before though. We looked a right pair, Dave slouching along, happily wrapped up in his bright blue waterproof mac, and me swaying along like a ship in a force-ten gale.

"Can't believe ya didn't bring ya raincoat," Dave remarked as I stepped in a puddle right up to my middle. Well, the middle of my leg nearly.

"Yeah." Water was pouring into my boot quicker than if it'd been the Titanic.

"Enjoy the protest, did ya?" He didn't wait for me to answer, "Though ya kinda looked funny – dressed for a protest."

"I did, didn't I?" I made a feeble attempt at something resembling a laugh. "I was the odd girl out all right."

Suddenly Dave stopped. Not feeling him walking beside me anymore, I turned to see what had happened. He was standing in the middle of the street and his face looked as if someone had lit a match behind it. "I never told ya it was a protest, did I?"

"Nope," I shook my head and gave a shrug.

He walked up to me, really quickly, his head stuck out as if his brain was working. "What did ya think it was?" He stood beside me, his head bent down to my level. "Jan?" There was an edge of agitation in his voice.

I couldn't answer. He'd probably laugh if I said I got dressed up because I thought I'd be going on a date with him. I was good at that, making men laugh at me. Only, I didn't want him to do that, he was something special, even then.

"Did you think," Dave did a big gulp, I could see his adam's apple moving with the effort, "that it was a . . . a . . ." he couldn't go on – he gulped again, "a date?" His voice was very low.

Again I shrugged. The rain was pelting on top of me now, but I didn't feel it. All I felt was hot with total embarrassment. This was his cue to laugh.

Only he didn't.

"Christ!" He banged his head with his fist. "Oh, Christ."

"It's all right." I wanted him to forget the whole thing.

"No way," Dave caught me by the shoulder, "No, it's not all right." He peered at me again, "I'm sorry Jan. Christ, I'm sorry."

"It's fine." A tinkly little laugh escaped. I felt that if I went any redder, I'd spontaneously combust.

"Oh Gawd!" Dave did a big dramatic thing of stomping about and splashing water everywhere. Mostly on me. "Oh Gawd, oh Gawd!" If he banged his head any more he'd have brain damage. "Oh Gawd."

People began to stare at him from under bright umbrellas.

"Forget it," I tipped him on the arm in an attempt to stop him from drenching every inch of me. "It's all right."

He stopped. "I shoulda told ya."

"I should've known."

"No – ya shouldn't." He shrugged and said slowly, "It's not like I wouldn't like ta bring ya out . . ."

"Really?" I despised the delight and desperation in my voice. "Really?"

"Only, I got no money ta bring ya out." He paused. "They won't gimme the dole over 'ere no more."

"Won't they?"

"No – I'm available for work but won't work or

somefink like that, they said. So from now on, I got no cash."

"I can bring you out." The words I'd sworn never to say, and had said at least a million times before, rushed out of me. "I have money."

He didn't jump at it. His face clouded and he muttered, "Couldn't do that."

Either he didn't like me or was totally unlike the free-loaders I was used to.

"Why?"

"It's not right."

I'd come this far, I wasn't going to let pride stand in my way. "Why?"

"The whole thing was my mistake, I should pay."

"Rubbish," I waved my hand in the air. "It's the nineties."

We had resumed walking at this stage and the flat was looming closer. Two more doors and we'd be there, I couldn't go in without a decent progress report. "Please?"

"Aw, I dunno." Dave took for ever to decide. He hummed and hawed and eventually said, "Tell ya wot, come to the site and 'ave dinner one evenin' with the lads."

The last thing I wanted around us was 'the lads.' I tried to keep the smile on my face.

"It'll make up for tonight and then," he grinned at me, "you can do the 'onors."

It was better than I'd hoped. Two more chances to see him. "All right so."

"Great." He smiled at me. He indicated my clothes, "Wear somefink a bit warmer on the site though."

"Right."

"And bring ya raincoat."

"Mnn."

"And a sleepin' bag."

"Whha." That was me catching my breath.

"Maybe," Dave wagged his finger, "ya could stay a weekend, get a feel for the place."

"Yeah." I was weak with delight.

"Great." He gave me a manly slap on the arm. "Great."

We'd arrived at the flat. "Coffee?" I asked, trying to inject a world of meaning into the word. I read somewhere that when Americans invite guys up for coffee it usually means sex. I wished more than anything that we were in the US of A.

"Na," Dave turned to go. "'ate the stuff. Caffeine's the most addictive drug."

"A beer then?" I was desperate.

"I'm on nightwatch tonight, 'ave to be sober." He winked at me and began to walk away. Not even a kiss.

I watched him for a few minutes from the shadows of the pillar.

I consoled myself with the thought that I'd see him soon.

When?

Horror struck, I realised that we hadn't even fixed a day.

But not even I was desperate enough to hare up to him and ask when I'd see him again. I'd just have to hope he'd ring.

And something told me that he would.

He wasn't like anyone else I'd ever met.

CHAPTER THIRTY – SATURDAY

Dr O'Brien rang.

He rang early Saturday morning and I answered the phone.

"Janet Boyle?" he asked. His voice was breathless.

"That's me." I was hoping it'd be Dave. My own voice got a bit fluttery.

"Hi, it's Jim O'Brien here."

"Who?"

"Dr O'Brien," he clarified.

My heart took a nose-dive.

"I've the results of your tests . . ."

"Yeah?"

" . . . and I was wondering if you could drop by the surgery and have a word with me?"

This was not good. I didn't want to stir outside in case Dave rang. I had to pin him down on when I'd see him again.

"Can you tell me the results over the phone?"

Please get off the line, please get off the line.

O'Brien hesitated. Then, ignoring my question, he abruptly changed the subject. "Have you told anyone you've seen me and gone for tests?"

"No."

He said nothing so I added, "Nothing to tell."

"I see."

"So?" My interest was wholly in getting him off the phone to stop him blocking up the line.

"Eh, so . . . " He seemed to be stalling. "So, eh, how's the glands today?"

I hadn't felt them in days. I avoided looking in the mirror when I brushed my hair because a couple of the glands were plainly visible along its length. I'd stopped tying my hair up for the same reason. "Still there," I said. "They're still there."

Another silence. "I'd really like to see you, Janet," he said. "Come down this afternoon around one. I'll be able to see you then, it'll be my lunch-break."

I wanted to ask for the results again but something in his tone stopped me. Or something in myself stopped me.

"Bring someone with you," O'Brien said then. He said it so casually, so off-handedly that I couldn't understand why my breath suddenly caught in my throat and my heart started to lurch.

It was only after, after I'd put the phone down, that it dawned on me. It was the fact that he'd said it at all.

I didn't bring anyone with me.

What was the point? There was nothing wrong with me.

And I didn't want Abby and Beth knowing my medical business. Not that I'd ever minded before, some part of me reasoned. Another part of me, told that part of me, to fuck off.

The door of the surgery was locked. I pushed against it and couldn't get in. It was a quarter past one and maybe O'Brien had left. If he'd left, it couldn't have been that important . . .

"Janet," he appeared as if by magic at the door. "Come in, I was looking out for you."

"Oh," I tried a smile and it didn't quite come off, "great."

For the first time in my life, I didn't want to follow him down the hall to his surgery. For the first time I noticed the wallpaper in the hall, horrible standy-up fresco stuff. The tiles on the floor were worn badly too, in fact the whole place looked a bit tatty. I wondered if maybe coming here for the past couple of years had been a mistake.

"Here we go," O'Brien gave me a smile and held the door open for me to go through it. A real gent. It was probably because he was going to smack a twenty-quid bill on me for seeing me after hours. At twenty quid a shot, I'd hold the door open for Charles Manson and his friends.

I sat down and he sat opposite me. His desk looked tidier than it normally did, all the files that normally scattered it had been put away. The only thing open on the desk was my file. I knew it was mine, I'd seen it often enough.

O'Brien turned to it and picked it up. He looked at me over its edge, "Didn't you bring someone with you?" he asked.

"No." I wasn't being rude or abrupt, I just couldn't say any more than that. My voice sounded weird and small.

"I see." He opened my file on the last page and then he took a brown envelope from his drawer. "I got the results of your bloods yesterday Janet," he said, "and then I rang up looking for the results of your x-rays. They came in the post yesterday evening." Another breath. "I rang for them because I was slightly concerned when I saw your blood test results."

"Yeah?" There was a funny feeling taking me over. I could feel myself tensing up, every part of me like a cat getting ready for flight. My fists curled, my heart slowed down to long thump-thumps. The sounds of outside and the room receded. Time became an eternity and it was like watching myself in slow motion.

"The bloods showed that you're anaemic."

He waited for the words to sink in. Slowly, I came back from where I'd been going. Anaemic! I was anaemic! "So what then?" I asked, trying to sound normal when the whole lot of me was rejoicing, "Iron tablets. I can take those."

O'Brien held up his palm. "Not so fast," his voice was gentle – he bit his lip and stared hard at me. "It's not an iron-deficiency anaemia. It's . . . " he stopped. I think he was trying to gauge the effect his words were having on me. "It's not that simple."

"Oh."

"It's another kind, basically it means that something is wrong, though I can't say what."

"Oh." My palms were sweating, I could feel the heat of them as they sat on my knees. I tried to pull my skirt down, to sit right in the chair.

O'Brien then took the x-rays out of their brown envelope.

I wanted to tell him to stop talking but I knew he wouldn't. I didn't want to hear any more, it was too weird.

"I got the x-rays of your chest. There doesn't seem to be any infiltration on the lung, but there seem to be glands up in the media stinnum." He picked up the x-ray and held it to the light.

"What?"

O'Brien pointed to the x-ray. "See there – the spaces between the lungs – that's the chest cavity. There seem to be glands up there too." He paused for a second, studying the x-ray, before saying, "Being honest, Janet, they're quite alarming."

"They are?"

"You've glands up all over your chest," he took the x-ray down and looked at me, "It's not normal."

"It's not?"

"No." He said it quietly and kept looking at me. I said nothing. Suddenly, I didn't want to be me anymore. Well, it had never been the greatest knowing myself, but now, it was the pits. "I think you need to see someone more specialised than me," O'Brien said. "A consultant."

"I do?"

"I've rung a friend of mine, an oncologist in St Anne's. There's an appointment for you on Tuesday morning. It's the soonest I could get."

"A what?"

"He's an oncologist," O'Briens voice was very soft now. I took it as a bad sign. I wanted to ask what an oncologist was but I hadn't the nerve.

"He studies tumours," O'Brien said.

Tumours?

"It's just a precaution," he went on. "I just want to get you checked out."

I grabbed the thread with both hands. "So it might be nothing?"

He shrugged and didn't answer.

One thing about threads, they don't hold much weight.

"So Tuesday?" He held out a piece of paper to me with the time and date on it. "It's important you go."

My hand shook as I took it from him. The ink smeared with the sweat on my palms.

"I've given him your history," O'Brien went on, still in the gentle tone, "he knows about the weight loss and the night-sweats."

"I mightn't have lost weight." The aggressive way I said it surprised me, but not him. He looked at me calmly and nodded for me to go on. "I mean, your scales could be wrong and anyway," I tossed my hair back, then remembered about the glands and pulled it around me again, "Anyway, I hadn't weighed myself in years before I stepped on your scales."

"Do you want to weigh yourself now, get a second opinion on it?" He indicated the scales.

Was he trying to make me feel stupid?

"No." I shook my head. "No."

"Please go to see this guy on Tuesday."

I hadn't a choice. Slowly I nodded.

O'Brien seemed to relax. "Please don't upset yourself. I know it's a worry but as I said, it's just a precaution."

"Yeah." I couldn't look at him, I didn't want him to see the panic in my eyes.

"So that's it." He waited for me to say something and when I didn't he picked up some keys from his desk and said, "I think maybe you could use a lift home."

I said nothing.

"You've had a shock."

"I'm fine." The thoughts of spending any more time in his company panicked me. I jumped up from the chair and began to back out the door. The sooner I was away from here the sooner I could forget all about what he'd said. "I'm fine. I'm only five minutes away." My hand was on the door handle.

"I can drive you."

"No!" The word tore out of me and I literally ran down the hallway and out the front door. I can't even remember if I closed it, all I knew was that I had to get away from there as fast as I could.

I hated that man.

How dare he tell me stuff like that.

There wasn't a thing wrong with me.

CHAPTER THIRTY-ONE

When I arrived back, Abby and Beth were stuffing themselves with chips and burgers.

"Join us!" Abby held a can of Budweiser aloft as she waved me toward the table.

"Yeah," Beth grinned, a huge piece of masticated chip dangling from her mouth. "Abby's had a huge bonus in work."

"A huge, huge bonus!" Abby laughed and, taking a slug from her can, she aimed it somewhere between her nose and mouth and ended up with most of the alcohol dripping down her designer something-or-other blouse. "Shit!" She tried to mop herself clean and gave up, collapsing against the table, giggling helplessly.

They were drunk. Or very nearly there.

"She bought chips and booze to celebrate," Beth gave Abby a thumbs-up and turned to me. "She's very, *very, ver-ry* gen . . ." She stopped, shook her head and tried again, "genen . . . geno . . ." She took a slug of Bud, "Aw, feck it. She's very nice."

"Thank you."

"No," Beth slurred, pointing her finger at Abby. "Thank *you*." She jabbed Abby in the stomach.

"Joining us?" Abby held out a can.

Their laughter made my ears hurt. All the way home, I'd run and run. The sound of my breathlessness was what I concentrated on to keep my mind focused on nothing. The way my feet hit hard on the path and jarred me all the way up to my spine. The fact that it was hard to run in a tight skirt. All this had made me shut down the part of my mind that was screaming.

The can Abby held out looked inviting. Drink would make me forget for a bit. The feel of it filling up my head and flowing through my veins would be wonderful. The freedom of being drunk where nothing mattered and where talking about things never hurt.

I took it from her and joined the two of them in getting legless.

"Chips?" Abby held out a brown paper-bag of grease.

"Pass." I wouldn't have eaten them anyhow.

Opening the can, I lifted it to my lips and drank it down. Really quickly. Beth began a chant, *"Go. Go. Go. Go."* Abby began clapping along with her.

Ten seconds.

"Me next." Beth opened a can for herself and began to do the same.

"Go. Go. Go. Go. Go."

Nine seconds.

"Me! Me!" Abby wanted to be next.

"No, me." I opened my can before she did, leaving her open-mouthed.

"It's my turn," she began to whinge.

Ignoring her, I began to gulp it down again. Beth didn't count this time, I think she was trying to show she was on Abby's side. I didn't care. I downed it quicker than I had the first one. Then I took a third and began to do the same.

"You got a brewery installed in your stomach?" Beth asked.

They said some other things to me, but I can't remember what they were. My head was loaded. Spinning first in one direction and then the other. The floor, when I tried to stand up was like the Waltzer in Funderland. But I had to get to the bathroom. I had to.

"I'm going to puke," I said, trying to focus my eyes on them.

Next thing I knew, I was vomiting my guts up into the toilet. I don't think I'd ever been as sick before.

"Waste," Abby fumed as she slammed the door on me. "What a waste."

Wiping my mouth and without looking at either of them, I staggered into my room and collapsed onto the bed. The last thing I remember seeing was Brad's face, giving me the white-toothed sexy smile.

Buzzzz.

Buzzzz.

The noise was coming at me.

Buzzz.

There it was again.

Buzzz.

It wasn't part of my weird bumble-bee dream any more. It was coming from somewhere else.

Buzzz.

The front door. Someone was buzzing to come up.

The light filtering through the curtains had a rosy glow and it was hurting my eyes.

Buzzz.

I don't know how long I'd slept and I felt all weird. Totally disorientated. What had happened?

My head hurt when I moved it so I must have been drinking.

Drinking what? And when?

Without any warning, memory crashed in. Like a huge tidal wave it washed over me, leaving me shocked and cold. I had something wrong with me.

Or maybe I didn't.

I didn't know.

Buzzz.

"Oh fuck off."

Buzzz.

Why weren't Abby and Beth answering?

Buzzz.

Easing myself out of bed, I supposed that I'd better see who was at the door. On the way out to the intercom, I glanced at the clock.

Eight-thirty!

In the evening!

I'd slept for over five hours.

No wonder Beth and Ab weren't in. Beth was most likely at work and Abby'd be with Mick. Despite the horrible cold feeling inside me, I grinned at the state the two must have been in when they left. I reckon Mickey would've been mortified seeing Abby drunk. Abby got a bit prostitutey when she'd a few jars on her.

On second thoughts, Mickey'd probably be delighted.

Buzzz.

Reaching the intercom, I pressed it. "Yes?"

"Jan? It's me – Al."

What the hell was he doing here?

Glancing down at myself, I saw that I'd puked on my shirt. Then, after noticing that, I noticed the smell. Stale puke. From me.

"Come up." I buzzed him through the downstairs door and went in to change my shirt.

Dressed and presentable, but still smelling slightly, I gave my teeth a quick brush before I let Al into the flat.

He was all dressed up. Well, as dressed up as he could be, considering he was wearing jeans and he always wore jeans. He'd a pair of black Levis with a black tee-shirt. Over the tee-shirt he had a denim jacket. It was the tee-shirt that made me close my eyes and groan. On it was a picture of Bob Dylan. "Bob Dylan," I said faintly.

Al grinned at me. "Yep. All set?" His eyes looked me up and down. "Eh, Jan, don't take this the wrong way, but, like, I don't think a skirt is the best thing to wear."

I glared at him. "I'm not stupid."

263

"Oh." He looked down at his trainers. "Yeah, right."

"I forgot about it," I said brutally, wanting to hurt him. I don't know why, but I did. "I can't go."

His eyes met mine and I turned away from the puzzled look he gave me. "Sure you can, just throw a pair of jeans on and we'll head."

"No."

He pulled the tickets from his jacket. "It says nine, but Dylan won't be on until later, you've loadsa time, Jan."

"I'm not going." I wanted to see him squirm. I wanted to be on my own and I wanted to go over and over how I hurt him. I wanted to feel bad.

Al stared at me and I could see it was working. The shades were clanging shut over his face. He slowly began to put the tickets back into his jacket. "Why?" he asked quietly. He was looking at some space over my shoulder. "You said you'd come."

"Yeah, well," I gulped, "I've changed my mind."

"You could've let me know." There was a hard edge to his voice now. "I could've got someone else."

"Sorry." I said it like I didn't care.

"Did I miss somethin'?"

"What?"

"Did I do somethin' or, did you maybe hear somethin' about me?"

"No." I turned from him and walked over to the table. "No, nothing like that. I just don't want to go."

"Righ'," Al said. He didn't move. Then he said "righ'" again. He was standing there waiting for me to say something, but I didn't. I heard him going towards the door. I heard him opening it and the door squeaking as he pulled it wide.

"Al?" I said then. "Al?"

"Yeah?" He stayed by the door.

"Don't go." I hadn't known I was going to say that, it just tore out of me. All I wanted was someone to stay with me. "Please?"

I didn't know that I was crying, not until his arms were around me and he was patting my back and telling me it was all right. Whatever was wrong, it was all right.

Then he lifted my head from his shoulders and, bending down, he looked into my face. He had his hands on either side of my face and he began wiping my tears away with his thumbs. Then, putting his arm about my shoulder, he led me to the table and made me sit down. I couldn't let go of his hand.

"Just let me make you a cuppa," he said, pulling his hand out of my grasp.

I watched him like a child as he did the things I'd always taken for granted. Turning on the tap, filling the kettle, switching it on. We didn't say a word as we waited for the water to boil, though every so often he'd flash me a quick grin and somehow, I smiled back.

"So what's the story?" he said eventually as he put a mug in front of me and began to heap sugar into it.

"I don't take sugar."

"Me ma says it's great for shock," he replied, dumping another spoonful in, "and she should know."

"Is she a nurse or something?" I took a sip and almost gagged. Mega-sweet stuff.

"Something," Al replied.

He watched me as I sipped another bit. He didn't say anything and I liked that. Just to have him with me was all I needed.

"You look a bit rough," he remarked after a bit.

"I drank too much this afternoon," I stared into my cup. "I was upset."

"Why?"

It was hard to say. "The doctor reckons I'm sick."

"Huh?"

In a halting voice, I told him from the beginning. Every time my voice shook, he'd take my free hand and squeeze it. When I finished, I looked at him. "So I've to see this oncologist on Tuesday morning."

He didn't say that I might be fine, which chilled me and cheered me all at once. "Have you told Beth and Abby?" he asked.

"No." I shook my head. "I don't want them to know in case it's nothing. Beth will laugh her head off and say it serves me right."

"Huh?"

"And it does," I was blubbering now. "It does. It serves me right. I wanted there to be something wrong with me and now there is."

"Shut up," Al shook me gently. "No one deserves that." He moved his chair closer to mine. "Jaysus, I'd love to be always getting days off only I can't." He put his arm around my shoulder and rested his chin on my head, so I couldn't see his face. "If me ma didn't need the cash at home, I'd go sick too. In fact, I'd go sick so many times, they could sack me. I hate that feckin' job, you know."

I got the feeling this was a big deal for Al to admit. He was only doing it because I was so miserable. "Thanks," I whispered. The smell of him was so nice. So familiar and reassuring.

"I don't think Beth'd laugh," he said gently. "You should give them a chance."

"No." I shook my head. "No."

"So who's going with you on Tuesday?"

"I'm going on my own." I honestly hadn't thought that far ahead.

"If you want, I'll go as far as the hospital and wait outside for you." He pressed my hand. "Only if you want."

I didn't know what I wanted. But maybe it'd be nice to have someone with me. "All right so."

"Good." He smiled slightly. "If you change your mind, just tell me."

His voice made the tears come again. He was being so good and after I'd let him down about the concert and everything. After I'd called him a stupid fecker and ignored his jokes.

"I'm sorry about calling you a stupid fecker," I sniffed. "You're not. You're nice."

"Thanks."

"Thanks for listening to me."

"Any time," he whispered as he stroked my hair. He

pushed it back from my face and kissed my forehead. "Any time." Once again his arms came about me and he held me against his chest. I could hear the beating of his heart under his tee-shirt. "I won't let you be sick," he whispered fiercely. "I won't."

It was an odd thing for him to say, but I liked it. I enjoyed the feel of his hand rubbing the length of my hair, curling it between his fingers and pulling it gently.

Without thinking, which is typical of me, I held my face up to his. Exquisitely slowly, he bent his lips to mine and kissed me. Very gently as if he was afraid he'd hurt me. Then he kissed me again, just as gently. His eyes were half-closed and all I could see was the black colour of them. I put my hand behind his head and pressed his mouth onto mine. His hair felt soft and smooth. His tongue was pressing my lips apart, very gently, very easily. I opened my mouth to him and we kissed, just using our tongues to explore each other's mouths. I don't think I'd ever wanted a guy so much in my life . . .

"Jesus," Al pulled away and his face was white. He ran a hand over his face, the way he did when he was nervous. "Jesus Jan, I'm sorry."

I stared at him in confusion. "For what?" Then it dawned on me. Maybe my breath . . . after being sick and everything . . .

"I shouldn't do that, it's not right." Al had his head in his hands and was staring at the table. "Christ, I'm sorry."

"I don't understand?" I was disorientated. What had happened?

Al stood up and began pacing around the room.

"We can't do this – you're – well – you're all upset. You'd only wake up and wonder what the fuck you've done in the morning."

"That's par for the course," I said. I meant it as a joke but it came out sounding bitter and horrible. I know it startled Al because he came and sat beside me again.

"Yeah, well," he looked at me, "it shouldn't be. I don't want you to think I'm a mistake you made."

I was going to cringe when I met this guy on Monday. I'd told him too much. Then I'd made a fool out of myself by snogging him.

"Anyway, you're seeing someone else, aren't you?"

"I'm doing my best," I giggled. "He hasn't copped onto it yet." The giggle was a bad idea. I began to cry again. "He's supposed to be ringing me this week."

"Maybe he'll go with you on Tuesday?"

"No!" The thought horrified me. I grabbed onto Al's arm. "I want you there."

"OK. OK." He indicated my tea. "Drink up and I'll treat you to a pizza."

"I don't want to go out." I sounded like a kid.

"Well, I want to be seen with you. You've made me miss Dylan, the least you can do is have pizza with me."

"I look terrible."

"No." Al shook his head. "You're beaut – grand."

I drank my tea up and he gave me his jacket to wear. "Let's go." He opened the door for me and out we went. He never put his arm around me or touched me all night.

Nice but definitely weird.

CHAPTER THIRTY-TWO – SUNDAY

Sunday saw me weirdly calm. Overnight, my mind seemed to have adjusted to the shock and the voice of reason was telling me that I had nothing to worry about. All I was doing was going to a hospital and meeting guy a who specialised in tumours.

If you ask me, he was the one with the problem.

Imagine wanting to look at people's lumps.

Now that was sick.

It was after eleven when I crawled from the bed. Pulling on a pair of track-suit bottoms and a tee-shirt, I wandered into the kitchen.

Mickey was sitting at the table, dressed in trousers and a shirt. The guy was even wearing a tie. His hair had been freshly washed, no doubt using up our meagre supply of hot water, and he smelt of aftershave and shampoo.

He still managed to look about as appealing as a plate of cabbage.

"Jan," he nodded to me and returned to reading a big tome of a Sunday paper. He wasn't an avid fan of the *Sunday World*, I'd bet money on it.

At least he seemed to have made some tea – steam was coming out of the spout of the tea-pot. The first time it'd ever been used as far as I could remember. He'd also set the table. Knives, plates, cups and saucers. I thought saucers were extinct. An endangered species that you couldn't use.

"Did you stay here last night?" I asked as I poured myself some tea.

You'd think I'd asked him if he'd murdered Abby while she slept. His face went the colour of raw steak and he started to cough. In between the coughs he managed to splutter out a yes.

"Oh, ya boya!" I couldn't help it. The guy was moronic.

He blushed harder and stared harder at his paper.

"So where is she?" I joked. "Have you worn her out?"

"Very funny, Janet," he said. He actually glared at me. A really good glare. One that made me feel like I was some kind of a pervert for asking a question like that.

We sat the remainder of the meal in silence. His big Sunday paper had an article on the back page that caught my eye. It was something to do with Brad Pitt.

How come other people's papers always have things you want to read and when you buy a paper for yourself, it's always boring? I kept trying to read the article but it was impossible. It was like he knew I wanted to read it and he kept jolting the paper about.

Annoyed, I went to get dressed.

I spent the day by the phone, hoping Dave'd ring. He didn't.

CHAPTER THIRTY-THREE – MONDAY

"How's Jan?" Al caught up with me on my way up O'Connell Street Monday morning. The way he asked the question was funny. Normally he'd yank my hair and say "How's Jan." Today he said it as if he meant it.

"I feel great," I answered brightly. "Sure I've nothing to worry about really."

He smiled back but I don't think it was a real smile. "How was Sunday?"

"It was all right." I didn't want him to talk to me about the weekend any more. That was the problem when you told people things, you had no control over what they said.

"So you're in better form now than you were?"

"I'm in great form," I said firmly.

"Still want me around tomorrow?"

Was it tomorrow? It was scary when he said it like that. I kept thinking of it as Tuesday. "Yeah." My voice wasn't as calm now.

"I'll meet you outside your flat at ten then." For the

first time since we'd kissed he touched me. His hand sort of brushed off mine. "OK?"

"OK." I shook him off. The last thing I needed was sympathy.

"Right so." He sounded a bit hurt and didn't seem to know what to say after that. I saw him shove his hand into his pocket.

I changed the subject. "And your Sunday?"

He shrugged. "So-so."

"Did you go out anywhere?"

"Nah, stayed in."

Al never went out. I can honestly say that the only places he ever seemed to go were to do with running. "Do you ever go out?" I asked. "With your mates like?"

He shrugged. A blush crept up his face and I knew that I'd done it again. Just when things started to go right with Al, in I jumped and messed him all up. "Sometimes," he muttered, but the way he looked at the ground, I knew he was lying.

I let him away with it.

"So what did you do *in* all day Sunday?"

"Nothin', just watched telly, ate me dinner, went to bed."

"At least you had a dinner," I joked. "Last week, we had a dinner-party. That was the first real dinner I ate in ages."

"A feckin' dinner party!" He looked at me, surprised. "You don't look like the dinner-party type."

"I'm not. I hate cooking."

"So who cooked?"

"Abby." I then told him what had been on the menu and he laughed and asked what the fuck cassoulet was.

It was great to find someone as ignorant as myself. So we got onto food-disaster stories.

"My ma cooked ham once, " he said.

"Just once?"

He gave me a punch. "You know what I mean, " he grinned. "Anyway, she left it in the middle of the table and next door's dog comes in and gets stuck into it. Feckin' ham all over the gaff. So Ma sees him and throws him out the door, but she's going mental. Worrying about what we're all goin' to have for dinner."

"That's more than my ma'd do," I joked. "She hardly ever cooks dinner." Then I stopped, I didn't want to say anymore after the last time I'd mentioned my family to him. "So what happened?"

A big smile spread over his face. "She picked it up off the floor, dumped it on a plate and gave it to me da. He didn't know shit about it, so he ate it."

"No way."

"Yeah." Al nodded. "Me an' Bill – that's me brother – couldn't stop laughing. Da kept wondering what the hell was going on." He bit his lip. "In the end, Bill was told to go up to his room but he said it was worth it."

"Your da sends you to your rooms?" I could barely keep the laughter out of my voice.

"He did when we were kids, yeah. It was years ago."

I told him about all my culinary disasters in Home Economics. By the time we reached the office he was eating himself laughing. "And yer tart slid off the plate onto the floor?" he spluttered.

"Yep," I nodded. "I lifted the tart out of the oven and the whole shaggin' thing slid off the plate. It fell about three feet, splat!"

His laugh made me smile.

"And at the end of the class we had to display what we'd done. I had to scrape the mess off the floor and try to arrange it artistically on a plate. It was shite."

Al grinned. "So you're not a cook then?"

"Hardly."

It was funny now but it hadn't been at the time.

Still grinning, Al opened the front door for me and we began the climb upstairs.

Work was quite relaxing that day due to the fact that Henry still hadn't arrived. Someone had e-mailed us to say that they caught him flogging his jumpers in Mary Street over the week-end. Jimmy Madden was on the war-path wondering where he was and why he hadn't phoned in sick.

"Hate that," Lenny had chortled. "Madden's going to hang him."

Liz spent the day boring us all rigid about her new fella. She was full of it. Apparently he rang her on Saturday and Sunday. I kept my mouth shut. My red-hot Armchair Warrior, as Beth had cruelly christened him since he'd spent the night in the armchair in the flat, hadn't rung at all. When he did though, I'd get my chance to bathe in the sun. So I listened to Liz as she told me all the details of how she'd met Andy and what he'd said, knowing that when the time came, she'd have to repay the favour.

At five, Liz bolted out of the office. She was meeting Andy that night.

Al and I looked at each other. He nodded to me to go first. So I did. "Lenny, I need tomorrow morning off."

"Yeah, so do I," said Al.

"Both of ye? Tomorrow morning?" Lenny gave us a smirky smile. "Oh now, now. I don't want to be encouraging that sort of behaviour a-tall a-tall."

"Lenny?" I quirked my eyes and attempted to look pissed off. "It's sick leave, I'll have a cert for it."

"When don't ya have?" He laughed at that. Turning to Al he said, "And yourself?"

"Annual leave." Al was looking guilty. He managed to look guilty at any reference to himself and women.

Lenny peered hard at the office roster. "If Henry doesn't come in, there'll only be meself and Liz in tomorra mornin'."

"Your lucky day then – isn't it?" I gave him a wink and left. "See you tomorrow afternoon."

Al and I could hear him chuckling as we belted down the stairs.

CHAPTER THIRTY-FOUR – TUESDAY

"How come you're not in work this morning?" Beth was giving me one of her you're-not-pretending-to-be-sick-again looks.

We were sitting across from each other in the kitchen. I'd only just got up and, upon seeing me, Beth had dumped her magazine down on the table and started to glare at me.

"I'm not in work because I have to go somewhere." I began to file my nails. They were in a state, they hadn't been filed in ages and were full of white flecks.

"Where?"

I didn't see that it was any of her business. "Nowhere major, just out."

"Big secret,is it?"

"Yeah. Yeah, Beth,it is." The last thing I needed this morning was her sarcasm. I didn't have to put up with it and I wouldn't. My thumb-nail was looking worse since I'd started it. One half of it went up at a ninety-degree angle, the other side curved, the way it was meant to do.

Beth was staring at me. She was pretending to stir her coffee, but she was sneaking weird looks at me. I bent further over my odd-shaped nails.

"Sorry for asking," she drawled. "I was only making conversation."

"Well, don't." I was really narky today. I hadn't realised it until I'd opened my mouth. It was like PMT only worse.

At nine fifty-five, I began to gather my stuff together. Basically, that involved getting a jumper and shoving it in a bag in case it rained later.

Beth was leaving at the same time. I think she engineered it deliberately just to see where I was going. Together we walked down the stairs and out the front door.

Al was waiting for me, lounging against the gate, with his hands in the pockets of his jacket.

Beth's jaw dropped and almost hit itself off the ground when she saw him.

Al's eyes widened when he saw her. "Hiya," he muttered awkwardly.

"Hi," Beth replied agog. "Are you waiting on her?" She thumbed to me.

"Yes, he is." I linked my arm in Al's and dragged him off. "See you later, Beth," I called back.

"For one scary minute I thought she was coming as well," Al said as we made our way to the bus-stop. "I'd have killed you, Jan, if you'd brought her."

"You mightn't have to." It wasn't a joke. I said it to make him feel awful.

It worked. "I didn't mean to say that."

"So you shouldn't have said it then, should you?"

He shot me a quick look and didn't reply. It was a wise choice. I'd probably have said something even more horrible to him if he'd crawled.

We stood in silence at the bus stop. Al leaned against a wall waiting for the bus to arrive, I stood, sentinel-like beside him, ramrod straight. He reached out and touched my sleeve, "Relax Jan," he said softly.

"Huh, that's easy for you to say. You're not the one heading off to the hospital."

"Are you going to the hospital, dear?" An old woman, who'd been standing on the other side of me, inquired. She was the sweet old lady type, all white hair and pink cheeks. "So am I. I have piles. What's wrong with you?"

"Oh, just one thing," I answered, feeling sorry for her. At least there wasn't piles wrong with me.

I heard Al laughing and glared at him. Talk about insensitive!

The old woman insisted on sitting beside me on the bus. Al sat behind us. Every so often he gave a snort of laughter which I valiantly ignored. I hoped he wouldn't be laughing away at me when I got my diagnosis.

"I have to get them removed," the woman confided as she sat in beside me. She pulled her old-person's bag up onto her lap and turned to me. "Apparently they're like varicose veins only up your back passage."

"Pardon?"

"Piles." She smiled and half her teeth were brown.

"Some people say it's a painful operation, others say it's all right, but I'm getting assessed anyway."

"So am I."

"And what's wrong with you?"

"Nothing much, just a few swollen glands."

"Not as bad as piles," she settled her back against the seat. "I'd swap piles for glands any day."

Another guffaw from Al, the ear-wigger from hell. "Do you mind?" I hissed the first opportunity I got. "Stop laughing."

We all got off at the hospital and the old woman, who seemed to know her way around, told us where reception was. "I'm going over this way," she beamed at me and waved good-bye.

Al, in between nearly puking with laughter, explained to me what piles were. "I feckin' knew you didn't know," he kept repeating over and over again as tears began to light his eyes. "Aw, Jaysus, Jan that's the best laugh I've had in ages." And he'd start laughing all over again.

"Shut up," I gave him an elbow but I was grinning. When he didn't shut up, I elbowed him again, "Shut up, I'm telling you."

Even when we reached reception, he was still laughing.

Rolling my eyes, to show the girl on reception that I thought Al was really immature, I asked her for Dr Daly.

"Third floor," she said. She was still staring

curiously at Al, who was walking around in circles as he tried to calm himself down.

"Are there piles of people waiting to see him, do you know?" I asked the girl.

Her answer was drowned out by another belly-laugh.

She looked at me smiling. "Your fella, he's mad," she giggled. "What's so funny?"

"Don't ask," I gathered my stuff and then dragging Al by the arm, I took him as far as the lifts.

"Daly's on the third floor."

Al's smile vanished, though his eyes still glittered. "Want me to go up with you?"

"Do you mind?"

"Naw, course not," he looked around the foyer and said, "Just let me grab something to read in the shop and I'll be right with you."

"Fine." I looked at my watch as he left. It was ten to eleven. He came back a few minutes later with the Irish Independent.

The lift doors opened and we stepped inside. I felt sick. It pinged as it reached floor three. Stepping out, we looked around. It was a big, cool glassy area, newly designed and really modern-looking. "Like the *Starship Enterprise*," Al remarked as he wandered over to the window. "Look at the view, Jan."

The view was the last thing I was interested in. I'd probably throw myself out the window by the time I was finished.

"Come on, let's go," I said in a low voice, turning

right, the way the girl on the reception had told me to.

Daly's office was down the very end of the corridor. Arriving outside, we saw a glass door that read, *Department of Oncology*. Al pushed it open and I went through. He followed me and neither of us talked as we made our way down the hallway. A door, with Daly's name, was right at the end.

"Yes?" A woman of about forty, busy tapping into a computer screen looked up as we approached.

"I'm here to see Dr Daly?" My voice was breathless and I could hear Al taking a deep breath behind me.

She picked up a load of cards and flicked through them. "Janet Boyle?" she asked.

"That's me."

Standing up, she said, "I'll just tell him you're here."

She bustled through a yellow door and I sank into a chair. I couldn't look at Al, I couldn't look anywhere. This was it.

"All right?" Al whispered, sitting in the chair beside me.

I didn't answer, just nodded my head. This always happened me, I was never too bad until the final moment, when there was nowhere I could hide.

"He'll see you now," the receptionist startled us and we both jumped.

"I'll be right here," Al gave me an encouraging nod as I lifted myself off the chair and forced myself to walk into the room.

CHAPTER THIRTY-FIVE

I don't know what I expected when I walked into Daly's office but what I got was bordering on the boring. It just looked like the average doctor's surgery. No big, hi-tech talking computers, no ultra-modern tumour-detection equipment. Nothing, only a guy with grey hair sitting behind a brown desk at the top of the room.

"Janet, hi," he smiled at me and told me to sit down. Holding out his hand, he said, "Jim Daly."

We shook hands and I began to relax. I hadn't realised I'd needed to, but when I shook his hand, I could feel the tightness in my chest for the first time. Without trying to be noticed, I let out a long slow breath.

Jim Daly held up a file. "I got your lab reports and x-rays from your GP and he's also given me your case history. Do you mind if we go over it?"

"No."

"You first noticed a lump in your neck a few weeks ago?"

"Yeah." I began to stare at my hands. My nails were

pitiful. When this was all over I was going to get them filed properly.

Daly began to go into each of my visits to the surgery and what had been done. I agreed with him on everything.

"You've experienced weight loss," he said then.

It was a statement rather than a question. I didn't answer.

"How much, roughly?"

"Dunno." My hands could do with some hand cream too.

"Half a stone?"

"Maybe."

I could feel him looking at me, sizing me up. I could tell from his few seconds' silence that he was wondering what to make of me.

"It says here you've had night-sweats?"

"Oh them," I was picking a thread that had come loose in my sleeve. "Yeah, now and again."

"Any pruritus?"

I didn't know what *that* was but it sounded disgusting. "What?"

"Itching?"

My head shot up. "Itching?"

He nodded.

I smirked. "No."

Of course, when I said that, I immediately wanted to scratch my neck. Then the itch went to my leg, and my hand and my scalp. And I couldn't itch because he'd see it and think I was telling him lies.

He began to get up from his chair and, as he was doing so, I gave my hair a good scratch.

He began to walk towards me. "Let's just have a feel of these glands."

I bunched up my hair and held my neck towards him. It was too late for him to hide the way his eyes drew together when he saw my neck. The lumps were quite visible now. There were about three of them really big, two on the left side of my neck and one on the right.

Daly felt them and then asked if he could feel the one under my arm. I pulled off my shirt and lay down on his couch.

I could see the beating of my heart if I looked down the length of my body. It was like something from *Alien*, trying to jump out of me.

Eventually Daly finished up and he motioned for me to sit back down again.

This was it!

The moment of truth.

He knew what was wrong.

I took a deep breath and tried to control the way my heart was racing.

"We'll have to take a few more blood tests and run a biopsy – all right?"

He didn't know what was wrong? "Sorry?"

"In order to assess the situation, we'll have to run a few more tests."

"You mean, you don't know what's wrong with me?" Was that good or bad?

He lowered his voice and leaned over the desk, towards me. "There are a number of possibilities and we have to run tests in order to see which one of them it is." He began to tap his pen on his desk. "Ever played Cluedo?" he asked, startling me.

"Yeah." What was he on about?

"Well, it's like that. We have to examine every possibility and start to eliminate all the suspects until we're only left with the main culprit."

"Oh."

Daly still kept tapping his pen. He kept my eyes on him, I wanted to lower them but I couldn't. "We need to do tests to build up a picture of you – firstly, we'll do a series of blood tests, they'll tell us the state of your general health, they'll show us how your kidneys and liver are doing. We'll do a biopsy on the lump under your arm."

I didn't like the word lump but hadn't the nerve to correct him.

"That'll show us exactly what those lumps are and if you need . . ." he stopped for a second and began to twiddle the pen through his fingers, "if you need treatment for them. And then, we'll do a CAT Scan. That's basically like a 3-D x-ray that'll show us the state of all the other glands inside your body." He grinned. "And then we'll know what we're dealing with."

I said nothing.

"We'll try and arrange for you to undergo all these tests within the next week or so. Each test will take up only a few hours. It shouldn't interfere with your work or anything."

"Right."

"We'll know within the next fortnight."

"Great." It wasn't great at all but what could I say?

"Is there anything you want to ask me, Janet?" He was studying me again.

There was loads of stuff I could've asked, but nothing that I wanted to. Ignorance is bliss. "No."

"So you understand what's going to happen."

"Yeah." My eyes kept darting to the door, I was feeling as if I couldn't breathe.

"I'll get my receptionist to book you in for the tests."

"Yeah, right."

"If you want a cert for the week you'll be getting the tests done, that's fine." He looked at me. "Most people prefer to work though, unless, of course, they're too tired."

I wasn't too tired. I was fine. "I'm fine," I said firmly, eyeballing him. "I'm not tired, I'm grand."

"Good." He got up and walked to the door. Opening it for me, he let me pass. Following me, he asked his secretary to book me in for tests.

Al looked up as I came out. He raised his eyebrows and I shrugged in reply.

Daly nodded at both of us and went back into his office. His secretary made a few phone calls, pressed a few buttons on her computer and handed me an appointment card.

"I've booked you in for your bloods this Friday

morning, it shouldn't take long, then next Tuesday you'll have your biopsy."

That was one question I should've asked and now I couldn't. I'd feel stupid going back to ask after the event.

I think the woman must have seen my face, because she smiled and pressed my arm, "It's nothing, just a really fine needle that'll be inserted into the lump –"

"Gland," I interrupted.

She paused, "Gland," she conceded. "It won't take any length of time and it's done under a local anaesthetic."

"Oh."

"Thanks," Al said, nodding at her.

Who did he think he was. My mother?

"And your CAT scan will only take an hour or so." The woman smiled at me. "That's scheduled for Friday week. It's the earliest I could get."

"Fine," I shoved the appointment card into my jacket and without looking at her I said to Al, "Come on, let's head."

I pretended not to see him nodding yet another *thank you* to the woman. We walked down the hall in silence, out of the department in silence. Into the lift and out of the hospital in total silence.

"Want some lunch?" Al asked as we made our way to the bus stop. He jingled some coins in his pockets, "My shout?"

He hadn't asked how it'd gone. He hadn't tried to make me feel better.

He'd just been there for me. I stopped walking and

turned to face him. "I won't know what's the matter until two weeks' time, Al."

He said nothing, just reached out a hand and gently began to rub it up and down my arm. The sort of thing my mam used to do when I was a kid.

I caught hold of his hand and held it hard. "I'm scared, Al."

"I know," was all he said as he wrapped his arms around me. "I would be too."

He felt so safe. Like a rock in the ocean. Somehow, I thought that if I held onto him long enough, I'd be fine. "I'm sorry for being awful earlier." My voice was muffled into his jacket.

"When?" he pulled away from me and, cocking his head to one side, he attempted to look puzzled, "Earlier today or maybe yesterday or last week or last month or . . ."

He stopped and smiled as I laughed.

"Bastard."

"Bitch."

"Pig."

"Wagon."

"Do you want to see my neck?" I asked it suddenly, it came out of nowhere.

Al nodded slowly. "If you want to show me," he said gently.

I lifted up my hair and pointed to the glands. "See there."

I could feel his fingertips lightly touching them. "Are they sore?"

I wished he'd said that he could hardly see them, but I guess that would've been a lie. "No, they're not," I answered. I rearranged my hair about the sides of my neck. When I considered that the way I'd arranged it concealed the glands, I turned to him, "I don't know if that's a good or bad sign."

"Did you not ask the doctor?"

"No."

"You *should* ask Jan, you should find out everything and then maybe you wouldn't feel so bad about it."

I resented him telling me how I'd feel – he didn't know anything, he wasn't the one going for tests. "Drop it." I snapped, irritated, "What do you know anyhow?"

I'd done it again. He flinched under my tone. I felt awful but I couldn't bring myself to apologise.

"So," he asked, "lunch?" His voice was quiet. He nudged me gently, "Say yeah – go on."

"Yeah," I smiled.

"Good girl." The smile he gave me made me feel all weird. It made me feel warm and safe, as if nothing would make him hate me.

I suppose that's what friends are for.

CHAPTER THIRTY-SIX

The day wasn't all bad.

Some of it was good.

And the evening was sensational.

Work that afternoon was all right. Maybe I was just glad of the normality of it. Even if normal, for me, was working with three head-cases. Only two of them were in when Al and I arrived back after lunch. Henry obviously was still on the missing list.

"Oh now," Lenny wagged his finger at us as we came through the door, "where have you two been this morning?"

"Having breakfast together, I bet," Liz said slyly. She smirked at Al, "Does she do a nice piece of toast, Al?"

Al's reply had been to throw a bored look at her as he sauntered over to his desk.

Buoyed up by the fact that I hadn't been declared sick, I pointed over at Al. "See that?"

"What?" Liz looked confused.

"Al just walked to his desk."

"So?"

I gave a big lewd wink, "If Al had spent the night with me, there is no way he'd be able to walk."

The three of them laughed, even Al, who'd normally be mortified by a comment like that.

"Can I book yer services sometime," Lenny spluttered. "I'd like to experience that."

"In your case, I think I'd prefer to chop your legs off, Lenny."

Only Al and Liz laughed.

Lenny had the nerve to look surprised.

The rest of the afternoon went by in a tumult of crude comments, Henry-sightings and interview-swotting.

I spent my time typing about three letters.

A nice relaxing day.

Al walked down O'Connell Street with me after work. It was a nice familiar feeling, as if nothing had really changed since that morning.

"Listen Jan," he said as we reached my bus-stop, "If you want, I'll go with you when you're having your tests." He went red and his eyes slid from my face. "That's if you're still not plannin' on tellin' people."

"I'm not planning on telling anyone," I said.

"Right." He began to shuffle from foot to foot. "Don't you maybe think you should tell – "

"I'm not telling anyone," I repeated. My voice was brittle. "No one."

"Fine." He didn't make it sound as if he thought it was fine.

"There's nothing to tell."

"Yeah, but still you might want to – "

"And I'll get the tests on my own." I sort of threw the remark out before turning from him. The last thing I needed going for tests was him, nagging away at me to tell everyone.

"Come on, Jan, you know I'll go with you." He was talking to my back.

"I'll go on my own," I said.

"Jan, don't be a fuckin' eejet, you know I'll – "

"It's fine." I kept my voice calm, unaffected. People were looking at us. I couldn't see what Al was doing, I still had my back to him. Turning around, I saw that he'd begun walking away.

I felt a bit let-down, as if he should've stayed and tried to persuade me. But if he had, I probably would've told him to get lost.

"See you tomorrow," I yelled after him, making the woman beside me jump.

Al turned back and gave me the two fingers, but I knew he was smiling.

CHAPTER THIRTY-SEVEN

When I got back, Beth was in. She was supping tea and still reading the magazine she'd had in her hand that morning.

"Hi."

"Hi."

Our usual monosyllabic greetings exchanged, I went into my room, took off my shoes and shoved on a pair of old runners. Passing Beth on my way to the kitchen I asked, "Anything decent in the press?"

"Huh?" Beth was glued to her mag. "What?"

"Is there anything decent in the press to eat."

"Bread." She said it without taking her eyes off her magazine.

"Dinnerwise, I meant."

"Bread."

"Great." Opening the press, I saw she was right. Bread.

"Howd' it go with gormless Al then?" Beth asked.

"He's not gormless and we only went to a work

conference." I kept my back to her as I talked, Beth didn't just swallow things. All day I'd been practising the lie. "A work conference," I kept saying over and over to myself in the mirror of the ladies'. I smiled as I said it, I looked serious as I said it, bored as I said it. Eventually I settled for saying it without looking at her.

"Oh," she sounded interested, "Where was it?"

My heart lurched. "Eh, Ballsbridge."

"And what was Al doing waiting for you? Sure that's out of his way."

"Well," I stalled as I began to try and butter the bread. The butter was hard and the bread was soft. "He, eh, offered to show me where it was." The bread was getting all ripped up. "You know me," I gave a fluttery laugh, "no sense of direction." I shoved a huge, buttery piece into my mouth so that I wouldn't be able to answer any more of her questions.

"He fancies you," she pronounced instead. "The poor eejet fancies the knickers off you."

I couldn't defend myself as a whole load of bread was in my mouth.

"God Jan," Beth began to fold up her magazine, "I'm sorry for you." She loaded her voice with sympathy. "How the hell do you attract them?" Getting up from the table she headed into her room.

Bitch.

Al was a mate for God's sake! He didn't fancy me. I drifted over to the telly. Absently, I flicked it on. *Fair City* had just started and thinking it would take my mind off what Beth had said, I settled myself down to watch it. The idea that Al might fancy me was scary, I liked him too much for that. He was my friend . . .

"See you," Beth said, making me jump. She was dressed for work and had come out to put on her jacket. "Enjoy the night on your own."

"I will."

"Anyway, if you get lonely, give Al a call." Laughing at her supposed wit, she left, slamming the door after her.

I kept the telly on the whole evening. The noise of it numbed my brain. Thoughts of Al and the hospital kept trying to push through the barrier, but I wouldn't let them. At about ten, I took a can of Bud from the fridge and opened it, thinking it might help me sleep.

The sound of the buzzer startled me. Some beer spilt over my blouse. "Shit!" I began to wipe it down with my hand.

The buzzer went again.

It was weird for someone to be calling so late. Still, I didn't have to let them in.

"Yeah?" I pressed the intercom.

"Jan, that you?"

My heart literally leapt and then hammered down with such a thud it left me feeling weak. "Dave?" I said, shakily, "Is that you?"

"Yeah, you gonna let me in?"

My reply was a buzz to let him up.

Running into my room, I gawked at myself in the mirror. "Ohh," was all I could say. I grabbed a brush and dragged it hastily through my hair. Kicking my runners off my feet, I pulled on my boots. One of the runners hit Brad Pitt in the face. Not the Brad Pitt on the ceiling, the one on the wall. The glass cracked and the picture went sideways. "Oooh." I didn't attempt to fix him up. I pulled my beer-stained blouse over my head, and pulled another even lower-cut one on.

I was out just in time to hear Dave rapping on the door.

I flashed a smile at myself in the sitting-room mirror and, satisfied that I looked as good as someone like me can, I opened the door.

He stood in his horrific mac, with the gorgeous grin on his face. "Hiya."

"Hi," despite my best efforts, my voice was shaking because my heartbeat had gone off the scale. If it didn't slow down, I was liable to collapse of a coronary. "Come in," I held the door wider for him to enter and banged myself on the face with the edge of it. I reckon the smack could be heard downstairs.

"Ouch," Dave stared at me as I tried simultaneously to shut the door and stop the tears springing into my eyes with the pain.

"Oh, it's nothing," I breezed. "Nothing." I closed the door and wished I could kick it.

"You sure?"

"Nothing that a bucket of ice won't cure!" I gave a gay laugh, and then cringed at the sound of it. Trying to ignore the throbbing that was now pounding the whole upper half of my face, I asked, "So, what brings you here?"

From behind his back, Dave produced a bunch of half-dead flowers. "They were all right when I picked 'em," he shrugged. "I think the wind musta given 'em a shock on the way 'ere."

Touched totally, I gently took them from him. They were wild flowers, dog-daisies, buttercups, forget-me-nots and some others that I didn't know the name of. "Oh, Dave," I smiled up at him and touched a daisy with my fingertips, "Thanks – they're lovely."

"They were lovely, ya mean," he grinned. Nodding to the kitchen, he said, "Ya betta give 'em some water."

"Oh . . . right . . . yeah . . . OK." He watched me as I frantically tore the place apart looking for a vase. There wasn't one. In the end, I filled a mug with water and used that. I put the flowers in the centre of the table and we both stood back and admired them as they drooped.

"'Opefully they'll come round," Dave said.

I didn't care, it was enough to know he'd got them for me.

My next purchase was going to be a book on how to press and dry flowers so I could keep them forever.

It was the first bunch of flowers I'd ever got from a guy.

"I figured I owed ya a major apology," Dave turned to me. "And I 'adn't enough cash ta buy ya ones in a flower shop, so I picked those instead."

God, it was awful, I was going to cry. He was so nice.

"And," Dave smiled, "I was wonderin' if ya ain't

doin' anyfink this weekend, that maybe ya could visit the site."

Overwhelmed, I just whispered, "I'd love to."

"Great." Dave began to zip his mac up. "Well, I'd betta go now so."

"Go?" For a second it didn't register.

"Yep." He was making for the door.

"But sure, you've only just got here," I said stunned, "You can't go now."

"I only called to give ya the flowers." He had his hand on the door and was ready to exit out of my life for another few days.

"Stay for a – a – a . . ." I faltered. Placing my hand on the door, so that he couldn't leave, I tried to think of what he could stay for. "Stay for a – a chat."

Party animal Jan.

He shrugged but, to my amazement, moved away from the door. "You sure? You're not goin' out tonight or anyfink?"

"No." I shook my head hard. "I'm all on my own."

"'Right so," Dave winked at me, not suggestively unfortunately, just an ordinary run-of-the-mill matey wink. "If yar lonely."

"I am."

He began unzipping his mac. "Got no mates then?"

"Oh, I have, it's just that, well, they're all out and I didn't feel like going anywhere so, you know, I just said, well, it's me and the telly tonight and then I got a bit lonely and felt . . ." I was doing it again – saying stupid things and unable to stop. " . . . company would be nice and so I was thinking of . . ." If he didn't interrupt I was going to keep talking forever, " . . . maybe seeing a . . ."

"It was a joke." There was a slightly bewildered expression on his face.

My mouth clamped shut. "I know." I giggled. An awful giggle. "I know."

"Good," Dave began to take off his mac. "I wouldn't say something like that to 'urt yer feelings or anyfink."

"Oh, I know." Smiling, I offered to take his mac from him with the pretence of hanging it somewhere. I dumped it, and myself onto my bed. Alone, I began to do my totally useless but supposedly calming deep-breathing exercises. In through the nose and out the mouth, deep and slow. In, out. In, out.

After doing my breathing for a few seconds, I walked back into the room. Dave had sprawled himself across our good chair. His eyes were half-closed and his head was back. I could see the curve of his neck. It looked so kissable. His *Save the Whale* tee-shirt was bright orange and loose. It couldn't hide the width of his shoulders or the breadth of his chest. I thought I'd vomit with desire.

"I see ya didn't take my advice." He didn't look at me as he spoke. He kept his eyes closed.

"What?"

"The kettle. Ya didn't change it like I advised."

"Eh, no." I went red. Why hadn't I changed it? "Next week we're buying a new one."

"Oh, right. Good on ya."

There was a silence.

"We're getting an automatic one."

"Great."

Why was I telling these lies? "A Kenwood one."

He didn't even reply to that. Instead he picked up the remote control and began to flick through the television stations.

Desperately I searched for something to talk to him about. I spied my half-drunk can on the floor. "Want a can?" I picked up my Bud. "There's some in the fridge."

"That'd be great."

It's funny how I can stand silence when I've a can in my hand, but when I'm crutchless it drives me mad. We drank in silence for ages. The only sound was the television. Dave had found some nature programme and was busy watching two leopards savaging the hell out of some animal.

"They're beautiful," he shook his head in admiration. "Big cats in the wild are beautiful ta watch, ain't they?"

"In the wild is where they belong, all right," I answered, not having a clue what I was on about.

Dave did though. "Bloody right Jan. Ever see the way they suffer in zoos?"

"I don't go to the zoo." I meant it as a joke. Only kids and old people went to zoos.

"Fair play!" Dave studied me over his can. He tipped it against mine. "Aw Jan, you and me, we've so much in common. I 'ate zoos too."

"Really?" I gulped and then gulped a half a can in one go. "Really," I said again.

"Ever see the polar bears? They go mental in confined spaces."

"They do?" That shocked me. I liked animals though I hadn't had a pet in years. Living in the same house as Buddy was enough to put me off owning anything.

"Oh yeah," Dave finished his can and I rushed to the fridge to get us a refill. He came down to sit on the floor beside me. "Zoos are all very well for protecting rare animals, right, but animals need their freedom, just like us."

"Yeah."

"And zoos . . ."

I really hadn't a clue what he talked about. All I could concentrate on was the shine on his hair, the brightness of his teeth and the way his eyes literally burned in their sockets as he talked. He held my gaze as he spouted his animal rights doctrine.

I kept slugging back the drink as he talked. The more I drank the more gorgeous he became.

The more he talked, the more I drank, the sexier he got.

The sexier he got, the more I drank . . .

"Me feet are killing me so I . . . " Beth flung open the door and stopped mid-sentence. Her eyes widened when she saw who it was. "Dave," she grinned.

He grinned back. "Betty, ain't it?"

Beth's face whitened for just a second. It was weird,

one minute she was smiling, the next she looked shell-shocked. "No," she shook her head and said softly, "it's Beth."

"Oh right," Dave nodded. "You look more like a Betty though."

"Well, I'm not." Her voice was hard. "I'm Beth."

"Hiya Beth," Dave said amenably, stressing *'Beth'*, "'Ow's it going?"

"Fine," she snapped back.

I knew he'd let us both in for it. Somehow, he'd annoyed her.

She saw the cans of Bud on the floor beside us and her eyes narrowed. Going to the fridge, she yanked it open. "Only one can left," she said ominously. "Only one can."

"You 'ave it why don't ya," Dave smiled at her good-naturedly.

"Thank you, Dave," Beth said in a very scary voice. "Thank you very much."

Dave missed it completely. "Naw, don't thank me, I didn't get 'em."

I tried to stifle a mini-shriek. He was mince-meat.

"So what's happening in your life?" Beth took her can and sat herself above us on the chair. "Got tired of saving the world have you?"

Dave laughed. "Naw, just 'aving a break, you know 'ow it is."

"Yes," Beth stared pointedly at his can. "Just drinking other people's booze and generally slobbing out."

"Got it in one." Dave raised his can to hers. "Cheers."

"He brought me flowers," I interjected before her remarks got so pointed she'd stab him. "See them on the table."

"Put them out of their misery by picking them, did you?" she asked, still glaring at Dave.

How dare she say that about my flowers!

"They were fine when I picked 'em, they just died on the way 'ere."

"They're not dead, they're lovely," I said, trying to show some spirit. "I was really pleased with them."

"And that says it all!" Beth raised her can high into the air. "Jan doesn't need much and by Jaysus she doesn't get much."

It was as if she'd slapped me. I think it was the most horrible thing she'd ever said. The silence that followed even seemed shocked.

"I don't fink that was called for," Dave said eventually, raising his eyebrows at Beth. "I fink that was a bit much."

I couldn't say a word. I thought I'd be sick. Slowly, I raised my eyes to look at her.

She was glaring at both of us and then her head dropped. Staring at her hands, she muttered, "Sorry Jan," her voice was quiet, "I'm sorry."

Sorry wasn't good enough for me. Totally humiliated would have been an understatement of how I felt.

"Sorry," Beth said again.

"That's all right," Dave squeezed my arm. "It's OK, ain't it, Jan?"

I wished he hadn't heard her say that to me.

"Jan?" Dave was squeezing my arm again.

All I could do was stare at the carpet, I couldn't say anything. I'd been doing so well with him and now it was all spoilt.

Beth heaved herself up from the chair. "I think I'll go to bed," she said, sounding subdued. "Night Dave." She paused. "Night Jan."

"Don't go on our account," Dave seemed under the impression that things were fine. An apology had been issued and now things were back to normal.

"I think I should," Beth threw a glance at me before she left, but I turned away.

Dave bent his head down and peered into my face. "All right?" he asked gently.

"No," I sniffed, trying to stop my eyes from watering. "No."

"I don't think she meant it in a bad way," he said. "She's just stupid."

I choked on a laugh. "Don't let her hear you say that."

"'Ere," Dave picked my can off the floor, "finish that and get yourself off to bed."

"And what about you?"

"I'll go back to the site once you're all right."

"Don't go," I said, looking at him. "Please." Dutch courage was a great thing. I knew if I went to bed alone, I wouldn't sleep. "Stay."

"Jan," Dave said, "No offence or anyfink but another night on that chair is not a 'appy thought."

I slugged back the remainder of the can. "You can sleep in my bed."

He burst out laughing.

And I'd thought Beth was tactless!

I was about to throw the empty can at him and then burst into tears, when he said, "And 'ave you sleep out 'ere? Even I'm not that bad."

Dave was lovely, but he was slow. "No," I brought my face nearer his, hoping he wouldn't notice how red mine had gone at close range. "We can share my bed."

The penny dropped. It clanged to the ground. Dave pulled away from me and stared at me with his glittery eyes. "Did I 'ear you right?"

I was mortified, totally dissolve-into-the-floor mortified. It wasn't as if I led a virginal life, but I can safely say that never, ever, had I propositioned a guy before. Usually with me, it was a mutual-drunkenness-falling-into-the-bed-thing. But this was different.

"You heard," my voice shook, not from unbridled desire but from the terror of rejection.

"Share your bed?" Dave looked amused. "You sure?"

I wish he hadn't looked like that. His eyes hadn't steamed up with desire, he didn't grab me and tell me it was what he wanted. He just had a self-conscious sort of grin on his face.

"If you want to."

"I do," he said simply.

What next? He'd given his consent – what did I do next? Dave stood and holding out his hand, hauled me from the floor. He looked at me and I wondered what he expected. Did he want me to kiss him, or show him my room. Did he want another can?

I could have done with a flagon of vodka.

"Eh," I pulled him gently towards my bedroom. "It's in here."

To my wonderment, he followed me like a sheep being led to slaughter. That's not exactly an apt description, I wasn't planning anything like that.

Once inside my room, he turned to me.

He shouldn't have bothered. I looked everywhere but at him. Desire was ebbing away quicker than my confidence.

Dave sat on the bed and began to pull off his boots. First he unlaced them and then off they came. So I took off my boots too.

"Nice room," Dave looked around. "Who's the bloke on the ceiling?"

"Brad," I muttered.

He had his socks off now so I took off mine.

"Some bloke you know?"

"Film star." God, I was pathetic. What other person my age had pictures of a guy on their ceiling?

Dave grinned then. "The teenager in ya, is it?"

"Something like that," I found the guts to smile back.

"Come here," he held his hand out to me and shyly I went and took his. He pulled me down beside him on the bed.

My heart was starting to hammer again.

Slowly, he put his hands to my shoulders and began to massage me, very gently. His thumb pressed into my shoulder-blades and his face hovered inches away from mine. I could feel his breath across my face and the closeness of his lips was too much for me. Moving forward, I kissed him softly. He responded. His hand came up the back of my head and held my lips to his. My hands were in his hair now, my thumbs rubbing his ears and then they were on his face, feeling his stubble.

Pulling away from me, he began to unbutton my blouse. This was the moment I'd been dreading. This was the moment I dreaded every time I was with anyone. A voice from my horrible nightmarish teenage years always floated up to me. Telling me that if breasts were cabbages mine were . . .

"Oh you're gorgeous," Dave had his hand inside my bra and he was kissing my neck. "You're gorgeous."

The tension left, hurdle overcome.

"Oh, Jan," Dave's eyes had glazed, his pupils were black. "God, Jan." He pushed me down on the bed and moved himself on top of me. He put his hands behind my back and began to unzip my skirt. At the same time I began to unbutton his combats.

Of course, unlike the films, we had to wriggle out of our clothes – they didn't just end up on the floor. And unlike the films, I wasn't wearing nice lace knickers with a pristine white matching bra. But it didn't matter. Neither of us noticed what the other had on. It was literally seeing who could get their clothes off quickest. Producing a condom from my drawer I lay back, totally unembarrassed now and watched while he put it on. The more I looked at him, the more I couldn't believe that he was going to sleep with me.

He was everything I wasn't.

He even had a flatter stomach than me.

He was the sexiest man I'd ever met in my entire life.

He was quite big, by the way.

Dave let his eyes linger over me, before coming back to lie on top of me again. Once he began to kiss me, that was it. I couldn't control myself. Panting, kissing, holding hard to each other, we both finally came together. Dave had his eyes closed and sweat stood out on his brow.

All the other days in my life melted away compared to this one.

For the first time in my life, I felt as if I'd actually got something I wanted.

I was fifteen and still a virgin of the lips.

Somehow I knew that having a boyfriend would give me access to the cool gang. That was where Jessie hung out.

Peter, my first boyfriend, was a bit like me. Unaccepted, uncool but a tryer. We'd kissed a bit and I'd wondered what all the fuss was about. A bit of heavy petting was indulged in. Peter wanted to go all the way.

The fact that his face was like a badly made pizza didn't endear me to the rest of his body. Not even the ultra-cool people deserved this kind of sacrifice. So, I'd dumped him.

Soon it was all over school. I had breasts like brussels sprouts and was frigid.

Peter, with his sorry tale of rejection by a "hung-up on sex because her mother was a Catholic nutter" girlfriend, was finally accepted into the exclusive club of being hip, cool and popular.

I became the laughing-stock-cum-dork of the year.

CHAPTER THIRTY-EIGHT – WEDNESDAY

Dave left early Wednesday morning.

I'd woken up as he was pulling on his tee-shirt. I stayed very still, totally sick with disappointment. Was he just going to walk out on me now? I couldn't bear for him to see my face, so I turned over and snuggled back down, listening for the sounds he was making.

I heard him softly opening my bedroom door as he headed out into the kitchen. Silently he padded about, flicking on the kettle, fiddling about with the cooker. I couldn't believe that he was making himself breakfast before deserting me. Why had I been such a fool as to sleep with him? Last night, I'd been sure it was the right thing to do. Now, listening to him stealing about in the kitchen, trying not to wake me as he stuffed his face with our food, I knew I'd been a thick.

I could hear my mother. He'll have no respect for you if you offer yourself on a plate. I'd not only done that, but provided the knife and fork for him to cut me with too. I was lying in the bed, feeling miserable and foolish and ashamed when he walked back in.

"Jan," he shook me gently, "Jan."

"Yeah?" I looked at him, his face black with stubble, his eyes sleepy, but oh, so alive. "Yeah." I made my voice bored, just in case he was planning on letting me down.

"I've some grub made, d'ya fancy some toast?"

Glancing at my clock, I saw that it was six-thirty. An ungodly hour for eating breakfast. But he wasn't doing a full-bellied runner, he was making me breakfast and I smiled. "I'd love some."

"Stay right there," he jabbed his finger at me and left.

I sat up in the bed and pulled the covers up to my chin. It was cold in the room that morning. Last night, to my relief, I hadn't had a sweat. Sweat-free nights were a rarity, so someone must have been on my side, because last night I slept better than I had in years.

Dave arrived in, balancing two plates of toast on one arm and carrying two mugs in his other hand. He placed my tea on the bed-side locker and handed me a plate of toast. Five slices of toast to be exact.

He put the butter beside me.

"I'll never eat all that," I laughed. "Never."

He'd done the same amount for himself.

Beth would freak when she got up – there was probably no food at all in the press now. I felt a thrill at the thought. Serve her right.

Dave grinned and sat cross-legged on the bed beside

me. Soon the two of us were munching away. I kept glancing at him out of the corner of my eye and smiling ridiculously. I couldn't help it, he was brilliant.

"Good cook, ain't I? Dave flashed a smile at me and I caught my breath.

"Thanks," I said.

"No probs," he nodded.

He thought I was referring to the breakfast, but I'd meant everything besides the breakfast. Still, I let it go. There was no point in letting him see just what a paranoid wreck I was.

Dave demolished his food and started on the three slices of toast I'd left.

"I see you've put me picture on ya wall." He nodded across to the oak tree picture.

"Yeah, I like looking at it."

"I like looking at you," he said. It sounded sexy even though he spoke through a mouthful of mashed-up toast.

When we'd both finished, he leaned across and caught me in his arms. "I enjoyed meself a lot last night."

"So did I."

He began to nibble on my ear, "You look lovely without all that crap on yer face too."

He was only saying that because all my make-up was animal tested. That was another thing I'd been worried about, him seeing me first thing in the morning, with all my make-up wrecked.

"You've nice skin, nice eyes, you look great *au natural.*"

His French accent was as bad as my make-up-free face.

"Just one thing though . . ." his eyes were laughing as he waited for me to respond.

Here it goes, I thought, he wants me to get a breast implant. Or, he thinks we shouldn't see one another any more. Or . . .

"Your mattress," Dave made a big deal of banging his fist on it, "it's foam."

"So?"

"CFCs dahling," he tipped his nose. "Bad for the ozone."

I was about to say I'd buy a new mattress when he grinned.

"And," he continued, his eyes sparkling, "your quilt is down, probably made from the feathers of intensively reared ducks."

I had the courage to throw the pillow at him. "Dave, feck off!"

He laughed and, standing up, said, "I 'ave to now anyhow."

I hadn't the nerve to ask if I'd see him soon.

"See ya soon," he said as he let himself out. "I'll be in touch."

I thought I'd burst with happiness

I bounced out the door to work.

All along the bus journey, I thought about him. My heart raced as I thought of how he'd made me feel. The walk up O'Connell Street, that I normally hated, was too short this morning. I was in the office before I wanted to be.

For the first time in my life, I was the first in. It was weird being in the office so early. It looked nice, the miserable bit of sun that slanted through the windows looked nice, the peeling paint made nice shapes on the wall, my desk looked inviting. The whole world seemed a much nicer place to be in that day.

I suppose I was pathetic.

It was even nice being pathetic.

Al arrived in about five minutes later. Barely nodding at me, he sloped over to his desk where he began to bury himself in work.

"Morning," I grinned. "And how are you?"

He didn't take his eyes off his desk. "Crap," he mumbled. He began to sort out some files, the way he slammed them into the In and Out trays told me everything I needed to know.

"What's up?" I asked, going over and sitting on the edge of his desk. "Is it because of yesterday?" I really didn't want to fall out with him. Plus, the fact that I was happy, made me want everyone else to be happy too.

"Don't flatter yerself, Jan," Al dumped his last file into his Out tray and began the business of switching on his computer.

"Fine." Feeling a bit insulted, I lifted myself up and marched over to my own corner of the room. "Be like that."

He didn't reply.

Liz came in, full of the joys of life. "Andy dropped me off this morning," she explained, beaming at the two of us.

This was to let us know the obvious.

I seized my chance. "Dave would've walked in with me only he had to leave early."

"Dave?" Liz gaped. "But, but," she made gestures at Al, "But I thought . . . "

"Dave's my boy-friend," I said airily. "Al knows about him."

"Al?" Liz couldn't believe that he'd known and not her. "Did you know Jan was seeing someone?"

He looked up. Staring at me, he muttered, "She said something all right." His sharp voice was gone. Instead he had that weird look on his face that I'd only seen once before, the time when we'd chatted on the stairs. "So his name's Dave, huh?" he asked.

"Yeah, didn't I tell you?"

"Dunno." He looked at me so hard that I grew uncomfortable. I turned away first.

Liz was agog. "You've kept this a big secret," she came over and sat on my desk. "So, go on, spill the beans."

I didn't need to be asked. A blow by blow account was given. Somewhere in the middle of my story, Al left the office.

Neither Liz nor I noticed.

After work that evening I approached Lenny about the mornings off for the tests.

"I'll wait for you downstairs," Al said as he passed me on the way out.

"Naw," I waved him off, "You head, you'll miss your bus."

Al didn't answer, just slammed the door after him.

Lenny tut-tutted. "Aw, broken the lad's heart ye have," he joked. "Ye shouldn't be mouthing about your fella in front of him."

"Hilarious," I commented dryly. "Lenny, I was wondering if . . ."

"Mad about you, he is. Anyone can see that. And what do ye do, only go and break his heart."

I gave another obligatory smile and tried again. "Lenny, I need a few mornings . . ."

"That Derbhla wan now, she's mad after him, but will he have her? Oh, no," Lenny did a big head shake. "Not at all. A grand girl like that flinging herself at him, morning noon and night and what does he want? A flighty wan like yerself. I don't know at all at all."

I'd had enough. Not even bothering to be polite and do the expected grovelling, I snapped, "I'm taking Friday morning off and two mornings next week – all right." With that, I walked out the door and like Al, I gave it a good hard slam.

CHAPTER THIRTY-NINE – FRIDAY

Sitting in the hospital, waiting for my blood test, was not as big a deal as I'd thought it would be. In fact, I hadn't actually thought about the blood test at all, which was usually a sign that I was terrified. But that day, I really wasn't too bothered.

The main and only reason for this lack of fear was that Dave had rung.

He was going to collect me first thing on Saturday morning and bring me to the site. Saturday and Sunday morning would be spent there. He told me I'd need a sleeping-bag and, Beth, in a repentant gesture, had promised to lend me hers.

When I'd arrived in from work on Wednesday evening, Beth had made a point of coming over to me and holding out her hand. "I really am sorry about last night," she muttered. "You've got to believe me."

I shrugged and took her hand. "Forget it."

I knew neither of us ever would.

Abby had arrived later and almost had a seizure

when I told her what had happened between Dave and me. "So go on," she said totally agog, "is his dick as big as his mouth?"

I ignored the jibe. "It – was – brill." I said it slowly to build up the brilliantness of it.

"How brilliant?" she demanded.

"Very, very, brilliant."

"And?"

"And what?" I casually asked.

"And what?" Abby gave me a puck, "Was it a one-night stand or what?"

I was a bit hurt by that, no one I ever slept with was a one-night stand, it was always forever, at least on my part. On their part, it was usually a different story. But that was hardly my fault. So without meaning to, I snapped, "No. He's ringing me."

I saw the way her eyes widened in a you're-some-sucker way. She didn't say anything.

"He is," I said firmly. "He's dead nice."

Abby changed the subject. "Was it his idea?"

"Yes." At her intake of totally disbelieving breath, I was forced to lie again. "Totally his idea."

And I made up a story about how he'd fancied me from the word go. I wasn't proud of doing it, but it was better than having her know that I was the sole instigator of all the action. In the end, I almost believed it too.

"Janet Boyle?"

The voice brought me back to the present. "That's me."

The nurse beckoned me forward. "This way."

Following her, I was led into a room where about six nurses were taking blood samples. The ordeal was over in a few minutes and out I went, feeling great that once again I hadn't let myself down by closing my eyes and blubbering at the amount of blood they were taking from me.

The fear of needles was firmly in the past.

Henry was in work when I arrived back that afternoon. He was bouncing about, laughing and joking. "Hey, Jan," he greeted me when I walked in. "How's the form?"

"Fine." I looked at the others to see what the story was. All of them had their heads down, looking as if they were working.

"How's things been with you," Henry leered and, preening himself, finished, "since I was out makin' me fuckin' fortune?" He stopped. "Makin' me fortune," he repeated pointedly.

I did what he wanted me to do. "So howd' you make a fortune, Henry?"

"By being enterprising!"

Out of the corner of my eye I could see Liz giving me filthy looks. Obviously Henry had told his enterprising tales already that morning. I didn't care. At least he wouldn't ask me where I'd been now.

"Enterprising?" I asked, feigning massive interest.

Henry clapped his hands together. "Yep. I sold all me bleedin' jumpers – they were snatched outa me hand, so they were." He did a demo of himself. He got into the middle of the floor and yelled, *"Good quality v-necks seven quid each."* Turning to me, he nodded, "Fuckin' stampede. Couldn't sell them fast enough."

"So how come," Al said in a quiet voice, "you haven't been in for days?"

"Wha'?" Henry glared at him.

"Well," Al shrugged, his face all innocent, "If they sold that quick, you should've been back here a few days ago."

"Aw, fuck off, you," Henry snapped. "You're only an asshole."

"He has a point now," Lenny seemed interested. "The lad has a point."

I saw Al beginning to laugh quietly. He really hated Henry for some reason.

"He hasn't a fuckin' point."

"Well, now I think he has," Lenny was adamant. "I think that if it took you . . ."

"Shower of assholes," Henry pronounced before making a grand exit through the door.

We all breathed a sigh of relief when he left. The last few days had been tension-free when he wasn't around. I think we'd all been secretly hoping for some kind of a miracle so that he wouldn't return.

"If he'd made a fortune, he wouldn't have come back here," Al said, turning back to his VDU and his space-invader game.

"Good point, good point," Lenny began shuffling towards Henry's desk. Picking up his paper he said, "Might as well get meself a free read while he's gone."

Back at his own desk, he started thumbing through the paper and muttering out the headlines, before stabbing a page with his thumb. "See here now," he said sounding shocked, "some chancer's going around snatching babies."

He then began to read us out sections of the report. Lenny was famous for doing that. By the time he'd finished reading a paper, it was as if you'd read it with him.

"A young woman in her thirties – *do-be-do-de-doo* – yesterday made an attempt to snatch a four-year-old – God Almighty – *do-be-do-be-doo.*"

"She made an attempt to snatch God Almighty," Liz giggled. "That was an unfortunate choice."

Al and I laughed. Liz was in great form these days.

"And there's a piece here on some young fella that killed himself after being bullied." Lenny began slowly and laboriously to read out some story or other about school bullying.

I left after the fifth sentence.

No matter what I did, or where I went, it managed to haunt me.

The adds on the telly for Pacer Mint sweets were based on the fact that if you ate a Pacer Mint, everything turned green and white.

Our house had eaten a huge packet of them, that's what

Louise Johnson told everyone. "Janet Boyle's house is like a giant Pacer Mint."

It started off as a joke, at least I thought it did. Then it began to get personal.

"Janet Boyle's house has rats living in it."

"Janet Boyle's house is dirty/smelly/disgusting."

Jessie had the inside track on the weird Boyles. Jessie knew the way my dad pinched my mother on the arse all the time. My dad was a dirty ould fella. Jessie knew how my dad only wore cheap shoes. My dad was a smelly ould fella. Jessie knew that my mother listened to James Taylor and my dad liked doing the Hucklebuck. My dad was a sad ould fella.

Jessie knew that all my family were really mental.

For the first time, I saw the cars piled up outside our house. For the first time I noticed the peeling paint and the dirty windows. For the first time my eyes were opened on what a crack-pot family I had.

I felt ashamed of everything.

CHAPTER FORTY – SATURDAY

Seven o'clock Saturday morning. An unreal time to get up.

Somebody was up, however. And that somebody was buzzing our bell for all they were worth. Closing my eyes, I tried to ignore the sound in the vain hope that it would simply disappear.

Instead, the ringing became more insistent.

I'd give it three minutes. If it wasn't gone in three minutes, I'd answer it.

Three minutes later, the bell was still buzzing.

Three more minutes. If it wasn't gone by then, I'd answer.

Fifteen minutes later, still there.

"Shit," I stumbled out of bed and dragged on a dressing-gown. "Bloody eejet, whoever you are." Pressing the intercom so hard, it almost shattered, I spat, "Who is it?"

"Me."

Too tired to recognise the voice, plus the fact that a headache was beginning to march up on me, I said, "Am I supposed to be inspired?"

"It's me," the voice faltered, "Dave."

Dave.

Seven o'clock on a Saturday morning.

"It's seven o'clock in the morning, Dave."

"Yeah, and it's breakfast-time back home," he replied doing a brilliant take-off of someone taking off an *Orish* accent and eating Galtee rashers at the same time.

I smiled, but I desperately wanted him to go away. For one thing, I looked a state. Unshowered, unmade-up, he was bound to do a runner when he saw me.

"Gimme ten minutes," I said. "You got me out of bed."

I could hear him laughing at the other end. "Pity," he said. "I was 'oping to put you right back there."

It was the only thing he could have said to make me open the door. He was in the flat in less then a minute and in my room split-seconds later.

Afterwards, he made breakfast while I showered. I came out of the bathroom, my hair wrapped in a towel and my dressing-gown around me to find an enormous plate of scrambled eggs on the table.

"For you," he kissed my neck. Running the back of his hand down my face, he said, "And ya look beautiful like that."

I knew he didn't mean it – for one thing I had spots breaking out all over my forehead – but it was nice that he had the consideration to lie. "Thanks."

Dave pulled some toast from under the grill. "Two slices, yeah?"

"Thanks."

I watched as he buttered them, I loved the easy way he had about him, as if he'd lived in the flat forever.

Putting the toast in front of me, he sat down and looked at me as I ate.

I hate people watching me eat. It makes me drop food all over the place. Bits of egg were falling off my fork onto the floor at an alarming rate. "Are you not having – ?"

"Naw," Dave shook his head. "I ate earlier."

The egg came out my mouth now. I began to cough. "What time did you get up at?"

He shrugged. "Dunno, could've been five, six. I dunno."

I stared at him, half in wonder, half in horror. "Eh, I won't have to get up early when I'm on site, will I?" It felt really technical saying "on site".

His laughter made me smile. "Wait an' see," was all he said.

"Why on earth would you get up so early anyhow?" The concept that someone could willingly drag themselves from bed earlier than necessary was beyond my grasp.

Dave shrugged. "Everyfink is nicer in the mornin'," he said. "I get up to watch the dawn most days. Everyone should do that, it's really cool."

It was really mental, as far as I could see. But I smiled and nodded along. He looked gorgeous that morning. Not that he didn't always look gorgeous, but that day, he looked fab. There was something so clean and fresh about the way he was, something brilliant in the way he studied me and grinned at me and talked to me. His tee-shirt made me smile though. It was a *Give Blood* message.

He caught me smiling and, cupping his chin in his hands, he grinned back. "Wot's so funny?"

I reddened. I didn't want him thinking I was sneering at his clothes or anything. "Nothing."

"Go on," his eyes sparkled in amusement. "Wot is it?"

"That," I gestured to his tee-shirt. "Every time you wear one, it seems to have some kinda message on it." Screwing up my eyes, I tried to think of the others I'd seen him in, "There was a CND one, a whaling one, a . . ."

"Yeah," Dave nodded. "I like to make statements with my clothes."

"Literally."

"Very much so," he grinned.

Al unexpectedly popped into my head. Huh, if I'd criticised something he wore, he'd have sulked. Al was hyper-sensitive, that was his problem. Up-tight. Why couldn't he be more like Dave?

" – orf?"

I shook my head, what the hell was I thinking of Al for? "Sorry?"

"You all packed and ready for orf?"

"Yeah, yeah," I spooned some more egg into my mouth. I really didn't feel great, the headache had got worse, but I didn't want to insult Dave by not eating his breakfast.

"Free-range eggs are nicer," Dave said, as he took my half-empty plate away. "You lot should buy 'em the next time."

"We will."

"Just as soon as you get yer kettle, huh?"

I don't know whether it was a dig or a joke, so I ignored him. Getting up from the table and brushing off all the bits of egg and toast crumbs that had landed on my dressing-gown, I said, "I'm just going in to get ready."

"Right."

I'd packed the night before and left my Saturday clothes on the bed. I knew I couldn't wear skirts and stuff like that on site, so I was stuck with jeans. I'd decided on the Levis I'd worn to the march and a tight, short jumper. Unfortunately, the jumper didn't reveal what it was designed to reveal. In fact, it flattened what it was meant to reveal, but it was the nicest jumper I had.

Dave came into the room as I was drying my hair. Very gently, he took the hair-dryer from my hands and began to dry it for me. The way he ran his fingers through my hair was beautiful and I began to hope that we wouldn't be leaving just yet . . . then, quite suddenly, he stopped. With a stomach-churning certainty, I knew what he was about to say.

"You've a lump on your neck, Jan." He pressed it. "A gland or somefink."

"Yeah," I pulled my neck away and shook my hair free. "I know, it's just a gland."

"Wow, super 'ormones, hey?"

"Where you're concerned, yeah," I was quite pleased at my daring. Since Wednesday, I'd been wondering how I'd ever face him again. But since he'd suggested sex that morning, I was finding my pride and confidence were returning quite rapidly. I wasn't even making a fool of myself every time I opened my mouth and, just then, I'd said something that was flirty.

Dave pushed my hair back from my face and kissed me. "Wait until later," he whispered, his husky voice making me feel dizzy.

He watched as I put on my make-up.

"Ya don't need it," he kept saying as I lathered it on thick and brown.

But I did.

Then I began to unzip my bag and shove it in.

"Christ Jan, ya can't bring make-up with ya!" He was torn between amusement and stupefaction.

"I can." Closing the bag, I tried to lift it. It was seriously heavy.

"Wot's in there?" Dave's eyes had narrowed suspiciously.

"Just, you know, things."

"But yer only goin' for tonight."

"And I need everything here." In truth, I'd packed almost everything I possessed. Shampoo, conditioner, deodorant, spare socks, knickers, pyjamas, toothbrush, toothpaste. Spare clothes in case the weather changed and became sunny.

"Ya only need some gear to wear and a sleepin'-bag." Dave had taken the bag from my hands and even he balked at its weight.

"That's all that's in there," I smiled uneasily. "Honest."

He didn't look as if he believed me.

I didn't want to annoy him. "Well, just clothes and a few extras."

He threw his eyes skyward and hoisted the bag over his shoulder. "Like the bleedin' queen comin' for a visit," he muttered.

It was nine by the time we left.

I grabbed a packet of painkillers out of the press for my headache. Shoving them into my pocket, I raced after him as he sauntered down the hall.

This was the most exciting day of my life.

CHAPTER FORTY-ONE

The site was a sight.

I think I'd expected something along the lines of a tourist brochure. Set amid the Dublin mountains, nestling in verdant glades, cocooned in sunlit-dappled forests, please visit our eco-warrior sites.

I suppose the fact that it was raining didn't help endear me to the place. Or the fact that we had to walk about two miles from the bus stop. Or the fact that when we arrived, they were all sitting huddled about an enormous belching fire. Sam was stirring it with a stick, trying to coax the embers to light and Megan was wandering around with an enormous chicken under her arm. It was like something from the Viking era.

"'Ere we are," Dave, giving a groan, dumped my bag straight onto the ground. Straight into the mud.

"Oh, Dave," I tried to laugh to cover up my disappointment and horror at the place. "Don't." Dave had wandered off and was deep in conversation with Sam. Bravely, I tried to rescue my best travel-bag from the slime.

"Here," Megan came over and dumping the chicken on the ground, she took one handle of my bag and I took the other. Both of us hauled it onto cleaner ground. "Heavy, that," she nodded to the bag.

"I didn't know what to bring," I muttered, feeling stupid. At that moment, I felt I shouldn't even have brought myself, never mind the bag.

Megan sat down on a log. Gesturing about, she asked, "So, what d'you think?"

"Nice," I mumbled, unable to say any more.

I heard her give a laugh, but didn't look to see if it was me she was laughing at.

She stood up. "Dave'll show you around," she promised, "Stay there, I'll get him."

Dave was over at the fire. He too was poking it with a stick and trying to get it to light. Megan went behind him and squeezing him around the waist, she said something. I saw him throw back his head and laugh and a stab of pure jealously went through me. What made her so funny?

Then I saw her say something else and point over at me. Dave glanced over and tipped me a salute. I raised my hand back. Soon, he was coming across the grass towards me.

"Sorry 'bout that, Jan," he grinned, wiping his hands along his combats, "bleedin' fire won't light."

A cheer went up behind us and we saw a flame leap up. "And there she goes!" Sam whooped as the others laughed.

Dave grinned and held his hand out to me. Hauling

me up, he said, "Right, let's start with the introductions." He brought me over and introduced me to the people standing or sitting around the now-blazing fire. There were seven in all, including Sam and Megan. They were all dressed more or less the same. Combats, tee-shirts. Most of them wore layers of clothes with bandannas around their heads. I liked the way they looked.

"Give her the grand tour, Davy," one of the lads instructed. I'd forgotten his name as soon as I'd heard it.

There was a lot of good-natured laughter at this.

I could understand why.

Dave took me by the hand and led me up a small slope behind the fire. A massive tent, unlike any I'd seen before, was erected there. Huge plastic sides making a dome shape. "This is the kitchen," Dave pulled across the flap and I saw that some people might have called it that. There was loads of tinned food, most notably huge tins of beans. A bottle of gas and a hob stood just inside the flap. There were bags of dried beans, the red-kidney variety and other weird things.

"We're all vegan 'ere," Dave explained.

"Vegan?" The word meant nothing to me.

"Ya know, strict veggies."

"No meat?"

"No meat, no fish, no cheese, no milk, no cream, nothfink from animals at all."

I was going to starve for the next two days. "Chips?" I asked pathetically.

Dave laughed, I think he thought I was joking. "We 'ad to move our kitchen," he went on as we left. "It used to be further down. Around there." He pointed to a patch in the distance.

I was about to ask why they moved it when he continued, "Bleedin' rats kept comin' in and nickin' our food."

"Rats?" My headache was booming now.

"Yeah, so we 'ad to move it." Dave pointed to a spot about a foot away from where we were standing, "There's their nest."

"Oh, Jesus!" I grabbed onto him and tried to run. "Oh Jesus. Why don't you just get rid of it?"

Seeing that he wasn't going to leg it with me, I ran past the rat's nest and waited for him to catch up.

There was a weird look on his face. "Disappointed" would have described it honestly. "It's their 'ome," he said flatly. "We're the interlopers, not them."

"Get lost!" I actually laughed. I really thought he was having me on. But he wasn't.

"They live 'ere, we don't."

He had a point in a weird, twisted logical way. "You have a point," I conceded, mentally noting that there was no way I was walking over this part of the woods on my own.

We'd reached another tent. "This one is where the nightwatch go," Dave put his fingers to his lips and opened the flap. Four people were lying curled up on the ground.

"They stay awake at night?"

"Yep."

"Why?"

We were walking further into the woods now. "'Cause bunches of lads think it's cool ta wreck our gear. They keep nickin' stuff and burnin' stuff, so we 'ave to stay awake."

It was like Cowboys and Indians. "And what happens if they do come, who fights them?"

Dave gave a slow grin. "We don't fight 'em, most times they get scared if they 'ear us about. We've got walkie-talkies and telephones to communicate with."

"Right."

He showed me where the toilet was. I won't even attempt to describe that and then he showed me his tree-house.

He climbed up a rope to get to it. "Come on, Jan, it's easy," he coaxed.

In the end, he actually had to haul me up on the rope.

His tree-house was a tree-slab. And that's being technical.

The wood for the house was attached onto the tree by ropes. "We don't 'ammer nails inta the tree for obvious reasons," he explained.

"Like the fact it might keep you alive if you did," I joked.

He didn't laugh at that either.

Mortified that I couldn't seem to please him on his home turf, I tried to make amends. "It must be great sleeping here."

"Yep, when the wind doesn't blow the shit outa ya."

"Still, it's nice."

He smiled. "I think so," he said simply.

And that was when I realised what it was.

The reason I was so attracted to him. He cared about things. A guy who cherished the rights of rats was a pretty weird guy. But pretty special too. I mean if he cared about them, what did it say for his feelings on everything else?

He had something that I'd lacked all my life. A blazing passion to care about things.

I hadn't cared about anything in a long, long time.

CHAPTER FORTY-TWO

School was a nightmare from which I thought I'd never wake up.

They'd all started singing 'Alleluia' behind my back as soon as I'd walked in and sat down. They were slagging my mam. She'd sung so loud in Mass on Sunday that when she'd sung the wrong words, everyone had known.

Walking from class to class was torture. No one would walk with me. I had to pretend I didn't care.

So Tuesday, I'd drunk three cans of lager to make me feel good. I'd found them in the press and liked the effect they had on me.

I'd gone into school, puked into someone's bag and collapsed on the floor.

They'd suspended me for a week.

Mam and Dad had gone mental. He because his booze was gone, and she because I'd made a show of them. She told me never to let myself down like that again.

The only thing was, they were the ones letting me down. They should've known how miserable I was. And if your mam and dad let you down, what else is left?

And if they didn't care, then why the fuck should I?

CHAPTER FORTY-THREE

Megan was the cook. At lunch-time she disappeared into the dome-like tent and fifty minutes later she emerged with the most horrific-looking meal I'd ever seen.

There were about twelve people around the fire at this stage. The four that had been asleep had awoken, rubbing their eyes and complaining about the weather. They were Irish, one of them had the thickest Tipp accent I'd ever heard. He kept talking to me and I hadn't a clue what he was on about.

"Something – something – something – boya."

"Is that right?"

"Yerrah – something – something else – cem-ment."

"Wow!"

"A millin pounds, something."

"Expensive – huh?"

"Yerrah."

Dave handed me a plate. "'Ope ya like bean curry."

"So do I," I said fervently.

A few of them laughed at that.

"Ah, Meg's a great cook, you'll like it." Sam was grinning over at me. "Ever eaten vegetarian before, Jan?"

"Nope."

"You'll like it!" Some Neanderthal individual gave me a thumbs-up from across the camp-fire.

Another person yelled, "If you don't give it to me!"

"Yerra – mutter – puzzling guttural grunt – boya!"

"I'll give it a try anyhow." I smiled shyly around.

Megan was behind me. A huge ladle of the runniest sloppiest array of beans ever was dished up to me. I stared forlornly at it. It wasn't that I was a fussy eater. In fact I wasn't really a dinner-eater at all, but I did eat. I ate to live. I thought I was going to lose a lot of weight over this weekend. "I've brown rice inside for it as well," Megan said. "Don't worry, it's not all you'll get."

"Great." The garlic smell from the food was strong enough to wipe out all living creatures within a mile radius.

A hen walked by me, clucking and pecking. I have to admit, I was sorely tempted. Just a little pressure on its neck, it wouldn't feel a thing . . .

Suddenly I had a great idea. "Do your hens not lay eggs?"

The silence around the fire was instantaneous.

"Can I not have an egg?"

"We're vegans," Dave had gone red. I think I'd embarrassed him. "We don't eat animal produce."

"Then why the hens?" I'd never wanted an egg more in my life.

"Someone donated them to us," Megan said softly, as she began to heap rice on people's plates. "We just look after them."

Dave came over and sat down beside me. His plate was heaped with food. "Tell ya wot," he grinned, "Tomorrow mornin' I'll find an egg for ya and cook it, all right?"

Sam was about to say something and Dave stared him down. "Jan's a guest," he said firmly, "she can 'ave wot she likes." Turning to me, he smiled, "Deal?"

"Yeah." A whole eighteen hours away! But he'd stood up for me and that's what mattered.

"Bon appitite so," he lifted his fork up and clinked it against mine.

Everyone began to eat.

In fairness, the food was all right. Megan had done a good job with weird ingredients. I ate almost a quarter of it. The Tipp fella entertained everyone with stories of his exploits aboard some ship he'd worked on. At the end of each story, everyone would laugh or clap. I hadn't a clue what he was saying. But I pretended to laugh along.

We all had hot water and biscuits afterwards. The biscuits were horrible. Plain boring dry biscuits. I couldn't wait to get back to the flat and munch my way through a packet of chocolate digestives. I'd welcome every black-head and pustule on my face in return for the luxury.

Everyone washed their own plates and the lads washed the pots and pans Megan had used. They were better organised than our flat.

During the afternoon, some people disappeared, while others stayed around the fire and talked. The rain had eased off and sunlight was slowly filtering down through the trees, making patterns on the ground beneath. They whole place had a really easy-going relaxed feel about it, even their humour was a quiet gentle laughter, not like the snorts and jibes I had got used to in work.

"Come on an' I'll show you wot they're plannin' on knockin' down to build the 'ouses on," Dave held out his hand to me. "It's not far."

Slowly, I got up from the up-ended tree-trunk I'd been sitting on. I didn't want to go anywhere, I'd got nice and comfortable listening to their chat. Dave clasped his hand in mine and feeling a thrill at his gesture, I followed him.

He led me through the forest, I don't know how he knew his way, until we came to a small clearing, high up, where we could look down on the camp.

Out of his pocket, Dave produced a large, technical map. Squatting down, he laid it on the ground and held it there with a few rocks.

"See 'ere," Dave pointed to a part of the map.

I hated maps. I had no sense of direction. Orienteering held more terror for me than complex brain surgery. I knew Dave would lose me in a mish-mash of jargon and geography.

"Yeah," I replied, doing my best to sound interested. "I see it."

"Well," Dave pointed to a load of trees, "That's

those trees over there. They're talkin' about rippin' 'em up and building 'ouses over there."

It didn't look too drastic. "Mmm."

"I mean," Dave settled himself, crossed-legged on the ground, "fink of all the animals that 'ave nests in those trees, loadsa species of birds will feckin' die, ya know."

Think of all the birds.

I felt a strange sensation creep up my spine. "Yeah," I gave an incredulous smile. "You're right."

Empowered, Dave pointed to the map again. "They'll knock those trees, but like, there's no mention of the damage to the roots of other trees, right?"

"Absolutely." Slowly, I was beginning to understand.

"Plus," Dave jabbed the map, "The drainage will be affected, fuckin' crap drainage, all the remaining trees will dehydrate."

He started to talk about alignment plans and drainage problems and I got lost somewhere in the middle. But I knew what he was saying. And for the first time since I met him, I understood where he was coming from.

Folding up the map, he began to shake his head. "I can't understand it, Jan," he said. "I tried an' I can't."

"Can't understand what?"

"Why they do it, why they wreck all the good parts."

"What? Like why they build on mountains?"

"Yeah." He'd begun to stand up. Folding up his map, he shoved it in his pocket. "Like, can't they see what they're doin'?"

"They can," I whispered, "but they don't care."

He put his arm around my shoulder and pulled me close. Kissing me gently on the cheek he said, "Just as well we do, then, huh?"

"Yeah," I said, surprised to realise it was true.

I spent the day exploring the mountainside with Dave. We walked through the forest and came out the other side. The air was really clean, really fresh. The smell of bog and heather and green grass was everywhere. Dave seemed to know every inch of the place and I was knackered trying to keep up with him. In the end we sat on some damp ground and he kissed me. The two of us lay side by side, just together, feeling each other's faces and kissing each others' fingertips. It was as if we were the only two people left in the whole world.

Around six, the sun went down. From a height, it looked magnificent. The sky became a huge multi-coloured easel, with a blood-red sun dominating the scene. Red and gold light spilled across our patch of ground.

"Isn't it beautiful?" It just seemed a lovely end to the afternoon.

Dave shrugged. "'Alf the chemicals in the ozone layer are making it so beautiful," he said. He stared at it for a bit. "D'ya know what the irony of it all is?" Without waiting for an answer, he went on, "A nuclear sunset is meant ta be the most beautiful spectacle of all."

I felt like belting him. Why did he have to spoil it?

341

Standing up, he stared across the mountain. "There was this guy, an Indian, Russell Means, right, and he said that one day Mother Earth will retaliate against being abused, that things always come full circle, and that that's what revolution is – the flip-side of the coin." He stopped and stared at me, "An' it's 'appening, Jan, people are dyin' 'cause of pollution in the atmosphere, cancers are killin' people that never should've been allowed 'appen. Lung cancers, skin cancers, you name it." He shoved his hands into his combats.

I stood up to join him. He was losing me again. This kind of stuff was too deep for me.

"People get sick anyhow."

"Yeah, before their time," Dave shook his head. "I believe so strongly in it all, Jan, you can never even come close, d'ya know."

His words shocked me. I didn't want to know what he was saying. "Come on," I pulled his arm. "Let's get back."

He allowed me to lead him back to the forest. Once inside, he took over. He started pointing out all the trees to me and telling me what they were. "Ya can tell by the leaves," he said, pointing to a huge one. "This 'ere's an oak, a big Sissile oak." He banged it hard on the trunk. "Beautiful, ain't she?"

For some reason, my heart twisted. If I had two huge pins, I would've stuck them into him to stop him from flying. But then, he wouldn't have been so beautiful himself.

"Lovely," I agreed.

CHAPTER FORTY-FOUR

There was a party that night in the forest.

Drinking was not allowed on site. Apparently it gave a bad impression to visitors. The gas thing about the party was that everyone tidied up afterwards.

It had stared raining again. In fact, the night was totally miserable. Megan was off under a tree smoking a joint. She was lying back with a calm relaxed look on her face. Catching my eyes, she held it up to me. "Want some?" she mouthed.

I didn't care that my mascara was running down my face and stinging my eyes, which meant I was well on. I'd lost count of the number of cans I'd had. But it was easy to talk to people so I'd had at least five.

"Want some?" Megan again held up her joint.

Stumbling over, I sat in beside her. "Why not?" Taking it from her, I stared at it. I'd never had this stuff before. What was I supposed to do?

"Just inhale," Megan said. "Big deep pull on it."

So I did. I ended up coughing my guts up and somewhere, in the fog, she started laughing at me.

"Novice," she teased.

"I'll stick with this," I held up my can and took a gulp. "Safer."

Megan nudged me. "Here he is," she whispered. "Lover boy."

Dave was making his way over. He didn't look too happy. Sitting beside us, he said, "I'm on watch tonight, Jay's plastered."

"So?"

"So, you'll 'ave to go to bed without me."

"Can't someone else do it?" I stared at him. Spend the night in his tree-house without him? "There has to be someone else?"

"I was asked," Dave stood up. "Sorry, Jan."

"Dave!"

"Leave him," Megan pulled me down. "He won't listen anyhow."

"He will." Pulling myself from her grasp I ran after him. "Dave, come on," I tugged at his sleeve. "You can't leave me on my own."

"Watch with me then," he offered.

I blinked. "I'd never stay awake."

"Well, then," he shrugged, "it's your choice."

"She can stay in my tent," Megan came up behind us. "Stay in with me, Jan."

"Ta." Dave smiled at Megan and turned away. "See yas in the mornin'."

I couldn't believe it! The nerve! "Bastard," I muttered, flinging down my can. "He was going to leave me on my own."

"You'd have been safe enough." There was a hint of amusement in Megan's voice. "Well, from wild animals anyhow, I dunno about the lads," she gestured around at the ten or so fellas who were starting a sing-song.

I didn't smile. I'd wanted a nice romantic night in the forest, just me and him.

Megan began to lead me away from everyone. I said nothing as she brought me up the hill towards her tent. "In here," she unzipped the entrance and I crawled inside. It was a two-man tent, so there was room for both of us.

"I better get my sleeping-bag," I said.

Megan threw me a blanket. "Here, this'll do. Your bag's down in the kitchen, it's too far to walk in the dark." She turned and began pulling out more stuff. "I've got a spare inflatable mattress here and a double sleeping-bag, if you want."

I didn't even bother asking who usually shared the sleeping-bag with her. "Fine," I muttered, still feeling acutely pissed off. Just when I thought he was being a normal boyfriend and everything . . .

Megan, unselfconsciously began to pull off her clothes. She rooted around and found a tatty tee-shirt and pulled it over her head. "All right?" she asked.

I wasn't a bit all right. Sobriety had returned and I realised that I had no cleanser, toner and moisturiser to get my make-up off. I had nowhere to wash my face. I had no pyjamas to wear.

"I have to get my bag," I said. "I've, eh, no pyjamas."

"Here, have a tee-shirt." Megan tossed a tee-shirt my way.

"I've left all my make-up on."

I could see the curl of a smile. "Take it off in the morning."

"Oh, I can't."

"Well," Megan curled herself up inside the sleeping-bag, "off you go and get your bag, if you want."

I wanted to go, but things like the rats' nests and darkness stopped me. I knew when I was beaten. "All right," I began to wrench off my jumper and pull the shirt over my head. "I'll do it in the morning." When I was ready, I climbed into the sleeping-bag.

I lay for a while, staring into the blackness of the tent. The sounds of the party could be heard in the distance, the faint strains of music floated on the air.

"He's a nice guy," Megan said suddenly, "just don't get too involved."

I jerked at the sound of her voice, I thought she was asleep. "Dave?" I asked.

"Yeah," Megan confirmed. She was staring upwards and not at me at all. "I've known Davy a good few years, I've met him on loads of protests." She paused and said cautiously, "I've even slept with him on a few occasions."

It was just as well it was dark. My face burned. "So?" I managed to say. Suddenly I wanted to get out of that tent. What did she think she was doing, telling me all this?

Megan turned towards me and lifted herself up on

one elbow, "I'm not trying to hurt you Jan," she said, "I'm just telling you how it is. He's a nice guy but he's out to save the world, ya know?"

I turned away and stared at the wall of the tent. "I'm only having a bit of fun," I said. "It's not as if I'm hearing wedding bells."

"Good," Megan said. "Because the only sound Davy hears is the groaning of a planet waiting to be rescued. It's in his head all the time."

I turned to face her, though I couldn't see her in the dark. "Don't make fun of him," I said annoyed. "I like the way he is."

"I'm not making fun," Megan replied. "I'm just telling you how it is." A bit of a pause before she said, "Davy is a one-man crusade. If he didn't have us with him, he'd still go it alone." She stopped. "Has he told you how he got involved?"

"He was a builder who had a major attack of conscience, or something, that's what he said." I spat the words out.

Megan had a smile in her voice. "He was more than a builder," she said. "He co-owned a big property-development company. Him and his daddy. We're talking rolling in it Jan. The guy was loaded."

"What?" I gave a nervous laugh. "You're telling me he gave it all up?" I thought of the mud and the rain and the tents. "He gave it all up to come here?"

"Yeah." Megan nodded. "He donated every bean he had to every campaign he's been involved in and now, well, he's broke." She laughed. "Like the rest of us."

I didn't know what to say. Cute, handsome, artless Dave had actually owned a business. Cute, handsome, artless, totally mental Dave had jacked it all in to march about in Somme-like conditions.

"All I'm saying is," Megan went on, "that he's given everything up for what he believes is right." She sighed and said in a horrible pitying voice. "He's not going to stay around."

I wished she'd shut up.

My wish was granted. She turned her back on me and snuggled back into her sleeping-bag.

"Night, Jan."

She was only being possessive, just because he didn't want her anymore. Dave wasn't going to leave me. I tried to make my voice sleepy. Giving a yawn I said, "See you in the morning."

The tee-shirt and air-bed were soaked.

Stepping carefully over Megan's sleeping body, I went outside the tent and sat in the rain. It was early dawn and some birds were singing.

The rain drizzled onto me and I was glad of it. At least it meant that when she woke, I'd have an excuse for my damp hair and sopping shirt.

CHAPTER FORTY-FIVE

Megan couldn't believe that I loved the morning rain so much that I'd sit in it and get soaked. She told them all about my weird ways as we sat around the fire at breakfast.

By this stage, I'd managed to wash my face in a stream and cleanse, tone and moisturise it. There was no water to wash in and my hair hung lankly around my face. I'm sure I looked a state. I'd no make-up on as I'd forgotten a mirror. Feeling wet, tired and spotty, I sat down and watched Megan as she dished up the breakfast.

Most of them were eating dry bread.

A good fry-up was what I craved. Sizzling sausages, rashers, pudding and fried bread all heaped up on a plate.

Dave wasn't anywhere. Sam said that he was sleeping the night off in the other tent.

"Any trouble last night?" a tall blondy guy I thought was Jay asked. I glared over at him.

Sam shook his head. "Quiet enough, Davy said."

The guy beside me tipped me on the knee. "Sorry about last night," he said softly. "I forgot I was on watch, so I ended up getting smashed. Davy offered to take over."

I stopped glaring at the blonde fella and stared at the red-headed guy. "Dave offered?"

"Yeah. Sorry again."

Dave offered? It was like a blow in the stomach. He said he'd been asked. I began to swirl my tea about in my cup envisioning what I'd say when Dave woke.

Megan tipped me on the shoulder. She was grinning. Holding a piece of paper towards me, she said, "Dave left an egg for you inside – read that."

I recognised Dave's writing from the other note he'd written me. Heart pounding, in case it was a note to *her*, I began to read. A few of the lads gawked over my shoulder.

Megs, he'd written, *I've put an egg in the cooler bag for Jan. I spent about two fucking hours looking for it last night, following the bleeding hens everywhere to see where they laid. If you don't cook it, I'll kill meself.*

There was a guffaw of laughter from the fellas and Megan giggled.

"Head-case isn't he?"

I couldn't look up in case they'd see the tears in my eyes. The wild flowers were one thing but this egg had got to be the most romantic thing anyone had ever done for me.

"What'll it be?" Megan asked, "Boiled? Fried? Poached?"

I wished I could bring the egg home with me and look at it. But that was being stupid. "Boiled," I smiled back. Hoping no one would notice, I slipped Dave's note into the pocket of my jeans.

At least I could keep that.

I kept walking by the tent and making noise. In the end, when no one was looking I opened it up and went inside. Four people, like yesterday, were sprawled out on the floor. Dave was on the outside. He was lying on his back with his hands curled into fists on either side of his head. I smiled as I thought of him scouring the undergrowth for an egg for my breakfast and I forgave him for the fact that he'd volunteered to do a night-watch. He was just that sort of fella. Considerate.

And it was an alien concept for me.

I couldn't believe what Megan had said about him being loaded. He didn't look the business-tycoon type. But then again, I'd never met any business tycoons so I wouldn't know. I was just leaving when I heard a whisper, "Hi, gorgeous."

Turning, I saw Dave observing me through slitted eyes. A faint grin played about his lips, "All right?"

I stood in the doorway. "Thanks for the egg."

"That fuckin' egg!" He rolled his eyes and smiled. "Never again."

He emerged from his sleeping-bag. To my disappointment, he was fully dressed. Quietly, he crept out of the tent with me. "'Ave I missed breakfast?"

"Hours ago," I smiled up at him.

He clasped my hands and I walked with him to the fire. "Sorry, man," Jay said when he saw him. "I'll do your shift next time."

"Bloody sure ya will," Dave accepted some water from Sam and curled his hands about the mug. "Wrecked all me plans."

"Sorry."

Dave nodded and began to drink his hot water.

They were so civilised!

"We've a meeting tonight," Sam said, "it's about the appeal." Turning to me, he explained, "We've lodged an appeal against the planning permission and it's being decided next week. If it's refused, we have to decide what we're going to do about it."

Dave was munching some bread. "Crowley coming?"

"Yeah." Again Sam looked at me. "Crowley's our solicitor."

"A solicitor?"

"Yeah, he's taken our case on."

I couldn't believe it. Where would they get the cash for a solicitor? "That must cost you a fortune."

"He don't charge," Dave said, draining his cup, "he's dead on."

"So will you be here?" Sam asked Dave. He looked pointedly at me. "I mean, you've to bring Jan back."

"Aw, yeah," Dave nodded, "sure I'm 'eading 'ome with Jan in a bit. She's seen it all now, 'aven't ya?"

"Yeah," I answered.

"You'll have to come again," Sam said. He smiled at me, "We'll be here for ages yet."

"She'll be back," Dave answered for me. "She loves it 'ere, don't ya?"

I looked at the fire and the mud and the soaking tents. "It's grand," was about all I could manage.

"If she had a shower and a Jacuzzi, she'd like it, huh Jan?" It was Megan, creeping up behind me.

Dave's laughter rang out. "That about sums it up," he agreed.

I felt like killing Megan. It was all right for her, she didn't need cosmetics to make her beautiful, but I did. I smiled though, in case they thought that I couldn't laugh at myself.

"Come on, Jan," Dave said, putting his mug on the ground, "lets get ya 'ome where ya can feel normal again." He helped me gather up my stuff and together we began the two-mile trek to the bus stop.

"Did ya like it?" Dave anxiously scoured my face. "I know it's a bit rough, but well, what ya don't 'ave ya never miss."

"It's my turn to bring you out next, remember?" I poked him in the stomach, side-stepping the question. "So give me a ring during the week, right?"

His eyes seemed to cloud over, then he blinked and the openness was there again. "Next week, I promise."

And I knew he would.

CHAPTER FORTY-SIX – TUESDAY

I was getting used to the hospital at this stage. The biopsy would be a cake-walk. Hadn't the receptionist said so? No big deal, or something like that, was what she'd said. So I hadn't thought about it. I hadn't had the time to think about it.

Al had offered to come with me again but I'd told him I didn't need him. If he'd come with me, it'd be a sign that I was worried and I wasn't.

Rummaging through my over-stocked-with-useless-things bag, I located my library book. I'd brought it to read while I waited. Reading something, especially something as boring-looking as this book, would make me appear intelligent.

It was the second library book I'd got out in about ten years. The first was taken out last week after I'd slept with Dave. It had been brilliant. It was called, *How to Keep your Man*.

The librarian had given me such a look of scorn as she'd blipped it through on her computer, but I hadn't cared. She was probably just a hormonal old biddy.

Anyway, the book had advised me to cultivate the same interests as my man. So I'd got a book out called, *The Greener Earth*. This was the tome I was valiantly ploughing through as I waited for the biopsy.

It was hard to concentrate on reading because the noise in the hospital was unbelievable. Echoes of feet along the corridors, trolleys squeaking, kids crying, telephones ringing. The noise, plus my lack of interest in the Green Earth issue, made me fold up my book and lean back in my chair.

My biopsy was at eleven – it was ten past the hour now.

The hospital was hot, very hot. That's the thing I hated most about it, the fact that the air was so drenched with heat. I started to pull my jumper over my head when my name was called.

The most sickening feeling I had yet experienced took me over. I could literally feel the blood drain away from my head and, as I stood up, the ground beneath me shifted. Steadying myself against the back of the chair, I followed the nurse into a room. I couldn't let them see how I felt.

I was examined again. All my glands were felt and prodded.

"We're just going to take a sample of tissue from the gland under your arm, all right?" The girl was smiling at me.

I thought I should smile back. "Fine."

She injected the area and made it numb.

My poor arm.

A needle of the most horrifying length was produced and I knew I was going to faint. "Don't do it," I remember saying. "Please."

They didn't hear me, so I don't know if I really did say it out loud. Maybe my mind was so loud in my head, that it felt like I said it.

The girl smiled at me again. "It won't hurt," she said, "The tip of the needle is so fine, there won't even be a scar."

I wanted to tell her to stop smiling and lying to me.

But she was right. I didn't feel it. They explained what they were doing, taking a small amount of my gland and smearing it on a slide, so that some guy could look at it and decide what was wrong.

So simple.

"Done," the girl smiled. "Do you feel OK?"

I was afraid to touch my arm. So I just put on my shirt and didn't look at it. "Fine," I answered, the relief making me smile again. "I'm grand." I concentrated on buttoning myself up.

"See you so." She opened the door for me.

"I hope not," I managed a laugh. It was a joke, but I meant it.

I'd taken the day off work. It was a treat I'd promised myself, I'd go to the hospital, get the biopsy and then slob out for the day. I bought myself a bottle of wine and, despite my better judgement, had allowed myself to be persuaded to purchase two huge bars of chocolate and a giant bag of crisps in Rob's Foodstore.

I'd been fleeced of a fiver.

Bastards!

Letting myself into the flat, I dumped my purchases onto the table. All I wanted to do was to get drunk and watch telly. Munching on the extra-expensive crisps, I searched for a bottle-opener. Finding it, I opened the bottle of wine, and began to drink it by the neck. It was nice wine, really easy to drink. It slid down my throat and spread through the whole of me. Soon, as the bottle neared its end, I realised that nothing was ever too bad, that I had so much going for me that it shouldn't matter if I had the odd glitch now and again. I mean, I was Janet Boyle, I had a typing job and a nice place to live. I was sleeping with the sexiest guy I'd ever met and he was going to ring me.

What more could a girl want?

CHAPTER FORTY-SEVEN – WEDNESDAY

My head had exploded in my sleep. There was a burning pain in my neck and arm. My ears were on fire from the sound of my alarm clock. Very slowly, I opened my eyes. The glare of light through the curtains seemed to scorch them in their sockets.

I was in a bad bad way.

The alarm wasn't what had woken me. It had been another sound.

If I concentrate hard enough through the pain, I'd hear it again.

Knock. Knock. Knock.

Someone was tapping on my wee small door. The lines of the Walter de la Mare poem went flitting through my brain.

"Yeah?"

The door creaked open and Abby's face peered in. "Hiya," she whispered. "How's the drunken sailor?" There was a big gooey smile on her face.

An image of me singing began to solidify in my

head. "What?" I tried to lift myself up and my whole stomach revolted.

My neck burned with pain.

"Hey, ho, for the drunken sailor," Abby did a funny song and dance routine in front of my bed. "D'you remember?"

I searched my head. A painful snap-shot surfaced, foggy but crucifyingly mortifying. "Was Mickey there?"

I knew he had been. I wanted to die.

Abby nodded. "You tried to get him to do a dirty dance routine with you."

One bottle of wine was all it took for me to find any man irresistible. Bad eyesight would have been cheaper. "Sorry, Ab," I closed my eyes and lay back on the bed. "Tell him I'm sorry."

"He thought you were mental," Abby laughed. "He said that both my flat-mates were mental. He said that Beth was a manless frustrated thirty-something and that you were . . ." she stopped. I think she realised she'd opened her mouth too wide again.

"Well?" I lay still, wanting to hear the worst. That way, it'd be over and I could get up.

"He said that – that – " she began to flounder, "that you were a laugh," she finished weakly.

"You're lying, Ab."

"I know," she said, "but I wasn't supposed to say anything."

"What did he say?"

"Look Jan," she jumped up from the bed, making it

rise, the motion of which set my head into spin mode. "Do you want a cuppa and a solpadine?"

I knew she wouldn't tell me what strait-laced Mickey had said now. "All right," I agreed, "but get me two tablets. I feel rotten."

I lay still and listened to her making the tea. Five minutes later she was back in to me. She sat down on the bed and handed me the tea and tablets. "Thanks."

Almost gagging on the tea, I swallowed the tablets. "Thanks," I said again.

"So what happened?" Abby had her concerned face on. "Did Dave do the dirt on you?"

"Why?" I couldn't understand what was making her ask me that.

"Why what?"

"Why are you asking me that? Why do you think something happened?"

She shrugged. "Well, I just thought you must be drowning your sorrows by getting drunk last night." She gave a small smile. "A whole bottle of wine, Jan. Come on!"

"I just felt like a drink," I said. I took a cautious sip of tea, "I had a day off and so I just got drunk." The tea still made me feel sick, even the smell of it was revolting. I put it down.

"So it's still on with you and Dave?"

"Yep."

Abby looked relieved. "Great." Smiling ruefully, she said, "I was afraid it was another disaster for you, I was afraid you'd be suicidal today."

"Thanks for the vote of confidence."

"I don't mean that I really thought it was over," she reddened as she tried to smooth things out, "but, Jan, come on, you and men . . . "

"I know." I did know.

Sometimes, when things went badly for me I confided in Abby. It was her job to prop me up during the dark months of the soul. She did this by listening, by offering advice, which I never took and getting drunk with me. After a while, I'd calm down, swear I didn't need a man to feel worthwhile and spend the rest of the time looking out for one.

I think she was afraid I'd crash-landed again.

"Dave and I are fine," I said.

"I'm glad," she smiled at me as she left.

The tablets took a while to work, but eventually my headache and sickness seemed to be abating. I decided to venture out of bed. That went fine.

Getting dressed, I pulled on my clothes in slow motion. It stopped that horrible jarring sensation in my head. The pain in my neck and arm wasn't lessening though, but I'd just have to live with that. By nine fifty, I was standing at the bus stop, ready to head into work.

Work being the operative word. Henry was ready to erupt when I walked in the door. "Give the girl a fuckin' clap," he roared as I entered. "Round of applause for turning up."

Ignoring him, I muttered an apology to Lenny, who

didn't look too happy either. "We start work here at nine," he said. "Remember that now."

Normally Lenny's remarks would have me sniggering to myself. Today, I felt hurt. I had a hangover and I'd been in for tests. It wasn't fair.

Taking a deep breath, so that I wouldn't cry, I turned away and began heading to my desk. I'd just sat down when a letter was slapped in front of me. "Type that now," Henry hissed. "I needed it first thing this morning – righ'!"

The words of the letter fuzzed over as a rebel tear seeped from under my eyes. I took the letter up and stared at it, so that he wouldn't see me crying.

I wished I'd rung in sick.

"I want it in ten minutes," Henry shouted from across the office. "It's very fuckin' urgent."

"Give her a break." It was Al.

"And who the fuck is askin' you?" Henry snapped. "The girl was supposed to do it on Monday for me. Then she says she'd do it Tuesday and hey, she wasn't in yesterday." His voice was redirected over to me. "Isn't that right, Miss Boyle?"

I nodded. I'd my back to both of them and my hands shook as I tried to flick on my computer. More tears had forced their way out now.

"See!" Henry sounded triumphant. "See."

I heard Al getting up from his desk and coming over to me. He bent down in front of me. "Don't mind him," he whispered. "He's in shite form, has been all day yesterday. Jimmy Madden came down like a tonne of bricks on him for being out."

"Yeah," was all I could manage back.

"Hey," Al had seen my tears. "Don't." I don't think he knew what to do. "Don't Jan."

"You got that letter yet?" Henry shouted.

"Will you leave her alone," Al shouted back.

"Now, now lads," Lenny said mildly. "Calm down."

"I'll have it in a minute," I said, my voice was shaking and I gave a big sniff. "Just give me a minute."

"Are you all right, Jan? Liz spoke for the first time. She'd had her head buried in one of those self-help interview books and, at the sound of my snivelling, had taken an interest.

"Fine," I said shakily. "Fine."

"You don't sound fine," Lenny was stating the blindingly obvious for anyone who'd missed it.

"There's no fuckin' major hurry with that letter," Henry said, his voice sounding a bit guilty. "Just today would do."

"No, no," I couldn't look at any of them. "I'm doing it now."

"Great girl," Lenny said. "Great."

Al stayed for a few more seconds beside me. Then he give me a quick rub on the shoulder before wandering back to his own desk.

Soon the only sounds to be heard was the scrape of pens and the click of my computer keys. It was oddly comforting.

CHAPTER FORTY-EIGHT – THURSDAY

I wasn't allowed eat before my scan. That's what had been written down on my appointment card. When I got to the hospital I was given a liquid thing to drink and then, when I finally made it to the x-ray department, I had to drink the stuff again.

At this stage I was getting totally fed up with being in the hospital. Everyone was being really nice to me and I was being really nice to everyone. They smiled, I smiled back. Everything was done with an air of calm about it, but hey, this was me and I wasn't calm. I wasn't sure how I was when they led me into this room with what looked like a Stephen King instrument of terror in the middle.

"Just lie there," yet another smiley person told me. She pointed to a flat slab. It was like something in a mortuary. "And stay very still."

Climbing up, I lay down on it. I don't think I could have moved for the terror invading me. Above the slab was a big hood. The nurse tapped a few buttons and explained, "This," she pointed to the hood, "is going to rotate about your body taking pictures of your tissues and bones. That way we can build up a 3-D picture of you."

Who'd want a 1-D picture of me, I wondered glumly. But, I smiled gallantly and thanked her for explaining it to me.

"So just stay very still," she said again. "It should only take about forty minutes."

I really can't remember too much after that. I closed my eyes and blocked out the humming and whirring of the huge camera that could see more of me than I ever would.

I closed my eyes and thought about Dave. His phone call was the only thing keeping me going. He'd rung last night and after a horrible day it was just what I needed.

"Hi gorgeous," he said, his accent making me weak. "Wot's the story?"

"I'm bringing you to the cinema," I said, "Saturday."

"Great." He sounded as if he was smiling. "Look forward to it."

"So will I." I was smiling too. Then I thought of my book. *How to Keep your Man*. "How did your meeting go?" I asked, "Did your solicitor have good news?"

"So, so," he replied, "won't know till next week." Someone said something to him. "Eh, Jan," he said hastily, "'Ave ta go, someone else wants the line."

"Right, see you at eight, outside my place on

Saturday," I yelled, hoping he hadn't switched the phone off. "And be on time!"

The line had gone dead.

I was vaguely aware that the machine had stopped. Opening my eyes, I saw the girl coming towards me. "You were nice and relaxed," she joked, "I was wondering if you'd gone to sleep on us."

"Not a hope," I said.

She gave a sympathetic smile. "It wasn't too bad though, was it?"

"It was grand."

I was using that word a lot these days – grand. A real nondescript word. A word that meant big and not fine at all.

Maybe that's why I was using it.

CHAPTER FORTY-NINE – SATURDAY

Dave was half an hour early for our date. I was disgusted that Beth and Abby weren't there to note it.

Beth had gone to visit her dad. She'd been in a weird mood all week and both Abby and I were glad when she left.

Abby wasn't in because she spent the whole day with Mickey. He'd called for her at twelve and the two of them had gone off for a picnic. A picnic in April. It was pathetic.

And Dave was early and no one to witness it.

He bounced in the door, all beautiful six foot two of him. "Jan," he smiled down at me, "I missed ya!" He was dressed in jeans and a sweatshirt. A sweat shirt with a big tree on it. To be honest, if I'd seen any other man wearing a sweatshirt with a tree on it, I'd have stayed well clear. But it was Dave and he lived in a tree – what more can I say?

"Did you really?" I asked, giving my hair a final brush before I left.

"Wot?"

"Miss me!" I gave him a belt. "You said you missed me."

"Oh, I did." He grinned. "I missed ya loads." He held the door open for me and together we walked out of the flat. "So, Jan," he slung his arm about my shoulder and pulled me to him, "'ow was your week?"

It was then that I decided not to tell Dave about my tests. Not unless there was something to tell. I wanted to enjoy being with him, laugh with him, not burden him down with problems. What fella went for a girl with problems? "It was all right," I answered. "I had work."

"An' that says it all," he smiled.

"And yours?"

"Not too bad. We 'ad a right session on Wednesday night, I got legless."

I felt the tug on my heart. The thought that he could enjoy himself without me. Gazing up into his face, I saw that he was grinning.

"Some geezer donated a pile a booze an' we all got stuck in."

"Megan too?" I had to ask. It was childish, but I had to.

"Oh yeah," Dave nodded. "She's a real party girl, is Megs."

I wondered if he'd sleep with two women at the one time.

"Her fella 'ad to drag 'er back to 'er tent."

"What?"

"Megan's fella. Wot's 'is name," Dave made a face as

he tried to remember. "The tall geezer with the dog, remember 'im?" Then he shook his head. "Naw, you wouldn't, 'e only arrived Monday. Anyway, 'e 'ad to 'aul 'er back to 'er tent."

He couldn't understand why I squeezed him around the waist. Gazing into my face, he gave a slow smile. "I like your 'air like that," he remarked as he kissed the top of my head.

I knew it was going to be a great night.

The film was good, I enjoyed it. Dave grumbled about people spending millions on films when there were trees to be saved.

"A quarter of the budget for that film and the mountains could be saved," he said, as we made our way out. "It's crap, Jan, so it is."

"Good film though," I wasn't going to let him spoil it for me. "They did a good job with their millions."

He gave me a shove. "Capitalist."

I shoved him back. "Idealist."

"Naw, realist," he corrected. His eyes grew serious. "I live in the real world, ya know. I'm not some 'ippy dope 'ead."

I'd offended him. "Sorry," I said. I didn't want him to think I made fun of him. "It was just a joke."

"I'm a realistic idealist," he grinned. "'Ow about that?"

"Done."

He began to pull me towards O'Connell Street. "Let's find a nice boozer," he said, "And I'll buy."

That was an offer I couldn't refuse. We were

debating which pub to give our custom to when we heard, "Jan!" The voice made my heart lurch. "Jan!"

"Is someone calling ya?" Dave began to look around.

I tried to keep my head buried. Maybe they were calling another Jan.

"Janet, we thought it was you!"

Still staring at the ground, I could see the white Nike runners my mother always wore and the shiny squeaky shoes my dad wore.

"Hello, hello," Dad said. "Now there's a surprise."

"Mam, Dad, hi," I smiled lamely.

"Out for the night?" My mother was busy sizing up Dave. She stood beside me expectantly, awaiting an introduction.

"Yeah, I was."

Dad put his arm around my mam and gave her a squeeze. "We went to see an ould romantic film," he said. "She's gone all frisky on me."

"Dad!" I reddened as Dave gave a guffaw behind me.

"She has now and no mistake."

"Oh Des," Mam flapped her arm at him. "Stop it."

"Dave." Dave surprised me my shoving his hand out to both of them. "'Ow's it goin'?"

"Hello, Dave," Mam had her posh voice on. "I'm Margaret and this is Des."

"Pleased ta meet ya."

"And you too son," Dad was pumping Dave's arm up and down. "Very pleased to meet you indeed."

There was a silence. I didn't know what to say, I just wanted them to go away.

"Well," Dad smiled, "I suppose we'd better be going home, it's getting fierce late now."

"D'ya want ta join Jan an' me for a drink?" Dave asked and I could have kicked him. "We're just 'aving one."

"Oh, now, I dunno," Dad muttered. "We don't want to cramp your style."

Mam said nothing. She gazed at me.

I turned away.

Dave nudged me and I ignored him.

Dad was hopping from foot to foot. He didn't want to agree in case Mam ate him out of it for going into a pub.

"Jan'd like it," Dave said. "Wouldn't ya?"

"Yeah." I said it without too much conviction and I despised myself for it. The last thing I needed was Mam and Dad boring Dave senseless as they talked about their extension. He'd be sure to go right off me if Dad started onto him about the horrors of living in a house with four women. And if by chance he should launch into a description of the house, I'd die.

Mam got the hint. Very gently, she began to drag Dad away. "Another time," she smiled, "when we're not in so much of a hurry."

"But we're not – " Dad attempted to say before she told him to shut it.

"Bye now," she said, smiling at the two of us.

They walked hand in hand down the street.

"They're young, your folks," Dave remarked, staring after them. "They seem like a good laugh."

"They're great," I felt I had to say something to make it up to my parents. "Really nice."

"And the shoes yer dad 'ad on – great."

"Ha, ha," I wasn't amused. In fact I was a bit disappointed. I didn't think Dave'd be into making smart comments on Dad's patent plastics.

"No leather in 'em at all," Dave enthused, missing my sarcasm. "Cool guy."

I wanted to say that Dad was actually quite a sweaty guy, especially when he wore those shoes, but I kept my mouth shut.

Dave took my hand again and began to lead me to one of the pubs he'd plumped for earlier.

I made no protest, I just wanted to get off the street before I met anyone else.

Fumbling about in the pockets of his jeans, Dave pulled out a handful of loose change. "So wot's it to be?" he asked.

I decided on a vodka and coke and watched him as he made his way to the bar. I knew I was meant to find a seat for us but I couldn't take my eyes off him. I was so lucky. He was such a decent guy and he was all mine. I watched every move of him, the way he paid for the drinks, the way he nodded to the barman, the way other girls scrutinised him and, best of all, the way he didn't seem to notice it.

Turning back and making his way towards me he shook his head. "That's a great seat ya found there, Jan," he mocked. "Brilliant."

"I'll stand if you will."

"Cheers," he handed me my drink and we clinked glasses.

CHAPTER FIFTY – SUNDAY

The phone rang. I jumped to answer it in order to get myself away from some potentially nauseatingly romantic exchange between Abby and Mickey.

We were sitting in the kitchen eating a late breakfast. Dave, after spending the night, had left really early and I was stuck with the gruesome twosome as breakfast companions.

"Hello?" I said into the phone.

"Janet." It was my mother. She's the only one who calls me by my full name. "So you're up."

"Obviously."

She laughed a bit at that. "Just calling to make sure you got back from town last night."

"Safe and sound." I knew she wanted to ask about Dave but I wouldn't make it easy for her. Anyway, when she heard he was an eco-warrior, the shit would probably hit the fan.

"Was that boy your boyfriend?" She attempted an off-hand, throw-away tone.

"What boy?" I did the same.

There was a brief silence. "Dave."

"Oh him," I laughed. "He's a man."

"Very droll, Janet." She didn't sound as if she thought it was in the least bit funny. "So is he your boyfriend?"

"Yeah, he is."

Now would come the twenty questions.

"He seemed nice," she said. "Your dad liked him," her voice dropped, so that Dad wouldn't hear. "Well, anyone that invites your father to the pub gets his vote."

We both laughed a bit at that.

"So how did you meet him?"

Question number one.

"I met him in town a few weeks ago." I wondered if I should elaborate and save her the trouble of thinking up tactful questions. "He was staging a protest against building on the mountainside."

"Oh."

"He's an eco-warrior."

That stumped her. "Sorry? He's a what?"

"A New Age traveller." I don't know if they're the same thing or not, but that's what I said.

"A *traveller*?" She sounded a bit shocked. "He's from the travelling community?"

"Not exactly."

"What do you mean 'not exactly'?" Her voice had risen. "I mean, it's not as if I've anything against travellers as *people*, it's just that, well, I don't want my daughter going around in a caravan with them."

She was being very open-minded. Very PC.

I decided to put her mind at rest. "He's not a *traveller* traveller. He's more an environmentalist. He travels around the world trying to save it."

"I see." Whenever she says that it means she doesn't see at all. The bigness of Dave's aims hadn't impressed her one bit.

"He's a nature lover."

"I see."

"He lives in a tree-house." Why I said that, I don't know. I think I must've been trying to shock her.

"A tree-house."

"Yep."

Abby and Mickey were gone quiet behind me, either they were listening in or had left the room. Turning around, I saw Abby making slashing motions with her throat and rolling her eyes.

I grinned and rolled my eyes back.

"Janet," Mam said, in what for her was a reasonable voice, "why don't you get a nice normal boy, one who does normal things."

This was the woman who talked about normal? "Like Dad, you mean?"

"Yes, like your father."

She meant it too. Her voice brimmed over with conviction. "He's got a job, he's ambitious, funny, dynamic, interested in doing things."

I couldn't think of anything to say in the face of such blind adoration. Dad was not normal, Dad had never been normal, Dad was a one-off. Dave at least had other people like him.

"Dave's a nice guy," I defended him. "He treats me well and that's what's important."

"*Hear,* hear!" Abby shouted from behind.

"Who's that?" Mam asked.

"Just Abby – she's talking to someone."

"Oh," Mam replied. Then back on track, she said, "He's English, isn't he?"

"Yeah."

"Catholic?"

"He calls himself a pagan."

"Wonderful."

"Paganism pre-dates Catholicism," I said what Dave had told me, "Easter is an old pagan feast meaning rebirth," she paused. "Or fertility."

"Great." The conversation was coming to a close. Whenever she used words like 'wonderful' and 'great' in a sarcastic context she was contemplating putting the phone down.

"I'm glad you liked him though," I couldn't resist saying. "He's really nice."

She went on, "I just don't want to think of you with some weirdo," delicate pause, "like that other time, the time . . ." She couldn't even bring herself to finish the sentence. It was the only time she'd ever met a guy I'd been with and unfortunately she'd got totally the wrong impression of my life style.

"Dave's not like that."

Her voice dropped, it became really unlike her. "I hope not," she said. "Janet, we worry, your dad and I, we don't understand what you want out of – "

I didn't need this. "Dave's a great guy," I said firmly.

"I'm sure he is." She didn't sound sure.

"An orgasm on legs," Abby chortled, whispering it in my ear, so that Mickey wouldn't hear.

Pushing Abby away and trying to keep my voice straight, I said, "Anyway, I've to go. I'll talk to you soon."

"Talk soon," Mam said as she put the phone down.

"Bye." I put the receiver down and turned on Abby. "You are dead."

She squealed as I picked up the cushion and aimed it at her.

I was twenty-one, two years out of home. Living life in the fast lane, enjoying my freedom and all the rubbish a weekly wage packet could buy – booze, make-up and more booze. I was working in a chipper and every week after getting paid, we'd all go on the tear.

It was the Saturday after my twenty-first and Mario, the guy that owned the chipper, had suggested that we all head out for a drink. So that night, whoever was off early headed down to the pub. By early, I mean four o'clock.

I drank cocktails through a straw. From four to eleven..

I got smashed. So smashed that after nine, I can't remember a thing. So smashed that I woke up the next morning and there was a fella beside me in the bed and I didn't know who he was. The only thing I can remember about him is that he had red hair and freckles and a smell of booze off him that would intoxicate a horse. I felt sick when I realised what I'd done or must have done.

How could I face him?

So I kicked him, hoping he'd waken and sneak away like some of the horrible sleazy guys I'd met. *Please go*, I willed. *Wake up and go.*

He woke up all right. He woke up and puked all over the bed.

I don't think he knew where he was.

Then the doorbell began to ring. And as there was no one in the flat to answer it, I had to drag myself from the bed, shove on my dressing-gown, go out to the intercom and say, "Who is it?"

"It's me."

And my blood ran cold.

"Mam," I whispered. "What are you doing here?"

"I rang this morning and no one answered. I thought something had happened."

My head was hammering. "Nothing's happened."

"Oh good." She gave a shaky sigh and asked, "Well, aren't you going to let me in?"

"Eh – no. Not just now."

"What?" Her voice rose. "That's a fine way to treat your own mother, I must say." Then her voice broke. "I was so worried about you – I really was."

So I buzzed to let her in.

Before she arrived at the door of the flat, I ran into the red-haired guy and said, "Don't move from there."

He stared at me with zombie eyes. Then he gave a slow, and I don't mean sexily slow, I mean slow smile and slurred, "Whatever ya say, Baby."

Of course my mother arrived in and of course Red Hair arrived out on his way to puke up in the bathroom.

I can still see her face. Pure shock. And I don't blame her.

"Is he," my mother stammered, "is he," she could barely get the words out, "with you?"

I contemplated lying but I knew she'd catch me out. "Yeah." I was mortified, I couldn't look at her.

"He's your boyfriend?"

"Eh – sort of."

"So what's his name?" I think she was doing her best to adjust.

"Peter," I said.

"Jason," he said.

That did it.

I could see her revulsion. "Janet Boyle, I thought you were better than that!" She didn't give me a chance to reply, she just turned on her heel and left.

She'd never really forgiven me. The rift had grown wider.

CHAPTER FIFTY-ONE – THURSDAY/FRIDAY

The phone call came on Thursday.

Beth answered it and then, turning to me said, "It's for you."

"Who is it?" I think I knew, but felt I had to ask.

Beth shrugged. "I dunno." Handing me the receiver, she walked back to her seat at the television.

Surely it was too late for the hospital to ring? They wouldn't ring someone this late? Maybe it was Dave, ringing from Kildare. He'd gone down on Tuesday night to visit some guy he'd met on a protest once.

"Hello." I said it cheerily, just in case it was Dave.

"Hello – Janet Boyle?"

I'd only heard her voice once, but I recognised it. Glancing quickly at Beth and Abby, I saw that they were absorbed in watching *Home and Away* and weren't paying any attention.

"Janet?" the woman spoke again.

"That's me." A buoyant upbeat note.

"This is Julia Davies, Dr Daly's secretary. He has the

results of your tests back from the lab, he was wondering if he could see you tomorrow afternoon?"

"Can't you just tell me over the phone?"

"I'm afraid only Dr Daly knows the results," she said, smoothly. "It's just my job to pencil you in for two thirty tomorrow providing the time suits you."

"Yeah, that's grand."

Beth and Abby were laughing at something in the background.

"And bring your partner with you." Again the off-hand manner.

"My partner?" For a second my mind dulled. "What?"

"Someone. Just bring someone with you, it's always nice to have someone there."

I wanted to crash the phone down. Just to be rid of her voice. "I'll see," I replied.

Like my mother, I didn't see at all.

I couldn't sleep. I spent the night tossing and turning. Dreams, when they came, featured dead birds and rotting trees. Voices swam in and out and at one stage, when I drifted off, I was back to being twelve and finding the dead bird beside our house.

I woke up, panting and sweating.

Two fifteen, making my way up in the elevator to the third floor. Lenny hadn't raised any objections when I said I had to take another half day. He'd given me a weird look and told me to go ahead. I almost wished he'd refused me permission. That way, I wouldn't have to be here.

The lift bleeped as it reached my floor. The last time I'd come here had been with Al and I missed his presence like an ache. I'm sure he would have come if I'd asked but something told me I'd be better off on my own. That way I wouldn't have to be thinking of him, I could just focus on myself.

Funnily enough for me, I remembered my way to Dr Daly's office. I've a terrible sense of direction and have mega problems remembering left from right. So, when I found myself standing in front of Dr Daly's secretary, I was surprised.

"Hi," I said, "I'm – "

"Janet," she gave me a warm smile. "I remember you." She stood up and then something struck her. "On your own?" she asked.

"Yes."

"OK, right." Again the smile. "I'll just tell him you're here."

I watched as she disappeared into his office. The waiting outside was worse than all the waiting for the tests I'd gone to. I could hear a dull rumble of their voices through the door and then footsteps as Julia came back out. "In you go," she said, holding the door for me.

It seemed weird that my legs did exactly what I didn't want to do. I think I was on some kind of auto-pilot. In I walked, making sure to close the door behind me. Then, slowly I walked towards Dr Daly. He didn't say a word until I'd sat myself down opposite him.

"Hello, Janet," he said. A slight pause before he continued, "I believe you're on your own?"

"Does that make a difference?" My voice was surprisingly strong and sharp. I looked from my hands to his face.

Dr Daly didn't flinch. "It's just that most people like to bring someone with them when they're getting test results," he explained.

"Well, I'm not most people." That was true. A human disaster is what I was.

"Fine." He didn't sound angry, not even baffled. I suppose he was used to all kinds of weirdos in his business.

He didn't say anything for a few seconds and that made me look up. The minute I did, he said gently, "It's never easy giving results to patients. If you don't understand something, just ask, all right?"

I nodded. What was there to understand, either I was sick or I wasn't?

"The aim of the tests was to find out what was causing your glands to swell up." He kept looking at me as he talked. "The biopsy we did came back yesterday. It tells us what the problem is."

A lurch of my stomach. I wanted him to go on but I wanted him to stop. I kept thinking that a few minutes from now and I'd know. A few minutes from now and it'd be over. A few minutes from now and I could just –

"The other tests we ran were able to tell us how serious your disease is."

"My disease?" I whispered it. The words seemed to float on the air.

"Yes."

There was a silence as he studied me. "Do you want to call someone?"

The question chilled me. Suddenly I felt alone, totally alone. I wished Al was there, I needed him there. "Is it serious?" The words jerked out of me. I had to know.

Slowly he nodded.

I blinked. "Is it?" I asked again. I was hoping my eyesight had been wrong.

"The biopsy confirmed that you have what's known as Hodgkin's Lymphoma. It's a disease of the lymph glands."

"Hodgkin's what?" It really didn't sound too bad. It wasn't as if I had AIDS or cancer or anything.

"Lymphoma," Daly said. "In simple terms, your enlarged lymph glands contain cells – we call them 'Reed-Sternberg' cells. A tell-tale sign of Hodgkin's Disease."

"Right." I was glad I hadn't called Al now.

"The CAT scan showed up more swollen glands but luckily for you, there's none below the diaphragm."

"Lucky?" It was if a weight was being lifted off my shoulders.

"Your bloods came back clear for kidney and liver functions."

A smile was breaking out on my face. It was ridiculous the panic I'd let myself get into. Not that I'd worried too much but still, I had been worried, I could see that now.

"So," Dr Daly began tapping his pen on his desk. "Are you with me still?"

"Yes."

He bit his lip. "We've established through the tests and through your medical history that you've got Stage Two B Hodgkin's. Basically this means that all your enlarged nodes are above the diaphragm but you are experiencing 'B' symptoms, the weight loss, the night-sweats."

"Right." I wanted to learn all I could about this.

"The 'B' symptoms mark your disease out as that little bit more serious."

"I see."

Daly stopped again. "We've decided initially on a eight-month course of treatment and depending on the disease, maybe radiotherapy to finish up."

"Treatment, like antibiotics?"

The longest pause yet occurred. For no reason, my heart, which had been beating quite normally began to skip in my chest.

"Chemotherapy," Dr Daly said.

Chemotherapy! I knew the word. "But chemotherapy is for people with cancer," I blurted out. "I don't have that."

He said nothing.

"You said I had Hodgkin's Disease, not cancer."

I knew what he was going to say before he said it. "Hodgkin's Disease is a form of cancer," he said.

Shell-shocked, I stared at him.

"I'm sorry." He shook his head. "I'm sorry."

It was too big. The word was too big. Cancer. I had cancer. I was only twenty-five. I couldn't have cancer.

From far away, I registered that he was talking again. His mouth was opening and closing but I couldn't hear him.

It was a mistake. It had to be. I was only twenty-five.

He was holding the phone out to me. He wanted me to call someone. I wanted to be on my own. Shaking my head, I stood up.

Suddenly, someone had their arms around me. I don't know who it was. He must have called someone.

"Let me go," my voice tore up, into my numbness, "Please, let me go."

The hands released me and I sank back down into the chair. More words were said, I don't know what, I'm sure I heard them but I don't remember.

A card was given to me. Some booklets were handed to me. I was patted on the back.

All I wanted to do was get away, be on my own and wake up.

It had to be a dream. It was like being underwater, I couldn't reach the top to say that I was drowning.

I know I didn't scream or cry or do anything much. I just nodded and took stuff and acted maturely. Then I left. I walked down the corridor, stuffing my appointment card into my bag, shoving those horrible books in as well. I got the lift down to the entrance and walked out into a day of dazzling sunshine.

The heat was like a slap in the face. The fact, that while I was sitting being told I'd cancer, the day had been heating up and people were walking about with no coats on. And my life had tilted in a weird direction. Tilted so that nothing looked the same anymore. The whole world had gone into a funny angle in the last hour.

I stopped just outside the hospital and stared at people as they bustled by. How could they not know about me? It was like screaming and no one to hear.

Nausea hit me with the speed of lightning. I vomited all over the pavement, all over someone's shoes. Then I began to walk away. I don't know if people yelled at me, Anyway what did it matter if they did? They had their sunshine and their summer to look forward to. All I had was a weird trapped vacuum.

I walked miles. Miles and miles. People seemed to be everywhere and I wanted just quiet. I didn't want laughter, even if it was coming at me from a distance, I didn't want shouts or car noises or humming, banging, clanking, drilling. I wanted to curl up and be on my own. Just to nurse my pain and lick my wounds on my own.

A church loomed in front of me. Its doors were open and inside I could see the gloom. That's what I wanted, somewhere away from garish sunlight and good-humour.

I walked in and the coolness wrapped itself around me. The dim light filtering through the stained-glass windows lit up the tiled floors. The echo of my feet on the floor was the only sound. I slid into the very back seat and just sat there. I hadn't come to pray, I never prayed anymore.

The silence was great. It seemed to ease itself into my head and I didn't think. I spent ages in there and I didn't think. My eyes stared at the altar and at the candles and at the way, when the light shifted, things looked different. Women went in and out, but I stayed.

Sometime later a man sat beside me. "Are you all right?"

I jumped at the voice. Turning, I saw a young priest gazing at me. "You've been here for hours, " he said. "I was just wondering if you're all right?"

No, I felt like saying, I've got cancer. But I didn't. Saying it would have been too painful. "I'm grand."

"If you want to talk . . ."

"I don't."

"OK." He left me then to walk the length of the church. I watched as he genuflected before the altar. I watched as he blessed himself, showing respect to a God that let birds fall from trees and people get cancer.

I left.

CHAPTER FIFTY-TWO – WEEKEND

No one had been in the flat when I got in on Friday. I can hardly remember what I did, except that I went into my room and curled up on my bed. I didn't even get undressed, just lay there, hugging my pillow and staring at Brad Pitt's smile on the wall. That was the thing that got to me most. The normality of everything. It was like going on holiday and coming home. You expect things to have changed and you can't believe it when nothing has. That's the way I felt.

I lay there all night, listening to the noises in the flat. Beth packing up to go home. Abby chirping away, laughing over the phone with Mickey. Both of them heading out, none of them coming back. I was on my own. I liked it that way.

Saturday morning and the phone rang. I didn't answer it. I heard the answering machine click on and then Dave's voice. I couldn't even be bothered answering it, it was like a wallop of something I was going to lose.

The phone rang again later and once again another message was left on it.

Abby arrived home sometime in the afternoon. I heard her bustling about in the kitchen. She was making herself something to eat. I held my pillow tighter and wished I could be her. Yesterday, I was her and for twenty-five years I was her. Now, I didn't know who I was or what I was or what I was going to become. The numbness in my head was wearing away, pain and grief were wriggling their way inside me.

"Jan?" Abby called.

I stiffened.

"Jan?" she knocked on my door. "Are you in?"

I wanted to stay quiet. I didn't want her near me. But she'd poke her head in the door if I didn't answer.

"Yeah," I said.

The door opened. "You're popular with the fellas these days," she smiled. "Dave and Al both rang you."

"Did they?"

"Yeah, you should check your messages."

"I will."

"Hello?" Abby came further in. "Hello? Jan are you receiving me – I said Dave rang."

"I heard." I turned from her. I really couldn't sustain a conversation.

"You haven't gone off him?" She came around to gawk in my face. "You couldn't have."

"No, I haven't." I wanted her to leave me alone. "Just leave me alone, Ab – all right?"

I could almost hear her mind wondering whether to go or stay. She stayed. Kneeling down by the side of my bed, she asked, "Is everything all right?"

Her concern was not what I wanted. Telling her was not what I wanted to do. The words were stuck inside me, the horrible disgusting words that I wasn't going to say. If you said them, they created sound waves, waves that spread out and were there forever and ever. Words that became concrete and permanent. I wasn't going to give them that dignity. "Just leave me alone."

I closed my eyes, so that she couldn't see anything in them. "I'm tired."

"All right so," Abby stood up. "If you do want to talk, I can stay in tonight if you like."

"I want to be on my own."

"Dave left a message for you to ring him," Abby said, "and Al said he'd ring you later."

I didn't answer. When she was gone, I'd lift the phone off the hook.

She went out. Before she went, she poked her head in at me. "Do you want tea?"

"I'll make it myself."

I heard her whisper to Mickey that Jan was in a funny mood.

Then they were gone.

I got up then. I could be on my own. I was zonked from tiredness because I hadn't slept well in the last two days, but that made things easier. My mind was fuzzy. I couldn't think too clearly.

I made myself some tea and sat in the good chair. It was nice, just holding the hot cup of tea in my hand and snuggling into the softness of the chair.

The phone rang. The noise from the outside made me jump. Someone was on the other end. I curled harder into the chair, wanting to push the noise away. After seven rings the answering machine should come on.

It was Dave. After Abby had delivered her sexy message, his voice came on. "Hiya gorgeous," he said.

I caught my breath. I should've taken the phone off the hook.

"Rang ya earlier an' I'm ringin' ya now."

I flinched at the sound of his voice.

"I'm 'eading out so I won't be 'ere if ya ring. I might see ya Monday, maybe Tuesday, all right? Loadsa news for ya."

He hung up.

It was a while before I realised I was crying. Silent tears were eeking their way down my face. I knew it when I tasted the salt on my tongue. I put my hand to my face and it came away wet. I let the tears fall, they plopped into my tea, they ran over my nose and onto my lips. And I still felt nothing.

Al rang much later. I didn't answer the phone for him either. He just left a message that he'd ring me on Sunday.

It had grown dark. I sat in the chair in the dark, holding the cup and trying not to think too hard.

I fell asleep in the chair. The whole night long I slept. I woke up at seven, drenched to the skin. The teacup had fallen onto the floor and a dried-in tea-stain now adorned the carpet. For a second or two, I didn't know where I was and then it all came crashing back.

The numbness wasn't quick enough. The pain got there first.

I curled up defensively against it. If I didn't acknowledge it, it would go away, or at least lessen a bit.

I hadn't the energy to even get out of the chair, or have a shower or change my clothes. Anyway, I didn't want to look at myself. I hated my body. There was something wrong with it. Something inside my body was killing me and there was nothing I could do. I couldn't make it stop. I couldn't tear it out. I couldn't control it. It was eating its way into my glands and destroying them. The sense of powerlessness was horrifying.

Every little while, a thought would sneak up through the numbness and it would be there before I could quench it. I tried to block it out. I tried to think of other things, but there was nothing else to think of. The more thoughts that sneaked through, the bigger the hole they made in my mind. The bigger the hole, the more thoughts that came through. Before I realised it, all sorts of mad things were swirling about my brain. The noise in my head was getting too loud. I was thinking of all sorts of weird things, things about me, about being sick, about my life, my past, my . . .

I grabbed the remote control and flicked on the telly.

Mass was being celebrated on one channel. I flicked over, some American chat show where two girls were beating each other to bits and being pulled apart by two guys. Over again, Homer Simpson was getting a heart transplant or a heart by-pass or something. There was no fears in his world. He was getting a special deal done on it. He made me laugh.

I laughed so hard I cried.

When the phone rang, I'd jumped.

I knew it wasn't my mother because she'd rung earlier and left a message.

This was someone else.

I'd lifted myself off the chair to get a can from the fridge. I'd decided that the only way to stop the horrors was to get drunk. The telly wasn't working anymore. My mind was telling me I had to think and I was trying to stop myself from listening to it.

I wanted to get drunk, I wanted to fall down and sleep. I wanted to wake up tomorrow with such a hangover that I didn't care if I died.

The phone kept ringing and the answering machine clicked on.

"Jan?"

It was Al.

"Pick up if you're there."

Al! He knew. He'd understand. I wouldn't have to explain anything to him. I probably wouldn't even have to say how sick I was. I made a grab for the phone and held onto it as if it was going to save me.

"Jan, is that you?" His voice brightened. "You're there so?"

"Yeah."

"It's just when you went on Friday, I thought . . ." he let his voice trail off. "Well, I guess I was wrong."

"I got the results." My voice sounded hoarse, as if it was rusty. "I got the results on Friday."

"And?"

I couldn't say it. I couldn't say it.

"Jan?"

I wished I'd never picked up the phone. But I held it to my ear all the same. I wished he'd just keep talking go me.

"Are you still there?"

"Yeah."

He hesitated, then said, "Do you need company?"

"Yeah."

"I'll be right over."

He arrived half an hour later. I was still cradling the phone in my hand when he banged on the door. I buzzed to let him up and then I let him in the flat.

I held the door open and he stood outside. I didn't have to say anything, he just held his arms out and I fell into them. I buried my head in his shoulder and clung onto him. He rocked me from side to side and I felt him rubbing his hand up and down my hair.

We stood like that for ages.

He made me tea. He wrapped a quilt around me and made me sit in the chair. He sat on the floor beside me and held my hand. Pressing it to his face, he said, "You're still cold."

I got the words out. "He said I have cancer."

Al's only response was to tighten his hold on my hand.

CHAPTER FIFTY-THREE – MAY

Sometime during the following week, my mind shifted up a gear. All I know is that I went to bed Monday afternoon, after Al had left, and slept straight through until Tuesday morning. When I woke Tuesday, I felt different. The half-numb, shell-shocked world that I'd inhabited since Friday seemed to have lifted.

I lay there for a while, staring up at Brad Pitt. He was a fine thing. If ever I made loads of money, I'd have breast implants and liphosuction and a face lift. Then I'd go after him. He was smiling down at me from the ceiling, blond floppy hair and happy eyes. I liked Brad a lot.

Sunshine was coming in through the window and it made the room look golden, it lit up the yellow wallpaper and the bare boards. The whole room seemed to vibrate with light. I wanted to stay there, safe in the warmth but some part of me, the part that seemed to have emerged while I slept told me I couldn't. I had so many things to do.

Al had told me that I had to tell people. People that mattered. He was going to tell Lenny that I was sick this week while I sorted things out.

Then, he'd made me get my appointment card and look at it.

That had been scary.

I pulled the books out of my bag, while I looked for it. Al picked them up and asked me if I'd read them. "They're all about what you have," he said.

It was unreal. "I don't want to know," I said. I shoved him away and then I shouted at him. He put the books on my bed and told me that it didn't matter.

I found the card. I had to go for an injection on Wednesday. A vaccine against all sorts of stuff.

A week later, the real treatment would start. I had to check into hospital Wednesday morning and I could go home Thursday. After that, the receptionist had written, I could get all my treatment as an out-patient. She'd stuck in a letter with the appointment card, explaining things. She'd written that with the shock I mightn't remember.

Al had offered to come with me on Wednesday and I'd agreed.

This Tuesday morning, Abby was in the kitchen, singing along to a song on the radio. She had a horrible, high-pitched singing voice which normally grated on my nerves. Today it made me smile. She was murdering the Sting song "Fields of Gold". I think she was trying to inject feeling into her words or something, but it was painful.

"Shut the fuck up!" Beth shouted. She must be up as well.

"*. . . in the jealous sky . . . dum de dum de dum . . .* "

"Abby, I'm going to go mental!"

Abby didn't take any notice. If anything her voice began to screech even worse.

"JESUS!"

I heard Abby laugh as Beth stomped about the place. They really rubbed each other up the wrong way in the mornings. Beth and I were not morning people. Abby was. She loved getting up early, she talked incessantly all through breakfast and then chirpily set out for work. The fact that Beth and I never answered her didn't bother her at all. She just talked away to herself.

"Hi," I said as I came out of my room.

Abby stopped singing. "Awake at last, huh?" She gave a grin. "You must've had a hard weekend, you were conked out when I got in last night."

The breakfast scene, which I'd seen almost every day for the last few years twisted something inside me. Beth glowering into her coffee, Abby bouncing about the place looking for her bag or her coat. I felt that I didn't belong in it anymore, that I was somehow like an outsider, it was weird.

"You'll be late for work," Abby said as she began to dump her cup and plate into the sink. "It's after eight thirty now."

"I'm off this week," I said. I gulped. "I'm off sick."

"Again?" Beth rolled her eyes. She turned back to her coffee.

"Yes." I slid into the seat opposite her. My heart was thumping, Al had told me to tell people. I tried to go on. I tried to say the words but I couldn't.

"What's wrong with you?" Abby asked as she liberally sprayed the place with perfume. "Your glands again?"

"Yeah." This was it. "I have – "

"Abby will you go easy on the perfume, I can taste it off my toast!"

"Sorry," Abby drawled. She gave a final spray just to annoy Beth. Shoving it into her bag, she rushed to the door, "See you later. Bye!"

"Abby," I forced the words. "Just hang on for a sec."

"Can't Jan, I'm late."

The door was slammed behind her.

Beth and I were left alone.

Slowly, my heart resumed it's normal beat. Now wasn't the time to break the news. Later on in the week would do.

On Wednesday, I still didn't manage to tell anyone. Once again, I got up for breakfast and the words died in my mouth. I don't know what held me back, I think it was the fear that they would change towards me, that I'd no longer be Jan but "the one who has the cancer".

Al met me outside the flat on Wednesday. He grinned in approval when he saw me. I had the war-paint on and I'd washed my hair so that it gleamed. "You look great," he smiled.

"Thanks." I loved him for the compliment. I'd lost

more weight and it suited me. My face had cheek-bones, my legs had knees and my arms had wrists.

But inside, I felt horrible. It wasn't the tiredness or the worry. It went deeper than that. Inside, I felt as if I was rotting. Something horrible was trying to kill me.

I didn't want it to show on my face.

We went to the hospital, I got my injection and I survived. Al waited for me and when I came out, he said, "It's the first step to gettin' better."

"Yeah." I wanted to believe that. I had to believe it.

After Wednesday, I had one week to tell people. I'd promised myself that I'd tell people once the injection was over.

I felt as if I spent the whole week running faster than I could. It was like watching myself run and then trying to catch up with myself. A roller-coaster of emotion battered me. One minute, I was so positive that everything would be fine, the next I'd bawl my eyes out. On Thursday evening, just before I told Abby and Beth, I'd been feeling great. Cancer was curable nowadays, everyone said so. Once it was caught in time, you'd live. I was going to live.

Then Dave rang. Without thinking, I picked up the phone. "Hiya, Gorgeous," he said.

The image of myself as gorgeous began to mock me. I had cancer.

I slammed down the phone and burst into tears.

Abby had found me sitting in the dark, staring at the blank TV screen when she came in from work.

The phone was ringing.

I was so glad to see her. "If that's Dave, tell him I've gone out."

She looked at my face, which I'm sure was a state and handed me a tissue. Then she answered the phone. "No, Dave, she's gone out. No, I don't know when she'll be back. She said if you rang, she'd contact you later." Abby raised her eyes to me as she said that and I nodded. "Right, right, I'll tell her." She listened a bit more and then said, "Fine. Yeah, I'll let her know. Bye now."

"What did he say?" I was wiping my eyes and blowing my nose.

"He said there was a demo on the developer's office at the weekend and if you wanted, you could go."

"Oh."

"And he said to tell you he's sorry he missed you at the weekend."

"That's nice," I sniffed.

Abby patted me on the shoulder and went to put on the kettle. She said nothing as she made us both a cup of tea. Handing me one, she took one herself and sat down on the floor beside me. We both sipped in silence.

"You can tell me, you know," she said after a while. "Whatever it is."

"I keep trying and I can't," I said.

"Is it so bad?"

"Yeah." I began to stir my tea with my finger. It burnt it, but I liked the sensation.

"Hang on right there." Abby jumped up. She ran into her room. I heard her opening her drawer before arriving back out with a big box of chocolates. "Mickey gave them to me," she said smiling guiltily. "I hid them because I knew you and Beth would eat them on me." Opening the lid, she offered me one. "The more you tell me, the more chocolates you can have."

I had to smile. "Smart woman."

I took the caramel and nut one. I like those.

"So," Abby put her elbows on the chair. "I've all the time in the world here."

"Not seeing Mickey tonight?"

"No." She popped another chocolate into her mouth. "Jan, I know something's eating you. You've been in a funny mood since the weekend."

"I know." I was afraid to take another sweet in case she did expect me to talk.

"You're not – " she paused. "I mean, it's not – " Again the pause.

I looked at her, she was blushing like mad. "What?"

"Well, don't take this the wrong way, but, well," big gulp, "you're not pregnant, are you?" The last part came out in a rush.

I gawked at her. "No." I tried to keep my face straight. "No."

Abby shrugged. "Well, I had to ask."

"I'm sick." I said then. I don't know how it came out. "Really sick."

Abby did a double-take. "What?"

"I've got cancer."

There, I'd said it.

The shock on her face was reflected in the way she said, "No!"

Three small words. I've got cancer. Changes everything.

I told her I didn't want to talk about it. She knew now and that was it. I'd talk when I was ready.

Beth came in later and found the two of us sitting in the dark. The box of chocolates were gone, except for the coffee ones, which we both hated.

"Oh great," Beth opened the door and arrived in. "Is the electricity gone?"

"No," Abby stood up, I think she was still a bit dazed. "Jan and I were – were chatting."

"In the feckin' dark!" Beth switched on the light. She spied the decimated box of sweets on the ground. "Who owns those chocolates?" She came over and picked the box up. "Oh, great, none for me."

"We kept the coffee ones for you," Abby said.

"I hate the shaggin' coffee ones."

Before she said anything else, I said, "Beth, I've, eh, some news for you."

"Really?" She didn't sound too interested. Nothing I'd ever said to her had ever interested her before.

"Yeah, it's important."

"Let me guess." She stood in front of me and folded her arms. "You've lost your job again and can't pay the rent."

"Beth!" That was Abby. "Please."

"What?" Beth began tapping her foot. I think then

I realised how much I got on her nerves. It was hard to tell someone who basically thought you were a waster that you were sick. In fact, if it had been a comedy show, I would've laughed.

"I've got – " I hated saying it, so I changed course. "Last Friday, I went to the hospital. I'd been in for tests."

Beth stopped tapping her foot. "About the sweats you were having?" Her face drained of colour.

I couldn't believe she remembered. She hadn't said a thing about them since I'd told her that day in the bedroom.

"You knew?" Abby said, looking from her to me. "You knew she was sick?"

"No," Beth said. "I knew she wasn't sick." She turned to me. "Was I right?" Her voice belied her words. It wavered a bit.

"No," I said. I couldn't say it and look at her. "I've Hodgkin's Disease. It's – it's a sort of cancer."

She said nothing. Then, she laughed. The sound of it made Abby and I jump. "You don't have cancer," she scoffed. "Gimme a break."

"I do." It was funny, saying that. Admitting it.

Beth picked up her coat off the chair. She began to put it on.

"Where are you going?" Abby asked.

Beth's fingers shook as she zipped herself up. "Shit," she said, "I've just remembered I have to meet someone at six."

"Beth!"

I said nothing as she stumbled towards the door. It shook as she slammed it closed.

I caught the bus home the following day. Back to Beiruit. I'd rung my mother on Thursday night. "I've something to tell you," I'd said. "In fact," I went on, "It's not just you, it's everyone."

"I see." I think she was in a huff because I hadn't called her back on Sunday.

"I'm coming home tomorrow morning, will you all be there?"

"Janet," she said, "your father'll be at work, Lisa'll be in school, God knows what Sammy'll be doing. So, no, we won't all be there."

She was *definitely* in a huff.

"Will everyone be in tomorow night then?"

She hummed and hawed. "I suppose," she said at last, "unless Lisa's going somewhere. She goes out far too much and her Leaving Cert's coming up."

"Try and make sure she's there."

"I'm a bit worried about her. She says she's going out with friends but I don't think she is."

I don't know why she was telling me this.

"She's gone difficult, she was always so easy to manage . . ." her voice trailed off. "So easy to manage," she repeated.

"I'll be over tomorrow so," I said, hoping she wasn't going to chew my ear off about difficult teenagers.

"What is all this secrecy about anyway?" Mam was back on track.

Maybe other people told their mother things. I didn't.

I thought it would be better to tell the whole family at once about my illness.

So I just said, "See you tomorrow," before putting the phone down.

There was an air of expectancy around the table on Friday evening.

"Now," my mother said, eyeballing me, "Janet has something she'd like to tell us."

Silence.

"Well," I licked my lips and gulped down some water. "It's not good news – "

"You've lost your job again," Sammy said. "I knew it! I knew it!" She grinned at Lisa, "What did I tell you?"

"No," I shook my head, took another gulp of water. "It's not that."

"Oh." Sammy looked put out.

"It's worse than that."

"Pregnant," my mother said. "Is that it?"

"Oh, now, now," Dad patted my mam's hand. "Janet wouldn't do something like that."

"That fella we met last week lives in a tree," Mam said. "I wouldn't put anything past him."

"I'm not pregnant." My voice caught in my throat. If they didn't stop, I was going. It was hard enough without them shoving their oar in.

"Is it worse than that?" Lisa asked breathlessly.

"Yes."

"Oh," Lisa heaved a sigh. "That's all right."

Everyone looked at her. "What's that supposed to mean?" Sammy asked.

"Oh nothing," Lisa shrugged. "Nothing."

"Lisa!" Mam's voice was sharp.

I was forgotten about. All eyes were on the demure eighteen-year-old at the top of the table.

"Can I just tell you – " I began.

"All right," Lisa said. "*I'm* pregnant." It sounded as if she was telling them she'd got blue eyes. Pointing to me, she said calmly, "But Jan's got worse news so it shouldn't matter."

"I knew it!" My mother jumped up. "I knew you were! Always feeling sick and out every night, I knew this would happen."

"Well, you should have told *me* then, shouldn't you," Lisa said back smoothly. "Then I wouldn't be in this mess."

"Oh, the cheek!"

"Now, now . . ."

"Shut up you," Mam whirled on Dad. "Now, now, my arse. Is that all the contribution you can make to a conversation?"

"Now, now . . ."

"AAGGGHHHH!"

Dad shut up. He slumped in his chair and gazed hopelessly at Lisa.

"So," Mam caught Lisa by the shoulder and dug her nails in. "What's the story, madam?"

That was it. I got up to leave. My head was lifting and all I wanted to do was sleep.

"Hang on you," Mam bawled as I made my way to the door. "Let's get all the news over with at once. What have you done?"

"It's worse than – " Lisa attempted to pipe up.

"Shut up."

Lisa cowered away in her chair. "She said it was worse than – "

Mam gave her a look that would have killed someone with less composure.

"Now?" Mam asked, turning to me.

I don't think I'd ever seen her so angry. Normally she tolerated things by whinging or moaning or if she was in good form, she'd laugh things off. But I'd never seen her like this before.

"Are you going to tell us how you've managed to mess your life up again?" Mam advanced towards me. "I don't know what I did wrong, I really don't know." She stood in front of me. "Go on, spit it out, I can take anything at this stage."

I looked at them all. My mother, red in the face, Lisa sulking in a chair, my dad, looking totally bewildered and Sammy with her head down, not looking at anyone.

The words came out. Very slowly, so that I could almost touch them, I said, "I've got cancer."

My mother hit me across the face.

"Margaret!" My dad was on his feet. "Jesus!"

"How dare you," my mam's voice was shaking. "How dare you! Do you think that's funny?"

I put my hand to my face and stared at her. She'd flipped, big-time. "No," my eyes blinked rapidly. "No."

It must have been the way I said it, because a look of complete horror crossed her face. She put her two hands up to her mouth and her eyes widened. "Janet?" she whispered.

"I've got cancer," I said it a second time.

She came over to me and I backed away. She caught my hand and pulled me nearer her. She ran her hands over my face. "Please say it's a joke."

Dad was beside her now and Lisa and Sammy were on their feet.

"It's true." I was numb again. I was looking at this family as if I was an observer.

"No," Mam shook her head. "No."

"It's in my glands."

Dad put his arm around my mother. He looked at me. "My big girl," he said it softly.

That's what he always used to call me.

Mam kept shaking her head. She kept reaching out and touching my face.

It was all very strange.

I left early on Saturday. I couldn't take any more questions. I told them that I was going into hospital on Wednesday morning and Mam and Dad said they'd come with me.

They wanted me to stay in the house, but I couldn't.

I really didn't want them to talk to me about it.

CHAPTER FIFTY-FOUR

When I got back, there was a message from Dave on the answering machine. It was good to hear his voice.

"Hiya," he said, "Listen Jan, if ya want ta meet me today, I'll be marching outside the developer's offices from around noon." He gave me the address and said, "Please come. If ya don't, I'll just figure ya've gone orf me."

That frightened the hell out of me!

I didn't want him to think that!

After the trauma of the last couple of days, he was just what I needed.

All the way into town on the bus, I tried to think of the words to tell him I was sick.

All along the walk to the developer's offices I envisioned scenarios of how I'd broach the subject.

When I saw the huge grin he gave me, I knew I couldn't say anything. He was my normality. The lifeline to the real world. The one I didn't want to treat me with kid gloves. I just wanted him to be the Dave I'd met that rainy day in town. Committed, dedicated, slightly nutty Dave. I wanted nothing to change between us, so when he jogged over to me and said, "Ya still loike me so?

I smiled back and said, "More than ever."

That Saturday was a good day.

I marched about in circles, holding my placard and chanting slogans. I laughed and chatted with the other protesters, I brushed off the sneers and abuse of passers-by.

I was me again. Just for those few hours.

Dave spent the night with me.

"Have you told him?" Abby whispered to me at breakfast.

"No." I shoved my head nearer hers. "And I'm not going to, so just button it."

"Jan!"

"No," I bit my lip. "Not yet, Abby. I can't."

She didn't say anything else. I think she'd told Beth not to mention it either. She didn't have to bother, Beth was avoiding me like the plague. Her only acknowledgement that I was even in the same room was a sidelong glance and a muttered, "Hiya."

Abby on the other hand, was all concern. Overboard. I thought she'd get over it.

On Monday, I bit the bullet and decided to go into work. I couldn't hide forever. Anyway, I had to tell Lenny that he was going to be seeing a lot less of me.

It was over a week since I'd been diagnosed and the time I dreaded most was when the dark came and I had to go to bed.

Every night, visions paraded themselves in front of me. It depended on the mood I was in. The most horrible thoughts came when depression would hit. It hit me almost every day at some stage. The thoughts I had were of the cancer, working away inside me and I couldn't do anything.

The day of treatment was a day I dreaded, yet welcomed.

That Monday, I knew I couldn't spend another day on my own. Abby had offered to spend it with me, but the sorrowful looks she kept throwing in my direction when she thought I wasn't looking drove me mad.

So I went to work.

"You're so brave," Abby had said. I almost expected her to wave me off.

"I'm so bored," I answered back.

"I'm cooking a nice meal tonight," she said then. "A nice dinner for the three of us."

Beth and I looked at her suspiciously.

"Just an idea," she said brightly.

"I won't be here," Beth got up from the table. "It'll be just you and her." She wouldn't even say my name.

It hurt.

Derbhla was in our office when I got in. She had a load of envelopes in her hand and was giving them out to everyone. "It's notification of the dates for your interviews," she announced as she began to rummage through them.

"Oh, oh, folks," Lenny was rubbing his hands. "It's getting closer to D-day." His eyes followed Derbhla around the office.

"Liz." Darbhala announced.

Liz caught the envelope mid-air and began to rip it asunder.

"Henry."

Henry took his envelope and without trying to appear anxious opened it by the flap.

"May 30th," Liz howled. "I'm on May 30th. Next . . ." she ran to her desk calendar. One of those ones that has all the cute angels on it, "Wednesday week!" She dropped into her desk. "I'll never be ready."

"I'm on the 30th too," Henry said. "First thing in the morning."

I'd been handed an envelope too. In all the fuss of the past weeks, I'd forgotten to pull out of the interview. "I'm not doing it," I gave the envelope back to Derbhla. "I pulled out."

She gave her head an emphatic shake. "No you didn't. Anyone that pulled out was put on a list. Your name isn't there." She replaced the envelope back on my desk. "You're in."

I refused to open it. There was no way I was doing an interview. No way.

Derbhla looked around for Al. "Al not in yet?" she said, her voice sounding disappointed.

"Nope," Lenny shook his head.

"Tell him to call down to me for his letter," she said, "I wouldn't like to leave it on his desk. It might get lost." Then, head high she swept regally by us as she left the room.

"So, Jan," Lenny said, "What date's your interview on?"

"I dunno and don't care."

"Oh now, that's not the attitude," Lenny chortled. "That's just nerves." He wrinkled up his nose, wiped it along his sleeve and said, "Open it up now, there's a good girl."

I hadn't the strength to argue. Where was Al when I needed him? He'd promised to come in today, to be there when I told Lenny. Giving a big heavy fed-up sigh, I opened it. "May 29th," I said wearily. "Whatever day that is."

Liz consulted her calendar. "Tuesday week," she shrieked. "What time?"

"2.15."

"You're in first of all of us." She smiled. "At least you'll be able to tell us what they asked you. You'd want to start swotting."

"That's what she's been doing," Henry pronounced. "That's why she was off last week. She was swotting for her interview, weren't ya?"

I flinched.

"No way," Liz's face creased up in annoyance. "That's not fair."

"I think it shows initiative," Lenny defended me. "If everyone showed that kind of commitment we'd have great interviews altogether."

"And no one in work," Liz countered smartly.

Lenny chortled. "True for you, true for you." He slapped his thigh.

Gathering an arm full of files, Liz said, "Seeing as Jan is in today, she can work while I study."

"I was sick over the week," I answered, finally able to get a word in. My voice kept remarkably steady. "And I'm not doing the interview."

"Sure." Liz gave me a catty smile and dumped the files on my desk.

"I'm a typist," I stuttered.

"And now you're a filer."

I looked to Lenny for support, but he was humming away.

Why did I have to work with such a thick shower of morons?

"I wasn't studying for the interview," I gulped out.

"Give nothin' away," Henry leered at me across the office. He tapped his nose. "Keep all your knowledge to yerself. That's what I'm fuckin' goin' to do anyhow."

"And what knowledge would that be now?" Lenny asked. "How to flog faulty jumpers or something?"

Henry shuddered to a halt. "What?"

Lenny looked up at him. "You heard." He looked back down at his newspaper.

Henry went over to Lenny's desk and placed his palms flat down on it. Shoving his head almost into Lenny's, he said again, "Wha'?"

"I heard," Lenny began in a sing-song voice, "that all your jumpers were faul-ty."

415

I sat back in my chair and watched the scene with a nice air of detachment. Normally their bickering got to me, but today, I didn't care. I suppose hearing you've got cancer does that to you.

"And who the fuck told you that?"

"Oh, now," Lenny tapped the side of his nose. "Can't reveal my sources."

Liz had her head stuck into insurance stuff. Stuff she thought she'd be asked at the interview. The rowing was not going to bother her.

"Who the fuck," Henry sprayed spit everywhere on the obscenity, "told you that?"

"I just heard. A little dickie bird told me," Lenny sat back in his seat and folded his arms, "that all your jumpers ran in the wash."

I'd bought two of them.

Henry gave a placating laugh. "They don't," he said in a big smarmy voice, "they just," he pursed his lips, "they just fade a bit."

Lenny chortled. "Jimmy Madden says that one of the lads in his office is suing you. The jumper wrecked all the washing."

"The fuckin' bastard."

The phone on my desk rang. I picked it up just as Henry slammed out the door. Lenny gave him a wave. "Bye, bye promotion," he laughed gently.

"Hello, accounts," I said into the phone.

"Jan, Al here."

"Al, where are you?"

He coughed. "Eh, listen, I'm awful sorry about this, Jan – but – well – I won't be in today."

I stared at the phone. He had promised. He'd promised to be with me while I told Lenny I was sick. "You promised."

"Something happened at home, all right."

"I can't do it without you."

"I feel terrible, Jan, you know I wouldn't let you down." He did sound sincere.

But all men sounded like that.

"So I'll tell Lenny you'll be in tomorrow, will I?"

"Jan – "

"Well?"

"I'll be in on Wednesday," he said. "Unless you want – "

"Right, I'll tell him."

Without listening to what he had to say, I put down the phone. Then I wished I hadn't. But he'd deserted me.

He was probably sneaking in study for his interview.

Somewhere, the fair-minded part of me attempted to speak up for Al, to tell me that he wouldn't do that. But I didn't want to know. It was easier to be angry with him. If I kept the anger, I wouldn't feel so alone when I told Lenny.

He was frankly shocked. "Well," he said, looking me up and down. "I'm frankly shocked."

"So I won't be in a lot," I muttered. "I've – I've to get treatment."

"Of course you have," he agreed. "That's how they'll cure you."

He made fumbling noises, I don't think he knew what to say. "Well, Jan, that's terrible," he said. "And now, I don't suppose you'll be doing the interview."

I hadn't planned on doing it anyway. "No."

"Pity." Lenny shook his head. "The extra money would have helped you with the bills."

That shook me.

For the first time I wondered how the hell I was going to pay.

I was not a saver. I was not an investor in serious illness policies.

"Jan?" Lenny was nudging me. "Are you all right?"

A weird question to ask. "See you in the morning, Lenny." I picked my coat off the hanger and left.

And that was it. I'd told everyone except Dave. I'd said the words: I have cancer. On the surface I'd said it. Inside, my head was still trying to get round it.

Acceptance was a long way off.

CHAPTER FIFTY-FIVE

The sound of a car horn blaring woke the whole street Wednesday morning. I was sitting nervously in the kitchen waiting to go to the hospital. At my feet was a small overnight bag. It contained some night things and clothes for Thursday.

Thursday seemed a long way off. I wished I could transport myself into tomorrow and have the first session of treatment behind me. At least then, I'd know what to expect.

The car horn stopped and then started up again.

"What the hell is that?" Abby had made me some breakfast. She'd virtually force-fed me with two slices of brown toast. She went to the window and looked out. "Some ould fella blaring his horn for all he's worth," she clucked. Opening the window, she yelled, "Do you mind, there's sick people in here!"

I suppose she meant me.

Gritting my teeth, I did my best to stay silent. I didn't want a row this morning.

There was a buzzing on the intercom. "That's probably for me," I said. Mam and Dad had decided that they were coming with me this morning. For support. "Hello?" I pressed the button.

"Only us," Dad's voice came back. "Jan, we've a taxi here – can you get yourself down now?"

"Sure." I turned around to pick up my bag.

Abby handed it to me. She passed it over and wouldn't let go of the handles. "Good luck," she said. "I'll be thinking of you."

We both dropped the bag together and she hugged me.

Mam and Dad smiled at me as I came out of the front door. Dad patted me on the back and Mam kept smiling. She smiled all the way into the hospital in the taxi. She sat in the back with me and kept smiling every time I glanced up at her. I got tired of smiling back, so eventually I just sat and stared out the window.

They checked me in. They took complete control of everything. I was led up to a ward and told that I had an appointment with the consultant at three o'clock.

Hours to kill.

They took more blood tests.

"Why are you taking those?" Mam asked. She was flitting around nervously, arranging my stuff in the locker.

The nurse started to explain about blood counts and while she was doing this, I started taking my things out of the locker and putting them back in my bag. Mam and Dad were listening avidly.

I studied the ward. There were five other people in it, besides me. Two women who looked about my age and three oldies. There were vases of flowers everywhere. People had cards hanging out of their beds. They had sweets and lemonade on their lockers. I'd always wanted to go into hospital when I was a kid. I knew it meant attention and sweets.

"Thanks very much, nurse," Dad said, making me cringe. He was the only dinosaur left who called nurses "nurse".

They watched the nurse leaving and I rubbed the part of my arm she'd pierced.

"That was very informative," Dad said, turning to me.

Mam was about to agree when she saw my bare locker. "Janet," she exclaimed, "What did you do that for?" She bent down to start taking stuff out of my bag again.

I caught hold of her hand and held it. "I'm not staying, I'm going home tomorrow, you know."

They didn't say anything else.

Dad wandered off to grab a smoke and a coffee. He came back with a coffee for each of us.

We sat in silence – not able to talk.

At three we were able to go to Daly's office. I dreaded this. Dad seemed to have a list of questions with him. I knew he'd make a show of himself. His shoes squeaked as he walked along the corridor. It sounded like a herd of giant mice were invading the hospital. With every squeak more and more of me cringed.

Daly was waiting for us. He held out his hand and shook my mother and father's hands. "How do you do?" he said. He pulled out chairs for them to sit on and then sat himself behind his desk.

Mam began to arrange herself in the chair. She folded her skirt under her as she sat down. She pulled the collar of her blouse out over her jacket. She smoothed the sleeves of her jacket and smiled expectantly at the doctor. For the first time it hit me that she actually looked very smart. Dressing up for her daughter's chemotherapy.

Dad crossed his legs, looked about, uncrossed his legs, coughed a bit, shifted a bit and reached out and patted my hand. "Good girl," he said, for no reason.

Daly studied us. "I always like to talk to patients and their families just before their first treatment," he began. He turned to me. "Janet, did you read the literature I gave you about Hodgkin's and the chemotherapy treatment?"

I stared back mutinously, "No."

"Janet," my mother said, "Don't talk to the – "

"It's fine," Daly held up his hand. "A lot of patients don't like to know the full facts. It's perfectly normal."

I was glad someone thought I was perfectly normal. A perfectly normal cancerous human being.

"The treatment Janet will be getting," Daly went on, "is a drug treatment. A number of different drugs all working together to kill the cancerous cells in the body."

"Ah," Dad said, as if the doctor had just accomplished the Second Coming. "I see."

"It works by killing off the bad cells," Daly went on, "Unfortunately, good cells get killed off too. Cancer cells don't recuperate as quickly as the good ones, the idea being, that after enough chemo, all the bad cells get eliminated." He stopped and handed a leaflet to my mam and dad. "That's basically how chemotherapy works."

"Very clever," said Dad. He squeezed my hand. "You'll be fine."

Oh ye of massive faith.

Daly sat on the edge of his desk. "Chemotherapy drugs have a number of side-effects too," he said. "I've told Janet this already, but with the shock patients tend to forget."

I didn't remember at all. Fearfully, I looked at him. What side-effects?

"It's like taking a narcotic to relieve pain – it also makes you sleepy," Daly said. "The side-effects of these chemotherapy drugs are weighed against their advantages."

I was beginning to hate this guy, every time I saw him, he'd bad news for me.

"The drugs work by killing off cells, cells that divide. Each drug has its own side-effects. The drugs Janet will be on may cause nausea. However, we've made great strides in anti-emetic preparations in the last few years. She shouldn't suffer too much."

He waited while that sank in.

I don't think my dad knew what nausea meant but he didn't embarrass us by asking.

"Secondly," Daly said and this time he was looking directly at me, "there is a risk of infertility. During treatment, your periods may stop, and you might never be able to have a baby."

It didn't register. I saw Mam looking at me but it didn't register. I wasn't big into babies and also I could well do without being doubled over in pain every twenty-eight days. So I shrugged and returned my attention to praying that my father wasn't going to make a show of us.

"She might never have a baby," Mam said.

Aren't you lucky Lisa's pregnant so, I felt like saying.

"A lot of patients do go on to have children," Daly said. "In fact, infertility seems to affect more men than women."

"I see," Mam said. She too, reached out and clasped my hand.

"Another side-effect," Daly said, "and only a temporary one is that patients tend to suffer hair loss."

That got me. The words penetrated my shell. "Hair loss?"

"That's right."

Slowly, I said, "Are you telling me that I could lose my hair?"

"Just while your having treatment. It'll grow again."

The only thing I liked about myself. I was going to lose that only thing that people admired about me. "But I can't lose it," I shook my parents hands out of mine. I clenched my fists and stared at Daly. "I'm going to look awful without my hair."

"No, you won't," Dad attempted to pat my hand. "Sure haven't you a beautiful – "

"I'd rather die."

"I don't think you would," Daly said gently.

"You can get a nice wig," my mother said soothingly, shoving her oar in with the delicacy of Hitler's invasion of Poland.

"I don't want a wig!" I stood up and screamed into her face. "I'm not wearing a wig!"

"Now, now . . . "

"I'm not beautiful, I've still got spots, I've flabby thighs, a big arse – "

"Janet!" Mam was mortified.

I continued on. "A crummy job, a horrible life and now," I began to pant. "And now, I'm going to lose my hair!"

I stood glaring at the three of them. I know I was going to cry. Angry tears. "I'm going to lose my hair."

My parents sat looking baffled. Dad wanted to say something but was afraid. Mam sat with her lips pursed. She wanted to say a lot. I don't think I'd ever screamed at her in my entire life.

Daly seemed to take it in his stride. He came towards me and said calmly, "Would you like to sit down now, Janet?"

I hadn't much of a choice. If I stayed standing, I'd only feel stupid. I nodded and sat down in between my parents again. Dad clasped my hand and Mam, after a few minutes, did the same.

It was more than I hoped for.

And then it was back to the ward. That was when my treatment started. I hadn't read about it, I didn't want to know what it involved, and yet, I couldn't wait to have the whole thing over with so that I'd know what to expect the next time.

The nurse was expecting me. She sat me down and explained what she was going to do. I drifted off somewhere in the middle.

The first thing she did was to start looking for a vein. "I'm just going to get a vein in the back of your hand," she said.

I've horrible hands. Big veiny hands, hands like a washerwoman. That day, my hands were vein-free. Soft and smooth and white.

She then took a needle, "It's called a butterfly," she explained, "because of the tabs on either side."

"I see that all right," Dad said.

Mam gave him a dig.

As I was watching, the nurse inserted the needle into the back of my hand. Some blood flowed out into the tube attached to the needle, and she smiled. "Bingo." She patted my arm. "You've good veins." The needle was then taped to my arm.

I really couldn't believe this was happening.

I didn't feel like I was sick and yet everyone else was

acting as if I was. It was like a play that I'd just walked in on.

"I'm just going to inject a small amount of fluid into the vein," the nurse said, bustling about, "just to make sure it's in properly."

In the fluid went.

"Any pain?"

I shook my head.

"If you do get any burning or swelling at the vein, tell me, OK?"

"She will," Dad said.

And then the scary part happened.

Bags of fluid were brought over. She explained what they were. "This is your chemotherapy, this is hydrating fluid and this is your anti-nausea medication."

"What is nausea?" Dad whispered to Mam.

She whispered something back and he nodded. "Right."

The nurse began to hook me up.

"It may feel cold and you might feel faint," she warned.

The stuff began to leak into my veins.

The three of us watched it with horrified fascination.

I was basically poisoning my system. This stuff was going into my body, into my blood and going to attack everything in its path. I was going to be sick, going to lose my hair and I was allowing it to happen.

Mam sat on one side of my bed. She stared at me and then stared at the medicine.

Dad couldn't take his eyes off it.

The feeling of surrender was alien. In order to live, I had to kill parts of myself, good parts. I had to surrender all I'd been told about not eating stuff that was bad for me and lie back on a bed and watch this poison dripping slowly through every part of me.

I lifted my hand and ran it through my hair.

It had never felt so soft.

CHAPTER FIFTY-SIX

I looked at the world through grainy eyes the next morning. I don't know whether it was lack of sleep or the fact that I'd slept too much. Before I could fully register where I was, more blood was being taken from my arm and more tablets were being shoved into my mouth.

Slowly my brain began ticking over. Hospital beds. Hospital smells. Hospital noises.

Memory began to filter through. Raising my hand, I held it close to my face and peered at it. A tiny bit of redness where the needle had pierced it. A tiny bit of redness where the poison had been injected into my system. I rubbed it gently with my other hand, trying stupidly to caress it, trying I suppose to apologise for what might happen to the rest of me. I felt deeply sorry, as if I'd betrayed myself.

I think I must have fallen asleep after the chemo the day before, all I can remember was that Dad and Mam both kissed me before they left. Weird, hesitant kisses.

Awkward cradling of their faces to mine. Then they'd gone. His arm around her shoulder, her head on his shoulder, bound together by each other.

And I was left, looking after them.

They arrived in sometime during the morning. I heard them before they even came near the ward. Dad's shoes and the rumble of his voice, Mam's voice, set higher as she answered him. I saw them coming down the ward to me. They stopped in front of my bed and Mam's face broke into a smile too bright for the situation. She tried to tone it down. "The nurse said you had a good night," she said.

"Had I?" I couldn't even remember. I didn't want to remember.

"You did." Dad was beaming at me. "You didn't even have that noxious thing the doctor thought you'd have."

Mam and I looked at him.

"What?" she asked.

"You know, the, the puking."

"Nausea," Mam corrected, withering him. She turned to me. "You didn't feel sick, did you?"

I wanted to tell her I didn't feel much of anything. "No," I said. "I wasn't sick."

They both smiled encouragingly at me, as if I'd done something wonderful. "She's strong," Dad said, patting my arm. "You wouldn't be a Boyle if you weren't."

"Oh please," Mam rolled her eyes. "Don't start."

Dad gained the courage to look offended. "I'm going for coffee," he said. "Anyone else want some?"

Both of us nodded.

He left and it was just me and her. She sat down on the chair beside my bed. "So," she swallowed, "How are you feeling – really?"

She didn't want to know.

"Not too bad."

"The doctor said Hodgkin's is very curable."

"Well, he should know I suppose." I didn't want to talk about it anymore.

"He should." She nodded emphatically. "He's paid to know."

I didn't answer. All I wanted was to be left alone. I turned from her and stared fixedly at the wall. We sat in silence until Dad came back, balancing three coffees on his arms.

"Here's Dad now," Mam said brightly. The relief in her voice was so obvious.

Dad sat down on the edge of my bed and handed us each a drink. "Doctor's on his way," he announced.

We sat waiting for him to come. Trying not to look as if we cared.

I was discharged, I was handed a pile of pills, given the amounts to take each day and told to report back to the hospital the following Wednesday.

"You'll get the injection as an outpatient," the doctor explained. "Then you'll take more tablets that week, there'll be a break in treatment of two weeks and back to us again."

"Why the break in treatment?" Dad asked.

"To allow the body to recover. Then when it has, we resume treatment."

"Oh, that's fine so," Dad gave the doctor a smile.

"Janet will be getting treatment for two weeks out of every twenty-eight days – that's the regime she's on."

"I see. Thank you very much, doctor," Dad sounded impressed.

He gave the doctor another smile, then turning to me, he said, "Right, Jan, let's get you home."

Mam picked up my bag, Dad walked in front opening doors for us and I tagged along behind.

At least I was going home.

That was good, I suppose.

I hadn't been sick.

Was that good or bad? Did that mean the drugs weren't working?

My hair was still there. I'd glanced at myself in a mirror and it still looked all right. Was that a good sign?

There was so much I wanted to know. There was so much I was terrified to know.

Mam had insisted on staying with me for the afternoon until either Abby or Beth came back. I didn't want her to, but she wasn't taking no for an answer.

The flat was deserted when we let ourselves in. Abby had left a note telling me all the food that was in the fridge. At the end she'd written, *I'll be back around four to mammy you!*

That was all I needed.

"Isn't that nice?" My mother picked up the note and read through it. "That's very considerate of her." Putting the note back on the table, she went to the fridge and began poking around in it. "Don't you lot eat well?" she remarked.

Food was virtually falling off the shelves. Melons, yogurts, eggs, milkshakes, things that had never seen the inside of our fridge before had now taken up residence. Abby must be on a health-food drive, I thought absently.

"I can make you a sandwich," Mam said. "How about that?"

"All right." I sat down at the table and watched while she poked about our kitchen, putting on the kettle, slicing cheese and tomato, looking for meat, buttering brown bread.

"Is there no white bread?" I asked.

"No – I looked," Mam gave the bread another huge scraping of butter.

That was strange. None of us ever ate brown bread.

Two thickly buttered, triple-decker sambos were put in front of me. She made tea for us both and I ate while she watched.

"I suppose that's why you got so thin," she said, a few minutes later. "You were sick."

"Suppose."

"I honestly thought you were on a diet."

I didn't want to discuss it.

"I was worried about you."

"Please Mam," I said quietly, "I really don't want to talk about it."

She winced. I think she thought that because she was my mother she could start unburdening herself to me. And vice-versa. But she took it on the chin. "All right," she said. Then, she stood up, "More tea?"

I didn't but I knew she'd take it personally if I refused. "Please."

She poured us both another cup and sat down again.

I could see her mentally searching for something to talk about.

"What's the story with Lisa?" I said, wanting to help her out. "How is she?"

"Pregnant," she said, dryly.

I think I'd just picked something she didn't particularly welcome discussing.

Silence.

"Nearly two months pregnant," she said, almost to herself. "And she's doing her Leaving next month." She bowed her head. "Christ."

"Who's the father?"

"I don't know and I don't care." She sounded totally pissed off.

It had been a bad subject choice.

Another long silence.

"Your father thinks it's the big lad he had building for him. The young fella."

"Claude?" I surprised myself by remembering his name.

Mam looked at me. "Yeah," she said slowly. "I'm surprised you remember."

"Why?"

She went red. She stood up from the table and looked flustered. "Oh, oh, no reason," she said in a high voice. "No reason."

"Why?" I asked again. I didn't take my eyes off her. "Well?"

She gave a really false cheery laugh, "Oh, you know," she was rinsing her cup under the tap. "You were in a mood that day. Sulking." She made it sound like great fun.

"I wasn't in a mood."

"No." She turned around and nodded reassuringly, "No, maybe you weren't." Another syrupy smile. She eyed my plate. "Eat up now."

I pushed it away. "I think I'll go to bed."

It was a relief for both of us.

CHAPTER FIFTY-SEVEN

I decided to take Friday off work. It wasn't that I felt bad, it was just so that I could get my head together. I needed to get used to remembering which tablets to take. I needed to feel like talking to people before I ventured out into the real world.

Wednesday had been a major slap in the face. The chemo I'd received had confirmed that I was sick. I suppose, at the back of my head there had been a little banner of hope fluttering away. I'd wanted someone to say that there'd been a mistake, that I didn't need any medication. That I was fine. With each test, with each tablet and finally with the injection of drugs, this banner had been quashed.

Depression had set in big time.

Abby couldn't understand it. "You look fine," she'd announced when she'd arrived in on Thursday. "Doesn't she look fine?" she'd asked my mam.

Mam had nodded.

"I mean," Abby had looked me up and down. "For

someone who's just had toxic drugs pumped into them, she looks great."

She hadn't taken it too well when I'd turned my back and slammed my bedroom door on her.

Mam had tapped on it nervously as she was going. "Bye, love," she called.

"Bye." I'd turned over and stared at Brad.

I'd heard her leaving.

Then Abby had tapped to come in. She hadn't even waited for me to tell her to fuck off. In she came. "Sorry," she said. "Sorry, Jan." She stood shyly in the door frame, staring at the floor. "What a tactless thing to say."

"True though." I lifted myself up on the bed. "What you said was true."

She'd reddened. "I know, but it was stupid. " Looking over at me, she continued, "I was trying to buck you up."

"Don't ever try to make me feel bad then." A feeble joke, but it made us laugh.

Mickey had arrived to take her out that night. He handed me a card. "Abby told me," he said. "Hope you don't mind."

I did, but what could I say. Another person who believed I was sick.

I was sitting watching telly when Beth came in. She stopped dead when she saw me and looked around fearfully. "Abby not here?"

"No."

"Oh." I saw her gulp and come further in. She began to rub her hands up and down her jeans. "How are you?" she mumbled.

"Cancerous." I know it was awful, but she was looking at me as if I was a leper.

The word made her jerk. "That's witty, Jan," she said, turning away. "Nice one."

I felt guilty, but I didn't answer. I turned my attention back to the telly.

The fact that she sat in the furthest seat from me and avoided looking at me all night only served to depress me further.

Midway through the afternoon on Friday the buzzer went. I knew it couldn't be Dave because he'd know I was working.

"Yeah?"

A hesitant voice. "It's me – Al."

"Yeah. What do you want? Come to gawk at me?"

"No."

"Well then?"

"If you fuckin' let me up, I might tell you."

It was like a bucket of cold water all over me. Refreshing.

I buzzed him in.

He arrived with a bunch of flowers. "Here." He shoved them at me. "Put them in some water."

"I've no vase." Trying not to look pleased, I took them from him. "I'll shove them in the sink for the moment."

"Whatever," Al shrugged. "I just thought you might like them."

"I do." I filled the sink with cold water and put them in it. Turning around to him, I said, "Thanks."

"No bother." He came over towards me. "Sorry about Monday," he said gruffly. "It couldn't be helped."

"Suppose not." I was back to being annoyed with him again.

"I mean it," he said earnestly. "Honest, Jan, I'd never let you down." He looked hard at me and when I didn't reply, he said intently, "You know I wouldn't."

"Everyone lets you down at some stage, it's no big deal." I said carelessly. Moving away from him, I occupied myself with throwing the wrapper of the flowers in the bin.

"I hurt me arm," he said, sounding strange. His voice was low, so low I could barely hear it. Rolling up his sleeve he showed me a horrible gash that had been stitched together. "I was in bits with the pain."

"God," I couldn't take my eyes off it. "God," I said again.

He started to roll his sleeve back down. He flashed me a bleak smile, "So, that's why I wasn't in."

"What happened it?"

"A knife," he was buttoning his shirt sleeve, "It got cut with a knife. Fuckin' stupid accident."

He sounded angry. The way he pulled his jumper over his shirt looked angry.

"I managed to tell Lenny about me being sick

anyhow," I said, hoping it'd make him feel better. "It wasn't too bad."

"Good." He looked at me and I looked at him. Al's looks always made me uncomfortable. Starting to babble, I indicated the chair, "How about a cuppa to say thanks for those flowers?"

"Fair exchange." He sat himself down at the table.

Glad to turn away from him, I put on the kettle and searched the press for a packet of biscuits. Oatmeal ones filled the shelves. "Sorry about these," I said unwrapping the packet, "Abby's gone roughage mad."

"I'll eat anything." To prove it he took one and started munching.

He waited until we were both drinking before he asked about Wednesday. "Howd' it go?" he asked, "Or do you want to say?"

I liked the way he asked me that. As if it was my choice to talk about it. "It went fine," I answered. "Weird though, I felt as if everyone was just accepting the fact I was sick." I laughed a bit, to make it seem as if I thought I was being stupid. "It was a bit scary that way."

Al didn't laugh though. "I bet it was," he said.

"The chemo wasn't too bad," I said, realising for the first time that it hadn't been. "I didn't even feel sick from it."

"That's good."

"Does it mean it's not working if you don't get sick?" I couldn't help myself, the question came out of its own accord. My voice quivered as the horrible fear was voiced. "Say the chemo doesn't work, Al?"

He put down his cup and studied me. "It'll work."

I gave a laugh. Hysterical. "And how the fuck do you know?" When he didn't answer, I said again, angrier this time, "How the fuck do you know?" I liked the way he looked stunned. So, I stood up and glowered across at him. "Are *you* a doctor?"

Al stayed sitting. "Sorry," he said. He crumbled the biscuit between his fingers. "I suppose I don't know."

"No, you don't." I still couldn't sit down. "Nobody knows."

Al shrugged hopelessly. "What do you want me to say, Jan?" he said. "That maybe it won't?" He shook his head. "I can't say that."

His words hit me. Sinking back down into my chair, I mumbled out a "sorry".

"Forget it," Al attempted to smile at me.

"Will you do something for me, Al?" I don't know how I dared to ask him. Maybe it was because I knew he'd agree. "Will you promise that whatever happens you'll tell me the truth." I swallowed hard. "If I look like shit, you'll tell me."

He bit his lip. "I dunno, I – "

I struggled to explain, "I want to know the truth. People tell me I look fine and I can't believe them. I need someone I can trust. Please, promise you'll do it," I stopped. "For me."

"Jesus Jan," he gulped, "you'll hate me." He gave a small grin.

"So what's new?"

"Right," he said, "I promise to be honest if you promise not to fall out with me."

"That's a toughie," I smiled back.

"I mean it." He was looking sombrely at me.

"I promise."

We shook on it.

CHAPTER FIFTY-EIGHT

I didn't leave the flat for most of the weekend. Saturday was spent huddled in front of the telly, wrapped in a quilt while the sun baked the streets. Anxious phone calls plunged me further into depression. Mam was on at least twice, wondering how I was.

Sunday morning, I woke up and felt different. It was like peeping out from under a blanket and seeing some light. For some weird reason, I felt slightly more upbeat.

Abby managed to ruin it.

For the third day in a row, she tapped at my door. "I just thought you might like some breakfast," she whispered. I think she thought that I'd acquired sensitive ears during treatment. "Do you want it in bed?"

"I'll get up," I tossed the covers off and pulled on my dressing-gown.

"Are you sure?" she looked at me doubtfully. "I thought you might be tired."

"If I was tired, would I be getting up?" It was an attempt at light-heartedness.

"I guess not." She really had a disapproving face on.

Ignoring her, I pushed past and went into the kitchen. Before she could see, I had shoved my quota of tablets into my mouth and washed them down with water. I hoped they zapped the fuckin' cancer out of it.

"I poured you a bowl of Bran Flakes," Abby gave a nervous smile. "And some orange juice."

"Bran Flakes?" She had to be joking. "I don't eat them."

"Well, I just thought," Abby said breathlessly, "that you know, you'd want to eat stuff that was good for you."

"Abby," I made a big production of pouring the Bran Flakes back into their box, "I want to eat stuff that I like."

"But you'll like these once you try them."

"Only, I'm not going to try them." The last of the Bran Flakes went in. Wiping out my bowl, I turned to the press. "Now, where are the Frosties?"

"Only kids eat Frosties." She had a face on her. "Beth and I didn't buy any this week."

My good humour was disappearing. "So what did you buy that I might eat?"

"Bran Flakes," Abby said weakly.

"Great. Great." I turned to the bread part of the press. "I don't suppose there's any white bread here to make toast with?"

"No."

"Why?" I stared at her. "Why?" I shook my head. "I hate brown bread toasted, it goes all hard."

Abby didn't answer. She shoved the orange juice at me. "At least you like this," she said brightly.

I was forced to drink most of the carton.

She hovered about me all afternoon. It was like we were magnets. If I sat down, she asked if I was tired.

"No, I'm just sitting down."

If I stood up she asked if I was tired.

"No, I'm just standing up."

"Oh, I thought you were off to bed."

Even if I went to the jax, she asked if I was sick.

"Yep, I'm puking my guts up in here."

"That's not funny, Jan."

"Then why did you fuckin' ask?"

"It's all right, I understand."

AAAGGGHHH!

Only the fact that I was in better humour stopped me from killing her. Pity oozed out of her every pore.

At about two, the phone rang. It was my salvation. Dave.

Pressing the phone hard up to my ear, I managed to cut Abby's sombre advising tones off. "Dave, hi," I said, "How's things?"

"I got good news for ya." He sounded lovely.

"Yeah?"

"Yeah." His voice was tripping over itself with glee. "Ya know the geezer I went to meet in Kildare?"

"Uh-huh."

"'E's putting me an' Sam on the radio, some environmental show an' we're goin' to put our case before the nation."

I smiled at his excitement. "That's brilliant!"

"Yeah," Dave said, "It's goin' out on Thursday, live – brill, wot?"

"Excellent."

"So," Dave continued, "Wot you doin' tonight? Fancy meetin' me ?"

I would've said no if he'd asked me Saturday. But I knew Abby was more lethal than chemotherapy any day. "I'd love to."

"I ain't got no dough so it'll be dull enough."

He didn't know that being with him was never dull, at least not for me.

I ignored Abby's advice to wrap up, to keep warm, to walk slowly.

I was going out.

CHAPTER FIFTY-NINE

The following Wednesday morning I was due back at the hospital.

Abby sat grimly at the top of the table watching me eating Frosties. "You should have some toast to go along with that," she said primly, "something sensible."

In order to shut her up, I agreed. Two cardboard slices of toast were handed up to me. "A little something I made earlier," she smiled.

As I sat, doing my best to eat them, she said, "I read somewhere that it's important to eat and drink before chemotherapy."

I hated the sound of that word.

"Stops you from feeling as sick."

I had tablets for that.

"You have to eat healthily, Jan."

"Abby, I don't want to talk about it." I said it calmly. I concentrated on the sound of the toast in my mouth.

"But you have to, it's important for your mental health. You can't keep hiding away – "

"I said I don't want to talk about it."

"You haven't talked about it all week. All you talk about is Dave's big interview."

Couldn't she see that's all I did want to talk about? I wanted to talk about anything but me. I would even have listened to her when she talked about Mickey. But Abby wasn't happy with that. She had suddenly turned the expert on cancer, on treatment, on symptoms, on caring for sick people.

On patronising her flatmates.

Without saying anything, I picked up my bag.

Abby stopped mid-flow. "Where are you going?"

"Out."

"Where?" she looked at her watch. "It's only eight. Your dad won't be here for another half-hour."

I didn't answer. Grabbing my coat from the sofa, I unlocked the door and exited. I ignored her cajolings to come back inside and finish my breakfast.

I gave the front door a huge slam as I left. I knew she was watching me from the window, so without hesitating, I strode purposefully along towards the bus stop without a clue as to where I was going.

I needed some peace.

There was a small coffee shop beside the chemist at the top of the road. I decided to see if it was open. Maybe I could get a nice fruit scone with tonnes of butter and a coffee.

They were open and I walked in. "Scone and a coffee," I said. I paid my money and sat down at a table.

I chose one beside the window because then I could look out and see my dad when he came.

I didn't have to wait long. He drove past the coffee shop in a fancy red car. He didn't even see me as I waved frantically at him. I ended up legging back down the road to the flat. He was just climbing out of the car when I arrived.

"Where did you nick that?" I slagged.

Dad chortled a bit, but didn't answer. "How are you?" he asked. He looked me up and down. "You're looking fine anyhow."

I rubbed my hand along the car's bonnet. "It's nice."

"Watch this." Dad fumbled about in his pocket until he found the keys. Holding the key-ring at arm's length and aiming it at the car, as if he was going to zap it, he made the door locks pop up. "There now." He beamed at his gadget. "Isn't that great."

"Great."

He held open the door for me and I climbed inside. "Where did you get it?"

Dad tapped his nose. "I hired it for the week. It's a surprise for your mother, she's very down in herself."

"She is?"

"Well," Dad said, starting the car and revving the engine so much it screamed, "what with you being sick and Lisa being the way she is and Buddy up in court next week . . ."

"Buddy?"

Dad nodded. "Yeah, he went for Mrs Johnson's cat,

and then, when Mrs J tried to intervene, sure didn't he try and bite the arse off her."

"He did?"

"Oh yes," Dad was driving the car at a safe twenty miles an hour, sitting right up in the seat and peering out the window. "Went for her as if she was a lamb chop."

I laughed. For the first time in days, I actually laughed.

Dad turned around to smile at me and almost ran an OAP into the ground. "It's good to hear you laugh," he said.

It was good to laugh.

Once in the hospital though, the sweaty palms syndrome took over. I couldn't remember much of anything from the week before.

They took more blood from me and we had to sit around for ages while they analysed it. Then it was time for the chemo.

Once again the needle was inserted, really smoothly. I felt nothing. Dad sat with me, patting my hand and not saying very much. Occasionally he wandered out for a smoke, but he always came back in again.

At one stage, he had a packet of boiled sweets with him.

"Your mother and I read that book the doctor gave us," he said, half-embarrassed, "and it said to suck these while you're having," he nodded at the needle, "that."

Everyone seemed to know more than I did. My

fault, I know. The books were still in my room, I just couldn't get around to reading them. Even their covers gave me nightmares.

"Thanks, Dad," I took the sweets from him. "Thanks."

It was over within the hour. Because I'd taken the sickness tablet, I didn't feel bad at all.

"Now remember," the nurse said, "you take your tablets for another week and then don't come back for two weeks."

"Thank you so much," Dad smiled at her. "You've been very helpful."

"Not at all."

I allowed Dad to lead me from the hospital. Another blow to the shock-absorbers. More poison inside me. More crap masquerading as "treatment".

I didn't talk all the way home.

Dad insisted on coming into the flat with me.

"If I don't, your mother'll kill me."

"Dad, all I'll do is go to bed. I don't need your help to do that."

"No nonsense now, Janet." He lit himself a cigarette as we got out of the car. "I've taken the day off work to be with you and that's what I'll do."

I hadn't asked him to do that.

"Besides," he said, "your mother needs some space on her own. Then, I'll surprise her with the car."

There was no getting rid of him.

He came in and I made us tea. "Oh by the way," Dad said, pulling a leaflet from his pocket. "Just in case you're asked, it's your VHI number."

"I don't pay VHI."

"Well and sure I know that," he gave a mildly exasperated shrug, "that's why I do. I knew when you moved out there was no way you'd pay for any of that stuff." He shoved the paper to me. "So I do."

My VHI number!

"It won't pay for everything mind, but it'll go a fair way. And your mother and I will do what we can."

I had tried not to think of cost. It had flitted briefly into my head, but knowing that I was broke, I had shoved it aside. And now . . . now I had a VHI number.

"Dad," I looked at him. My dad.

"What?" he smiled benignly at me as he took a sip of his tea.

"I just want to say – "

"Jesus, girl, is there no sugar in that!" He spat some of his tea back into his cup. "Get us a bit of sugar, would you."

"Sure." I got him the sugar and watched while he dumped half the bowl in on top of his tea.

"Now what was that you were saying?" he asked.

"Nothing," I shrugged, the moment was lost. I held up the VHI number. "Just – just – thanks for this."

He looked baffled. "For that? Sure what about it? Amn't I your father?"

Abby was horrified when she arrived back.

Dad had left and I'd gone to bed.

I was asleep, actually having a nice sleep when her screech penetrated into my comatose state.

"There's smoke in here!" I heard her banging open windows. "That's terrible!"

"What of it?" That was Beth.

"What of it?" I could picture Abby trying to grab armfuls of smoke and dump it out the window. "Jan is sick, it's not good to have her in a smoky atmosphere."

"Oh feck off," Beth retorted. "She'll be fine."

"Beth," Abby was at her condescending best, "Jan has," her voice lowered respectfully, "cancer." Voice back up again. "It's no picnic, she'll get worse before she gets better."

Well, that was nice to know.

"If she ever gets better, that is."

Jesus!!

"Abby give it a rest, willya." I heard Beth sit down. "I feel I'm living in Emergency Ward 10."

"You'd want to start showing some concern," Abby sounded like my mam now. "You're hurting Jan by not being nice to her."

"Abby, I really don't want to discuss this."

"Well, I do. I mean, what is your problem?"

There was the slam of a bedroom door.

The conversation was closed.

CHAPTER SIXTY

I forced Abby to listen to Dave that Thursday night. "It's very interesting," I told her.

She wanted to listen to the other Dave. Dave Fanning. It was a phase she was going through, pretending she was into obscure music.

But I got my way.

I was sick after all.

According to Dave the programme was to start at eight. Sam and him were meant to be on first.

That night there was great excitement – on my part anyhow. Abby arrived home from work with cans of fizzy drinks. "You can't drink, remember," she said. "It might react with the drugs."

I didn't argue, I wanted to stay on her good side.

Mickey arrived with crisps and dips and popcorn. "Thought I might as well," he said. "It not often you get to hear the saviour of the world live on air."

Abby clapped her hands and giggled uproariously at his wit.

It was funny how he suddenly developed a spine when she was around.

Mickey dumped his purchases on the table and started looking for little bowls to put them in. "Have you any bowls for the crisps?" he asked, "Might as well do it right."

They were like some old married couple, clucking away over a few cracked bowls. Abby did the artistic arranging of things on the table and by the time eight o'clock came, all the food was gone.

There was a big ceremony as the dial was turned to switch on the radio. Mickey started humming the "Alleluia".

"Shut up," I scowled at him across the table.

He went red as Abby said, "Jan, that's not nice, you shouldn't talk to Mickey like – "

"Shut up!"

Compassionate understanding crossed Abby's face. "It's the cancer talking," she big-mouthed over at Mickey.

"It's fuckin' me talking," I spat back.

"Oh," Abby looked as if she just singed her fingers, "Oh, oh, Jan you weren't meant to hear that."

"I'm sick, not deaf."

There was an uncomfortable silence. Abby broke it. "I know you're not deaf," she said benevolently.

She was going to send me over the edge.

Luckily for her, the news ended and some crappy diddlly-aye music came on. "And now," the announcer said, "it's time for The Green Machine."

More crappy music, which died out.

"How yez, and a very big welcome ta dee Green Machine!"

The bogger voice shocked the three of us. Abby and Mickey exploded in mirth, I sat, stony-faced, waiting for them to shut-up.

"And ta-day, or ta-night radder, we have two men wid us who are camping out in dee woods near dee Dublin moun-tins. Dave and Sam. Hi, guys."

"Hi." That was Sam.

"'Ello." My Dave.

"Now, what's dee pint, lads?"

More cackles from Abby and Mickey. "Shut up," I snarled. They were not going to ruin it on me.

Sam began to talk.

And talk.

And talk.

The interviewer couldn't get a word in edgeways.

Sam went on.

And on.

And on.

Abby and I looked at each other. "What is he talking about?" Abby asked, baffled.

I pretended not to hear her.

Mickey was listening though.

"This is boring," Abby gave a huge yawn.

"Quiet," Mickey hissed.

"Oh, excuse me," Abby made a face at him.

"Well, now, dat's fascinatin' stuff, rite enough," the

interviewer said, interrupting Sam's flow. "How about you, Dave, what's your story?"

A big intake of breath from the three of us. I made shushing motions with my fingers.

"Why are you here, in Ireland, in our mountains?"

"They're not just yah mountains though, are fey?" Dave replied.

I'd heard that the first time I'd met him.

"It's our world, it's our kids' world, it's our grandkids' world. It's 'anded down from one generation to the next, each generation 'as a responsibility to protect it for the next generation." He stopped. "Like an 'eirloom, I guess."

I was pleased to see Abby and Mickey both listening now.

"So wat's wrong wid a few men wanting to build a few houses on a mountain?"

Dave laughed. "So wot's wrong with a few men destroying eco-systems? Killin' rare wild-life, knocking down a few great oak trees, cuttin' into the earth and makin' loadsa dough? You tell me, mate."

Dave answered a few more questions. Then he was asked why he was doing it.

"'Cause I believe it's the right thing for me ta do. I love this earth, we all come from this earth in one way or another. We destroy it, it'll destroy us." He paused, "Fink of it this way, we use CFCs they burn a hole in the ozone layer, we get skin cancer. We pollute countries with black smoke, we get lung cancer. Wot goes around, comes around, ya know."

There was silence after he'd finished. On the radio and in our kitchen.

Then the interviewer thanked the lads and went onto his next guest.

Abby, Mickey and I couldn't look at each other.

I got up and went into my room.

CHAPTER SIXTY-ONE

The two weeks I was off medication were like school holidays. Even though I tried not to think about being sick, I suppose it must have been there at the back of my mind.

No, who am I kidding? It was always there at the back of my mind.

The day I took the final tablet that finished my first course of chemo was unbelievable. I hadn't planned on the sense of release that invaded my body. As far as I was concerned, I was normal again. Poison-free, tablet-free. Not a scratch, not a scar, to show for the two weeks of hell I'd been through.

Hell. More mentally than physically.

I wanted to go out. I wanted to do things. I wanted people to see me living and say, oh, look at her, she's just like us.

In fact, I felt so happy that I was determined to work Monday to Friday without a break.

Slowly I walked up O'Connell Street, enjoying the

madness of rush hour. I'd actually always enjoyed rush hour, because if it was really busy, I had an excuse for being a few minutes late, which chopped a few minutes off the day.

"Well, how's it goin'?" Al came up behind me and pulled at my hair. "In for the week, huh?"

"In for the week."

He looked really nice that morning – he always did when he smiled, he had lovely Tom Cruise teeth. And I liked his jeans, the really really washed ones, faded unevenly to a white. He had a faded denim shirt on too, rolled up at the sleeves. His hair flopped over his forehead as he grinned down at me. "That'll be a shock to the system. Jan Boyle workin' for a week."

"Feck off!" I gave him a belt.

He caught my hand and held it. "Fancy goin' for a pizza tonight, to celebrate?"

I wish he'd let my hand go. "Celebrate what?" I asked. I had nothing to celebrate.

"The first month of getting better?" He let my hand drop. "Well, what d'you say?"

"On one condition."

"Name it."

"That you don't talk about me, all right?"

"Jan," Al said patiently, "I intend on having a good night. Not boring myself stupid."

I belted him again and ran as he made a grab for me.

Lenny gave me a paternal smile as I walked in. "And how are you?" he asked.

"Thin," Liz spat from her corner of the office. "Thin, that's how she is."

I froze, with my hand on the coat-hanger. Al rolled his eyes and moved past me to sit as his desk.

"I mean," Liz said, "what are you on? How come you look so good all of a sudden?"

That was the best thing she could have said. My hand relaxed and I almost collapsed with relief.

Lenny giving me a wink, said, "Yep, she looks mighty all right – a fine girl is our Jan."

"Not as fuckin' fine as Derbhla," Henry sneered. "Everyone knows what you think of Derbhla."

I hurried to my seat before I got caught in the crossfire.

"I think Derbhla's a lovely girl, a fine, well-made woman and I don't deny that." Lenny looked at the rest of us. "Do I, lads?"

None of us reacted.

"An ould lad like you, saying yur fuckin' prayers you should be."

"Well, and I do that too. I pray for a woman like Derbhla every night."

"Jaysus, Our Lord has fuckin' better things to be doing than listening to a male-menopause victim like yourself."

"He has indeed," Lenny nodded pleasantly. "He has your court cases for faulty v-necks to be sorting out for one."

"Ya bollox. Don't you start that again."

The bitching went on all morning.

When lunch-time came, it was a relief to get out of the office.

I went into the canteen, bought a sambo and tea and carried my purchases down to a table. I didn't have to remember to take tablets. Wonderful.

Angela and Liz joined me. Angela hadn't really spoken to me since I'd lost weight. It was a surprise to see her heave herself into the chair opposite and unwrap her Rivita biscuit.

"Hello, Jan," she said. "How's the diet going?"

Liz sat in beside me. "She swears she's not on a diet," she said sarcastically. "I mean, come on."

"Have you been for interview yet?" Biting into my ham sambo, I looked at Angela, desperately hoping for a change in subject.

"That proves you're dieting," Angela pronounced. She took a small nibble out of her cracker and nodded wisely. "Side-stepping the question."

"She is, isn't she." Liz was excited. She gave me quite a sharp poke in the ribs. "That proves you've something to hide, Jan."

Something snapped. Maybe it was because they were ganging up on me, maybe it was a throw-back to my miserable adolescence or maybe it was because I was totally pissed off. Fuck them, was all I could think of. "OK," I said, "I give in."

Shock and hope lit both their expressions.

"You want to know how I've lost weight?"

"Yeah." Liz leaned so far into me that her elbow squashed the second half of my sandwich.

"What did I say?" Angela had recovered herself and was gazing at me in scorn. "There was no need to lie about it."

"You want to know the best way to lose weight? You want to know how I did it?" My voice was rising and people were looking over.

Liz, who'd been busy rubbing my sambo from her sleeve, paused briefly. Out of the corner of my eye I saw Angela giving her the nod to proceed with the interrogation.

"Yes," Liz said, "what's the secret?" She was breathless with anticipation.

"No secret," I shrugged. My voice was hard. I had to keep it like that. "I just caught cancer."

Angela stopped eyeing up my squashed sambo. She turned shocked eyes on me.

Liz gave a bark of a laugh. "That's in horrible taste, Jan."

"It's true though." I banged my cup down and stood up. "Now will the two of you just fuck off and leave me alone."

Al and I were sitting in Pizza Express. In front of us there was a massive twelve-inch pizza with everything on it. It was aptly called The Works.

"So you told Liz and Angela," he said, as he poured us both a glass of water. "You know it'll be all over the place by tomorrow."

I stared at my slice of pizza that I suddenly didn't

want. "I know, but sure, they'll have to know sooner or later."

"I guess so," Al agreed. Then, tapping my plate and grinning, he scolded, "Eat up now, before it goes cold."

"You sound like an ould one."

"I didn't pay for a pizza to go to waste, cancer or no cancer."

That made me smile.

The subject of me was dropped. He told me all the news I'd missed. Everyone had been for their interviews. "To be honest," he said, "the place was mental last week. Feckin' interview mania took over."

"Oh yeah," I smiled at him over a slice of pizza, "how'd' you do?"

"Aw, I dunno," he shrugged, "I wore in me good suit – "

"The one you wore to work your first day?"

"The very one."

"You looked like a prat so."

"Thanks very much," Al pretended to look offended. "Anyhow, the interview wasn't too bad. Jimmy Madden asked me some right shitty questions though."

"Not as bad as the ones he asked Henry, I bet."

Al exploded in a laugh. Bits of pizza sprayed everywhere. "He crucified Henry," he chortled. "Feckin' cruicified the poor bastard."

"How?" His laugh, as usual, was making me laugh.

"Aw, Jaysus, Jan," Al shook his head and wiped his eyes, "Aw, Jaysus, you never saw a guy more broken in yer life."

"How?"

"Firstly, right, Henry said that Madden wore a red v-neck to annoy him." Al nodded as I began to giggle. "He swore Madden did it on purpose."

"No."

"Yep and then, Madden started asking the weirdest questions, really mad stuff. Even Lenny had never heard of the stuff Henry was asked. So Henry reckons Madden was making stuff up."

"He couldn't do that."

"Henry says he did," Al's face was animated. "But the best was, an' you're not goin' to believe it," Al had started laughing again, "The best was the end of the interview."

I wished I'd been in work. "What?"

Al pointed to himself, "I'm Henry right – just imagine I'm Henry, right?"

"Right." I'd never seen Al so animated.

"I'm Henry arriving in after the interview, OK?"

"OK."

Al coughed, and then in a perfect take-off of Henry's voice, he said, "I couldn't answer a single fuckin' question."

I coiled up laughing.

"But I fuckin' got him. I fuckin' got him." Al was wagging his finger and doing Henry's jabbing gestures. "At the end of the interview, right, fuckin' Madden turns around, smooth as a fuckin' piece a diarrhoea and asks *ME* have I any fuckin' thing I'd like to ask. An' do ya know what I fuckin' said?" Al glared at me. "Do ya fuckin' know?"

"No." The tears were coming out my eyes.

"I fuckin' said," Al was beginning to grin now, "I fuckin' said to him, right, I fuckin' leaned over and I fuckin' said to him, "'Here, tell us, where did ya get that *fuckin' whore* of a jumper?'"

I screamed with laughter. "No way!"

Al was grinning broadly. "Yep. That's what he says anyhow."

"I don't believe it." I was laughing really loud and people were looking over. "That's brilliant."

Al grinned.

"And Liz," I asked, as I composed myself, "how did she do?"

"She won't tell anyone," Al made a face. "Not telling anyone what she was asked."

"Typical." I grinned.

"You should've done it, you know," Al said. "If you were all right, like, you should have done it."

I gave a laugh. "Who'd give me promotion," I scoffed. "Sure they all think I'm a waste of space."

"You're not a waste of space," Al said softly. He shook his head. "Don't say that."

"You know what I mean," I said. "I'm not going to win Team Member of the Year, am I?"

"No," he grinned. "But you're not a waste of space."

"I do think that's the nicest thing you've ever said to me." I smiled at him.

"You asked me to tell you the truth," he said. "I'm just doing my job."

He insisted on getting the bus back and walking me home. "So," he said, turning to face me, "how are you – really?"

"Al – " I shrugged and turned away.

"It's OK, I was just askin'." He went red and gave a small grin. "Put my foot in it – huh?"

"No." Impulsively, I stood on my tip-toes and planted a kiss on his cheek. He smelt nice. "You've been great."

His hand came up to his face and he rubbed it where I'd kissed it. "The nicer I get, the bigger the snog?" He looked at me half-hopefully.

"Yeah – nicer as in archangel material."

He gave a laugh and something about it made my heart go all buttery. Maybe it was the way he stopped all of a sudden and seemed about to say something. Or the way the grin stayed on his face and his eyes gazed at me. Or maybe it was just him.

Anyway, he never got to say what he wanted because someone grabbed me around the neck and planted a kiss on my head. "Wot's the story 'ere?" Dave said. "Jan out with strange blokes?"

"Dave!" I was thrilled to see him, but I felt a bit let-down for some reason. "What are you doing here?"

"Just comin' ta see ya. We got news on our appeal today." He planted another kiss on my hair. "It's getting 'eard in the next couple of months."

"Really?"

"Yeah. Crowley," he looked at Al and explained, "that's our solicitor." Turning to me he continued, "He

467

rang Sam and told 'im. We should know wot's 'appening with the land by the autumn at least." He started to nibble my ear.

Laughing, I pushed him off. "Willya stop!"

"Eh, listen lads," Al said, "I'll head off now."

"Oh, hang on," I eased myself out of Dave's grip. "Dave, meet Al, he's a guy I work with."

"'Ow are ya, mate?" Dave held out his hand and Al took it.

"Dave's my boyfriend," I said to Al. "He's an environmentalist."

"Nice to meet you." Al shoved his hands into his pockets and smiled at the two of us.

"Come on in," I said to him. "Don't go yet."

Al shot a glance at Dave and shook his head. "Naw, naw, I'd better go, Jan." He nodded to Dave. "See you again."

"See ya, mate." Pulling me after him, Dave made for the front door. "I have a special present for ya," he said, beginning to kiss my hand. "Very special."

As he pulled me in the door, I shot a glance after Al. I really wished he'd come inside.

CHAPTER SIXTY-TWO
JUNE

The night before the second batch of chemo I had terrible dreams. I was in a nest that didn't belong to me. All the other birds were trying to push me out. The more they pushed, the harder I screamed. The harder I screamed, the more they pushed. Until, in one major scream, I was sent falling through the air. My wings wouldn't work. I woke up before I hit the ground.

Abby, who'd done a great job of being normal for the past while, had her mournful face on at breakfast. "Hello, Jan," she said. "How are you today?"

Jesus!

It was like coming back to reality after a good holiday.

Beth breezed out from her room. Dressed in her work-gear of black skirt and a green shirt, she nevertheless managed to look good. Slight hesitation as she saw me and then a cheery, "Hi folks, gotta rush."

"Jan's back at the hospital today," Abby said.

"Oh, you'll do great, won't you?" Beth didn't even look at me as she talked. She looked past me to the door. "Cancer's very curable these days." Shoving a hat on her head, she grabbed a piece of toast off the table. "See you later."

"That was Jan's slice," Abby yelled after her.

Glancing at my watch, I saw that I had about ten minutes to kill before I left. I did not want to spent the time listening to Abby trying to be perky and uplifting when all I felt was a grinding pissed-offedness. "I'm going to wait for the taxi outside," I said, "get some fresh air."

I knew she couldn't argue with that, so out I went.

The air wasn't that fresh as it happened. It was a dull, drizzly, heavy day. A real manifestation of pathetic fallacy.

Mam was in the taxi that picked me up that morning. I'd hoped it would be Dad. At least I could have a conversation with him. Obviously, the two of them had decided to take turns shepherding me to and from the hospital.

"Hello Janet," Mam said, opening the taxi door for me, "you're looking well."

I hated when people who knew I was sick said that. I couldn't trust them. It was scary, the people I confided in were the ones I'd normally trust. Well, I never trusted anyone completely, but they were the people closest to me, and yet, I kept wondering if they knew something I didn't. I kept wondering if the doctor had told my parents stuff about me that I didn't know.

But because I was such a yellow-belly, I was afraid to ask. And if they denied it, how would I know if they were telling the truth? It was a crazy circle that kept going around and around in my head.

"You don't have to bring me to the hospital," I said, slamming the door of the car and sitting in beside her. "I can get a taxi there and back myself."

"We don't mind," Mam said. "We like going with you."

"What? Like seeing me getting poisoned? Is that what you like?"

Mam closed her eyes. "Don't be ridiculous, Janet," she said wearily. "That's not what I meant."

I shifted away from her. "Well, that's what it sounded like."

She pursed her lips and didn't reply.

I wanted her to though. I wanted a fight with her. "I'm able to get a taxi on my own, you know."

"I'm sure you are."

My blood boiled. "Don't patronise me."

I saw her steal a glance at the taxi-driver and I knew I'd done it. Made her embarrassed. Now she was going to come after me. I prepared myself for the onslaught.

She said nothing. She folded her arms, lay her head back on the seat and stared at the ceiling.

Bitch!

At the hospital, I got out before her. Almost running up the steps, hoping I'd lose her, I entered the hospital.

The heat overwhelmed me. The smell of it, up my nose, in my hair, all over me. I had to stop and catch my breath. I put my hand against the wall to steady myself, the sweat coming off my palms made patches on the paper. The biting anger that had cushioned me since breakfast was gone. I only felt despair.

Mam's hand on my shoulder made me jump. "All right?" she asked. It was in a gentle motherly voice. A voice I hadn't heard in years.

"Just a bit dizzy," I shook her off. "With the heat and everything."

She didn't attempt to touch me again. Still, she walked beside me as we made our way to the part of the hospital reserved for people like me.

I saw her wince as they did another blood test and she turned away when they started injecting the drugs. I just sat still as they bustled around me. Answers to questions they asked, I replied in monosyllables. Someone asked had I been sick.

"No."

"She's been lucky," Mam said.

I wanted to kill her.

Treatment over, it was time to go. Mam pushed the door open for me and let me go in front. I came face to face with a woman.

A thin-faced, weary-eyed woman. She was getting to her feet and her scarf slipped. Her scarf slipped and floated to the ground.

I couldn't take my eyes off her. Her head was completely bald. Totally bald. She was bending down to pick up the scarf and I could only stare. Lifting herself upright, she saw me and nodded.

She smiled.

How could she smile?

She looked what I dreaded.

"Hello," Mam said to her as she came out the door. She held it open while the woman went in.

I allowed Mam to propel me away and out of the hospital.

She brought me back to the flat and I just wanted to go to bed.

I was so grateful for the tiredness. It meant that I could forget.

CHAPTER SIXTY-THREE

The buzzer rang and we all ignored it. *Eastenders* was on.

It rang again.

And a third time.

"Jesus!" Abby leapt up and pressed the intercom. "What?" she barked.

There was a silence and then, "Is Jan there?"

"Yeah, who's asking?"

"It's Al," I said from my position on the good chair. "Buzz him up."

"Come up," Abby said. Turning to me, she warned, "You'd better talk quietly." Despite her overpowering sympathy at my predicament she just would not tolerate noise during a soap.

There was a tap at the door.

"It's open," I called.

"Quiet," Beth hissed.

"Hiya," Al smiled over at me as he came in.

The glares he received from my flatmates made him stop.

"We're watching *Eastenders*," I whispered, beckoning him over. "Another fifteen minutes and I'm all yours."

This remark didn't even cause a raised eyebrow or a smutty comment.

Al stood awkwardly by as the three of us ignored him.

To be honest, I wanted to talk to him but I hadn't the nerve. Every so often I'd smile at him and he'd give a nod back.

When the programme ended, the three of us turned to him.

I could see the way he hunched himself up, the way his fists curled and I wanted to die for him. "Just, eh, just called to see, eh how you were," Al focused desperate eyes on me and blushed.

"She's great," Beth answered for me. "Sailing through it, aren't you?"

"Well, I think . . ."

"Tea?" Beth asked, hauling herself from the floor. She reached out a hand and touched me briefly, two quick taps on the shoulders. "Jan hates going on about it."

I suppose she was right, but the way she said it annoyed me.

"Tea?" Beth asked again, going to fill the kettle.

"Eh, well . . ."

"Take it while it's going," Abby laughed. "It's not often Beth offers."

"He will." Now it was my turn. "Won't you, Al?"

"Suppose." Al sat on the sofa and smiled over at me. I know he wanted to go because the others were there, but I didn't want to let him.

"How was work today?" I asked, hoping I'd get some mileage out of it.

Al shrugged and studied his hands. "All right."

"Any news on promotions?" I wanted him to look at me, just one look so he could see it was me he was talking to and not the others.

"Nope." He sat back in the sofa and then sat up straight. It was like he didn't know what to do with himself.

"Any more news on Henry's jumpers?" I asked then, thinking that at least it would get a smile.

"Dunno." His voice was flat, dull.

Abby giggled. "You're a mine of information all right."

Beth laughed then.

I don't think they meant to be unkind. It was just a joke. In fact, I even smiled.

Al's head bowed further. I saw him bite his lip – it's what he does when people upset him – before standing up and saying, "Listen, eh, sorry about the tea, but, eh, I haveta be somewhere."

"Al!" I couldn't believe it as he walked to the door. I got up off the chair and went after him. "Al!"

I didn't take any notice of what the other two were doing as I ran out the door after him. "Al, hang on would you?"

"What?" He turned to me.

"What is it with you? Why wouldn't you stay?"

He glared at me. His face looked angry but his eyes didn't. "And have them laugh at me?" he said in a furious whisper. "You think I'm that stupid?"

"Hey," I reached out to touch him, but he jerked away. "It was a joke. Abby was joking." I didn't want him to walk away on me. "You should hear the things they say to other people. It's not just you."

He didn't say anything.

"Please don't go."

"I only called to see how you were anyhow," he said sulkily. "That's all."

"And I appreciate that. And, well," I gulped, "I'm grand." He was like a kid. "Thanks for calling."

"No problem."

"And call again."

His eyes met mine.

"I mean it."

"Right," he exhaled a slow breath. "I'm sorry."

The relief I felt was weird. After all it was only Al.

"I can't blame you," I whispered, "after the way they treated you the last time, you're bound to be suspicious."

The wrong thing to say. I knew it was the minute the sentence finished. More dark surly looks. "Why'd' you have to bring that night up?"

I'd had it.

Pleasing Al was like walking on eggshells. "Fuck off," I said. Not exactly the most reasoned response, but definitely the most satisfying.

Both of us walked away from each other.

CHAPTER SIXTY-FOUR

I screwed up the courage to go into work the next day. Normally if I have a row with someone, I try my best to avoid them. But there was no way I was spending a day on my own in the flat. Being alone meant thinking and thinking involved hard work.

I'm not into hard work.

So, hauling myself and my copious pills to the bus terminus, I caught the bus to O'Connell Street.

As I disembarked, I saw Al in front. I knew it was him because he has the sexiest arse of anyone. Dave's is nice, but Al's has a Bruce Springstein "Dancing in the Dark" look about it. I decided not to bother catching him up, it was more enjoyable to watch him from behind. That, plus the fact that I was a trembling wreck of a coward made me decide not to confront him until I actually met him in work, surrounded by Lenny, Henry and Liz.

I gave him plenty of time to get settled into his desk before walking into the office. I would've run right back out again only he saw me.

He had been the first in and I was second.

Neither of us spoke as I hung my jacket up and walked to my desk. There was silence as I switched on my computer. He said nothing as I sifted through my dump of a desk looking for something to type. Finding a coffee-smeared effort of Lenny's I began to set up the word processor on my screen.

"Little Miss Industry today," Al threw the remark from across the office. He sounded amused.

"Sorry?" I arched my eyebrows and stared at him.

"You," Al gave a gesture. "Workin'."

"That's what I get paid for." My words were snappy but I was smiling over at him.

He smiled back. "Friends?"

"Friends with you?" I threw my eyes upwards. "A touchy bastard, that's all you are."

"I know." He surprised me by agreeing with me. "I can't help it."

"I like touchy bastards."

"Good."

We didn't need to say any more. He turned back to his running magazine and I turned back to trying to make sense out of Lenny's English grammar.

Liz was the only one in the office that got promotion. A phone call came from management that afternoon to tell her.

To give her credit, she didn't scream or jump about or go mad. She put the phone down and said, "Listen guys, just to let you know – I got promotion." She glanced at Henry and Al. "Sorry, I know you both went for it too."

"Well, that is marvellous!" Lenny came over and clapped her on the back. "Good girl, good girl yerself."

Henry went over too. "Congrats." He stuck out his hand. "Well done." As she took his hand, he said carelessly, "I made so much fuckin' money from flogging me jumpers, I don't need promotion anyhow."

"Well done, Liz," I smiled at her across the office. "I knew you'd get it."

"You knew more than me so," Liz laughed. She picked up the phone. "I'd better ring me parents and Andy too, just to tell them."

"I vote we buy a cake to celebrate," Lenny was digging his hand into his pocket. "A nice cream sponge or something."

"I'll go." My hand shot up. Anything to get out for a few minutes.

"A willing messenger, that's a great girl," Lenny handed me some silver. "See what you can get out of that."

I took the money from him and shoved it into my pocket. Turning to go, I saw Al's face.

I don't think I ever saw someone look as gutted.

He saw me looking and his face changed. "Hurry back," he smiled. "I'm starving."

Getting up from his desk he went over and slapped Liz on the back. "Well done," he laughed. "It must've been the short skirt that did it."

She laughed and flapped him away.

I felt bad for him.

Of course, Liz wanted us all to go for a drink to celebrate.

"Can you drink, Jan?" she asked anxiously. "You know, with – with – with what you have?" She blushed a deep shade of red. It was the first time she'd directly referred to me being sick since the day I'd told her and Angela in the canteen.

She'd been nice to me though, taking all her files back and asking me if I wanted anything typed. I suppose it was her way of saying she was sorry for me.

"I don't know," I shrugged. And I didn't.

"Small doses," Al piped up from his corner. "Otherwise it might disagree with you."

How the hell did he know?

"How the fuck do you know?" I glared at him. It wasn't his business.

Lenny began to hum, his way of extracting himself from the exchange, I suppose. Henry threw an uncomfortable glance around before picking up a file and exiting. Neither he or Lenny had ever referred to my illness since the news of it had crept around the building like a fungus. Lenny kept smiling at me though, every time I lifted my head from my desk, there he'd be, smiling away. He was trying to be nice, but it was seriously weird. Henry had done a massive willpower job by not asking me to go into the gory details of my illness. I guess it was his way of saying he cared.

I liked that they didn't talk about it, that they were silent in their support. But I would've liked to be able to talk about it if I'd wanted. Which I didn't. But still.

There's no pleasing me, I guess.

"Well?" I asked Al. "How come you're such an expert on chemotherapy?"

Lenny began a louder mindless hum.

Liz began to shuffle some papers.

Al shrugged. "Saw a programme about it on the telly," he said nonchalantly. "Drink in moderation."

He was lying. I could smell when he was lying. But because he'd said I could drink, I let him away with it. "I'll go so," I said over to Liz who was pretending not to listen to us.

She smiled. Looking at the others she said, "Well lads, any other takers?"

Lenny said he'd go and then, Henry arriving back agreed as well.

"Al?" Liz asked.

"I'll go for one," Al said reluctantly.

I was surprised, he normally never went out with the office. This was a big deal for him.

"Don't sound so fuckin' enthusiastic," Henry jeered. "Be gracious in defeat, Al. She got the promotion and you didn't."

I thought Al was going to plant him. I really did. He stood up and scowled over. "Would you ever give your mouth a rest for once in your life," he snapped. "Just for one bloody time."

Then he walked out.

"It'll be a good night this," Lenny joked, rubbing his hands together. "I can feel it in me waters."

We were sitting in the pub that adjoined our office building. Henry had insisted that we all go there. The idea was that time spent searching for a pub would be better spent boozing. Derbhla and Angela had tagged along with the rest of us.

Derbhla was sitting as close as she could to Al without actually sitting on top of him. Al was trying desperately to talk to Lenny and ignore the fact that Debhla was flaunting tonnes of flesh for his perusal.

Angela and I were sitting either side of Liz.

"I wish I hadn't bothered," Liz grumbled. She was drinking some sort of fancy cocktail thing that Lenny had insisted on buying. "I mean," she gestured around at the three lads, "was I dreaming when I thought I'd enjoy spending a night in their company?"

Angela laughed. "I don't know how you work in that office, Liz – pack of weirdos."

I coughed.

"Except you," Angela said hastily. "You and Liz are normal."

She wouldn't have said that a fortnight ago. Being sick suddenly made me a normal person. The miracles of modern diseases.

"Thanks," I said sardonically, raising my glass.

I wouldn't have done that a fortnight ago either.

I was gratified to see her blush. Stupid fat cow. Stupid fat healthy cow.

I was drinking a Southern Comfort because I was only allowing myself one drink. This was a strong drink and it might do something for me. My head was a bit shaky actually. I felt tired, all I really wanted to do was to go back to the flat, but Jan, the good-time girl part of me wouldn't let me. I was free from hospital and I was living.

Living people got drunk.

I ordered another one. I knocked it back.

My head was light. If you drank at speed it was cheaper to get drunk than drinking slowly.

Angela and Liz were talking to each other now, I don't know what they were saying, something about hairstyles and fashion. Angela was big into stuff like that.

Angela was big, full stop. I grinned at my internal wit.

"Great to see you smiling," Henry bellowed in my ear.

There was music coming from speakers behind us.

"How are you?" he shouted again. He was slightly drunk. He never would have dared to ask me that if he was sober.

The others, hearing the question, tuned in. Angela and Liz put on concerned faces. Lenny just put his pint on the table and studied me. Derbhla even stopped laughing at everything Al said to listen.

"I'm grand," I said, "except for a lump or two here and there, I'm fine."

They laughed. They thought how brave I was to say that.

I know they did.

I was just drunk. Or feeling a bit drunk.

"Well, fair play to you," Lenny said. "That's the spirit."

"Another spirit would go down very nicely, Lenny," I tipped my glass at him.

He jumped up, eager to show how obliging he was. "Begod, I will. What is that you're drinkin'?"

"She's had enough, I think," Al's voice cut through the conversation. "Come on, Jan, I'll bring you home." He stood up, knocking Derbhla sideways so that her skirt went right up her backside.

Lenny and Henry sucked in enough air to vacuum-pack the room.

"I have not had enough," I said crossly. "I have not."

"Jan," Al said, as if he was talking to a moron, "just come on." He held out his hand to me.

"Get lost," I waved him away. "I don't need a baby-sitter. I don't need you."

Lenny sat back down again.

"Lenny," I said, "I want a drink."

He stood back up again.

"Shove a Southern Comfort in that." I held out my glass and he hesitated to take it.

"Maybe Al's right," he said, not meeting my eye. "Maybe it's best if you went home now."

I was furious. Out of proportion furious. "He just wants to get away from her," I pointed to Derbhla. "She frightens him."

I don't know who I'd embarrassed more, Al or Derbhla.

She opened her mouth to say something, but then closed it. She hoisted herself upright in the seat and glowered at me. But she couldn't say anything because I had CANCER. I could see it in her face, the horrible things she wanted to say, but she wouldn't.

She was as frustrated as me.

I'd underestimated Al though. He wasn't a pushover like the others. He went red, like he normally did. He ran his hands through his hair and bit his lip, like he normally did. But he let none of that stop him. "Thanks, Jan," he said, sounding bitter, "Ruin the night, why not?"

"Now, Al . . ." That was Lenny trying to butt in.

"She's not ruining . . ." That was Liz. About to say that she was having a great time.

"I'm enjoying myself anyhow." That was Angela who probably was because all the muck raking was at everyone else's expense.

Henry just slugged back his pint and for once said SFA.

Al pointed to his watch. "I'm heading off, Jan, if you want to come, come. If not, don't bother."

Who the fuck did he think he was?

"All right," I stood up and the world tipped eerily. "I'll go with you, you stupid bastard."

"That's the girl," Lenny stood up to let me out. "That's the girl."

I felt like thumping him.

"Come on," Al's voice had changed. He caught me by the arm and escorted me out of the pub.

I held onto him as we headed to the door.

The hum of conversation around the table resumed.

Al and I walked to the bus stop in silence. He had his arm around my waist to steady me as we made our way to it. I liked the feel of his arm about me. It was reassuring.

"I'll walk you to the flat," he said as the bus arrived. "Make sure you get home all right." His voice was gentle now, as if I hadn't called him a bastard. I don't think I'd ever called someone that before, in a serious way. My language seemed to be falling apart along with the rest of me.

"I'm sorry for calling you a bastard," I mumbled, half-ashamed as Al guided me to a seat at the back of the bus. "I was just angry."

"I know." He took his arm from around my waist and stared out the window. He began to trace patterns on the wet glass.

"No, you don't," I said, wanting him to look at me. "You don't know, Al." I felt like crying all of a sudden. "Since I've been, you know, since I've been sick, it's like I'm out of control. Everything is out of control."

He'd stopped his tracings and was looking at me.

"I get so mad." I tried to explain how it happened. "One minute I'm fine, I can be normal and the next, it's like – like a white-hot feeling in me. I just want to hurt people." I blinked my eyes hard. "So I say horrible things, then I feel guilty, and then I get depressed."

I don't think Al knew what to do. He began to look about in case people were staring at us.

Once started, I couldn't stop. My voice hic cupping dangerously, I continued, "Everything is out of my control. It scares me." Tears began to seep out of my eyes and I wiped them away with my sleeve.

Al was mortified. "Jan, don't," he said, squeezing my hand. "Everyone will think I've hurt you."

"Sometimes," I said, my voice rising, "I think I'm going mad."

Al gulped, he gave a wary smile, "And you're only realising it now?"

I couldn't laugh. I'd just spilled my guts out to him and all he could do was crack feeble jokes. "You are a bastard," I pulled my hand out of his grasp and sat, staring straight in front, trying to blink back tears.

Al was right, people were staring. They turned away when I glared at them.

I was aware of Al shifting restlessly in his seat. Just before we got off the bus, he bent his head down so his face was level with mine. His eyes looked hurt. "Jan," he said quietly, "I don't know what to say to you. I try me best and it's all I can do."

"Am I going mad?"

He gave a smile. "You've got cancer. I think you're doing great."

"Really?" I sounded like a five-year-old looking for approval.

"Really."

He took his face away and stared out the window again.

CHAPTER SIXTY-FIVE

I hadn't the strength to resist Mam when she insisted that I come home for the weekend. She'd heard that Beth and Abby were not going to be in the flat and there was no way her daughter was spending the weekend alone in a flat. No way. Her daughter was sick. What was the point of having a lovely home to go to if she didn't go to it? Her sick daughter was not going to be on her own over any weekend.

"I'll have the cancer for company," was the only horrible comment I could make.

She'd shrivelled me with the look she gave. "That really is in very bad taste, Janet," she'd said.

"I have bad taste," I replied.

She'd looked at my orange top and leather skirt and shrugged. "I can't argue with that."

I knew she was going to piss me off.

How would I stick her for the two days?

Dad had insisted on picking me up in a taxi. There was

no way, no way on this earth that any family would let their sick daughter, their very sick daughter, arrive home via public transport. No way. If she was coming home, it'd be in a car.

I hated to admit it but when Saturday came, I was glad of the lift. Lately I'd been feeling more tired than usual. Not that I was a debilitated wreck or anything so dramatic, but I was tired. So when Dad collected me in the car, I didn't gripe that I could have got home by myself.

I wasn't cutting off my nose to spite my face.

Though on my face, I doubt it'd have made much difference.

"There you are," Dad said, stating the blindingly obvious when I appeared outside the flat with my overnight bag. He gave a discreet nod to a bright white Mercedes parked on the roadway. "I ordered one of those Merc taxi jobs as a little treat for you."

"Thanks," I smiled.

"They've electric everything in them," Dad said, taking my bag and ushering me over to the car. "They even have this thing under the seat that heats your arse up for you in winter."

"Brill." I tried to sound fascinated.

Dad opened the back door and I climbed inside. It was gorgeous. White leather everywhere with a mahogany dash. Dave would go mental, I grinned to myself. I was sitting on some dead animal's hide that had no doubt been bleached by some horrible chemical thing. The wood in the dashboard was probably donated by a section of rain-forest.

It was still beautiful.

The journey was conducted in silence. Dad sat in front and spent his time staring out the window, hoping that everyone would see him travelling in a Merc.

Every mile we got nearer the house increased my heart rate. The taxi driver would see where we lived. Sweat broke out on my palms and I tried to mentally project myself away from the inevitable.

"Just here," Dad said. "Here we are."

I began to search for a button that would let me out of the car.

"That'll be . . ." the taxi man began pressing some buttons to calculate the fare.

My hands were so sweaty that I couldn't open the lock.

"Twenty-five quid," he pronounced.

"Naw," Dad shook his head. "That's too much."

At last, the lock opened and I ran from the car straight up the garden and into the house. Someone had left the front door open and I slammed it closed.

"That you, Janet?" My mother spoke from the top of the stairs.

"Yeah."

"Where's your father?" She began coming down to me. "He was meant to collect you."

"He's outside talking to the taximan."

I watched as she re-opened the door.

She looked out and then looked back at me. "Don't tell me he picked you up in that?" Her hand trembled a bit as she pointed to the Merc.

"As a treat," I smiled weakly.

"For who?" Her mouth suddenly turned into the straight line that terrified us when we were kids and still terrified Dad to this day. "Where in the name of Jesus did he think he was going?"

The fact that she'd taken the Lord's name meant she was seriously annoyed.

Her voice rose to a screech. *"How much is that yoke going to cost? How much?"*

I watched horrified as she began a death march up the path. Her hands on her hips and her backside shoved out. "Desmond!"

His full name meant there was no redemption for him.

Dad's white face peered out of the taxi. I saw him making the same frantic efforts as I had to get out of the car. Finding the lock, he exited as if his arse was on fire. Maybe the heater under the seat had overheated.

Mam stood by fuming as he counted out a pile of notes and handed them to the driver.

She dragged him in as he was waving good-bye.

"Do you think that you're a special type of person that you can blow your money on hiring fancy cars?"

"No," Dad held up his hands in a gesture of surrender. "If you'll just let me explain. I hired it – "

"Are you a millionaire in disguise?" She said that at reasonable pitch.

Dad gave a watery laugh. "No. But I just – "

"Are you a pop guru?" Lower than reasonable.

"No. I wanted to – "

"Are you a president of some country?" Very low.

"Indeed I'm not, I just – "

"But you're a moron, aren't you Desmond?" High decibel screech.

She pushed past him and stormed into the kitchen, slamming the door so hard she made the phone fall off the wall.

Dad quirked his eyebrows at me. "Isn't she a gas ticket altogether?" He made a move toward the kitchen and stopped. "Better let her cool off," he muttered. Coming back over to me, he picked up my bag and said, "Come on now and let's get your stuff upstairs."

Lisa drifted out of her bedroom as we neared the top of the stairs. "What was all the shouting for?" She pouted. "I'm studying in there and I can't think." Then she looked at me. "You don't look sick."

"Thanks." It was the best thing anyone could say to me at the moment.

"I'm sick every morning and every night." In a woebegone voice, she continued, "I puke down the jax if I even *smell* coffee." Turning her limpid gaze on Dad she asked, "Don't I?"

"That's what happens when you're pregnant," Dad was unusually firm. "You should have thought about that."

"Pig." Lisa went into her room and slammed the door.

"I'm offending them all today," Dad said mildly as he deposited my case on the extra bed in Sammy's room.

I began to dump all the rubbish off the bed onto the floor.

"You just have a lie down or whatever you want, I'll bring you up a cuppa," Dad smiled at me.

"Thanks."

I fell asleep before he came back.

I got up and went down for tea. It was the usual sambo mountain.

Lisa was busy opening all the sandwiches. Peeling them apart, she examined their contents before announcing that she couldn't eat them. "Ham, ugh," she pretended to puke over the floor. "Egg, ugh," another puking attempt. "I hate tomato!" That sandwich was flung down onto the table and never rejoined its rejected comrades on the plate. After she fussily went through the pile, she settled back with two cheese sandwiches which she proceeded to nibble wanly.

The rest of us had to eat her discards.

Sammy was sitting beside me. "So how's things?" she asked. "How are you feeling?"

"Grand." I pretended to look for another sandwich so that I wouldn't have to elaborate.

"A bit tired," Dad said to Sammy. "But that's to be expected."

Everyone seemed to know what was expected, except me.

"How's the fella?" Lisa changed the subject. "Mam said you have a fella?"

"Man-mad," Mam said. She sounded bitter.

"I am not!" I glared up the table at her.

"I meant Lisa." She sounded as if she could cry.

Dad put his arm about her. "Now, now . . ."

"I'm not man-mad." Lisa stood up. "How dare you say that!" She glowered at Mam and Dad. "The only guy I love is Claude."

"Yes, we know," Dad tried to placate her. "Your mother's just upset about things."

"So she calls me a slag, is that it?"

"Shut up, Lisa," Sammy dragged her down. "Just shut up."

"I'm going up to study." Lisa flounced her way out of the kitchen.

"Isn't she a bitch!" Sammy rolled her eyes and took another sandwich.

No one said anything for a bit.

I couldn't stand it. I had to ask. "So I take it high-rise Claude is the father?"

Sammy exploded in a giggle. "You're disgusting!" She shoved me with her elbow.

For a second I was confused. "I didn't mean that," I shoved Sammy back. "I was talking about his height."

Both of us started to giggle.

Mam had begun clearing up, banging cups and plates together.

"He's the father," Sammy confirmed eventually. "She announced it last week."

For a second I was stunned. No one had told me.

Mam pulled my cup from under my nose. "Finished?"

I nodded.

She banged the cup into another one and slammed the two down on the sink.

Dad trailed around the kitchen after her, not knowing what to do with himself. Every time she turned she banged into him. "Jesus, Des, will you stop shadowing me. Jesus!"

Another set of cups were banged down.

Sammy and I looked at each other. Slowly we began to get up from the table and try to make a discreet exit from the kitchen.

Mam came towards us and picking up the remaining sambos, she dumped them in the rubbish bag.

"Are you not giving them to Buddy?" I asked as the final piece of bread left the plate. "He'd eat them."

She stopped and looked at me. Dad stopped and looked at me. Sammy gave an audible gulp.

Then it hit me. Since I'd come, I hadn't heard a single snarl, a single growl, I hadn't been attacked and barked viciously at. Mam hadn't used the word 'fecker' at all.

"Where's Buddy?" I asked.

None of them would meet my eye.

"Where is he?"

Mam put the plate on the draining board and said, "Buddy's . . ." she swallowed, "Buddy's been put down."

"He attacked Mrs Johnson next door, remember I told you?" Dad said.

I couldn't believe this.

496

"So he's dead?" I said calmly. "He's dead and no one told me?"

Dad gave a strangled laugh. "Sure, he was mental, you hated him."

"So?" I looked at the three of them. Sammy was gazing hard at some spot on the floor. "Why didn't someone tell me?"

"We didn't want to upset you," Mam said.

My laugh was too loud. It wasn't a laugh really, more a shout. "Dad just said I hated him. How would it have upset me to have told me?"

No one said anything.

"First," I said, "no one tells me about Claude being the father of Lisa's baby and now, no one tells me about Buddy." I stopped. I thought I might cry with frustration. "Why?"

"You've enough on your plate," Dad said. He was the only one to look at me. "We didn't want you bothering your head about us."

"I'm not dead yet," I said. "Not yet."

"Janet – "Mam called, but I didn't hang around to hear what she'd say. I ran upstairs and threw myself on the bed.

I wanted to cry, but I couldn't.

A while later, there was a tap on the door.

"Can I come in?" It was Sammy.

"It's your room." I turned my face to the wall and didn't look at her as she came over to me.

"I wanted to tell you," she said. She was standing

up. "But they said not to. They said it'd only upset you."

"He was a horrible dog." I stared at the way the wall paper had been put on upside down.

"I know." Sammy gave a small laugh.

"He was a member of the family for the last eight years though," I said. I thought of Buddy when he'd been small. All wagging tail and bright eyes. He'd dug massive holes in the garden, and left shit everywhere, but he'd been so cute.

"I thought I hated him," Sammy said quietly. "But, you know, I bawled my eyes out when they took him away."

"At least you got a chance to say good-bye."

"They thought it was best, they didn't want to upset you." Sammy got up the courage to sit beside me on the bed.

"And I'm not upset now?" I turned to face her. "The fact that he's gone, that I never saw him before he left, that everyone acts as if I'm not here anymore, that's supposed to make me happy?"

"Supposedly – yeah."

The way she said it, in her deadpan voice, made me smile. "Well, they fucked up."

"They always fuck up," Sammy said. "But that's the way they are. They only do their best, you know."

I think she was trying to let her words sink in, before she said, "They're worried sick about you, Jan. I mean, when you think about it, Lisa doesn't know how easily she's gotten off because you're sick. Mam and Dad haven't the heart to make a big issue out of her being preggers."

And it was true. Her words hit me. Mam would have Lisa locked up in a monastery by now, if I hadn't got sick.

"Mam is in bits," Sammy went on. "Dad keeps trying to be the strong one, but," she shrugged and smiled, "you know Dad, he keeps saying the wrong thing."

I marvelled that she could laugh over what I always found mortifying.

"All I'm saying is," Sammy reached out and touched me. We both looked away, we weren't a feely family, "Just give them a break. They only did it for you."

She whipped her hand away and stood up. "Come on down."

Without looking to see if I was following, she left.

I did go down. Mam and Dad were in the sitting-room. They were both watching the lotto programme. They looked up as I came in.

"Aw, here she is," Dad said.

Mam nodded to me.

We all turned and watched the box.

The lotto ended with its usual brash signature tune and Mam picked up the paper and began to look through it.

Dad picked up the remote and began zapping from one TV station to the next. I saw Ma grind her teeth, she hated when he did that. Bits of programmes flashed momentarily onto the screen and were soon replaced by bits of other ones. Zap. Zap. Zap.

Eventually, Dad settled on an ad for sanitary towels. By the time he realised what it was for, it was too late to change the station without drawing attention to the fact that he was mortified.

"A grand girl able to roller-blade like that," he said, trying to show what a liberated man he was.

Neither Mam or I replied.

More silence as we waited for the next ad.

Sammy joined us in the room and sitting herself on the floor she asked what was on.

"Feck all," Mam said.

Andrex were the next to advertise their wares. A cute puppy was parading about the screen with a toilet roll in his mouth.

"He wasn't a bad dog," Dad said slowly. He shot a penitent glance in my direction.. "He was nice in his own way."

Mam looked sharply at him.

"And what way was that?" Sammy giggled. "When he was attacking bitch-face Johnson?"

Dad chuckled. "Exactly. His finale was spectacular."

Mam gave a small smile. "The poor dog, with that wagon's backside in his mouth."

"I'd say now," Dad leaned back in his chair, "if he hadn't been put down, the trauma of the taste of her big arse would have driven him to canine-cide."

They were trying to make me smile.

So I did.

"Do you remember when he ate all the washing off the line," Mam was looking at me. "And you were thrilled because he ate your school uniform?"

"Yeah."

"And the way you trained him to growl at Louise Johnson when she walked by?" Sammy asked.

"I used to say 'kill'," I said. "And he'd snarl like a Rottweiler."

The way I said it wiped the smile from their faces.

It brought back things they didn't want to think about.

"He was a grand old dog," Dad said. "A great fella."

Later that night, when I went to bed, I thought of Buddy. The poor dog, to get put down. I thought of the way he used to wriggle into my bed in the morning. Licking my face, he'd wake me up. That was when he was a puppy. Later on, as he grew older, I would have been lucky to have a face left if he'd been let near it.

I wished like anything I could hear him howling in the garden as I drifted off to sleep. But he was gone. And I cried because he was dead.

CHAPTER SIXTY-SIX

JULY

I woke up at 9.00am on 15th July. It was a Thursday, a bright morning, slightly misty but looking out the window, I knew it would clear and the day would be hot.

I'd survived my third batch of chemotherapy injections and I felt all right. Tired but able to cope. All I had to do was take tablets for a week and then I'd be finished with the hateful stuff for another two weeks.

There were a few hairs on my pillow.

Turning the pillow over, so that I wouldn't have to look at it I plumped it up and started to make my bed. Making the bed was stupid really, because, by midday, I'd probably end up wanting to sleep for a while. I didn't bother getting dressed. Once the bed was made, I went into the kitchen to see if I could rustle up some breakfast. Beth was there, buttering herself some toast.

"Hiya," she nodded. "Want some toast?"

"Yeah."

She passed me over a slice, poured me some tea and then, carrying her breakfast over to the television, she flicked it on. The noise of breakfast TV filled the flat.

There was a hair in my tea. I burnt my fingers trying to fish it out of the mug. Holding it up to the light, I saw it was black. It was one of mine so I didn't mind drinking the tea.

The toast tasted a bit off. I smelt it, to see if the butter was all right. It seemed fine.

"Beth," I shouted over the telly. "Does your toast taste funny?"

"Tastes fine." Beth said, her eyes still fixed on the box.

Maybe it was just me. I ate it anyhow. The only alternative would have been to eat Bran Flakes. Gone-off butter was preferable in my mind.

Beth carried her plate over to the sink. "See you later, Jan." She looked at me for the first time in ages. "Do you want anything brought back?"

She was uneasy, her hands clasped and unclasped. Her head kept moving, even when she'd finished speaking.

"No," I shook my head and tried to smile at her. "Thanks for asking." All I wanted was her to smile back.

"Fine so." The relief in her voice was unmistakable. She made a dash for her jacket and was at the door in seconds. "See you around lunch-time."

"Bye."

I heard her feet clattering off down the hall and I wished like hell I was her. Heading off to work.

I decided to have a shower. Might as well strike while the water was lukewarm. Gathering all my stuff together, I went into the bathroom. I let the water run in the vain hope that it would heat up before stepping underneath it. I washed myself first, using a moderately expensive smelly soap that I'd picked up in a Roches Stores sale. I wanted the smell to linger on me after I'd finished washing. Lately, I kept getting whiffs of a funny smell around the flat and sometimes in work. A stale musty smell. I didn't know what it was, so I decided to perfume myself up to the hilt so I wouldn't have to smell the other smell.

The soap was gorgeous. Like Dove only with scent. Then I began to wash my hair. Soaking it under the water before dumping in the shampoo. Lathering the shampoo . . . a funny tingling sensation. Really strange.

I decided to wash the shampoo out quickly, maybe I was allergic to it. Maybe the drugs had made my head sensitive to it. Taking my hands away from my hair, I got ready to rinse the shampoo out.

Hair was entangled in through my fingers. Lots of it.

Hair was all over the shower floor, clogging up the plug-hole.

Hair was on my shoulders.

The nausea was instant. I had barely time to make it to the toilet before I vomited.

The phone was ringing. I was sitting in the bathroom,

beside the toilet with my dressing-gown on. The only thing I'd managed to do was to turn the shower off.

I don't know what time it was, only that I was cold and wet. The floor-tiles were slippy and dangerous and I wished I'd the courage to fall on them and break my neck.

The phone was ringing. I couldn't stop staring at all the hair in the shower. All *my* hair. It had started appearing on the pillow last week, but that was all. Everyone's hair thinned out at some stage during the year and then it grew back. I knew that. I'd convinced myself that's all it was. Until now.

The phone was ringing. I couldn't get sick anymore. I felt sick but that was it. What was I going to do without hair? I was going to look even worse than I ever had before. My hair was the way I wanted to be. Now it was gone.

The phone stopped ringing and started up again. I wanted to die. But I wanted to live. I wanted to live if I could go back to what I was, plump, spotty, Jan. Not this new skinnier, bald version.

I sat in the bathroom for a long time.

The buzzer was buzzing. I still didn't know what time it was. Wrapped up in my dressing gown, I felt so cold. Wouldn't it be nice to get a cold? The buzzer stopped. Footsteps coming along the hall. I didn't care, I didn't care who it was. A sound of a key, voices, panicky. The door opening and a "Jesus".

Looking up, my mother and Beth in the doorway. Both of them white. Mam comes in and crouches down beside me. Beth stands by, her hands dangling. Her eyes darting about the place.

Mam takes my hands and tries to get me to look at her. I can't. I feel so ugly.

"My beautiful baby," she whispers. "All your lovely hair."

I can't even get mad at her lies. I just point to the hair in the shower. I pull some off my head and place it in her free hand. She holds it to her face and then pulls my head into her.

Beth is gone.

Mam holds me for ages. We sit on the wet tiles, not speaking, just holding the hair and each other.

She makes me get to my feet. It's like I'm drunk. Nothing has ever hit me so hard before. She leads me to my room and tells me to get dressed. I see Beth's white face as a blur. Then I'm in my room and on my own.

I suppose I did get dressed. I can't remember much. Shock does that, cushions you. I know Mam checked up on me and that I was dressed. Beth lent me a cap and then Mam was trying to coax me into going outside.

But they didn't understand. It was just hair to them. For me, it was me. It wasn't vanity, it was identity, confidence, beauty. And it was gone.

I wouldn't go out.

"The doctor said it would happen," I remember Mam saying in a soft voice. "It's only temporary."

"I'm not going out."

They called the doctor.

He came and tried to talk to me. I don't know what he said.

Beth had to go back to work.

"You'll have to get it shaved," Mam said. "Won't she, doctor?"

He nodded. "It'll grow back," he said. "I promise you it will."

"And she was getting on so well," Mam said. "Really well. She was coping so well."

Snap.

Bang.

"I'm not coping," I shouted at her. I saw her take a step back and I followed her. I poked my face into hers. *"I'm not coping. I hate it."* I was beside the sink. I picked a cup up and smashed it. The noise was good. "I'm on a treadmill and I can't get off. It's pulling me along and I have to keep pace otherwise I'll fall."

Mam opened her mouth to say something, but O'Brien shook his head. Their understanding infuriated me. I hadn't been so angry in ages. "First I lose my freedom, I have to trust all these prats telling me what to take, how to live, then I lose my hair. What the fuck comes next?" I banged my fist off the table and it shook. So I did it again. "Why don't you piss off to your God and ask him why the fuck he did this to me? What the fuck have I done?"

"Janet!"

"Surely you've earned some brownie points over the years? Huh?" I began to march on her again. "Sinful, horrible Janet can't ask but you can." I pulled out another fistful of hair. "Bastard. Fucking bastard." I threw my hair at her feet. It floated down onto the floor.

She bent down and picked it up. When she stood to face me, there were tears in her eyes. "That's what I think too," she said. "I called him that last night."

"When you said your nightly prayers?" My voice was mocking. But it was no use. I didn't want to fight anymore. There was a hopelessness invading me now. Back-against-the-wall stuff. I knew I had to get my head shaved. I knew I had to get treatment. But I resented it. Every tablet, every injection, I resented.

My shoulders sagged. There was no point in fighting.

"Sit down, Janet," O'Brien's voice shocked me. I'd forgotten he was there. Always a bit wary of him, I complied.

He started to drone on about what a shock I'd had. How discovering you're sick is a big shock and everything else is just shock piled upon shock. He said people coped in different ways. He wondered if it would help me to talk to someone about how I felt.

Was this guy for real? "Don't you think it's bad enough to have this disease without talking about it too?" I rolled my eyes. "I'm not talking to anyone."

"Maybe it would help?" Mam said.

"Yeah, about as helpful as giving a bat a pair of glasses."

O'Brien laughed. Mam and I looked at him.

"I must remember that one," he smiled.

"Still witty old Jan," I muttered. "I can still make everyone laugh at me."

"No one laughs at you," Mam said back.

I didn't answer.

"Would you like a course of anti-depressants?" O'Brien asked. "Maybe they might help you come back to yourself."

Nothing would ever do that.

But I agreed. I mean, what was a few more pills?

I did get my head shaved. Mam called the hair salon that she went to. It was an old-biddys place, blue rinses and Queen Mother perms. I wouldn't have been seen decomposed in the place. But as it was, I didn't have to go. My mother did the sob-story routine and they agreed to send one of their staff to the flat with a razor.

What an enticing prospect.

The razor-person arrived in the afternoon. Mam and I were sitting at the table, drinking tea when the buzzer sounded.

Mam let the person up. "Josie," she said, "they sent you." Her voice lower. "She's in there. She's a bit upset."

Josie came into the room. "Hello there." She was all bright and cheery. "Janet, is it?"

I hated the way she smiled at me. "Yeah."

"You're getting your head shaved?" Now her voice was respectful.

I could see Mam hovering nervously in the background.

"It's not by choice." I knew I sounded like a horrible kid. But I didn't give a shit.

Josie nodded. "I'm glad," she said as she began to set herself up. "Shaving off lovely hair like that would be a terrible thing to do." She made me sit in a kitchen chair and she placed papers on the ground. "Beautiful hair," she said as she began to shave.

There wasn't a hell of a lot to take off. Every time a chunk fell to the ground I winced. My mother did too.

Josie finished up. She came around to look at me. "Do you want to see yourself?" she asked.

I shook my head. I never wanted to look at myself again.

CHAPTER SIXTY-SEVEN

I crawled into bed on Thursday night before Beth or Abby came back. It was hard to get the words out. "Tell them I'm asleep," I said to my mam. "Don't let them come into me."

No one was going to see me until I was ready.

I turned away as my mother's face sort of creased up, like as if she was going to cry. "Fine," she said slowly. "If that's what you want."

It wasn't what I wanted. It was what I had to have.

I burrowed underneath my covers. Curling up and wrapping my arms around me, I rocked myself to sleep.

Next morning, Abby tapped on the door. "Jan, Jan," she called. "Are you awake."

"No."

"Can I come in?"

Her voice sounded even more mournful than usual. It held the sort of tone people normally reserve for funerals.

"Why?"

That shook her. "Well, eh, you know, just to see if you're all right."

"I'm fine," I muttered. "Bald but fine."

"Oh, Jan, don't say things like that." Abby sounded shocked.

"Why not? It's true."

There was a pause.

"Mmm," she said then, "you're right, I guess." I didn't say anything so she asked again, "Can I come in?"

I didn't want her to. I really didn't want to face anyone. It was one thing telling people you were sick, it was quite another supporting a bald-headed banner and proclaiming it from the rooftops. No matter what happened now, people would never forget to think about my cancer when they looked at me.

That's if they wanted to look at me.

Still, I had to start somewhere. And Abby was bound to tell me how great I looked.

"Come in," I said. My heart was booming and I felt sick.

In she came. She saw me and stopped at the door. It took about three seconds to get the smile convincing. Her voice never quite made it. "You look great," she pronounced.

"Great for a neo-nazi."

"No," Abby said, her voice saturated in consideration. "Just, you know, great."

"For a lesbian?" I offered.

"No." She was getting flustered.

"For a cancer patient?" I made my voice cajoling. Oh, God, I was being a wagon. I knew it but I couldn't stop.

"I got you these," Abby said hastily, changing the subject. "Your mother told me you wouldn't wear a, you know, a . . ." She hopped at bit. "A wig. So, I bought you these last night in town." She approached the bed as if she was terrified, which I guess she was. I would have been nervous of me. "Here." She placed some coloured scarves on the bed. "My magazine did a feature on how to wear them a few months back so I dug it out for you." A copy of *Cool Teenager* was deposited on the bed too. "It's cool to have no hair," she said.

"Pretty cool when it pisses rain on top of you all right," I managed to joke. The scarves were so thoughtful of her. I picked them up and fingered them. The colours were lovely.

"The nicest I could get," Abby shrugged.

"Thank you." I bit my lip. "Thanks a lot."

"If you get up I could maybe help you put them on?" Abby was relaxing now. "There's a nice way where you can twist a couple of them together. Here," she sat beside me and opened up the magazine. "See?" She pointed to a gorgeous model with the scarf on her head.

"Sinead O'Connor I am not," I joked. I screwed my eyes up. "I probably look more like ET than anything."

Abby didn't know whether to laugh so she tittered

awkwardly. Then shrugging, she said, "Well, even ET wore a scarf, you know. And he was cute."

She persuaded me to come into the kitchen. Telling me to sit down, she stood behind me. "Here's my favourite one." She began knotting two scarves together. When that was done, she studied the magazine picture for ages before attempting to put them on my head. Only they wouldn't go. "Your head is too big," she grumbled. She came in front of me and glared at my head, "It looks much bigger with no hair."

Why had I agreed to this?

"It must be my brain," I said dryly.

"Maybe," she was taking me seriously. "Well, whatever it is, it's ruining any chance you have of wearing a scarf." She stomped back behind me again. The fact that she couldn't get the scarves to go over my head began to piss her off. She started trying to tie them really tightly and hurting me. "OOOH," she shrieked frustrated. "This is not the way it's meant to be." Picking up the magazine she glared at it.

"Abby, just go to work," I said. "You'll be late."

"No, I have to figure this out." She started reading the article and muttering away to herself. In the meantime, I got up from the chair and began to make myself breakfast. I'd decided not to go into work that day, it was one thing showing Abby, but quite another having to face a whole building of people.

"I have it!" Abby made me jump. Tea spilled down over my pyjamas. Without waiting to let me rub the tea off, she propelled me to the chair again. "Now, just one more try."

An hour later, the scarf was balanced precariously on my head. She told me not to move too quick in case it fell off. "I'm going now, take care," she shouted as she left.

At least one of us was happy.

The minute I stood up the two scarves floated to the ground.

I picked them up and grinned. Abby was not a technical wizz. She even had trouble assembling the Happy Meal boxes from McDonald's. Running the scarves slowly through my fingers, I decided I'd better learn how to put them on. Somehow I had to make the best of this awful situation and covering my head was the most positive thing I could do for myself right now.

I picked up the magazine and studied it. Eventually, after messing about with them for ages, I figured it out. It would have been easier if the diagrams in Abby's mag hadn't been printed sideways. Anyhow, I got the scarf on and decided that I might as well wash my face and stick on some make-up.

My heart went thud. A big deep sick-to-my-guts thud.

How could I wear make-up with a big white scalpy head? I'd look weird. Seriously weird. Brown face, white scalp.

Horror piled upon horror as I realised that I'd have to get what all the magazines recommended, *a foundation to match my skin tone*. I could never see the point of that. I like the I've-been-in-Ibiza-for-ten-years look. Not the Janet-Boyle-skin-tone look.

I sat for ages in the kitchen, wondering what the hell I was going to do. I couldn't cover my head in brown, it would cost a fortune. Plus, I'd probably wreck the scarves with make-up and Abby wouldn't talk to me. There was nothing for it but to go whiter.

That thought frightened me more than anything.

Louise Johnson told me that I was ugly. One day, on the way home from school, she started singing, "She's a bald-headed chick, she's an ugly head. Haven't seen worse since I dunno when." There were more lines but I don't want to remember them.

CHAPTER SIXTY-EIGHT

Friday night was Dave's night to call. I'd been so wrapped up in my problems that I'd forgotten all about him. The anti-depressants were taking their time about working, I wasn't singing songs or cracking stupid jokes about my Kojak state by the time the buzzer went. In fact, I still hadn't even seen myself in the mirror.

All I really wanted to do was to get drunk. That was the best anti-depressant of them all.

But angel Abby was close at hand. Every can and bottle in the place had been stowed away. All that remained in the fridge were bottles upon bottles of Lucozade or Miwadi. And because I didn't want to go out, I couldn't even buy myself a can.

In fact, when the buzzer rang, I was bordering on the medium suicidal.

"Oh my God," I wailed suddenly remembering, "It's Dave." I turned to Abby. "I forgot!"

She looked at me. "Jesus Jan, you still haven't told him?"

"No." This was awful. What would I do? "Tell him I'm gone out."

Abby looked at me incredulously. "And what about next time? And the time after that? No Jan," she strode purposefully towards the intercom. "He's coming up."

I made a dive and got there before her. "Don't do this, please." I know it was awful, but I pretended to get faint. "Oh, Ab, I'll get sick."

She hesitated. She gulped and said, "Jan, you'll have to tell him."

"I can't." If she let him up, I knew I'd die.

"So what are you going to do? Every time he calls you'll be out? Maybe you should stop seeing him and never tell him?"

"I can't do that!" I was stricken with indecision. I didn't want him to see me, but I couldn't lose him either.

"It's your choice." Abby said. She walked away from the door and sat down in a chair. Folding her arms she gazed up at me. "I hate seeing you stressed out, Jan," she said, "In fact, you shouldn't be under stress. It's a contributing factor to cancer and . . ."

"SHUT UP!" I shouted.

The buzzer went again.

"Please tell him I'm out," I joined my hands in prayer over to her.

"No," she said.

"Well, he might just go," I said crossly, walking away. "I just won't answer at all."

Abby sprang across the room and buzzed him up.

"Abby – " I thought I was going to collapse. She couldn't make this happen.

"Sorry, Jan," she said. "But I had to."

"You're supposed to be looking out for me," I spat. "Jesus, some friend you are."

Abby didn't answer. The minute Dave entered, she exited.

"'Ow's life, Ab?" Dave asked as she passed him. She pushed by and he stared after her. "She in a funny mood?" He turned to me.

I was standing by the window, having run the length of the flat as he came in. I was hoping the distance would do something to help my situation. What exactly it was to do, I don't know.

Dave blinked and blinked again. He came further in and shut the door closed with his foot. "Jan?" he said uncertainly.

I was suddenly conscious of the way I looked. A crummy tracksuit, white face and a blue scarf tied around my head. I'm surprised he didn't do a runner. "That's me," I tried to sound cheery but my voice was breathless. The shame was going to kill me before the cancer.

"Wot 'ave you done to yer 'air?" Dave moved up closer. "You got a new 'airstyle."

"Yeah," I attempted a grin now, "the style being that I have no hair."

"Christ." Dave looked faintly disturbed. He began rubbing his palms up and down the sides of his combats. "Bit radical, huh?"

"Yeah." I didn't know how to tell him. I was more afraid of his reaction than anything else. "Do you like it?"

He shrugged. "I liked your 'air," he said. "But ya know, if you like it, that's wot matters."

"So you don't like it?" Where was time when I needed to stall it?

"It's all right." He reached out and touched my face. "I like your face though, nice soft skin." He bent his head and kissed my cheek.

"Good." I wondered could I get away with still not telling him. That's me, the least said the better. "So you thinks it's radical?"

He shrugged. "Whatever."

He didn't seem impressed. Maybe he'd go off me?

There was no way out. I had to tell him. I took a deep breath, screwed up my courage and stuttered, "Dave, I, eh, well, I didn't get my hair like this by choice." I couldn't look at him. If I did, I'd bawl.

"No?"

"No." This was it. The words tumbled out of me, sounding hollow because I still felt it was like being in a film and I was acting and I wasn't really sick, "I'm sick. I'm getting treatment and the drugs they gave me made my hair fall out."

"Wot?" He took a step back. "Sick? Wot's the matter?"

I gave a shrug and raised my eyes to his.

"Somefink bad?" His voice was stunned. "It's not . . ." he stopped. "Wot is it?"

Another shrug. Gulpy voice. "Cancer."

"Christ," he said slowly. "Christ." He hit his head with his palm. "Shit." He stared at me and his face clouded over. "And ya never told me?"

"I'm sorry." He looked hurt and I felt awful. "I couldn't tell you, Dave," I began. "I didn't want to."

"Great." He sounded dejected.

"Dave, please," I touched the fabric of his jacket, then pulled my hand away. "I needed to forget, to pretend it wasn't happening to me. When I was with you, it made it easier because you didn't know."

Dave frowned. "Run that by me again?"

Tears were forming in the back of my eyes. To my shame I broke down and said the dreaded words that men hate, "Please don't leave me, Dave, I couldn't bear it."

His face went white, the shock I guess.

Then slowly, he wrapped his arms around me.

I knew he wouldn't let me down.

CHAPTER SIXTY-NINE

It took me a week to screw up the courage to go into work. At that stage, either because of Dave or the antidepressants, I'd slowly begun to emerge from the bottom of my barrel.

I went in on a Friday so that everyone would have the weekend to get used to my bald state. That way Monday wouldn't be as bad.

O'Connell Street was a nightmare. In fact, from the moment I stepped out my door it had been a nightmare. I was convinced that everyone was looking at me. The girl with the pale face, no hair and funny smell. The smell wasn't funny at all as it happens. The smell seemed to be following me around. A stale dull odour. I had thought I was imagining it. Then Abby started to smell it. She kept sniffing, wondering what it was. Then she stopped, went red and looked at me. Then she said nothing more.

So I knew it was me.

I actually screwed up the courage to ring the

hospital. It was the first time I'd done it. As long as I was off the tablets, I'd tried to forget about being sick. Hospital, pills, treatment, didn't feature in my vocabulary two weeks out of every month. But I found I just had to know what the smell was.

"I smell," I barked down the phone. "I'm having," I gulped, "chemo."

The nurse or councillor or whatever she was, was so nice that I was in tears by the end of the conversation. But I was on my own in the flat and she didn't know me from Adam, so it was all right. She told me it was normal. It was just the drugs digging themselves in for the long haul. She started to tell me other things to look out for, that were also normal. And also horrible. Changing tastes, tingling of fingers and toes, constipation, to name but a few. "It's all in your booklet you probably got from the hospital," she said. "I can send you one out if you like."

"No, that's fine," I said hastily. I didn't want to know.

She started to ask me how I felt and how I was getting on and that's when I began to cry.

Walking up O'Connell Street, I pushed the phone call out of my head. As far as I was concerned, I didn't smell anymore. I had sprayed enough deodorant on me to open my very own hole in the ozone. This was backed-up by a half bottle of White Linen. Unfortunately, there was nothing I could do with my face. It looked pale. No more brown make-up for a while.

"How's Jan?" Al's familiar greeting made my heart twist. There was no hair-pulling to accompany it.

I found I couldn't look at him as I muttered, "Bald."

"So I see," he said. "Feckin' can't yank your hair anymore."

I gave a small smile. "No."

We walked the rest of the way in silence.

Standing outside the office, my heart started to hammer.

Al opened the door and in I walked.

"Hi," I said.

None of them looked at me. "Hello," they replied.

I took off my coat, walked to my desk and began to work. No one said anything.

An hour went by, still silence except when the phone rang. Did I look so awful that they couldn't say anything?

Eventually Liz said, "You look nice with that paler make-up, Jan."

It was as if she'd decided to hold them at gun-point. Anxious looks passed between them all. I looked over at her. "Do I?"

Liz nodded. "I always thought that other stuff you wore was too dark."

"Tarty," Henry couldn't resist it from his corner. The silence was killing him. "Sometimes you reminded me of a satsuma."

I suppose it was the best I could expect.

"And your – your – " Lenny flapped his hands, "that

coloured thing that you've on your head, that looks nicer than I thought it would."

"Really?"

"Indeed." Lenny smiled, proud of having pleased me.

Al spoke. "The make-up is nicer," he said. He blushed and turned back to his files.

"Lucky you," Liz smiled at me. "Derbhla would kill for that compliment." Then she stopped. "Eh, not kill," she stammered. "Eh – "

"I know what you mean," I said. "It's fine."

"Right."

I knew what Al meant too. I waited until he looked at me. "Thanks," I mouthed. He winked over at me. "Just doin' me job," he mouthed back.

CHAPTER SEVENTY
AUGUST

The week after my August chemo, Dr Daly rang from the hospital. He wanted to see me and my parents.

"I've the results from your CAT Scan and bloods," he explained. "I just want to discuss your progress with you."

I'd been getting CAT Scans and blood tests on a regular basis. To be honest, I hadn't given them a thought. I was a veteran of the hospital at this stage, injections, needles, tests, drugs were just something to be endured. On no account were they to be thought about after the event.

"We'll be there," I said, putting the phone down.

Mam and Dad both came with me. Daly asked to see us Friday morning at ten. We arrived early. Julia, as I'd come to call his receptionist, told us to go on in. "You're the first on his list today," she said.

"I'd love that," Dad whispered loudly. "Starting work at ten in the morning, must be marvellous all together."

"Shut up, Des," Mam snapped.

It was her mantra these days, telling Dad to shut up. His only response was to pat her on the shoulder and roll his eyes at me.

Daly was sitting at his desk. In front of him he had a load of charts and books and notes. His desk would have fitted well into our office. "Hello again," he smiled at us.

Mam and Dad nodded, I didn't say anything.

Daly watched us as we found somewhere to sit. He steepled his fingers and put them to his lips. I sat down first, Mam and Dad seemed to take ages to settle. Then Dad started to cough and Daly had to pour him some water and Dad had to drink it. "That's better now," Dad smiled around as he put the glass onto Daly's desk. He banged his chest with his fist. "Bit of a cold."

Mam began to tisk and I clenched my hands. I was afraid she'd say something about all the fags he smoked, but she didn't.

"So what's the Johnny McGory?" Dad asked.

"Pardon?"

"About Jan," Dad thumbed to me. "How's she getting on?"

I studied the carpet. A dull brown. Talking about me as if I wasn't there.

"Janet?" Daly said, startling me. "How do you feel?"

I shrugged. "OK, a bit tired maybe." I volunteered the information with a bad grace.

"She doesn't talk about it much," Mam's voice was high and anxious. "She's on tablets for depression."

Daly knew that, she didn't have to tell him.

"We got the results of your scans. It tells us how the treatment is progressing," Daly said, shuffling and juggling bits of paper. He stopped for a minute. I didn't like that. Pauses and bad news seemed to go hand in hand in this place. Glancing up, I saw Mam and Dad staring transfixed at him. Mam reached out and caught Dad's hand. I saw him squeeze it.

"There has been some shrinkage in the tumours," Daly said. His started to make circular movements with his thumbs, back and forth, back and forth. We all watched him. "Unfortunately," he continued, "not as much as we'd hoped."

You could have heard a feather clanging to the floor.

Mam gave a funny gasp and Dad closed his eyes and let out a long breath. I just looked at Daly.

"So what now?" I heard myself asking the question and was surprised. I was not into knowing what came next. My hand strayed to my neck and rubbed the bumps underneath the skin. My skin, my neck, my bumps.

Daly seemed to like the fact that I'd asked a question. He smiled at me. "Well, for a start we'll up your dosage of chemotherapy and see how that works . . ."

"See how that works!" Mam made us jump by the screech she let out of her. She sprang out of her chair and pointed to me, "This is my daughter you're talking about. She's not some guinea-pig you can try out . . ."

"Now, now Marg . . ."

"Shut up you!" She shouted at Dad without even looking at him.

I wanted to die.

"Mrs Boyle . . ." Daly tried to get a word in.

"She's only twenty-five you know," Mam said. "Her whole life in front of her and all – you – can – do is say you'll *TRY OUT* stuff." She stood trembling and heaving. "You'd better do more than that."

"Margaret – "

"Shut up!"

Dad glanced across at me and shook his head hopelessly.

Daly didn't seem too worried. "Please let me explain," he said mildly. "Treatment is not an exact . . ."

"This is my daughter," Mam shouted, jabbing her finger over at me and advancing on Daly at the same time, "*My* daughter. Do you have children? Do you?"

I wished I could be anywhere else. Why did she have to go off the deep end?

"I do," Daly nodded. "Three kids actually."

"Mam, please stop," I said quietly. "Please don't do this."

They were making a show of me, just like they always did.

I should be the one jumping about and yelling. It was my life they were on about.

But for some reason, I couldn't have been bothered. I'd shouted and cried when I heard I was going to lose my hair and where had it got me? I'd still gone bald.

Nothing she could say would change anything.

"Just let's listen to the doctor," I said.

Mam slumped. Dad stood up and put his arm around her, he managed to get her back into her chair.

Dad shot an apologetic smile at Daly and me.

"Sorry," Mam said, her voice muffled and sniffily. "I'm sorry."

"It's perfectly all right," Daly said. "I'd be the same if I was you."

That shocked me. I couldn't imagine him yelling like a banshee at someone.

"I've heard worse in here," Daly said. "You were quite the lady actually." He smiled at my parents and they smiled back.

"A lady is what she is, right enough," Dad said, patting her shoulder.

This was bizarre. I couldn't imagine anyone else being worse than my folks. Maybe he was only saying it to make them feel better.

"It's understandable you should be annoyed, " Daly went on. "Most parents in your position would be."

More incredulity from me.

"It's just," Mam gave a big sniff, "We thought she was doing well."

"She is," Daly said. He gazed at me. "She's doing very well indeed."

I don't think he meant my treatment. He meant more than that.

The upshot of it all was that my chemo dosage went up. If there wasn't the expected results within a certain time frame, I'd have to have radiotherapy.

I thought the blow of hearing that I hadn't reacted properly to treatment would have sent me reeling.

But it didn't.

It took ages before I realised why it hadn't.

For some reason, I wasn't so scared anymore.

It wasn't a passive acceptance, it was just the lack of fear.

I had nothing to lose.

Not anymore.

CHAPTER SEVENTY-ONE

Lisa scraped her Leaving Cert. Four passes, three miserable fails. Better than mine. I'd got Ngs, she got Es.

"She's delighted," Mam informed me over the phone. They had obviously decided to keep me abreast of all developments concerning home. "She's going out celebrating tonight."

I remembered my Leaving Cert celebrations. A bottle of vodka and a stomach pump.

"So Janet," she changed subject. "How are you?" Her voice grew soft and a bit shaky. "How'd you feel about this stronger treatment you'll be getting?"

"Tell Lisa to enjoy herself, won't you?" I said.

She didn't reply.

I bit my lip. "Mam," I said. "Just let's take it one day at a time, huh?" I couldn't bear to think of how the increased dosage would make me feel in the coming months, so I blanked it. I'd deal with things when they happened, just like I'd always done.

I didn't stop to think just how far that had got me.

Old habits die hard.

CHAPTER SEVENTY-TWO
SEPTEMBER

I was tired and felt rough. I told myself that I felt so tired because I wasn't used to the amount of drugs they were giving me. It'd just take time for my body to adapt, then I'd feel grand.

My hand hurt where they'd injected the September chemo. That was nothing either, just a collapsed vein or something stupid like that. I hadn't listened when the nurse had been talking.

The flat was deserted as I peeled myself from the bed and wandered into the kitchen. Black thoughts seemed to be haunting me and I was doing my best to chase them away with logic and reason. In my chaotic head, logic and reason were quite hard to pin down at the best of times.

That day was not one of those good times.

There was a note on the table and I concentrated on reading it to make the thoughts go. It was from Abby telling me there was some milk-shake made up in the fridge. She told me to ring her if there was anything, anything at all that I needed.

What I needed was nothing she'd ever be able to get for me.

Shut up, Jan! (That was logic and reason)

I had decided to settle for pouring myself a milk-shake when the phone rang.

It was Al. He always made a point of ringing me the day after the chemo injection.

"How's it going?"

His voice made me feel even sadder for myself. "Awful," I said mournfully. "I feel awful."

There was a brief silence. Al never knew what to say to me when I was depressed. I think he knew that no matter what he said it'd be wrong. He opted for, "Why?"

"Why?" I barked out a laugh. "Why do you think? Because the bra I wanted to wear is in the wash?"

"Jesus, Jan – "

"Because I feel bad, that's why! They upped my chemo and now I feel bad."

There was a silence, while he thought about what to say, so I hung up on him.

He'd ring again anyhow.

The milk-shake Abby had made was apple. My least favourite.

Great!

A can of something, that was more up my street. And Al had said that I could drink little bits.

I knew Beth had shoved a few cans of Bud in the fridge. She'd hardly mind if I had one. Just one, that's all I wanted. Something to relax me. I went over and opening the fridge, I spied about three cans on the top shelf. Taking one out, I rubbed it against my cheek. It was lovely and cool and sort of dewy. Like a can in an advert.

Abby had warned me to 'never, ever drink from cans in my weakened state'. Of course, she'd been talking about cans of Fanta and Coke. I grinned. It was like I was rebelling or something.

The Bud looked so inviting. Lifting it to my lips, I couldn't wait to taste its cool, slightly raw flavour.

I couldn't wait to get drunk either.

I was unprepared for the fright I got, it's like when you're a kid and someone gives you a taste of beer. You know the fright when it doesn't taste nice? Well, that was me. It was as if someone had poured stomach acid into my mouth.

I spat it out all over the floor, all over my clothes. Beer dripped everywhere.

Tears blurred my eyes and I smashed the can so hard down on the table that more Bud splashed out. Then I looked around. I looked at the four walls, I looked at the furniture, I looked at the spilt beer and finally, I looked at me. Ugly, wasted, rotting. I hated myself.

I picked up the can and flung it across the room.

Then, I sat down and wept.

CHAPTER SEVENTY-THREE

Anger came. Anger at everything – my life, my sickness, other people being healthy. I'd been angry before, but not in this pounding thumping murderous way.

There was nothing I could eat or drink that tasted nice. Alcohol was vile. I couldn't even get smashed drunk and forget about things for a while. The crutch I'd used to avoid reality in the past didn't cut the mustard anymore.

Life was suddenly a very scary place to be.

And I resented that.

Very much.

Day after day, I lay in my room and let it fester. I ignored Abby, I abused Al every time he rang, I refused to talk to my wagon of a mother. I ate like a robot, hating the taste but doing so to live and feed this emotion that was buoying me up. The only one I let near me was Dave. Because I didn't want to lose him. When he came I smiled and acted fine, then when he went, I stomped, and snarled and frightened the shit out of everyone. Everyone except Beth who avoided me like you would a Joe Dolan concert.

That pissed me off big-time.

And the anger gave me strength.

Just like it had before . . .

She'd slagged off my hair. My hair. The only thing that ever looked good. I knew if she destroyed that on me I'd never survive. So I'd snapped.

I'd got Buddy to snarl at her and back her against the wall in our garden. I'd left him growling at her for three hours. Mam and Dad had found me sitting on the grass, slightly drunk, laughing my head off as Louise cowered against the wall.

I'd been so ashamed of my anger. I'd never got so angry again.

Beth was in the kitchen. Humming away to the radio. It was fine for her to hum, she wasn't sick and she wasn't too bothered about me being sick by all accounts.

Who the hell did she think she was?

So I went out.

I went out and stared at her as she hummed.

She turned around and saw me staring and jumped. "Oh, Jan," she said, "I didn't know you were there." As usual, her eyes slid away from me.

I said nothing, enjoying the way I could make her squirm by just being in front of her. I had power over her.

"Eh, how are you today?" she asked. She fumbled with a piece of paper she had in her hand. "Feeling all right?" Her voice was bright and ready to snap.

"I feel crap actually," I said in an even tone. "Really crap."

"Oh," Beth turned away, just like she always did, "you'll be fine."

She didn't want to talk about it.

"And how the hell would you know?" I asked. I wasn't even afraid of her. It was like I was behind a huge see-through shatter-proof wall. "Go on, tell me. How would you know?"

Something in my voice made her jerk and I was glad. Serve her right. "Well?" I asked.

She gulped. The paper that she held fluttered to the floor. "You'll be fine," she said again.

"Why do you say that?" I pressed.

"Jan," she turned to look at me, "just drop it, please."

"No," I answered. "No, I won't." I saw her make for the door and because I was nearer, I pressed myself against it. She wouldn't dare shove me out of her way. "You said I'd be fine and I want to know why you said that." I was enjoying this, I felt strong again. Strong and in control.

I was more in control than I thought because Beth began to back away. She looked terrified.

"Why did you say that I'd be fine when you don't know?" I asked calmly. I moved nearer her, wanting her to cower away. "Why did you say it when you hardly ever bother to talk to me anymore?" I saw her close her eyes and I spat out, "Why don't you want to look at me?"

She didn't answer, just kept her eyes closed. "WHY?" I screamed, the anger flinging my voice so hard out of me that it smashed against the walls. "WHY?"

It was like my words hit her. She jerked underneath them and then slowly, she raised her head and her eyes met mine. "Because," she said, her voice quivering, "Because *you* remind me of my brother – all right?" Big tears stood out in her eyes. She gulped. "All right?" she repeated, though softer this time.

It was as if I'd been run over by a steam-roller. I knew what she meant yet I didn't. "Brother?"

Another flinch. "Yeah, he got sick like you."

"Don't – " I shook my head afraid of what she'd say, "Don't, Beth."

"He had sweats like you. And pains. And sickness. And in the end, he – he – " she took a gulp of air. "In the end he died." Tears started seeping from her eyes. She put a hand up to stop them.

I knew I should put my arms around her, but I couldn't.

"He died," she repeated. She was crying. "I'm afraid you'll die too." Her eyes were fixed on the floor. "I can't bear to look at you, I can't bear to be near you."

I wanted to turn back the clock and not listen to her. I didn't want to hear of people dying. "I'm not going to die," I said, wanting her to stop crying. "No way."

"I feel that if I don't look at you then nothing bad will happen."

"I'll be fine," I said desperately, "I really will."

"How do you know?" she heaved. "How can you say that?"

"Because I believe what you said a few minutes ago?"

She didn't laugh like I thought she would. "I didn't think John would die either," she said tearfully, "He wasn't meant to – he was my twin, you know."

"Beth, please – "

"He was fun, Jan, you would have liked him."

More tears started to flow and I didn't know what to do. I'm dreadful in those kind of situations. "Beth – "

"He used to call me Betty, it was his name for me." She stopped like as if she was remembering, then she went on, "We were so close and now he's dead."

Her words chilled me, I didn't want to hear anymore. But it was like she couldn't stop.

"I took such good care of him," Beth had her arms wrapped around herself and she was rubbing her hands up and down her body, as if she was cold. "I cooked for him, watched over him, talked to him, read to him . . ." she let her voice trail off.

I stood like a thick watching her, afraid to listen and afraid not to.

"Did no good," Beth said disconsolately. "Whatever I did, it did no fucking good."

"I'm sure he appreciated it." That was me with my pathetic comment.

Luckily, Beth didn't seem to notice. "Worst year of my life, that was," she went on. She walked to the table and sat down. "Worst year."

I stood like a spare, totally unable to do anything.

Neither of us talked for what seemed like ages. I stood, my back pressed against the door and Beth stared at her hands.

"He left me, you know," she said after a while, "I was engaged and one night I come back to our flat and find him in bed with someone else."

I hadn't a clue what she was on about. "Yeah?" I said.

"Said I neglected him, said I spent too much time with John," Beth gave a laugh that wasn't a laugh. "I said," she continued bitterly, "I said to him, well, when you're dying of cancer I'll be sure and dance attendance on you, how about that?" She shook her head. "Then I threw him out. Then John died. Then the folks separated. Then I was left on my own to pick up the pieces."

For the first time since I'd been diagnosed, I actually felt sorry for someone other than me. "I'm sorry, Beth." I moved towards her.

She put up her hand to fend me off. "Don't," her hands came to her eyes. "Don't touch me, Jan."

But I had to. I reached out and patted her shoulder and she began to cry. Big heaving sobs. I held her as she cried and I felt that at least I still had some use.

Much later, she told me about her folks.

"John's death wrecked what little marriage they had and now all they do is bitch about each other." She took the coffee I offered in a shaky hand. "I hate heading home to visit either of them, I just hate it."

So I admitted to something I'd never told either her

or Abby or before. "I hate going home too." I reddened with shame. "You should see our house."

I'd been hoping for a mutual sympathy thing, but Beth laughed at my stories.

She stunned me by saying, "At least your folks don't hate each other."

"No."

"And I think your dad is sweet."

"Yeah, as sweet as a fruitcake."

Beth smiled. "And your mother lives for you. She drives Abby mad with all the instructions she gives."

I couldn't say anything. There was a lump in my throat for some strange reason.

"You're lucky, Jan."

I gazed down at myself. My thin spiky body, my brittle nails and dry skin. "Come again?"

Beth laughed gently. "You know what I mean."

I'd never looked at things from another angle before. Not in my whole life. It was a weird experience.

CHAPTER SEVENTY-FOUR

Getting angry at Beth had been good for the two of us. My "why me?" neurosis abated. Instead I began to focus on crawling back up the barrel again. It was easier this time because Beth began to make huge efforts to talk with me. She didn't scurry away every time I came into a room and if, on the odd occasion she flinched when I brushed off her, I didn't feel ashamed. It wasn't me and it wasn't my fault.

The days greyed up though. Even when I was off the tablets, I felt as if I was still on them. Nothing seemed to sparkle anymore, but eventually, as the month wore on it became my normality.

Feeling more tired and only working when I could became my normality too. If someone had told me that I'd hate leaving work and coming home to an empty flat I'd have told them they were mental. But it was true, I began to dread coming back to the silence. Rattling around on my own, making tea that suddenly didn't taste so good, or crawling into bed and trying to have a kip didn't hold the same appeal it once had. Oprah began to get on my nerves. Rikki Lake I detested. So, I began to watch documentaries, yep, Janet Boyle used the telly as an educational tool. Animal programmes mostly, so that I could impress Dave with my knowledge of the animal kingdom. And, even harder to believe, I began to listen to *The Arts Show* on Radio1. RTE 1 was my dad's station. I used to tease him that RTE stood for Radio Terrible Eireann. But it wasn't terrible, it was interesting.

Sometimes in the afternoon, Dave called up, usually to fill me in on the campaign. We'd lie on top of my bed and talk. Well, he'd talk and I'd listen. We'd sometimes just sit in silence and watch the sky go by. Dave would point out the different types of clouds to me and tell me their names. Apparently, the puffy clouds meant rain, the stringy, wispy ones normally meant a good day.

And I liked the way looking at the sky made me feel. Totally anonymous. A small cog in a massive world. It was like my problems didn't amount to a hell of a lot.

Dave brought me presents too, feathers and stones and things. Beth thought it was a real cheap-skate thing to do, but I didn't. Feathers and stones meant something to Dave, and because he gave them to me, they meant something to me as well. I had a world-class collection of stones arranged all along my windowsill.

The Tuesday before my October chemo, Dave arrived. He was a bit manic. "Our case is up next month," he said. "We'll know about the land by mid-October."

543

He gawped around at Beth and me looking for a reaction.

"Brill," I smiled. "Great." I turned my attention back to the telly. We were watching *Brookside*.

Beth glared at him. Pointing the remote at the telly, she raised the volume. Liverpool accents boomed out of the box.

Dave laughingly gave her the finger. "I'll take ya with me when I 'ead back 'ome, Beth. Dump ya in Liverpool. Ya'll never want to see that programme again."

We flashed tense smiles at him, hoping he'd shut up. Dave was liable to talk all the way through a soap unless someone told him forcibly to button it.

"Crowley's comink out –"

"HEEEELLLPPP!"

Abby's shriek from the bathroom stunned us and then sent us running. Dave got there first, Beth second and I hobbled up last. When I got there, all I could hear was Dave laughing.

"What is it?" I asked. "What's wrong?"

Abby was curled up in a foetal position beside the bath. Her fluffy bathrobe was pulled around her. Eyes wide and shocked, she pointed to the shower. "Look," she squealed.

Dave was still laughing and Beth looked as if she badly wanted to maim him.

Inside the shower, just beside the handle, was the most horrific hairy black-legged spider I have ever seen. Horrendous was too nice a word.

"Oh God," I whispered.

"Take him out," Abby said. "Please." She turned tortured eyes on Dave.

"That's what men are for," Beth said. "The only use they have."

"Take him out, please Dave," I added my plea to the others.

The three of us were spider-phobic. Beth was the bravest, but not even she would handle a job as big as this.

Dave's laughter faltered. "'E's only thirsty," he replied. "'e'll go when he has a drink."

I thought he was joking, but he wasn't.

"Spiders are our friends," Dave said, beginning to leave the bathroom.

"That lad is no friend of mine," Beth said. "He'll have his fill of drink when I drown him." She put her hand on the shower button and the spider made a run at her.

The three of us shrieked and Dave, pushing Beth out of the way, scooped up the spider and brought it out of the flat. "Ya plonkers," he muttered.

He came back about ten minutes later, the grin gone from his face. "Just called to tell ya that the case is being heard next month," he said. "Thought ya might like ta know."

He turned on his heel and left.

I think somehow I'd let him down.

CHAPTER SEVENTY-FIVE

OCTOBER

I lay awake all night worrying about Dave. Why hadn't I been nicer to the spider? Why did I have to shriek and make a fool of myself? What must he think of me? How could I best salvage the situation?

The fact that I had chemo the following day didn't feature in my worry list. It was all Dave, Dave, Dave.

My head was pounding as I took my place at the breakfast table.

To make matters worse, Abby was bustling about, humming to the radio and making me scrambled eggs.

"They're nutritious, delicious and easily digested," she said cheerfully. "Just the thing to start the day with."

Beth emerged from her room. Sleepy-eyed.

"Hello, sleepy," Abby joked. "You look happy today."

Beth made a face behind her back and then, shoving a plastic Roches Stores bag nearly into my face, she said gruffly, "Thought I'd wait until today to give you this. I thought, you know, it might cheer you up."

"A present?" Abby left the eggs and rushed over for a gawk. "Why are you giving Jan a present?"

Beth said nothing.

Inside the Roches Stores bag was a kettle.

"Automatic, to save energy," Beth said shyly. "I figure we might as well all do our bit to help the environment."

I know a massive apology when I see one. "Thanks."

Abby was looking from me to Beth. "What is going on here?"

"I've been awful to Jan, " Beth muttered. "And awful to Dave."

"So you bought a kettle?" The gesture was lost on Abby. She rolled her eyes and when Beth wasn't looking mouthed over to me, "She's a spacer!"

Her eggs all burnt. I got away with not having to eat a breakfast.

The nurse couldn't find a vein.

It really hurt as she tried to put the needle in.

"Ow," I said, pulling my hand away and blinking back sudden tears. I tried not to look at the bruises the needle had made.

"Sorry, pet," the nurse said, "It's just getting harder to find a vein." Taking the needle away, she said, "I'll just get you something to warm your hands on, hopefully that'll make the veins pop up."

Mam watched her as she left. "Everything in this

place is 'hopefully'," she sniped. "Do they know what they're doing at all?" She glanced at my hand and shook her head. "It's in bits," she whispered. "In bits."

I wished she wouldn't say those things.

The nurse came back. She gave me a hot-water bottle to hold and told me to relax. "Being tense only makes it harder," she said.

"How can she relax?" Mam couldn't resist it. She was dying to have a go at someone. Every month she was getting more and more agitated. "How can she relax?" Her voice shook.

The nurse took no notice. Wrapping a blanket around me, she said, "I'll be back in a few minutes." After tucking it in, she walked away.

"Wagon," Mam fumed. "Who does she think she is?"

"She's only doing her job, Mam," I said. "She can't help it if my veins are shite." To be honest, the idea of another attempt at an injection scared me stupid, but I couldn't let Mam see that. It'd only freak her out more if she thought I was getting upset.

More jabbing, hell of a lot more pain. Mam was tensed up like a piece of elastic ready to snap.

In the end, I told her to leave. I was afraid she'd throw a wobbler at the doctors. I told her to go and say a prayer for me or something. Out she went, full of piety to pray for her daughter.

Sucker.

I don't know if she made it to the oratory or not, because when at last the injection was given, she was waiting for me outside the door.

"Jan," she said, beckoning me over. "Come here." She was standing beside another patient that we knew as Kathy. She was the woman I'd first seen a few months back when her scarf had fallen off. I didn't like talking to anyone else that was sick. So, hanging my head, unable to look Kathy in the face, I slunk over to the pair of them. "Kathy's last treatment is today," Mam said. "Isn't that great?"

"Yeah – brill." My attempt at enthusiasm flopped.

"How are you, Janet?" Kathy asked. Her voice was like her smile, soft.

"She's having trouble with her veins," Mam answered for me. "They've difficulty starting her off now." She looked at me. "How did it go?"

"Fine." I wished she'd get us away from this place.

"I've a Hickman line," Kathy said. "It's a sort of under-the-skin tube that they installed to pump me with drugs." She grinned. "Works great – any time they use it, I puke my guts up."

Mam managed a smile but I couldn't. Black humour was never my forte.

Kathy gently patted my arm. "Best of luck Janet, you'll do fine."

"And you too," Mam said.

Kathy gave a nod and left us to go and get her treatment.

The relief that she was gone made me feel faint. I hated when we met her, but Mam, good Samaritan, had to talk with everyone. She couldn't see that I hated it, but then again, she could never see anything properly when it concerned me.

CHAPTER SEVENTY-SIX

During the following week I had the usual phone calls. Mam rang about a million times to check up on me, Al rang the day after chemo to see how I was. He always remembered to do that and he mostly managed to cheer me up. Abby checked every day to see if I was OK and even Beth rang when she managed to get a free moment.

Dave didn't contact me at all.

I suppose it was because of the court case but still, I was hurt.

He called up at lunch-time the following Thursday. I know I should've been annoyed with him, but what would be the point? Then I might never see him again.

He knocked on the door and came in.

Slouched in would be a better way of describing it. Hands in his pockets, head down. "'Ow's my girl?" he asked. There was no smile, no kiss, no hug, no telling me I'd look better if I ate proper foods.

For some reason my stomach lurched. "What's wrong?"

He didn't answer. "Sorry 'bout not being in touch," he said instead, "It was the case, it took over everyfink."

I didn't say that it was all right, I wasn't that much of a thick. "Oh."

"They threw the fuckin' appeal out of court." His bitterness surprised me. He plonked himself down at the kitchen table and stared at his hands. His voice low, he muttered, "It's all gotta go."

"Aw, Dave – that's awful."

"Yeah." He sounded broken-hearted. When he looked at me, I could see he was. "You saw it," he said earnestly, "You saw 'ow beautiful the place was, and now . . ." He let his voice trail away.

I slid into the seat beside him and putting my arm about his waist, I laid my head on his shoulder. I felt bad for him, but I couldn't help thinking that at least he'd be around a lot more.

"It ain't right," he said a few seconds later. "It ain't right." His voice rose. "If we don't stop soon there'll be nothfink left."

He rested his head top of mine. "We've to be orf the site by next week."

I liked the feel of him so close. "So what's the story now?" I asked. "Is that it?"

"Yeah, we've ta pack up and go. I was thinking of maybe 'eading over to Sellafield with Megs."

I jerked upright and looked into his face. He was meant to stay around to be with me. Hadn't I told him

I couldn't bear it if he left? His casualness stunned me. "But – " I stopped. I shook my head. He couldn't leave. I couldn't understand.

"Yeah?" Dave gave me a questioning look.

"I thought, you know, you'd – " I gulped, "stay around here."

"Naw," Dave said surprised. "Sure there ain't nothfink to protest about no more."

"But you *promised*, you *promised* you'd stay with me." I couldn't help it. Pure panic tore the words out of my mouth. I couldn't go on, the bewildered look on Dave's face stopped me.

"I never." He shook his head, confused.

"You *did* promise." I was going to cry. I grabbed his sleeve and tugged it as I sought to explain, "I told you I couldn't bear it if you left me and you hugged me, you *hugged* me and you stayed around."

His eyes had widened. "Naw," he said perplexed. "That wasn't it. I 'ung around." He nodded. "I 'ung around 'cause I wanted to. But like, I thought you knew I'd 'ave to leave when the campaign ended. I *told* you that, Jan."

My head wouldn't believe it. There had to be a reason why he was leaving. There had to be. Going to Sellafield with *her* . . . I pulled away from him. That was it. Almost spitting out the words, I asked, "Is it because she's beautiful and I'm not?"

"Wot?" He looked stunned. "Who?"

"Who do you think?" I began to sniff. Oh God, I thought, I can't cry. "Megan. Who else?"

"Megs?" He made a face. "Wot?"

"Are you leaving with her because she's beautiful and I'm not?"

It took a second for my words to sink in. I could see his mind ticking over. "Wot?" he said at the end. "Wot are you on about?"

"You fancy her, don't you?"

"Naw." A really puzzled look came over his face. "Jan, you're the one that's gorgeous, Megs ain't a patch on you."

"Oh come on!"

I was sick but I wasn't stupid.

"You are, even without yah hair, you've one gorgeous face, ya really have." Dave touched my face. "That's why I 'ated all the crap you wore on it. You kept trying to cover yourself up. Your make-up was like a bleedin' mask."

I think he meant it. Dave wasn't a compliment-giver. There wasn't room in his world for niceties.

"So why are you leaving?" I asked with renewed hope. "If you wanted, you could stay here."

His smile wavered. "I'm leaving 'cause I want to, Jan. I don't want to live in anyone's place. I've 'ad all that. It drove me mental. I'd go crazy."

My tears stared to come again. I couldn't believe he was just going to walk out of my life. "So you used me," I whispered. "You just used me. Good time Jan, what?"

"Naw!" He sounded hurt. "No way." He cupped my face in his hands and said softly. "I do care about ya, ya know."

"But not enough to stay."

He flinched at my words. Then slowly he shrugged. A slow shake of his head. "Naw."

I felt sick. A tear trickled down my face and I let him see it. I wanted him to know how he'd made me feel.

He took his hands away from my face and turned from me. "I get up at dawn every day." He spoke quietly, as if it was just him in the room. "I get up and I see how beautiful a new day is. And I get up the next day and I feel exactly the same. And in ten years from now, when I look at a dawn, I want to feel the way I did this morning. And if I don't, then I'll know it's time to quit. But until then, I have to keep going." He looked across at me. "It's wot I do, Jan. It's who I am."

I remembered something from months back. When he'd showed me an oak tree on the site and I wanted to pin him down and keep him with me. And I remembered thinking that he wouldn't have been as beautiful if I'd done that.

It was who he was.

A horrible sadness was washing over me.

"It's like the other day with the spider," Dave said, "It just showed how different we are, you and me."

"Yeah." I wiped my face. I'd been a fool. Again.

"So?" Dave was studying me.

"If you want to go, just go," I said dully. I didn't know how'd I'd get over this.

He stood up and said uncertainly, "I'll see ya before I go – yeah."

I shook my head. "Just go."

He came over to where I sat and put his hand on my shoulder. I shrugged him off.

"Thanks for your support, with the marches and all."

"Yeah."

He stood behind me for a few seconds. Then he made his way to the door. "Take care, gorgeous."

I didn't answer.

Much later, Abby came into my room. "Want to talk about it?"

I turned over and sat up. I couldn't cry any more. "He's gone, Ab," I said dully.

"Dave, huh?" She sounded sad but not surprised.

"He's gone and I don't know what I'll do." Abby's arms encircled me and I clung to her. My voice rose. "Abby, what am I going to do?"

We didn't talk. I didn't even get drunk.

That was why it hurt so much. No cushion to numb me.

It was back to just me and Brad – again.

CHAPTER SEVENTY-SEVEN

Without Dave, I didn't know who I was anymore. How had I existed before I met him? What had I done? When I'd been with him, the world could see that I was worth something – how else would I manage to hang onto such a beaut? And now, there was nothing left. There was just me, on my own. And that wasn't worth talking about.

A big hole existed inside me where he'd been. I moped about the flat with no interest in anything. I no longer acted like a maniacal control freak where my bedroom was concerned. It was so messy that it reminded me of a real live Picasso painting (my arts show listening) I didn't bother dressing up. What was the point? I didn't even bother to put on any make-up. Every so often, when I'd be lounging miserably in a chair a sharply focused snapshot of Dave would surface. O'Connell Street in the rain handing out pens, drinking with him in a pub, the coloured hat he wore, the earrings. And every time this happened, the knife twisted a little more inside. The hurt was a raw physical ache. I didn't think I'd ever get over it.

Al rang the following week. I was watching a programme about swans and how they only have the one partner in life. I was in the middle of wishing fervently to be turned into a swan when the phone rang.

"Hello," I made my voice deliberately dull to show whoever it was that I was in mourning.

I knew by the hesitation that it was Al on the line. If ever I seemed in bad form, he'd get nervous. He couldn't seem to cope with me biting his head off.

"Jan, how's the form?" he made himself sound cheerful.

"I suppose you know Dave's gone?" I barked out. I knew he didn't but I wanted to tell him.

"Eh, no," he said. He didn't sound surprised either. "Sorry to hear that."

"I don't want to talk about it."

"Oh, fine so." He gave a gulp. "Got news for ya."

I *did* want to talk about it as it happened but Al was so thick he took my word at face value. All men were thick. "Well, it better be good," I snapped. "I don't want bad news."

"Laura Delaney from the cash desk is coming to our place to work."

Laura was the female equivalent of Al. The day she'd started in work, all the lads could have licked their shoes clean, their tongues were hanging so far out of their mouths. The thoughts of her in our office were vaguely disconcerting. "Is she doing *my* job?"

"Naw, she's being trained in for when Liz leaves."

"'Cause I'll be back, you know." It suddenly seemed important to say that.

Al's voice dropped. "I know," he said.

His tone made me sniff.

"You're not cryin', are you?"

"Just a bit," I wailed. "Dave's gone and I'm so miserable."

"Don't." He sounded panicky. "Look, I'll ring you everyday from now on and if you want to talk you can, how 'bout that?"

"Why don't you call out?" I tried to keep my voice steady. It was silly crying. "Come over to the flat."

He hadn't called since he'd walked out the last time.

"Naw, I'll ring."

More suppressed sobs from me.

I could sense his indecision. "Well," he eventually said, "I'll call out after your next injection in November, OK?"

"I'd like that," I said sniffing. "I miss not seeing you." And I did funnily enough.

"Likewise." I could tell he was smiling.

CHAPTER SEVENTY-EIGHT

NOVEMBER

Abby was polishing her shoes and Beth was morosely stirring her coffee when I got up for breakfast the day before the November chemo. For the first time, I'd actually devoted my time to thinking about the injection and the way I'd feel. It staved off thoughts of Dave.

My humour was bad. It really was a major case of wallowing in self-pity.

The minute I appeared, Abby left her polishing and began cooking my breakfast.

"I don't want anything," I grouched.

"You have to eat," Abby said in her nurse's voice.

I gave a sigh to show her how fed up I was.

"So," Beth said, "How's the form?"

"Crap." I slumped down at the table. "I mean how would you feel if your fella did a runner?" Then I remembered that her fella actually had. "Oh, sor . . ."

Beth waved me away. "Dave was just an eco-wanker." I think she was trying to comfort me. I know she didn't really believe that.

"Yeah," I agreed morosely.

"He wasn't," Abby said from her position at the cooker. "He was just your usual unreliable type."

"What?" I thought the remark was a bit callous, seeing as I was sick, especially from Abby who was bent on agreeing with everything I said these days. Beth joked that if I crapped, Abby would crawl out of my arse. Crude, I know, but how true.

"Well," Abby said, cracking an egg into the saucepan, "you always seem to go for lads that let you down."

"That's all there is out there," Beth remarked, still on my side. "Unless you count the drips."

"Mickey isn't a drip!" Egg forgotten, Abby glared at Beth.

"Or the desperately intent on marriage ones."

"He's not like that either."

Beth shrugged. "Whatever."

"I don't pick fellas like that," I said, finally able to get a word in. "That's a horrible thing to say." I was hoping she'd back down and be nice to me again.

"But you *knew* what he was like," Abby said, "You *knew* he'd leave sooner or later." She said it as if she couldn't believe I was so stupid.

I suppose I had known but what had that to do with it?

"You pick them because you prepare yourself in advance for disappointment," Abby pronounced. "You think they'll let you down, so you pick the ones that don't disprove your world view."

I barked out an uncomfortable laugh. "That is crap. Crap."

Beth was staring at Abby, agog.

"You won't let yourself trust so you don't let yourself get caught."

"Oh, shut up!" I stood up, wishing I'd never come out. "Shut up!"

Abby licked her lips. It was like she was on a roll. I think she was making it up as she went along, but because it made alarming sense, she kept plugging away. "I mean the guy told you he wouldn't be around, he virtually spelled it out for you, so you think, 'Oh, goody, I'll have him and he can dump me and I can feel bad about it but at least I'll know I was right not to trust him'."

"Wow!" Beth said.

"Fuck. Off." I said.

Abby began to remove a dripping egg from the water. The sight of it made my stomach turn. "That's what Mickey says about you anyhow." She shrugged and looked at me. "I dunno, maybe it's true."

"Is it true?" Beth asked.

"Don't be stupid," I virtually shrieked. "What does a prat with creased trousers know about me!"

"I just said maybe it's true," Abby said calmly. "Don't upset yourself over it, I only said it to help you." A poached egg was put in front of me.

"Help me? Huh, that's a laugh." I shoved the egg away. "And you can keep your egg."

"It's just the way you appear to Mickey."

Her calm manner infuriated me. "Well, tell him the

next time I'll appear to him as a – a – " I sought for something.

"A man-hating ball-breaker," Beth offered.

"Yeah. A man-hating ball-breaker." I didn't wait for Abby's reaction, I stormed into my room and slammed the door.

How dare they discuss me behind my back. How dare they!

I almost broke the bed, the thump I gave it.

I was just unlucky in love, that was all. Unlucky and let-down. That was it. Unlucky, let-down and a bit stupid. That about summed me up.

I *did* trust people.

Well, maybe not trust exactly . . . but I believed in people.

I believed in them despite the fact that I couldn't trust them.

Didn't I?

CHAPTER SEVENTY-NINE

The November chemo was a nightmare. But I didn't care. I deserved it. I was so depressed and angry at my life. Dave leaving and then, Abby having the *cheek* to try and analyse *me*. And to put the tin hat on it, Mam spent her time shouting abuse at the doctors and sniping at nurses. It was mortifying. I couldn't even bring myself to talk to her as we came back in the taxi.

"Don't come up with me," I hissed at her as the car drew to a halt outside the flat. "I don't want you to come inside." I opened the lock and tried to slam the door on her.

Ignoring me, she got out and paid the driver. Without saying a word, she followed me up the path. "I don't need you," I said. "Just go home."

Mam did a big martyr sigh. "Janet, whether you like it or not, I'm coming in. Now, just open the door and let's get inside."

I did as I was told, there was no point in arguing with her. I'd go to bed when I got in and leave her to twiddle her thumbs and bore herself stupid. Though that wouldn't be hard –she was stupid.

"Why did you have to embarrass me?" The question came out without me thinking about it. When I saw her go red, I was glad I'd asked. I'd take my bad form out on her.

"What do you mean?"

"What do I mean?" I almost laughed. I shoved open the door to the flat and we went inside. "You – shouting and giving out to everyone in the hospital, why do you have to do it? It's mortifying so it is."

Mam had been about to fill the kettle for tea. She had the tap on and water was splashing into the sink. "I do it for you," she said quietly. "To make sure they're doing their job right." Filling up the kettle, she said, "Anyway let's face it, you're easily embarrassed."

"And what's that supposed to mean?"

Mam shook her head. "Nothing, forget it."

"No, I want to know. What are you on about?" I wanted her to stop fiddling with the damn kettle and tell me what she meant.

"Just go into bed and have a sleep, you're tired."

"And annoyed," I glared at her. "What do you mean I'm easily embarrassed? If my mother making a show of herself in the hospital isn't embarrassing, I don't know what is." I couldn't believe I was shouting at her, usually the way we communicated was through massive silences or sweeping things safely away under the carpet. It worked well for us.

Mam looked sort of sad. "Well, Janet," she said

softly, "Let me ask you a question – why did you leave home?"

"Ha!" I said, in my weaker chemo voice. It was a near as I could get to a bellow. "Ha!"

"Well?" Mam had her arms folded and was studying me. "Go on."

She was only pissed because I'd moved a few miles away and never visited. "Because I had a job and I wanted my own place."

"Why did you want your own place?"

"Because I wanted to be independent." Where was this leading?

"You never visited us at first until you lost your job and needed money," Mam said.

Suddenly I didn't want this conversation to continue. "I'm heading to bed."

"You come home and you're like Lady Muck turning your nose up at everything," Mam's voice rose. "It's like my own daughter is a stranger in the house." She shook her head. "You couldn't get away from us fast enough, could you Jan?" She gave a small sad laugh.

"That's, that's not true," I lacked the conviction of my words. "I just wanted my own space."

"If you really wanted independence, you would have hung onto one of your jobs," Mam said, "All you wanted was your cake and to eat it. Live away and come home when you'd nothing better to do." I was about to deny it, when she said, "I wouldn't have gone so mad at you for leaving only I knew you were running out on us, running out on everything you were."

"Mam," I said, "I'm tired."

"You used to slop around in jeans and the minute you leave, there you are dressing like a – a – " she sought for a word to describe how she felt about me. "Tart," she finished. "Skirts up to your arse, make-up up to your eyeballs, a new person."

Her words hurt me, I blinked back tears. That was all I seemed to do lately, cry.

I think Mam was forgetting that I was sick, she was determined to keep going. "It hurt us Janet, it really did. I mean, what did we do to make you feel like that about us? Are you ashamed of us? Ashamed of yourself?"

How did she know all this? "Nothing. You did nothing. You've got it all wrong."

Mam shook her head. "I know you like the back of my hand, Janet. I know all my kids. You've never talked to us, everything you feel gets shut up inside good and tight. Even now, being sick, you never – "

"I'm going to bed." This was awful, I couldn't take it. Talking about me was never a subject on my agenda.

Mam didn't say anymore and I went into my room and curled myself up against my thoughts.

CHAPTER EIGHTY

Unfortunately, Al chose the following evening to call up. My mind was still slamming about, like a fly against glass, wondering what the hell was happening to me. It was as if I'd lost myself and couldn't get back. Or maybe I'd lost myself a long time ago, I dunno. My whole life was falling apart. At least it was in keeping with the rest of my body, I guess.

Al shuffled into the room, bearing chips and burgers. Beth and Abby gave him wary nods and he nodded back. I think they'd decided not to talk to him in case they said something wrong. They'd made the incorrect decision, it only made me more aware of how weird everyone I associated with was. Why couldn't Al just be normal and grin and smile at them. I knew the two would snigger at him when he left. I'd had enough of being laughed at to last me a lifetime.

"What do you want?" I said sulkily.

"Just came to see how you were," Al slid into a seat beside me. His jumpy air got on my nerves. "I got some chips on the way, want some?"

"Are you trying to piss me off?"

Beth and Abby looked in our direction. "Naw, naw," Al stammered, "It's just, I thought you liked chips." He looked like a kid that someone had slapped for no reason.

"I like nothing anymore, Al," I said slowly and deliberately, "Everything tastes like shit."

His eyes slid from my face and I could see his Adam's Apple moving as he gave a hard swallow.

"Do you want a plate for those chips, Al?" Abby got up from the floor and smiled at him. "I'll get you one."

I shot her a horrible look which she valiantly ignored. I still couldn't forgive her for what she'd said about my choice in men.

Al got up from the sofa and followed Abby. "Thanks," Taking the plate from her, he dumped his chips on it. "I, eh, got two lots," he said, "Anyone else like some?"

"Just eat them and shut up," I snapped.

"I'll have some," Abby said brightly, "I'm dying for a few, how about you, Beth?"

"Fine." Beth said, "just a few."

"Sure you don't want to share your burger too?" I asked.

All three ignored me. I didn't like being ignored by Al. "Don't you ignore me," I said straight at him. "Don't you dare."

"Sorry?" Al said. This was what he always said when he felt a bit threatened. "Sorry, Jan?"

"Don't try and lick up to my flatmates by getting them chips, don't you dare."

"He's not licking – "

"Just cause you fucked up that night."

I'd hit him harder than I'd meant. I don't know why I said it. I don't think Al even remembered admitting to me that he'd felt so bad about the night with Beth and Abby.

He went white and his eyes gave me such a look that it twisted my heart and made me know just what an awful person I was. His mouth opened to say something and then he closed it again. He stared at the table and then stared at me again.

"What are you on about?" Beth asked. "Who fucked up?"

"Thanks," Al said. "Thanks, Jan."

Without saying any more, he left.

I suppose I should have run after him and apologised, but I couldn't. I wanted to feel bad, I felt I deserved it. When I felt better, I'd say sorry. I don't know why I wanted to hurt Al, only that he was there to be hurt. He was the only one I could get at and feel secure that he wouldn't turn on me.

Anyway, he'd probably ring.

CHAPTER EIGHTY-ONE

I spent the whole of the next day waiting on the phone to ring. I didn't even sleep in case it would be Al and I'd miss him.

But he didn't contact me.

The first call was from Mam to see how I was. She didn't make any reference to our conversation in the kitchen. That suited me fine. It scared me to think that she was right, that Louise Johnson had done such a good job on me that I'd disappeared into someone else.

I told Mam I was fine and she told me to take care of myself. And I said I would.

Abby rang.

More of the same.

Nothing from Al.

A whole week went by, I was in hospital for tests. There was only one session of chemo left.

Al hadn't rung.

For the first time thoughts of Dave began to abate.

Horrific thoughts of Al never ringing me again began to haunt me. He was my friend, I couldn't loose him.

The uneasy notion that I'd overstepped the limit with him began to solidify in my head. I felt ashamed of what I'd said and of how I'd treated him. If only he would ring I could tell him.

But he didn't.

By the time the end of November came, I knew I'd have to make the first move. I don't think in the whole of my life, I'd ever held out an olive branch to anyone. The pain of rejection was too horrible to think about.

So I searched the flat, top to bottom. I even went into Beth and Abby's rooms while they were out at work. Abby's room stunned me. Books on Cancer were everywhere. *The Cancer Diet, What you should know about Chemo, The Cancer Patient, Cancer Ward,* etc, etc. It was nice of her to be so interested in me, a warm feeling spread all the way up my body.

The warm feeling didn't last long when I realised that there wasn't a single hidden can of booze anywhere in the place. No Dutch courage. And there wasn't even some money left lying around for me to go to the off-licence. And I would have.

I wondered hopefully, if not finding any booze was a sign to leave well enough alone. Then I thought of what I'd said to Al and I came to the reluctant conclusion that it was up to me to apologise. So, heart thumping, I picked up the phone and dialled work.

Lenny answered and he recognised my voice

immediately. "Janet, how are you?" he said. "How's things?"

"Not too bad." My courage was seeping away. "Just called to say hi to everyone."

"And isn't that nice and you sick and everything." He lowered his voice, "'Tis a pity there's no one really in today atall atall."

"No?"

"Well, now, Laura is here, she's the new girl, a lovely girl indeed. She's here but sure you don't know her."

"And the others?" I didn't know whether I was relieved or not. Adrenaline had been flowing and now it had nowhere to go.

"Liz is off with Andy for the day, shopping for things for a new flat," he paused as if he expected me to comment, but I couldn't. I just wanted to find out about Al.

"Henry, now, he's up in court. Someone has him over a barrel with those ould jumpers he was flogging, it's all very up in the air. I don't understand it atall atall. Do-be-do-be-dooo."

"Oh, right." I gulped. "And, eh, Al, is he there?"

"Oh, well, now that's a terrible state of affairs."

"What?"

"Well, you know – his mother and everything."

"His mother?"

Lenny paused. "Aye, his mother," he said, "Surely he told *you*, sure doesn't he tell *you* everything."

There was a major nudge, nudge, wink, wink,

behind his words, which I ignored. "What about his mother?" I asked patiently.

"Well now and wasn't it in the paper and everything – his mother was attacked to within an inch of her life." He stopped, "Surely you read about it?"

"What?"

"She's in hospital and," Lenny assumed a newsreader's voice, "a man is helping the police with their enquiries." His voice dropped dramatically, "Rumour has it 'twas the husband – she told him to get out because he was a bit free with his fists and he went mental altogether. But sure, I don't know about that atall atall."

I was stomached.

"Do *you* know anything?" Lenny asked hopefully.

"No."

"Aw, well . . ." he sounded disappointed. "She's in the same hospital you're going to," he continued, "That fancy new one, St Anne's."

"Oh."

"Sure it's like a hotel, that place. I'm thinking I'll have to be getting sick meself and just go there for . . ."

I hung up and wondered what I was to do now.

The following day I had to go for a CAT Scan. Mam came with me. I told her that after the scan I wanted to go and visit someone.

"But you can't," she looked horrified. "Your immune system is way down, the doctor said . . ."

"I'm only going to see the person's son, I won't be in a ward or anything."

She looked doubtful but I knew she'd let me go. I think she was regretting calling me a tart.

I'd become really conscious of not looking tarty since. For hospital that day, I wore a pair of jeans and a sweat-shirt Dave had lent me and I'd forgotten to give back. It was big and sloppy and hid how thin I was. It advised people to *Grow up and not Blow up*. Good advice where me and Mam were concerned. A picture of a huge mushroom dominated the front of it.

The receptionist told me that Mrs Freeney was on the second floor. She was still on the critical list. "You can't go in," she said, "it's family only."

I didn't know whether Al would even want to see me with so much on his mind, but I, being totally single-minded, knew I had to see him. "Can you see if her son is there, Alan Freeney and ask him to meet me in the canteen?"

"You can't be going into canteens," Mam tut-tutted behind me. "For God's sake, Janet!"

I ignored her and the receptionist put a call through to the ICU place.

"He's there," she smiled at me. "He said he'll meet you in the television room on the second floor."

My heart lifted and sank at the same time.

"At least he has some sense," Mam muttered from behind.

Ignoring her comment, I said that I wouldn't be long and she could either wait for me or go home. Of course, she wanted to wait. She said she'd just pop into the chapel and say a prayer and maybe have some coffee in the canteen herself. A half an hour was all. If I wasn't back by then, she'd come looking for me.

I hardly heard her as I mentally ran through what I was going to say to Al. I'd never felt intimidated by him before but then again, I'd never be so horrible to him before. Apologising for me was scarier than facing chemo, and I really mean that.

After about five minutes, because I lost my way, I stood outside the TV room. To my relief the room was empty, the telly switched off. Al was already inside, sitting hunched forward on a chair. He didn't seem to hear me as I opened the door. "Hiya," I gulped out as I entered.

He looked up at me and nodded. He didn't look like Al because there wasn't even a hint of a smile as he gazed at me. Everything about him looked miserable, from his greasy hair to his white face.

Why had I been so rotten to him? "How's your mother?" I asked, wanting to sit beside him but terrified to do so.

His head slumped. "Bad," he muttered.

I closed the door and began walking towards him. Every step I took increased my heart-rate and sweat was clamming up my palms. When I was about halfway across the room, he looked up at me again. "So, Jan," he asked. "Why are you here?"

I stopped. I gave a small cough. "I, eh, just wanted to say that, eh," I stared at the wall behind his head,

"The night in the flat, what I said, well, I'm sorry." The word was out. Swallowing I continued, "I didn't mean it." I forced myself to look at him.

He gave a smile, not a nice smile, sort of cynical. "You meant it all right," he said quietly.

I gulped. "I didn't."

"Jan," Al rubbed his hand over his face. "I know you meant it, 'cause let's face it, it was true – right? I did fuck up."

"No!"

"Don't lie, Jan," Al stood up and faced me. He shoved his hands into his jeans and hunched his shoulders. "Please."

"I'm not." This was terrible, he couldn't do this.

"I have to get back to me Ma."

"Al – "

"Look Jan," he cut across me, "that night in the pub was one of the worst nights of me life." He shook his head, "and that's sayin' something – believe me."

"But I'm sick, I say stupid things, I don't mean – "

"You did mean it." His voice had gone hard. He was like the day in the office when I'd called him boring. "You did mean it and I deserved it. I made an eejet out of meself – but Christ, that's the way I am." He came towards me and stopped just in front of me. "I couldn't face you the next day, remember? I didn't show for work?"

I nodded.

"Then, just a while ago, I go to your flat to see how you are and I make a thick of meself by walking out.

You tell me your flatmates were only jokin', so I believe you and I – I – " he bit his lip and turned away, "I fuckin' visit you with chips and what happens? Huh?" His voice lowered as he said, "You say that to me."

"I'm sorry." I put my hand on his arm but he shrugged me off. "I was in bad form."

"You are not the only one with a shit deal, Jan," Al said gulping hard. "OK, I know you're sick and I took everything you hurled at me. It was always me, you know, I was the one in work that was the eejet, the fucker, the baby-sitter. It hurt but I know you and I – I – well, I liked you and I told meself Jan doesn't mean it, she's sick. But like," he shrugged, "I can't take it anymore, me Ma is sick, really bad. And anyway, you have your ma and da and your mates. You don't need me."

But I did. It was only then I realised how much I needed him. "Al – "

"My da beat her, do you know that?" He said it out of the blue. He didn't wait for me to answer, he went on, "We barred him from our house, but he doesn't listen. He came in a few months ago and tried to hit her, so I jumped on him. He held my arm down and ripped it with a knife."

I felt sick.

"He used to beat us if his dinner wasn't on the table. He shouts all the time, I've never heard him talk normally, can you believe that?"

"Al – "

"So Jan, my life is shit, really shit, and I liked you

and I had a laugh with you, but you think the same as him. That I'm a complete fuck-up. I don't blame you. I really don't. Who'd want me around?"

I tried to touch him again. I wanted to tell him that I'd have him around. I wanted to hug him the way he'd hugged me when he'd found out I was sick. But he wouldn't let me.

"I gotta go now," he said, when he saw me attempting to touch him. "Thanks for the apology, but it doesn't matter, honest."

"Please – " It was worse than losing Dave. It was worse than anything I'd ever had to deal with before.

"Bye Jan. I'll ring you sometime." He stared at me for a second before turning and walking out the door.

I let him go. I'd just lost the best friend I'd ever had.

As far as I was concerned, I was the biggest fuck-up of all time.

Back at the flat, lying on my bed, staring at the sky, real shame came to haunt me. Pure, undiluted humiliation worked its way inside my head and for once I didn't fight it. For once I admitted to myself that perhaps I deserved to feel this way. Mam and Dad had been great to me and all I could do was worry about the state of their house, Al had been so supportive and because I felt crap, I punished him with the words I knew would hurt him. I'd even treated Dave badly. I was a horrible, horrible person. I know I was sick and sick people said hurtful things, but sometimes that wasn't enough of an excuse.

FLIPSIDE

I lay awake all night and finally in the early hours of the morning, I got up out of bed and left the flat. I wanted to walk and think. I'll never forget that day. I walked out just as dawn was breaking. The sky blazed with colour. It turned blood red with the emerging light. Everywhere was silent and the whole world looked new, as if it had been reborn during the night. I stood for ages in the drizzle just watching the sun come up and the world coming alive, like a flower uncurling its petals. First there was silence, then there was the odd bit of noise and soon the whole day was just bursting with sound.

I remember Dave telling me that everyone should see a dawn. And now I knew why.

And wherever he was, I knew Dave had seen daybreak with me. Putting my finger to my lips, I blew him a kiss, just to say good-bye.

I was over him and I'd realised it far too late.

CHAPTER EIGHTY-TWO

DECEMBER

I'd never believed anyone when they said getting wet led to getting a cold. I, Janet Boyle had once slept with a medical student. He'd told me that colds were caused by viruses and you couldn't acquire a virus by merely getting wet.

Impressive stuff.

It actually turned out that the guy in question, Claude Bernard, wasn't a medical student at all. Just a medical head-case. But what he said rang true and I believed him.

So when I met Daly a couple of days before my final batch of chemo and he told me the tumours had disappeared, I decided not to tell him about my sore throat. A sore throat wasn't a big deal anyhow.

Focusing my thoughts on the final chemo was what I used to take my mind off Al.

The next day, my throat began to burn and I started to cough. Nothing major, just coughing. It didn't worry me. I gargled with salt and water and decided to have a lie-down. I woke up at lunch-time drenched in sweat and burning up. Rising up on my elbow, I tried to see across the room and my vision blurred. I couldn't even get to the telephone.

"Help!" I called, but my voice was scratchy and my throat screamed in pain.

Maybe it would go. It could just be the drugs.

I lay back down and closed my eyes and tried to concentrate on just breathing and staying alive.

It didn't work. I got worse.

I felt so bad that I wanted to die. Maybe I was dying. I didn't feel scared, just sad. Then I felt sad that all I could feel was sad.

There was so much that I suddenly wanted to do, that I could so easily have done and never did. There were so many things I should have said and hadn't. I'd had twenty-five years and no excuse. Twenty-five years was a quarter of a century.

I didn't even think of what it would be like to die, I just wondered what it would be like to live.

And now it was too late. I knew if I could just hang on until Abby got home, maybe I could tell her and she could pass it . . .

There was a bird flying at me. A huge bird with black wings and a big beak. He lived in the trees in the mountains and they'd knocked his home down. He was angry and he was going to pull me from my nest and shove me out . . . Now Dad had a paintbrush in his hand and our house was white and everyone else suddenly had a Pacer Mint house . . . Mam was crying

581

and reaching out for me and I was whirling away somewhere being pulled deeper and deeper and no one could catch me . . . I was falling down from a nest and I couldn't fly. All I had to do was spread my wings and I could save . . . Al was smiling saying sorry and that he loved me and that please not to go and leave him . . . there was the ground coming nearer and nearer to me and I tried to open my wings. I really did. I tried my hardest.

Bang.

And I was floating high on the air and I could see where I lived far down below and I was diving and wheeling and I was free and once again I was falling, falling, being pulled back into the ground and suddenly there was a noise.

A bleeping noise.

Voices and murmurs and smells. Noises and clicking and beeping.

It was too soon, sensations rushing at me when I'd been so light. I was heavy again, I could see blackness and I was scared. I was in a tunnel, or was I? My eyes seemed heavy, as if they were closed. Maybe they were closed. They were hard to open but light seemed to be coming from underneath them.

I tried harder and slowly and painfully they opened. The colours burst into them and everything seemed so bright. Relief washed over me.

I'd been let into heaven after all.

So had my mother.

My mother?

She was there too. Standing a bit away, crying. At least I think she was. She reached and pressed a bell. And she came up to me and clasped my face in her hands and kissed me. Warm kisses. On my face.

"Oh Janet," she said and her voice was softer than I'd ever heard it before, "we thought we'd lost you."

I didn't understand. How had I got lost? Where had I been?

Someone else came into my field of vision, dressed in white. My eyes followed her and for the first time I noticed all the things beeping away on the walls and all the tubes coming out of them and all the things going into me.

It was too much.

I closed my eyes again.

More noise. Rumbley voices. Another struggle to open my eyes. Daly was there, bending over me. He smiled and told me to rest. He didn't have to tell me.

Next day I could open my eyes and it didn't hurt so much. My mind seemed to be working too, piecing together sounds and sights and making pictures of explanations in my brain.

I thought I was in hospital.

"Am I in hospital?" My voice didn't make a sound.

No one explained where I was.

I was scared.

In and out of sleep for days and hours. Darkness and light. Injections and liquids and tests. My voice came back and then they told me.

"You had an infection," Mam said. "When Abby got home you were delirious and we really," she bit her lip, "we really thought we'd lost you," she finished.

I wasn't dead.

The thought was like a brightness in my head. The brightness became dazzling.

I wasn't dead.

I still had my chance. I was alive and I still had my chance to live.

That was when it hit me. The acceptance.

I was sick. But I was still alive. So I could still get better.

The fight could still go on.

I made myself get strong, I willed my blood count to go up. Little by little they stopped pumping me with antibiotics. Blood transfusions stopped.

My family were let into see me.

Lisa was huge, her baby was due after Christmas and she wasn't looking forward to it. She had a stockpile of horror stories about giving birth.

"Have you read some book on it or something?" Sammy asked after a particularly gory one about a baby that came out sideways and almost split the mother in two.

Lisa shot her a patronising look. "When you're in my position, you'll find out how it really is."

"And what position was that?" Sammy jibed. "Missionary?"

"Sammy!" Mam shrieked, as Sam and I cracked up laughing.

Dad looked totally confused. "You're never joining Trócaire?"

"Des," Mam said half-exasperated, half-laughing, "will you shut up and stop going on about things you don't understand."

"Women," Dad rolled his eyes and left to have a smoke.

Mam turned her attention back to me. "So how are you today?" She never got a chance to ask until Lisa had had her daily moan.

"Better," I nodded. "I feel much better."

"Dr Daly says you should have your chemo by next week at the latest. He's really pleased with you." She beamed at me as if I'd done something wonderful. Getting up and assuming a mournful face, she said, "I'll just go and peep in on Kathy." Kathy's cancer had come back and she'd been re-admitted to hospital. She was in the isolation ward.

Mam left and Sammy began rummaging in her bag. "Abby called up the other day and said to drop these off for you. They came in the post." She produced two envelopes and a postcard and handed them to me.

"Abby called to the house?" Nice, orderly Abby in our front garden. The thought was frightening.

"Yeah, she had this weird guy with her," Sammy made a face.

"He had creases in his trousers – imagine," Lisa added.

I tried not to think of Abby. There was nothing I could do. She'd come, she'd seen and she'd probably conked out. Ah, well.

I dug into the cards. One was from Dave. Printed on

recycled paper, it read, *Happy Christmas, Gorgeous. Calmed down yet? If not, I hope you're taking good care of yourself. Loadsa eco-friendly hugs – Dave.* I felt no tug reading it, just fondness. He'd been right to leave, I could see that now.

"Why does he say you're gorgeous?" Lisa asked, obviously having read my card. "Did he not see you before you lost your hair or something?"

"Lisa!" Sammy exclaimed.

"My hair didn't bother him," I smiled. "It's just hair."

"You're weird." Lisa rolled her eyes. It was as if I'd just declared that I wanted to join a convent or something.

The second card was from Liz. She'd wished me all the best and stuck in a picture of her new flat with a flabby Andy standing outside it. *You'll be able to visit when you're better* she'd written.

Hand trembling, I tore open the last card. It was from Henry and Lenny. Disappointment shot through me. Lenny had written something that no one could make out. Henry had scribbled down what he considered a funny remark. *Hope your recovery's quicker than your typing speed.*

There was nothing from *him.*

I did get my chemo a week later. Two days before Christmas. The hospital was winding down and they said if I was all right that I could go home for Christmas. All going well, I'd be able to stay at home until my check up in a month's time.

The chemo was horrible, I felt sick.

But I survived.

I was going home.

CHAPTER EIGHTY-THREE

Christmas day in our house was like any other except that we had turkey for dinner and exchanged presents. It was a bit embarrassing when I got gifts from everyone and the only person I'd managed to buy for was Dad. Two red jumpers.

"Be careful how you wash them," I warned, "I think they might run."

"They're wonderful," Dad was delighted that he was the only one that got something from me. "I'm touched by that. Two jumpers. Exactly the same. That's great."

Lisa was staring daggers at me. She'd got me a scarf. Every year I got the latest A-wear scarf from her. "If I'd known that you had nothing for *us*, I wouldn't have bothered," she grumbled. "I mean, I don't even work."

"Lisa," Mam was setting the table. "It's the spirit of good-will. Janet was sick. She wasn't in a position to be buying presents for everyone."

"Except me," Dad said proudly, from the top of the table.

"Yes, Des, except you." Mam gave him a brief,

clipped smile. "And with a bit of luck you could get a part-time job as a traffic-light."

"Now, now . . ."

"It's a joke," Mam clarified and, as Dad nodded, she said, "Sure you couldn't be a traffic light, you'd be stuck on red."

He was about to retaliate when the front doorbell rang. In fact it did more than ring. Dad had bought a new chime that played "Mistletoe and Wine". Every time the bell went, Cliff Richard announced it in booming tones.

"Who can that be?" Mam said irritably. She hated visitors on Christmas Day.

She exited to the hall and we heard voices. Then we heard her telling someone to come in. Then we heard the other person saying they couldn't and then we heard Mam saying that they could. Then we heard the slam of the front door and Mam arrived in followed by Mrs Johnson.

"Aaahhhh." Collective intakes of breath.

"Mrs Johnson brought us some chocolates," Mam beamed. "Isn't that nice?"

"Phewww." Collective sighs of relief followed by a stunned silence.

"I just came to, eh, tell you how glad I am that your Janet is all right." Mrs Johnson looked at me. "I hope you'll soon be better," she said softly.

"Thanks," I smiled at her. It must have taken a lot of guts for her to come into our house and bury the steel-bladed, super-sharp, many-headed hatchet.

"I know we haven't been on the best of terms but, well, with Christmas and all, what's the point of having grudges?"

"Life's too short," Dad nodded vigorously. Then he looked at me. Shaking his head, he muttered, "Oh, isn't that an awful thing to be saying."

"No, it's true," I agreed.

Mrs J stayed for a drink. She ended up getting locked. Staggering out our front door, she fell into the dug foundations of our new extension. Dad had to haul her out. She joked that if she wasn't our neighbour she'd sue us. We all laughed good-naturedly at her.

"Thought she'd never go," Mam said through gritted teeth, waving her off.

"I'm telling you," Dad chortled, his arm around Mam's shoulder, "that woman drank enough of our wine to shit grapes for a month."

"Dad!" Lisa was aghast. "That's crude. God, how can I bring a baby into this house?"

"Get your own house so," Mam said matter-of-factly, "Off you go."

That shut her up.

Later Dad got drunk and began singing. We left him in the kitchen and went inside to watch the Christmas Day films. I fell asleep at some stage and woke the next morning in bed.

Two big things happened that month to take my mind off the waiting.

The waiting was the worst thing I'd had to deal with where the cancer was concerned. I'd never have believed that finishing chemo and being told not to come to the hospital for a month could've been so scary. In fact it should have been brilliant, but it wasn't. If someone that month had asked me what the waiting was like, I would've said like the film *Jaws*. The suspense, the spooky music. Is he gone or is he just swimming below the surface? For eight months, the hospital had been my safety-net, the place where they pumped me with drugs and took pictures of my insides. And now, the net was gone and I was cast adrift. Back into the world to see if I'd sink or swim. A whole month of waiting. A whole month wondering if every little twinge or itch was the cancer coming back. A whole month of pretending to be optimistic while being eaten up with terror. A whole month of wishing each day was over. Seven hundred and twenty hours of waiting.

Lisa's baby was born on New Year's Eve. Amid much screaming, despite an epidural and gas, Jade Juniper arrived into the world. Claude was at the birth. Sammy said he collapsed when the baby came out. Sammy said Lisa could be heard yelling all over the hospital. Sammy said Dad cried.

Mam stayed with me. I was the one that had to be looked after, she said. I liked that.

I went in to see Jade the next day.

"She's like you," Dad said. "She has the fat face you had when you were born."

"Thanks, Dad," I took it as a compliment.

Lisa was at the end of her ward. As we entered, I could see Claude's head. He towered over everything in the room. "Oh look," he said, spotting us, "It's Grandad Dessie and Auntie . . ." He frowned. "What's the name of your sister that has cancer, Liz?"

I was mortified. It wasn't as if he'd whispered it. Every head in the ward swivelled in my direction. "It's Jan," I shouted. "I'm the one with cancer."

I'd hoped to embarrass him but I didn't. Instead, he laughed and everyone else got embarrassed. "Auntie Jan," Claude said. He lifted a tiny pink-clad baby up into the air. Putting on a ridiculous baby-sounding voice and waving the child's arm, he said, "Hello, Grandad Dessie and Auntie Jan. Hello. I'm Jade."

"Hello Jade," Dad waved back.

I didn't know which of them was worse.

Lisa was reclining on her pillows. She looked fantastic except for the world-weary face she'd on. "I'm aching," she announced the minute we came abreast of the bed. "It's the worst experience in the world."

"But look at what came out of it," Claude held the baby up to his face. "Guggery, guggery goo."

"I'd like to see you go through it," Lisa pouted.

"Your mammy is just getting the blues," Claude said knowledgeably to Jade. He was nearly swallowing the baby, his mouth was so big.

"Let Jan have a hold," Dad gave me a dig.

"Oh, I don't . . ." I was terrified of kids. They all cried when I held them. Whenever someone bought a baby into work and handed it to me, the kid would shriek. And then puke. "I don't . . ."

Ignoring me, Claude held the baby out. I gulped, as very gently he placed Jade into my arms. "Mind her head now," he said sternly. "Her neck muscles haven't developed properly yet."

They all looked at me as I self-consciously held her. I braced myself against the screams that I knew were coming. Very soon the angelic face would curl up and start howling.

But she didn't.

I slowly started to relax, I even rocked her a bit.

She had a cap of black hair, dark blue eyes and a smell. A lovely baby smell that seemed to come from her head. She was so tiny and yet perfect. I reached out and stroked her tiny curled-up fist. "She's beautiful, Lisa," I whispered, getting all emotional, "Beautiful."

My periods had stopped, I didn't know if I'd ever have a baby like this.

"She is, I suppose," Lisa said. "Do you want to be Godmother?"

"What?" I gawked at her. "Me?"

"Well, you have a job, you can buy her nice presents," Lisa smirked and then continued, "That's what all the best Godmothers do."

My Godmother had been shite. I'd never got a thing from her in my life. Lisa and Sammy had ones that bought them everything. Even now.

My very own Godchild. "I'd love that," I said, feeling touched. "Thanks."

I kissed the top of Jade's head.

Then she screamed.

CHAPTER EIGHTY-FOUR

The other thing that happened was that Kathy died. We found out about it when Mam rang the hospital to see how she was.

The news devastated me. Not in a bawling, wailing sort of way, it went deeper than that. I couldn't even cry. I suppose it was because for the past year Kathy and I had both been climbing the same tree, only somehow, she'd fallen.

Of course, Mam was going to the funeral. She was a real funeral-goer. Dad always joked that he should hire her out to mourn people. *"Rent a Mourn,"* he chortled. "I'd make a fortune."

Sammy said that Mam was like Eleanor Rigby from the Beatles song. She kept her funeral face in a jar beside her bed. *"Only to be applied on mornings of mourning."*

No one said this to Mam's face, of course. We all knew better. Funerals were no laughing matter.

But she did have a great pious funeral visage, a cross

between reluctant acceptance of His will and a deep sympathy with the bereaved. My mam was a pro.

She insisted that I go with her. "It'd be terrible if you didn't show your face," she said. "What would her family think of you?"

I didn't give a toss what they thought of me but I went all the same. I sort of felt I had to.

It was the first time I'd been in a church in ages. Ponderous organ music echoed off the walls. There was no way if I died, I was having an organ. I wanted songs like "Wind beneath my Wings" and "Honey". Songs to make people cry. When I went, I didn't want a dry eye in the house.

Mam paraded before me up the church. Her heels clicked off the tiles and people turned to look at us. I was terrified she'd head for the top seats but she restrained herself. A view from half-way was good enough.

She began to point out who was who in a big loud whisper. "That's her mother and father," she whispered, "lovely people. He has his own shop in Kerry, sells ornaments and stuff to tourists. And that fella there," she pointed to someone else, "that's the husband. He's broken-hearted."

She knew everyone.

It was a nice funeral, if you can say that about funerals. All went fine until the gospel. It was the one about God clothing the flowers of the field and minding the birds of the air and if he was so good to them, think of how much better he'd be to you.

I felt myself stiffen as each word was read out. I hated that crap. It wasn't true and someone should tell them that. Things never worked out that way.

Mam gave me a nudge, "Isn't that lovely? You used to love that story, remember?"

I stared at her incredulously. "I don't remember," I said coldly.

The gospel came to an end and the priest told everyone to sit down. I slumped into the seat and tried to stop my heart from hammering so hard.

He waited until we were all seated before beginning his sermon. When I was a kid, I'd hated sermons. Big yawns all around.

"God clothes the flowers of the field," the priest began. "He clothes them in spring, makes them beautiful and then winter comes and they die."

He wasn't a gardener that was for sure.

"They serve their purpose by being beautiful and then they go." The priest looked around. "The birds of the air come to stay, they sing for us, and in winter they fly away. Or some birds die. Or some live and produce new birds the following year. It's the circle of life."

My bird had died.

"Without sorrow, we wouldn't understand joy, without darkness we'd never appreciate the beauty of a new day. There's a flip-side to every coin. Kathy was a beautiful woman, beautiful inside. She was born, she lived and served her purpose and now God has taken her." He stopped and continued quietly, "He's taken her to look after her better than we ever could. Like a darkness before a glorious dawn, she dies and is reborn in God." He paused and in the silence I heard my mother beginning to snivel.

My head felt strange. What he'd said actually made sense. About the birds and the flowers. My bird had died. Maybe it was never meant to live that long. Maybe that was life.

The priest waited a few more seconds, blessed himself and Amened.

"Amen," went everyone. Mam said it really loud, but I hardly noticed.

The rest of the Mass went by in a blur. My mind was racing with what I'd heard. All my whole life I'd felt abandoned, ever since I found the bird and now, suddenly, I didn't feel so bad about it anymore. It wasn't that I believed in God, it was just so clear to me now that death is just a part of life.

The part that make us free really. Gets us to wake up and smell the coffee.

I didn't want to fly or live forever, like the words of the Fame song.

Nope, in order to live, I had to accept the fact that I would die. And if I accepted that, then I'd be free.

And the world would be my oyster.

CHAPTER EIGHTY-FIVE

At the end of January Mam, Dad and I went to see Dr Daly.

We were all knackered. Jade had kept us awake by screaming her head off the previous night. Lisa yelled into me that as I was her Godmother, I could get up and fix her her bottle.

"Jan is sick," Mam had screeched. "Get it yourself — you lazy little wagon."

"Naw, it's OK," I called out, "I'll get it." I got out of bed and went into Lisa's room. Jade was yawling, kicking her legs and punching the air with tiny fists. Picking her up, I cooed, "Come on, chicken, let's get you all fixed up." The minute I said that, she stopped crying and looked at me with her big blue trusting eyes. She was really intelligent.

To be honest, I was glad to be up and doing something because lying in bed, trying not to think about the visit to Daly, was doing my head in.

I rocked Jade in my arms as I descended the stairs. I

597

even crooned her some kind of lullaby in my awful off-key voice. Babies make you act really stupid. I rocked her around the kitchen as I put her bottle in the bottle warmer that Claude had bought out of his last weeks' wages. He'd made a big production of unveiling the present for his "girl". Lisa had been disgusted, she thought it was a present for her. I smiled as I remembered.

"Couldn't sleep either, huh?"

Mam's voice made me jump.

I shrugged. "No."

"Want some tea while you're feeding Jade?"

"OK."

Mam went and put on the kettle. The bottle was ready and I tested it on my wrist to make sure it was the right temperature for her. I was becoming good at doing mammy things. Sitting down, I put the teat into her mouth.

"She's a great little eater," Mam commented, putting a cuppa down in front of me.

"She is," I smiled into Jade's face. "She's the best little eater."

"Just like you were," Mam said. Her voice caught in her throat. "Jan – "

"Uh-huh?" I was still looking at Jade. I loved to see her little mouth sucking away. Sometimes her hands would clasp either side of the bottle. Dad said that was very unusual in a child so young.

"I know this is going to sound a bit, you know, off," Mam said, "But well, I just want to say that, well, me and your dad, well, you, eh, you know we love you, don't you?" The last part of the sentence came out in a rush.

The bottle jerked out of Jade's mouth. Ignoring her cries, I turned to my mother. She wouldn't look at me, she was picking some fluff off her dressing-gown. My voice was going to go all shaky if I said too much so I just said, "Thanks, Mam, thanks for everything."

"No need," she was back to herself. "No need." Pointing at Jade, she said, "Better feed that child or she'll throw a tantrum like her mother."

I stuck the bottle back into Jade's mouth. "I love you too," I said, not taking my eyes from the bottle. "You know that, don't you?"

Her answer was a soft pat on the shoulder and then she was gone.

Tears dripped off my face onto Jade.

Daly was beaming. He sat behind his desk and gave us a cheery smile. "I've good news for you, young lady," he smiled. "We've the tests back and they confirm that at the moment you're cancer-free."

It was as if someone had pricked the three of us with a pin. We slumped in our chairs. The relief almost made me dizzy.

"Of course," Daly went on, his voice grave again, "Cancer can re-occur. You'll be having regular check-ups for the next few years just so that we can monitor the situation. Your next one will be in six weeks, after that, three months, six months, one year and so on." he looked at me. "Anything you'd like to ask?"

There was only one thing. "Can it be cured a second time?"

My days of burying my head in the sand were over.

Mam and Dad looked at me. Then they looked at Daly.

Daly nodded cautiously. "With Hodgkin's the answer would probably be yes – in most cases."

It was the most I could ask for. I had a new shot at life and damned if I was going to fuck it up.

I went back to the flat the day after. I told Mam and Dad that I wanted to catch the bus back. It was about being normal again, I was cured and I had to start acting cured.

At the door, before I left, I took a look at our house. Yeah, it was bad. Really falling apart bad. But nobody else seemed to mind, Claude virtually lived in the place, Sammy's friends bunked down overnight on the sofa when they'd been on the tear. They thought Mam and Dad were really with it people living in a house like that.

"My ma keeps polishing her door knob," one fella had said. "Like, as if it's going to benefit society or something."

Everyone had sniggered.

"We don't have a doorknob," Sammy announced proudly. "Our dog, that we used to have, attacked it and ripped it off the door."

The only one who was bothered at all was me. I suppose I was just like that. I'd still be mortified bringing people home, but it was something I'd have to live with.

Hopefully for a long time.

Beth and Abby had bought a cake for my homecoming. They ate it while I imagined what it tasted like. We sat around and caught up on all the news. They'd kept in contact with me through phone calls over the past month but it was hard talking over the phone and anyway, most of their conversation had centred around me, which I didn't like, so our chats were always brief.

"I spent my Christmas on my own in the flat," Beth said.

"Oh, Beth, that's awful." I couldn't imagine being on my own at Christmas.

She laughed. "It was great." She poured herself some wine and slugged it back. "My parents had an almighty row about who I was to spend it with this year, so I told them both to get lost, that I wasn't spending it with either of them." She grinned at Abby and me. "I took the phone off the hook for a week and just sprawled out in front of the telly, ate crap and had a brilliant time."

Abby glared at Beth, "When I got back, she was up to her eyes in dirty dishes, dirty cups and the flat looked filthy."

"I was going to clean it," Beth said, sounding sulky. "How was I to know you were coming back early?"

"Well, seeing as the phone was off the hook, I don't know," Abby shot back.

"How did your Christmas go?" I asked Abby hastily. The last thing I wanted was the two of them rowing.

"Fine." A dreamy look came over her face. A big mooney sigh. "Mickey spent Christmas Day with my folks and we went to his for Stephen's."

I have to admit that during her hour-long description of Mickey's "wonderful" family and the amazing present he'd bought her (a gold chain) I fell asleep.

Because I'd been sick, I got away with it.

The next morning, Abby arrived in with tea. Sitting on my bed, she said, "The better you get, the less I'll do this, you know."

I smiled. Another thing to look forward to, being able to breathe when Abby was in the same room as me. "Thanks, Ab." I took the tea from her.

"No probs."

I touched her. "For everything," I clarified. Then afraid that she'd do a big *Walton* hug on me, I grinned, "For being totally overpowering and suffocating and all the rest."

"Oh," she beamed. "I didn't mind." She flung herself at me, almost up-ending the tea. "I really didn't mind." She squeezed me a bit more and then, deciding that that was enough emotion for one morning, she detached her vice-like grip on my neck. "Oh," she said as she stood up to leave, "I rang the hospital once a week like you asked. Al's mother was discharged two weeks ago."

During one of our phone calls, I'd asked Abby to

keep a check on Al's mother. "Thanks." I stared into my tea. "Has he, you know . . ." My voice trailed off. I hated asking because I dreaded the answer. "Has he been – "

"No," Abby said softly. "He hasn't been in touch at all."

"Oh."

She reached out and patted my arm. "Look Jan, it's none of my business, but to be honest, you were pretty sick and he couldn't even lift up the phone to see how you were. I think – "

"It doesn't matter what you think, Ab," I said abruptly. "It's what *he* thinks I care about."

"Jan, don't go upsetting – "

"But I am upset, Ab," I gulped. "I am." Putting my cup down, I got out of bed. "It's my fault and I have to put it right. Or at least try."

"Jan!"

"Life's too short, Ab," I said, sounding all business-like, but quaking inside. "I don't want to waste my time wondering if he'll ever talk to me again. Or wondering if I could have made it up with him."

"It's only Al," she said.

"Yeah, the best guy I've ever met. That's who he is."

"Oh Jesus," Abby rolled her eyes.

"And I think I can trust him, " I added softly.

That stopped her. She gave a small grin. "Just don't go making a fool of yourself."

I didn't answer. I'd been planning this for some time. If I made a fool of myself, so what?

I wanted to talk to him, before I lost him for good. If that hadn't happened already.

CHAPTER EIGHTY-SIX

I'd rung the office and when Al answered the phone, I'd hung up.

I knew he was in, I'd talk to him after work.

At five o'clock, stomach churning, I stood across the road from the office, watching the front door. It was ages since I'd been in and everything still looked exactly the same. It was strange to think that just because my life had changed, nothing else had.

I'd done my best to look my best. It was in the vain hope that he'd realise what he was missing if he rejected me. Make-up was subtle, the way he'd admired it in the office ages ago. I'd a jumper on that actually covered my middle and a pair of jeans belonging to Abby. She'd refused to let me out in a skirt, even though it was a long one. "You'll get a kidney infection," she said. What her logic was, I didn't question, especially when she dragged out her favourite and most expensive pair of jeans and insisted that I'd look great in them.

She'd also lent me her double-breasted jacket. I'd promised not to get it sopping wet this time.

Just after five, he came out the front door, his sports bag slung over his shoulder. He jumped the last two steps, the way he always did. He looked so achingly familiar. Tall, dark and for the first time I really noticed how handsome he was. I was just about to cross the street when he was joined at the steps by Laura.

They stood talking together.

That should be me.

A stab of pure jealously hit me. Then as if that hadn't done enough damage, a stab of pure despair stabbed me too. I stood, looking forlornly at them. He smiled at her a lot, she big-beamed up at him. I hadn't a hope.

I saw the way he brushed his hair from his eyes when it flopped onto his forehead, the way he shoved one of his hands into his pocket and nodded at her. Then I heard him laugh. The laugh that always made me laugh.

Then, to shove injustice upon injustice, both of them started to walk down O'Connell Street together.

For a second I was stunned. *How could he?* Then I was angry. *How dare he! How dare he replace me so easily!* That was it. Across the street I stormed, almost getting run over in my single-minded determination to catch up with him.

It was my life and I was in control.

"Al?" I shouted, "Al?"

He stopped abruptly, almost knocking her over.

Turning around, he saw me speed-walking towards him. I slowed down then, in case he thought I wanted desperately to talk to him. "Hi," I tried to smile.

Was it because I felt I was losing him that he looked so sexy?

"Jan." He couldn't even look happy to see me. "What are you doin' here?"

"Just, you know, just . . ." I couldn't lie and say I was shopping. I'd come to tell the truth, but I hadn't bargained on an audience. "Hi, Laura," I nodded to her.

"Jan," she said. "It's great to see you looking so well."

I rolled my eyes. More lies. "I don't look well," I said. "But I'm working on it."

She went red and I felt a sick pleasure. I was awful.

The three of us stood there in silence for a few seconds. I wished Al would tell Laura to get lost so I could talk to him. But he didn't.

"You heading to your bus stop?" he asked me.

I stared at him. I tried to will him to read my mind. No go. "Yeah," I muttered.

"I'll walk you so," Al said off-handedly. "Laura, get a pint put by for me, will you?"

"Sure," Laura gave him another irritating worshipful smile and was gone. "See you, Jan," she called out.

I didn't bother answering. "Huh," I said to Al, my nice grovelling speech lost among my indignation, "Huh, you never came out with me when I went drinking!"

He didn't reply, just slung his bag over his shoulder

and asked, a bit snappily, "Are you heading to this bus stop or not?"

"How come you never went out with me?" The nerve! The bloody nerve of him to go out with someone who was only a wet week in the place. "Well?"

He gave me such a look of pissed-offedness that I recoiled. "Me da was busy beating up me ma whenever I let her out of my sight, all right?"

Oh shit.

"Sorry."

"He's banged up inside now."

"You don't have to tell me."

His shoulders slumped. "Naw, I guess not."

We hadn't even started walking. He was staring at his scuffed shoes and I was staring at his bent head. "I hear your mother's fine now anyhow," I said gently. "I kept a check on her."

"Did you? That was nice." He looked dispiritedly into my face. "Let's head so." He started to walk and I had to run to catch up with him.

Silence.

"I got the all clear from Dr Daly yesterday," I said brightly. "Cancer-free now."

"Great," he smiled at me and his voice softened, "I'm glad."

It gave me courage. I touched the sleeve of his jacket. "That's why I came to see you today. I have something to say and you'll know I mean it."

"Jan – "

"You'll know it's true because I'm not dying and I

don't have to ease my conscience." The words were tumbling out of me. "Also, the fact that I have to work with you increases my humiliation factor by about a millionfold." I gave a nervous smile. "I just want to say – "

"Just don't. Don't." Al shook his head. "Don't go over that day in the hospital, Jan. What's done is done. Just forget about it, right?"

"I didn't mean – "

"Jan, you're not listening, I said forget it."

He sounded as if he meant it. As if he didn't want me to grovel. "But – "

"Look, I'm glad you're fine, I really am." He touched me briefly and said gently, "That's all that matters."

Double take. More stuff I hadn't planned on saying spewed out. In with both legs and two arms. "Well if it's all that matters, how come you never bothered asking how I was? How come you never rang when I was really sick? You *do* know I was really sick, don't you?"

"Of course I – "

"I almost died!"

"Take more than that to kill a narky cow like you."

I was speechless until he grinned. "My Ma was in the same hospital, remember?" he said. "I asked after you everyday with the nurses."

"Oh." Me and my big mouth. "Sorry."

"And I knew that you got your chemo and that you went home." He gave a rueful smile, "I dunno where you live."

"Oh."

"And I did ring you Christmas, but the phone was engaged."

"Beth had it off the hook," I muttered, wishing he'd shut up.

"See?" He was giving me a laughing smile.

"Yeah." I wasn't apologising again. I just wasn't.

Another silence.

"Sorry," I said meekly.

It was the quickest walk ever down O'Connell Street. Every step closer to the bus stop, I knew I had to say something. I had to tell him how I felt. I'll wait until this woman goes by, I thought, then I'll say it. The woman went by. Just until we pass this pharmacy, I promised myself, then I'll say it for definite. Past the chemist's shop we went. I'll say it while we're waiting at the bus stop.

Up to the bus stop. Silence.

Al shuffled from foot to foot. I desperately wanted to talk but I couldn't find the words. Eventually, Al said, "You do look nice, you know. Laura was right."

I looked up at him, but he turned his head away. "Anyhow," he continued, "I'd better head back." He gave me one of his gorgeous grins. "Take care now."

Oh God! This was desperate.

Where had the woman who vowed not to let humiliation stand in her way gone? Where had honesty, truth and vomiting my feelings up gone?

"Al!" I called shakily, "Please, don't go. I've something to say."

Everyone at the bus stop pretended not to look.

Al turned around. "What?"

"I, eh, well, I'm sorry about the night in the flat."

"I told you, forget it." He was blushing. People were listening and looking at him.

"I know I hurt you and I'm sorry."

"Jaysus, Jan – " He came towards me and dragged me away from everyone. "Will you shut up, I don't care, honest."

I had to keep going. "I don't know if I'm going to regret this or not, but well, I miss you. I miss you so badly, Al." My voice faltered. "I really do."

He'd stopped holding me. I couldn't figure out what he was thinking. Then, he ran his hand through his hair and gulped. "Jan – "

"I can't bear the thoughts of you with anyone else. I only realised it when you walked away from me in the hospital," He wasn't saying anything. He looked as if I'd just aimed a tank at him, but I had to go on. What was the point of it all if I didn't go for what I wanted? "I think, well . . . I think that . . . well . . ." Big deep composed breath. "I think I love you." I said "love" really hysterically high-pitched. I braced myself for what he'd say.

He didn't say anything. He didn't even look at me.

Time seemed humiliatingly endless. "I'm mortified, Al, please say something."

He bit his lip, a bad sign. Slowly his eyes meet mine. "Let's just be friends, hey?" He said it as if he was sad.

He didn't want me.

He held out his hand. "Friends, Jan." He sounded miserable.

I felt so sick with the anti-climax of it all. Then I felt angry. Then I felt sick again. I couldn't bring myself to clasp his hand. "I could quite happily die now," I joked.

"Jan – "

"Forget about it," I began to babble. My face was on fire. "Just forget it, you know what . . ." The bus was coming. Saved. "There's my bus, I've gotta go." I gave him quite a nasty shove out of my way and I legged it onto the bus.

The last I saw of him he was standing gazing after the bus as it pulled off. "I hope he chokes on his feckin' pint," I muttered tearfully, "I really do."

CHAPTER EIGHTY-SEVEN

A week later, I was sitting in the flat listening to *The Arts Show*. Mike Murphy was talking about a new book on the art of love. I was seriously considering buying it. I could do with a few pointers in that direction.

A few? Who am I kidding? A whole library of books wouldn't even touch the depths of my ignorance.

When I'd arrived back from town the week before, Abby had her I-knew-that-would-happen-face on. She'd been all sympathy though and blamed the drugs for making me act so out of character. "Imagine," she said, "throwing yourself at a fella."

"I used a cannon," I commented dryly. "I fired myself at him and out the other side."

For a few days, I wallowed in my stupidity. But I hadn't taken to the bottle. Mainly because I knew I'd wake up the next day with a hangover and think it was the cancer coming back. It just wasn't worth it.

Then, later, I began to feel that at least I knew what was what. At least I could move on.

But I still wanted to crawl under the nearest stone and never see Al again. And I did cry when no one was around.

I'd been rejected and I'd survived. Worse things could have happened.

Things in other ways seemed to have got back to normal. I was fighting with my Mam, as usual. Dad's jumpers had run in the wash and despite my protestations that I'd told Dad to wash them separately, she'd had a fit. *Do you think your Dad would remember something like that?* she'd screeched at me. *"Do you?"*

"Well, no but . . ."

"There you are. There. You. Are." A bit of righteous heavy breathing. Then, "And how are you, anyhow?"

And that was it. Except for the fact that she was going to demand my money back from Henry and ask him to pay for the damage to all her washing.

Suddenly, I wasn't too keen to be heading back to work.

Mike was asking one of his reviewers about the book when the buzzer went.

"Yeah," I said.

"Eh, Jan it's me." *It was him.*

Shame made my face crimson. "What do you want?"

Hesitation. "To talk."

"Well, talk so." I couldn't face seeing him. I'd die.

A brief silence, then Al said, sounding panicked, "I can't talk here, let me up, willya."

"I can't let you up." I tried to control the upward spiral of my voice. "I can't."

"Will you let me up if I told you that I made the biggest bloody mistake of me life by letting you go last week."

That was my imagination. It had to be. Things like that didn't happen to someone like me. "What?"

"Jan, willya let me up?"

"What did you say?" I asked again, really afraid I'd heard wrongly. "I didn't hear right."

"I said," Al's voice was low, "that if you want me, then I'm here."

I wanted to cry. But I couldn't. "I do want you."

"You gonna let me up?"

I buzzed him up. Opening the flat door, I waited for him. I heard his footsteps coming up the stairs. When he reached the top step, he saw me and stopped. "I'm sorry about last week," he said, his voice shaky. "I miss you."

"I miss you too."

He came over and held out his arms. I fell into them and we held each other tight. I could hear the beating of his heart through his shirt. He smelt of Al.

I felt his lips brush my ear and I raised my face to his. He put his hands on both sides of my face and kissed me. A really deep kiss. "Jan, I love you," he whispered.

I took him by the hand and led him into the flat.

He kicked the door closed with his foot and pressed me to him. Once more he kissed me, then his hand snaked up my jumper and unclasped my bra. I felt his hand work its way around until he was rubbing my nipples with his thumb. We both gasped and without hesitation, I pulled my jumper over my head. "I love you," he said again as he bent his head to suck my breasts.

"And I love you," I whispered. I raised his head, kissed him and began unbuttoning his jeans. He didn't help, just stood watching me as one by one the buttons popped open. I looked into his face as I did it. His eyes were black. He watched me as I opened his shirt, he closed his eyes and gasped as I kissed his nipples. I pulled the shirt down over his shoulders, he stepped out of his jeans. I was out of my trousers, our underclothes lay in a pile on the floor. He pulled me over to my room. "Come on." His voice was husky.

He had a lovely lean body, dark hair in all the right places. But he could have looked like a slob for all I cared. He was Al and that's what mattered.

He led me over to the bed and we both lay down on it. Slowly he began kissing me all over, starting with my forehead and working his way down. He didn't hurry, it was like he was making love to every part of me. Every so often, he'd raise black eyes to look at me, and my heart would start hammering. I wanted him inside me but I wanted him never to stop kissing me.

He kissed my toes. He took each one in his mouth and sucked it. I moaned in pleasure. However shy Al was with words, he knew the way to talk in bed. By the way he touched me and kissed me, I knew he really really loved me.

Slowly, he moved himself back on top of me. "You are so beautiful," he said softly. "I've wanted to do that for ages now."

I could feel his erection pressing against my thigh. "Oh, God, Al," I said, quivering, "Please . . ."

And he was in. He kissed me and called out my name as he came. My name! All I wanted to do was love him.

And I did.

In the words of the song, *I ain't never been loved like this before . . .*

Afterwards, a long time later, he lay, his head propped up on one elbow and stared down at me. "I'm sorry about the other day," he said. "I – "

I put my finger to his lip. "Shush."

He took it in his mouth and sucked it. Then, pressing my hand to his face, he said, "I was scared, scared that you'd let me down like everyone else has."

He sounded like me.

He lay back and stared at the ceiling. "All my feckin' life I've been scared," he said softly, "scared of me da, scared for me ma and me brother, scared in case I wouldn't get a job and we'd have no cash." He paused and said bitterly, "And then I met Carla."

"Carla?"

"Yeah," Al said softly, "Me first real girlfriend. I was crazy about her, told her I loved her, the whole lot.

Then, wanting to be honest with her, I screwed up the courage to tell her about Da." He gulped and said sounding hurt, "She dumped me quicker than lightning." He put his arm about me and cuddled me to him. "I only stopped feeling so bad after I got to know you. When I started work, I was petrified, totally shitting myself in case I'd fuck it up. Me da did that. Told me I was useless all the time."

"You shouldn't have believed him."

"Easy said." He attempted a smile. "Anyhow, you talked to me, made me feel all right. I liked you a lot, Jan. I fancied you like mad. But I was afraid in case you'd dump me too, I wanted to forget about home when I was with you, so I never told you. But 'cause I didn't tell you, I could never go out with you."

"Complicated logic that," I teased.

"I wanted to be honest with you, you know." He looked at me intensely. "You deserve so much and I didn't think I could give it to you." He hesitated before saying, "Last week, when you told me you – you – "

"That I loved you?"

"Yeah, well, I was petrified. All I could think about was what would happen if you changed your mind and dumped me or found out that I really was a complete fu – "

"You're not and I won't." I didn't want him to torture himself. "I really meant it, Al."

"Then, all this week, I couldn't get you out of my head. I never could before that anyhow, but last week, you looked so gorgeous." He kissed my forehead. "I knew I'd hurt you and I felt like shit, but I was scared. I felt you were outa my league, you know?"

"No." I shook my head. "I don't know."

"I couldn't even go into the pub," Al said sheepishly. "I ended up running all the way home."

"You ran?"

"Yeah. It lets me think and sort my head out." He stopped and said bitterly, "When I was a kid, I used to run for miles to get out of the house."

"Must've been awful."

He didn't reply. Instead, he said, "I wanted you so bad but I was petrified. But then, this week, I kept thinking how I'd feel if you found someone else. I couldn't let that happen." He gave a small grin. "I was mad jealous of that Dave guy you were with."

"You had no need."

Al rolled over and studied me. "I can't live without you," he said solemnly.

"You won't have to."

And slowly, he loved me all over again.

EPILOGUE

Something weird happened the other day. Dave would have called it serendipity.

I was at my mother's and Jade toddled into the kitchen with the decapitated body of a bird.

Lisa went pale and almost puked. "Get it out!" She frog-marched Jade to the door. "Ugh, get it out." She turned desperate eyes on me. "It's Mrs J's cat, it keeps doing that." As Jade came further into the kitchen, she screeched, *"Out!"*

Jade's little face started to droop and big tears welled in her eyes. "Burdy," she kept saying. "Likkle burdy."

Lisa was about to go mental. She couldn't bear to touch it or take it away from Jade.

"Come on," I said. "We'll dig a little hole and bury it." I took Jade by the hand and led her outside.

"Oh, thank you," Lisa said breathlessly. "Oh, it's disgusting."

Together, Jade and I buried the bird. She got all mucky and had a ball, I stomped down the earth when we'd finished.

Later, Al asked me what I wanted for my birthday.

I told him to get me some flower bulbs to plant in my parents' overgrown back garden. He looked at me funny but he didn't say anything.

I'm going to plant the bulbs and watch them sprout, flower and die.

I'm going to plant them where the bird is buried.

That way the bird can still be part of it.

Part of the circle.

Of life.